In the Absence of Light

Book Two

A Bad Man's Song

Andy Monk

Copyright © 2020 Andy Monk
All rights reserved.
ISBN-13: 9798575467144

Contents

Finding the Lady 1

The House of Mrs Crisp 26

Lady Henrietta's Cakes.. 58

The Dance of Delights... 73

A Room Above a Shop.. 111

The Workshop of Curiosities 150

The Courtesan.. 166

The Fields of Venus... 190

The Nature of the Beast 230

J'entends Ton Coeur.. 278

A Bad Man's Song 303

Love Burns 337

The Things We Leave Behind 362

A Matter of Commerce 390

The Frost Bride... 410

Caleb Cade 460

Ghosts in the Blood 474

Chapter One

Finding the Lady

The Old Dick Whittington Tavern, London - 1687

Crispy Pete sat back and folded his arms across his scrawny chest, "Pick a card, Billy Boy, show me where that lady's hiding." He revealed the blackened tombstones of his teeth with an encouraging grin.

Daniel took another slow, careful sip of the ale he'd been nursing for the last hour as Billy Bottles hunched forward, frowning deeply. He nodded at each of the cards Crispy Pete had moved around the beer stained table top in a blur of motion a moment before.

"Tricky..." Billy muttered, scratching behind his ear. Being a young man of limited vocabulary, Billy categorised most everything as being either "tricky" or "easy."

Daniel's attention was distracted as Emma, one of the barmaids, passed by clutching a collection of empty mugs in each hand. Billy had often used the latter of his two adjectives to describe her, the word usually accompanied by a boyish snigger.

Regulars whispered luridly of her and the other girls that worked in the tavern, even the ones who weren't as pretty as Emma. However, the ferocity with which she'd slapped Daniel's face when he'd drunkenly tried to fondle her heavy and well-advertised breasts, indicated it was better to take those lewd tales with a hefty dose of scepticism.

Only when her swaying hips had disappeared around the corner of the bar did his attention return to the table. Billy was helping his concentration by taking a big greedy swig of beer, fat heavy drops trickling through the soft bristles patchily covering his chin. Daniel looked down at his own drink and wished he could be so wasteful. Billy always had more money than him, even though they both had to resort to doing whatever they could to make a few coins. They laboured in the market and on whatever building sites required casual men, failing that the wharves around the Pool of London often needed to hire day labourers. Neither of them was apprenticed and so could only do the most menial of work, fetching and carrying mostly. It was casual, irregular hand to mouth work, but they were young, healthy and strong, and being local boys they were usually hired in preference to the Irish and Scots who formed the bulk of London's unskilled cheap labour.

Billy was a powerful brute of a lad who could carry bricks and timber on his back all day without breaking sweat. Although a couple of summers of labouring had bulked him out with muscle, Daniel was still a much slighter build, and if it came down to a choice between the two, they'd always pick Billy. Besides, Daniel was known to have a lot of learning in him, and there were plenty who would hold that against a man.

"C'mon Billy Boy!" Crispy Pete chided, clamping the long slender stem of a clay pipe between his lips, "you never usually take this long to get your hands on a lady!"

Billy's shoulders shook as he let out a deep rumbling guffaw and nodded his head vigorously enough for the limp, greasy rat tails of his hair to dance about his shoulders, "Billy's good with the ladies!" He declared, glancing at Daniel for confirmation.

"They love those big muscles," Daniel agreed.

Billy Bottles flexed his arm theatrically so that his biceps bulged beneath the dirty grey cotton shirt he wore under his faded red waistcoat. He turned his head towards the bar to check if any of the serving girls were looking. While he was looking away, Crispy Pete glanced at Daniel and rolled his eyes.

Daniel didn't smile back.

"Girls too busy today," Billy decided, propping up his chin with his hand.

"Then let's find the lady here then, eh, Billy Boy?"

"Tricky..." Billy's brow folded back into its natural furrows once more.

"You can do it, Bill," Daniel encouraged, almost wishing he would.

"Yeah, this time..." Billy finally reached out to place a thick grubby finger on the left-hand card of the three that lay face down on the table, "I watched real careful this time. That pretty lady is here."

Billy flipped the card over to reveal the Ace of Diamonds.

"Damn it!" Billy declared, though he uttered the words with incredulity rather than anger, "I was sure I got her this time!"

"The Queen of Hearts is a deceitful little doxy," Crispy Pete grinned leaning forward to reveal the Queen had been the right-hand one all along. He swept Billy's penny from the table and added it to the pile he had already won off him, "Maybe you'll be luckier next time?"

Billy finished his drink before rising unsteadily to his feet, "Need a piss first."

Crispy Pete laughed once Billy was out of earshot. "Oh, you done well bringing this one to me Danny boy. I do believe I could live off this one for a good long time."

"Perhaps you've taken enough of his money for now?"

"Don't you mean *we*?" Crispy Pete replied, taking a few coins from his pocket and sliding them across the table, "your cut Danny boy as agreed; more to come, especially if you find me other meat heads like poor old Billy."

Daniel stared at the coins for an instant before scooping them up and depositing them into his pocket.

"We make a good team, thee and me," Crispy Pete sucked thoughtfully on his pipe, "Unlike most around here, we're clever fellows, we use our brains, which can be a much more profitable than selling your brawn to whatever chap needs some shit shifting."

"There's always shit that needs shifting," Daniel offered, looking forlornly into his mug after he'd drained the last of his beer.

"And any number of coves who can do it too... you seriously want to be on the same level as the likes of Billy? Sweet fellow an all, but really..."

"What are you suggesting?"

"Opportunities, that's all! We uses the brains God gave us, and we make a little money, I'm talking about more than just skimming a few pennies from the likes of Billy mind. Enough to keep life sweet is what I'm talking about, eh, Danny Boy?" Pete smiled again and pushed his battered hat a little further back, so his eyes were no longer half hidden by its broad and saggy felt brim. There was something sly about those eyes; Daniel thought they were the kind of eyes that looked upon everyone as a potential victim.

Crispy Pete was only a few years older than Daniel and Billy, but he wore those years heavily, his flesh hanging loosely from his bones like a cheap and ill-used suit. He never removed his battered wide-brimmed hat that he wore at a pronounced angle, not for a jaunty effect, but to cover the burns that had left his right ear and the flesh above it hairless, shrivelled and discoloured; the scars of some childhood trauma that had unkindly earned him the name *Crispy* Pete.

Daniel couldn't actually remember how he'd made his acquaintance, which suggested he'd been quite drunk at the time. This wasn't entirely surprising as that was how he'd been spending more and more of his evenings; at least when he had been working enough to earn some pennies anyway.

Daniel didn't know why Crispy Pete had shown him how the three-card monte trick worked, rather than simply using it on him. Pete had said he was looking for a new partner, but Daniel found it difficult to trust the man even if there had been something sweetly compelling about his words. He genuinely didn't want to spend his life shifting shit.

The one positive such work had brought him, namely upsetting his father, had worn thin a long time ago. Without really thinking too deeply he'd introduced Crispy Pete to Billy, who was too fascinated by Pete's tricks and games to realise he was being fooled out of the money he had spent the last few days earning by shifting timber at Hermitage Dock. Daniel had played the game first, following Pete's coded gestures to find the Queen and won a few pennies, much to Crispy Pete's mock despair; the simple ruse had easily snared poor Billy.

He hadn't worked himself for a week, and this morning he had only a single penny in his pocket, now he had several and all he'd had to do was make an introduction and egg Billy on a little now and again. What could be easier?

"Always open to opportunities," Daniel finally replied.

"Good boy... we'll have words later," Crispy Pete finished his own beer before sliding the mug across the table, "now gets a fresh one for me, thee and the meathead too."

Daniel left Pete to his pipe and his smirk and made his way through the crowd of merry afternoon drinkers. Catching Emma's eye, he ordered three more beers and hovered to collect them as she filled the mugs from one of the large kegs stacked behind the bar.

She deposited the drinks on the counter with a thud that was hefty enough to send some of the frothy ale splattering onto the scuffed wooden surface, as well as diverting Daniel's attention away from the deep shadowy valley of her cleavage.

"Thrupence," she demanded, rubbing her hands dry on the soiled apron she wore.

"Careful!" Daniel exclaimed, "You're spilling more than I'll get down my throat."

"'tis still thrupence," Emma cocked her head and favoured him with a thin exasperated smile as she thrust out her palm, which hard work had aged faster than the rest of her young body. Other than her breasts, everything about her was small and petite. Sadly, her temper was as short as the rest of her.

However, Daniel found both her breasts and her sharp tongue almost equally fascinating, though being a young man of little experience both had the effect of leaving him flushed and tongue-tied in her presence. He had been engaged in a somewhat ham-fisted attempt to woo her for some time though the twin obstacles of his own awkwardness around girls (particularly pretty ones) and the fact she didn't appear to like him much had quite stalled his attempts at romance.

"You working all night?" He asked hesitantly as he fumbled with his small collection of coins, though he had long since memorised her hours and knew she would soon be leaving as she did housework for her mother on Thursday evenings.

"Not tonight," she replied, flicking a loose strand of blonde hair from her eyes.

"Perhaps... I could walk you home?"

Emma's eyes widened slightly and the look that crossed her pretty face suggested his approach was about as welcome as an invitation to be buggered by a gang of drunken syphilitic sailors and their overly endowed pet monkey.

"I don't think so."

"Oh," Daniel shrugged, dropping coins from his suddenly sweaty hand into Emma's, whose fist clasped around them in the manner of a swineherd gripping the balls of a pig before castrating it.

"Shame on you, Daniel Plunkett," she hissed, leaning forward on the counter.

Daniel blinked, "I only asked to walk you home-"

"Not that!" She rolled her eyes and shook her head.

Although her reaction took him aback, he couldn't help but think how pretty she looked with a faint flush of anger in her cheeks, "God knows, compared to what I get offered every evening that's nothing. Even if I do know you want more than a five-minute walk off me."

Daniel tried to protest his innocence, but Emma was starting to build up steam.

"You're not a bad lad Daniel, but what are you doing mixing with the likes of *him*," her head darted in the direction of Crispy Pete, "and don't think I don't know what you're doing to poor Billy. Everyone knows he's a bit simple on account of being dropped on his head when he were a boy by that drunken waster of a father of his, God rest his soul. You proud of stealing money off that harmless oaf, are you? He thinks you're his friend and what's more..." she added after only the barest of pauses in order to breathe, "you think I might be interested in the sort of fellow who gets himself into those kinds of underhand dealings. Do you?"

Daniel assumed it was a question and tried to answer, but Emma was having none of it.

"I see all sorts in here Daniel, and just because I got a couple of tits swinging around in front of me, don't mean I haven't got eyes in my head or brains to know what I sees. I don't want nothing to do with wrong uns Daniel and that Crispy Pete is a wrong un, and if you keep his company, you'll end up a wrong un too. Mark my words. So, don't you be asking me out for walks or any other kinds of such nonsense while you're going around and getting yourself involved in shady dealings. You got some brains and some learning, everyone knows that. You start using them gifts as God intended and make something of yourself, or you'll come to no damn good at all Daniel Plunkett."

She straightened up and placed her hands on her hips when Daniel remained rooted to the spot.

"Well, got something to say for yourself, young man?"

"Don't worry, keep the change..." he finally managed to mumble.

*

"Remember Billy Boy, keep your eye on Queenie here," Crispy Pete was saying, though Daniel wasn't paying much attention. He was thinking too deeply about Emma and all he really wanted to do was to retreat to some distant quiet nook in the tavern to nurse his beer and feel sorry for himself.

During his absence, Pete had somehow persuaded Billy to up the bet, and now a silver shilling sat next to the twelve pennies he had already won off him.

Billy had simply grinned happily when Daniel had commented on the size of the bet while Crispy Pete allowed a vaguely smug expression to float across his features.

He held the three cards lengthwise by their top and bottom edges, with the face of each card towards Billy. One card in his left hand, a second in his right hand between his thumb and middle finger, while a third was above it, between thumb and forefinger. Billy could clearly see that one of the two cards held in Pete's right hand was the queen.

"I'm watching her," Billy muttered leaning forward, resting on the burly arms he had folded on the table.

Pete tossed each card face down onto the table, one at a time until they sat side by side. Billy had no idea Pete had thrown the queen when he had tossed the cards on the table. As the cards were dropped, he had moved his right hand sideways to separate the two cards. Billy thought the lower card had fallen first; however, he'd pushed the top card out slightly early, swapping the positions of the two cards. Even though Daniel knew what he was doing, Pete was so smooth even he hadn't seen him do it, so as Billy leaned even closer to the cards he had already lost his shilling because the card he was watching Pete slide around the table wasn't the queen.

Daniel let his eyes and attention drift, sipping his beer and feeling the nervous sweat that Emma's words had created dry beneath his shirt. He felt angry, not to mention a little embarrassed. Who was she to lecture him on what he did with his life? He didn't listen to his own father on that subject, so why should he listen to some doxy who spent her days pouring beer and getting her arse pawed by drunks; like she was some big success!

He took a generous gulp of beer and when that didn't calm him down, he took another. It wasn't like she was that pretty anyway. No, he was better off forgetting her, she was clearly nothing more than a sharp-tongued scold, he'd be better off sticking with Pete, once he had some more coins in his pocket the girls would show more of an interest in him anyhow. He wouldn't have to worry about mouthy barmaids. He'd seen women hanging around Pete before, drunken flirty girls, girls who knew a thing or two; girls who would be far more amenable to fumbling than some prissy barmaid, at least if you had a few coins.

"I made me mind up," Billy announced, Daniel could almost see Pete's fingers twitching to pick up the fat, juicy shilling.

"Go for it Billy, I just knows you gonna be lucky this time," Pete purred.

Billy reached out towards the left-hand card, but before he could flip it over a metal-tipped walking cane cracked down on top of the middle card.

"I'll think you'll find that's the Queen," a voice boomed out unexpectedly from behind them.

"Hey!" Crispy Pete protested.

Although he'd recognised the voice, Daniel was still mildly surprised to turn around and find Uncle Jonathan looming over them.

"'tis definitely this one mister," Billy said, unfazed by the intervention.

"How many times have you picked the right one today son?"

Billy thought about this for a moment before replying, "None."

"Turn the middle card," Jonathan insisted.

Daniel glanced at Crispy Pete, expecting to see him spitting with fury, but the little trickster was sitting meekly, looking up at Uncle Jonathan with wide, nervous eyes.

Billy shrugged as if losing his last shilling was of no great importance, and turned the middle card.

"What do you know," Pete said shakily, "there she is, told you your luck was changing, eh Billy!" He rose swiftly to his feet, stuffed his cards into one of the pockets of his ill-fitting coat. "Well it's been fun Billy, but I gotta be going, see you around eh?"

Both Daniel and Billy watched perplexed as Pete rushed out of the tavern without even finishing his beer.

Billy looked slightly disappointed; he carefully scooped up his winnings before looking up at Jonathan, "Do you know any good games, mister?"

Uncle Jonathan only smiled and winked at his nephew.

*

"What was that all about?" Daniel asked once he and his Uncle were settled into a nook at the rear of the tavern, fresh beers before them.

"Just doing a good turn," Jonathan smiled, fumbling for his tobacco pouch.

"How did you know where the Queen was?"

"I didn't, other than it wouldn't be the one your friend was going to pick. 'tis a very old trick."

"So you might have been wrong?"

"Fifty-fifty chance; if I was wrong, your friend wouldn't have been any worse off," Jonathan smiled contentedly when he finally found his pouch, and he began to fill the bowl of the clay pipe, "you should be careful playing cards with the likes of that boy."

"Crispy Pete?"

Uncle Jonathan nodded.

"You know him?"

"I know his sort."

"Does he know you?" Daniel asked, recalling the way Pete had hurried out of the tavern. He'd initially thought he'd simply been embarrassed about being caught out, but it didn't quite seem like Pete to scurry away with his tail between his legs.

"I shouldn't think so."

Daniel sipped his beer, not entirely convinced.

"How are you, Daniel?"

"Not starving."

"Still working around the market?"

"When I can."

"And drinking the afternoon away in the company of rascals when you can't?"

"You're starting to sound like my father."

"Heaven forbid," Jonathan exclaimed from behind a cloud of grey smoke as he got his pipe going, "how is the old misery anyway?"

"Still breathing," Daniel replied with a shrug that suggested he didn't much care.

"Do you see him often?"

"I'm not a debtor; I don't have to live within the Rules of the Fleet."

"But you can visit him?"

"If I wished, but I'm old enough to choose which rascals I spend my time with now. If you're so concerned why don't you go and see him for yourself?"

Uncle Jonathan chuckled at the idea.

Daniel stared glumly into his pint, any mention of his father tended to sour his mood. Despite the years that had passed since Caleb's death, he had never forgiven his father, and he could not imagine ever feeling anything but contempt for the man. After his mother had died his father's moods had become blacker and his fists even freer. He spent all his time writing sermons to rant at people from atop a wooden box he carried around as a makeshift pulpit;

street corners, outside taverns, cockpits, dog fighting rings, markets, bawdy houses and theatres. Wherever people congregated, Nathanial Plunkett considered a suitable place for his gloomy ministries; especially if they were gathering for reasons other than wanting to be told how they were all going to burn in Hell. The few teaching jobs he had were sacrificed to allow more time for preaching, and as he only ever preached in places he wasn't wanted he received virtually no donations. It had only been a matter of time before the money had run out, and the debt collectors came to haul him off to the debtor's prison.

Luckily for Daniel he had been old enough to no longer be considered a dependent and, unlike Jacob, had not been taken too. Until his father could pay off his debt he would remain living in the squalid confines of the Fleet Prison. Of course, it was not such a straightforward matter to pay off your creditors once consigned to the Fleet for as well as an institution of punishment it was also an excellent mechanism for generating profits for the warder of the prison, who had bought the contract to run the prison in return for the right to extract as much money as possible from the debtors within its confines. Therefore, Daniel's father not only had to find the money to pay his debts. He also had to pay for his lodgings and meals within for himself and the various associated fees (such as the key turning fee or the removing of irons fees) within the prison and once those were all paid for then he had to find the money for his departure fee to be allowed out of prison.

For debtors with some means or relatives prepared to help them life could be quite tolerable within the prison, with good lodgings and food available, not to mention all the comforts of life such as ale, wine, tobacco and prostitutes. Wealthy prisoners could rent lodgings outside the prison in the surrounding streets and alleys, which were known as the Rules of the Fleet, so long as they paid the warder for his loss of earnings of course. They could even leave the Rules for the day, so long as they paid for a Keeper to accompany them and ensure they returned by nightfall.

At the other extreme were those unfortunates left to hunt for rats and fight for the best spots at the begging grill in the Farringdon Road wall of the prison from which to thrust their hands and their pleas at passers-by.

The bitterest part of Daniel's mind had hoped that would be his father's fate.

However, his father had somehow been able to find enough money to rent a relatively comfortable room in the Rules. If it wasn't for the fact he knew he would never accept charity from his brother he would have suspected Uncle Jonathan of having something to do with that.

"How is Jacob?" Uncle Jonathan asked, summoning Daniel back from his thoughts.

"He is like the dumbest of dogs," Daniel muttered sourly, "the worse my father's beatings become, the more Jacob loves him; as if he could only show enough devotion the beatings would stop."

In his own twisted mind, Nathaniel Plunkett blamed himself for Caleb's death; he blamed himself for the sins of weakness and leniency. If only he'd been stricter, then his oldest son would not have fallen to the wickedness for which God had insisted he paid the highest penalty. Daniel he'd considered spoilt beyond redemption and his beatings had become ever more half-hearted as Daniel grew older. But little Jacob, he was still young enough to mould as he saw fit. And if that mould was not working, why, it was easy enough to break him open and start again.

"I offered to look after Jacob when your father was sent to the Fleet," Jonathan shrugged; he didn't need to explain what his brother's reaction had been.

"He cares for only himself and his God," Daniel said with a shake of his head, "I thought when they took him away it was some kind of retribution for what he'd done, but I get the feeling he rather likes the Fleet. There are no end of sinners there for him to lecture."

Jonathan laughed with grim amusement.

"Are you here to scold me for not visiting my father and Jacob?"

"No," his uncle sighed, "it would do no good, my brother will survive, and in a few years, Jacob will be old enough to make his own decisions. I will ensure no harm befalls him until then."

Daniel raised an enquiring eyebrow, but Uncle Jonathan didn't elaborate.

"I'm here to talk about you."

"Me?" Daniel snorted, "I am fine."

"Are you really?"

"You think I ail?"

"You have been ailing ever since Caleb died."

"That was a long time ago."

"Yet you still carry the pain, Daniel. You used to be a bright, fun loving boy blessed with a good brain and rather too much cheek. How such a boy could develop under my brother's tutelage is a mystery to me, but that is not the point. Six years have passed, and you have grown into an insular and bitter young man who is in danger of shunning the world."

Daniel stared at his uncle coolly, "If I wished to be insulted, I'd visit my father."

Jonathan reached over and gripped his nephew's wrist in his plump but surprisingly strong fingers as Daniel made to rise, "I mean no offence, please hear what I have to say."

"You're going to say I shouldn't be wasting my life drinking and gambling, that men like Crispy Pete will lead me down a path that will end in Newgate and Tyburn, that I should be using my brains rather than shifting shit around the market."

"That covers most of it."

"Do you know any of the barmaids in here?"

"Pardon?"

"It doesn't matter," Daniel sank back into the shadows of the nook, "get the lecture over with, then I can go get drunk and fondle whores."

"Do you spend much time with whores?" Jonathan asked plainly.

"No, of course not; I'm too scared of the pox," Daniel shuddered slightly, he'd seen too much of what the pox could do to go with a harlot, no matter how much he yearned to feel a woman's body properly for the first time. Not that he was going to tell his uncle that.

"Spend too much time with the bottle and you'll lose that fear."

"I can't afford to drink that much."

"You have a choice," Jonathan said, sucking thoughtfully upon his pipe, "but you do not have long to make it. You can continue as you are and, as much as you may not want to hear it, you will end up in the gutter or the end of a rope. I've seen enough to know that is true. Even you've seen enough to know it is true too."

"Perhaps, but I fancy I'd enjoy myself getting there."

"The alternative," Jonathan continued, ignoring the remark, "is that you find yourself some proper work, apply yourself diligently and make something of yourself."

"You have something in mind, given I'm too old for an apprenticeship now?"

Again, Jonathan sighed, "I did offer to pay for one of those too..."

"My dear old father," Daniel concluded, "still, don't know if I'd much care to be an apprentice boy, it would have interfered with my drunken lewdness."

"My dear boy, I know you find this hard to accept, but I do care for you. You and Jacob are the closest things I will ever have to sons. If my brother was not such a pig-headed fool I could have helped you more than I have, but that is the past and I cannot change it. However, you are a man now, and it is no longer your father's choice whether or not to accept my help. It is yours; I'd like to think you had a little less foolishness about you than my brother."

"I'm listening."

Uncle Jonathan leaned forward, resting his fleshy arms upon the table, "I know a man, Greaves, and he is the Duke of Pevansea's butler at their residence in St James' Square."

"You do move in high circles."

Uncle Jonathan waved off the sarcasm, "A position has arisen in the house, a junior footman, the work will be hard and tedious, but you will be well rewarded, good references from such a household will open many doors. If you apply yourself fully, it will be an excellent opportunity."

"And the Duke of Pevansea is given to employing market labourers then is he?"

"No, 'tis a much sort after position."

"Then what makes you think-"

"Let us say that Mr Greaves owes me a favour, the job is yours if you want it."

"What kind of favour?"

"He has an unfortunate fondness for cards."

"I didn't know you were a gambler?"

Uncle Jonathan looked at his nephew plainly as if to suggest there was plenty about him Daniel didn't know.

"But I have no references, no testimonials-"

Uncle Jonathan delved within his jacket and produced a sealed envelope that he slid across the table, careful to avoid the bear splatters, "I think you will find this will suffice."

Daniel looked at the envelope quizzically, "These would be false then?"

"Do try not to be dense boy, of course they're false. Greaves knows they are false, but by calling up my favour, he will not check them. They are quite glowing; the job is yours."

"If I want to spend my life polishing brass and waiting on a bunch of nobs?"

"'tis a good opportunity; you will have money, food, a bed, a position. You will be able to find a good wife, raise your own family. Make something of yourself."

"What makes you think I want a wife?"

"Every decent man wants a wife Daniel; a good woman, not some street corner doxy."

"Perhaps I'm not a decent man?"

"I'm not your father, stop trying to fight me."

"Why can't I just come and work for you? If you look on me as a son..."

"That's not possible Daniel. I'm sorry."

Daniel leaned forward, "I've always wondered Uncle, what exactly *do* you do?"

"I'm just a merchant, I buy and sell things. Nothing more."

"Then why do you never talk about it; couldn't I help you... buy and sell things?"

Jonathan let out a slow exasperated sigh, "Firstly your father would never stand for it, secondly, there is no position you could fill. I'm very much a one man business. Now I don't have all day Daniel," he said tapping a finger impatiently on the envelope, "do you want this job or not?"

Daniel looked glumly at the envelope. He had no desire to go into service, however grand his employers might be, but he wasn't exactly overwhelmed with better offers. He had only a few pennies to his name, no greater likelihood of work tomorrow than he did today, and nothing to look forward to other than a cold night curled up on the flat straw mattress that sat in the dampest corner of the room he rented with Billy Bottles and three older lads who stank even worse than he did. He could take Crispy Pete up on his offer, but he knew in his heart of hearts Uncle Jonathan was right, the kind of opportunities offered by the likes of Crispy Pete would probably end in his dancing in mid-air for the entertainment of the Hanging Day crowds at Tyburn.

"Where and when?"

Jonathan beamed and pulled another envelope from his jacket which he tossed across the table with less care than he had the first. It landed with the metallic thud of coins rattling inside.

"Friday morning at ten o'clock sharp. The address is in the envelope, there's money for you to buy a presentable suit, visit the bath house and get your hair cut," Uncle Jonathan looked at him sternly, "Don't drink it."

Daniel opened the envelope and poured the coins into his palm. He wasn't quite sure if he'd ever held so much money in his palm before.

"A nice suit," Uncle Jonathan said gently.

"I don't quite know what to say."

"Thank you will suffice."

Daniel grinned, "Thank you."

A Bad Man's Song

Uncle Jonathan finished his beer before rising to his feet, "Splendid, now I must be a rushing, I'll drop in on you soon to see how you're getting on."

Daniel rose and walked with him to the door, "Are you not staying?" Uncle Jonathan asked him.

Daniel glanced back to where Billy Bottles was rolling up his sleeve to show Emma his bulging bicep.

"No, I don't think so," he said following him outside, where the afternoon light was unexpectedly bright after the gloom of the tavern. Not for the first time in his life he wished Jonathan had been his father. He wished he could think of something to say, but he was unused to either expressing his feelings or to someone showing him kindness, so he just shook his Uncle's hand and found another piece of paper pressed into his palm.

"If you need anything, remember you can always call on me." Uncle Jonathan smiled.

"I will." Daniel nodded, he'd never visited his Uncle's home, and he didn't even know where it was. When he'd been younger he sometimes even wondered if his Uncle was some kind of wizard who just appeared out of thin air, so little did he actually know about him, but the address scrawled on the scrap of paper suggested his residence was earthly enough.

"Your father never wanted you to visit us, but now you're your own man."

"Why does he treat you like this?"

Uncle Jonathan smiled a distant little smile, "He's never really approved of me I'm afraid."

"Well, I approve," Daniel said, slipping the address into his pocket.

"I'm glad to hear it," With that his Uncle slapped him lightly on the shoulder before bidding him farewell and heading off down the street.

The coins weighed heavy in his pocket. He hoped no one had seen his Uncle give him the money. His brother had been kicked to death for a few measly pennies and Daniel often had nightmares about suffering a similar fate; when he wasn't dreaming of talking trees or thieves dancing on the end of a rope anyway.

It was no fortune, but the price of a good suit was enough money to enjoy himself royally for weeks. All the beer he could drink, beef suppers and a hearty breakfast. No need to hang around the market before sunrise in the hope of finding work. He decided he liked the feeling of having money. He could buy a good woman with it too, he thought darkly, his stomach churning excitedly. Not one of the rough streetwalkers either. Oh no, he could find himself a real pretty Miss who would show him all the things he yearned for.

He stamped down on the thought.

The constant lectures from his father about bube-ridden harlots haunted him. A mixture of spite and the belief that his father was always wrong had ensured he had tried pretty much everything else his father had warned him off, but that was the thing that had stuck in his mind. The briefest of glimpses of the pitiful creatures that lurked in the deepest shadows of the darkest alleys to hide their pox-eaten faces had always been enough to overcome

Daniel's prejudices and admit, in this one thing, at least, his father probably had a point.

He wanted a woman and his Uncle was right, he needed a job if he was ever going to find one. He would try to make the most of the opportunity Jonathan had handed him. He had nothing to lose, even if they didn't give him a job he would have earned a new set of clothes. The thought of him working for some high and mighty Lord would probably send his father into apoplexy as well; which would be an added bonus.

And if he was extremely lucky, maybe there would be some pretty young scullery maid there who might take a shine to him. Daniel smiled at the thought and headed off to buy his suit before he stumbled across some enticing tavern that might tempt him to change his mind.

Chapter Two

The House of Mrs Crisp

Duck Lane, London - 1708

Caleb found Harriet on her hands and knees in the kitchen vigorously scrubbing the flagstones.

"Am I so terrible you would rather scrub the floor than lie in bed with me?" Caleb asked from the doorway, only half-jokingly.

Rising to her knees Harriet pushed back several locks of unkempt hair that had fallen across her face whilst she worked, "Father likes the house to be clean," she offered by way of explanation. Caleb thought it a little odd, given the dusty state of the shop itself, but he didn't press the matter further.

The sun had barely climbed above the horizon, and the sky to the east had not yet entirely lost the last pink blush of dawn. He had woken from a fitful doze to find Harriet gone and had momentarily feared she might have been carried away over the rooftops by Louis Defane for some unspeakable purpose. The idea seemed only slightly fanciful in the cold light of the morning.

"How long have you been up?" Caleb asked, surprised he had slept soundly enough for her to rise without him realising.

"Not long," she smiled, rising to her feet with a grimace and rubbing the small of her back, "there's chocolate and bread if you're hungry?" She hurried to bring a mug and plate for him, "if the chocolate's gone cold I can make some more?"

"It will be fine," Caleb assured her, accepting the food, "have you eaten?"

"Oh.... I never eat early," she shrugged, wiping her hands on a cloth, "you have it."

"Are you giving me your breakfast?"

"Of course not."

Caleb was not convinced, but he ate the bread and chocolate all the same, partly because he did not want to offend the girl, but mostly because he was hungry.

"Don't you have a maid for that?" He asked between mouthfuls, nodding towards the bucket and scrubbing brush.

"Father can't afford a full-time maid, we have a girl who comes once a week to help with the laundry and cleaning, but she is not due until Friday and I can't let the house get dirty in the meantime. Father wouldn't be pleased."

Caleb watched her intently, the mug of chocolate poised at his lips, she looked like a ragged cleaning maid herself, which he supposed was not particularly surprising given that was pretty much how Brindley treated her. He finished the drink and carefully put the mug to one side before holding out his hand. She stood awkwardly before him, smiling uncertainly and fidgeting with her hair till Caleb beckoned her again to take his hand. Tentatively she reached out and entwined her grubby broken-nailed fingers with his and allowing herself to been drawn into his embrace.

He kissed her gently before holding her against him, she gripped him fiercely in return, her fingers digging into his back, "I thought you might just want to leave," she whispered eventually.

"Why would I do that?"

"I thought you might be... disappointed with me."

"Foolish girl," Caleb replied, kissing the mess of hair that was engulfing his face.

"I thought as I didn't let you... *know* me."

"I think I know you a lot better today than I did yesterday."

Harriet giggled softly and looked up at him, "As a man knows his wife?"

"Oh, *that* kind of knowing."

"My father goes to his Society meetings tonight; he always stays out all night. If you come back this evening... you may know me in any way you wish."

Caleb pursed his lips and looked closely at Harriet, did she genuinely want him to have her, or did she just want to because she thought he might disappear if she didn't give him that pleasure? It wasn't a thought that had much concerned him in the past. As long as he had his pleasure he had never been too worried about why he was getting it. But this was different, he thought, remembering he was trying to be a better man. After all these years, he was trying to be a man that didn't leave dead brothers or faceless women and broken-necked fools in his wake.

"Do not be so hasty... you are a good woman Harriet, you should save such a gift for your husband. It should not be given away so cheaply, especially on a scoundrel like me," his words sounded singularly noble, he decided, and he felt a faint tinge of pride that he was capable of such selflessness, especially as he actually wanted to rip Harriet's clothes from her body and have her there and then on the cold stone floor.

"I will have no husband," she muttered.

"Nonsense! You will make a splendid wife."

Harriet laughed bitterly, "I am but straightforward, plain little Harriet. I am not a beautiful Countess, I am just a mousy bookseller's daughter. I do not drive men wild with desire."

"You should be careful what you wish for."

Harriet pulled away, "I am sorry. That was thoughtless."

Caleb shook his head, for no apology was necessary, "I will call tonight, we can talk again then."

"Just talk?"

"There are *other* things we could do..."

"Really?"

"One or two my dear," Caleb smiled broadly, "one or two."

*

The shadows were drawing long again in Duck Lane and Caleb tried to make himself as inconspicuous as a man lurking in a doorway clutching a large box possibly could.

The book in Harriet's window signified her father was still at home, which consigned Caleb to an indefinite spree of lurking and wondering whether the old man had changed his mind about going to his meeting.

Caleb found his eye continually drawn to Harriet's window in the gable overhanging the shop. The more he looked at it, the more ridiculous the idea that anybody could have been hanging upside down outside it seemed, let alone the effete Louis Defane. Admittedly, the fellow was the strangest of coves, but playing tricks with cards and women's minds were one thing. Clinging upside down to the side of a building, which was the only conceivable way he could have done it, was another altogether. The man might be singularly odd, but he was not a human spider.

These had been thoughts that had reassured Caleb through the bright hours of rational daylight when he *almost* managed to convince himself that it had been no more than his recurrent nightmare of Jack Frost spilling over into his half-woken mind, merging briefly into something vivid enough to have seemed real. However, now the sky had darkened and the sun had foregone the world for another night, such rational explanations seemed increasingly tenuous.

He half expected to see some shadowy figure lurking above the eaves, but save for a few pigeons nothing moved above the skyline. He tried to visualise how a man might cling upside down above the window, but without the aid of ropes and assistants, all the possibilities seemed ridiculous. He had half toyed with the idea of climbing up there himself to look for evidence of ropes tied securely to some sturdy brace, but he could not even figure how he might get up there, even if the thought of being so far for off the ground on such a precarious perch did not make his stomach turn decidedly queasy.

No, it was better to believe that he had seen nothing at all. It made things much simpler that way, and he had always much preferred things to be simple.

With a little effort, he managed to drag his eyes from the rooftops and his mind from the strange events of the previous night. He had thought much about Harriet during the day, well at least when he wasn't imagining acrobatic Frenchmen were hanging outside his window. Perhaps it was time he did good by someone, he had spent decades being selfish and shallow. It had brought him pleasures aplenty to be sure, it had given him the kind of life young Daniel Plunkett would never have dreamed of, but it had brought him no happiness in the end. Not the lasting kind at any rate. Instead, he found himself racked by guilt, by disgust and the fear of what the future would bring now his youth had receded behind him.

Was it so difficult to be honest? Since he had been with Harriet, he found he had even developed something of a taste for it. It almost seemed easier than perpetually lying, he did not have continually to invent new stories, he did not have to fear contradicting himself, he did not have to walk forever on ice, the prospect of a single wrong move sending him plunging into the cold waters below. In fact, when he thought about it, other than telling her the truth about his past, there was little he had done with Harriet that he would have done differently if he had been trying to rob her. He had charmed her, made her laugh, wooed her and seduced her. All these things she had done willingly, without being fooled. Accepting him as the actual imperfect man he was, rather than the perfect man he had always pretended to be.

All he had to do was not disappear in the night with her jewellery box and he would have done nothing wrong at all! Well, apart from persuading the girl to give up her virginity out of wedlock, but that seemed such a trivial sin compared to the kind he usually committed, it was barely worth mentioning.

"That's a rather large box?" A familiar voice whispered in his ear, startling him out of his rambling thoughts on the ease of virtuous living.

Caleb whirled around to find the grinning face of Louis Defane just a few inches away from the end of his nose.

"Defane!" Caleb cried, involuntarily taking a hasty step backwards, forgetting he'd been busy lurking in a doorway, bouncing off the door and nearly dropping the box.

"Small world, eh?" He said with an extravagant wink, pushing the brim of his hat back with the tip of his cane.

"Good Lord," Caleb muttered, eventually regaining a little of his wits as he peered at the Frenchman, "have you become a Puritan?"

Defane run a hand down his plain black jacket and britches upon which Caleb could not detect a single piece of unnecessary or ostentatious embellishment. Even the buckles on his shoes were of dull brass. He wore an unfussy little periwig beneath a sober tricorn hat while his face was free of powder, rouge and beauty spots. Only his cane and his sparkling ice blue eyes were completely familiar.

"Oh, I awoke today feeling considerably less extravagant, you know how it goes."

"What are you doing here?" Caleb hissed, the coincidence seemingly too great for even the most rational part of his mind to protest otherwise. It had to have been Defane at the window last night.

"What am *I* doing here?" Defane repeated, looking mildly perplexed, "I was taking an evening stroll before quenching my thirst in a tavern or two. Several of my particular favourites are to be found hereabouts," he leaned close enough for the point of his hat to be perilously close to poking Caleb in the eye, "I believe the more pertinent question is what are you doing here, lurking so mysteriously in a doorway with a rather large box?"

Caleb stared at him balefully for a moment, "I'm waiting for someone," he eventually replied, tersely.

"Aaah," Defane said, knowingly, "a lady I surmise."

"And why do you surmise that?" Caleb asked pointedly, *besides the fact you were hanging outside Harriet's window last night*, he added silently.

Defane raised his cane and tapped the large oblong shaped cardboard box Caleb was clutching protectively to his chest, "The box my friend, 'tis a design commonly employed in the packaging of ladies' dresses, and unless I am very much mistaken, it was one purchased from Tanbury & Sons of The Strand. A very exclusive dressmaker to boot-"

"How could you know that, damn it Defane, why are you following me? This is ridiculous!"

"Following you!" Defane said, flabbergasted, "What makes you think I've been following you?"

"How else could you know where I bought this dress?"

"I've told you before Caleb, I know *everything*," Defane grinned impishly, "besides that card fell out of the box when you were juggling with it," he pointed the end of his cane at a card lying by Caleb's foot bearing the words "*Tanbury & Sons - Dressmakers.*"

"Oh," Caleb said, suddenly feeling rather foolish.

"You must like this Harriet of yours very much," Defane said, the playfulness fading from his tone.

"I do," Caleb agreed after a moment, "*like* her."

"You wouldn't lavish such gifts on me, would you?"

"I doubt it would suit you, Louis."

"Oh, I can carry off almost any style. I'm sure I could look quite ravishing in a dress..." it was a hollow jest, which brought a smile to neither of them.

"I should apologise," Defane said quietly, "you must think me the strangest of fellows after the other night."

"I thought you were the strangest of fellows long before that."

This time, a smile did ghost Defane's lips as he replied with a light shrug, "'tis a fair enough opinion, sometimes I speak too freely, too emotionally. I do not explain myself as well I should. Words can be temperamental beasts that do not always follow the path you intend for them," Defane sighed deeply before thrusting out a hand, "I hope we can still be friends."

"Of course," Caleb replied, juggling the box so that he might grasp the offered hand.

"So, tell me, my friend," Defane asked, "just why are you lurking here? Does this girl of yours have an inconvenient husband perchance?"

"No, just a father with a large stick he keeps close by to beat would be daughter stealers to a messy pulp with."

Defane laughed, "Oh yes, I have encountered that variety of animal myself, once or twice. Very tricky beasts."

"Best avoided," Caleb agreed.

"I should leave you to your affairs. Perhaps one day you would do me the honour of introducing me to Harriet. I would like to meet her."

"One day," Caleb smiled though he had no intention of doing any such thing.

Defane nodded, "Call on me some time, my friend, I really am not a monster," he spoke the words very softly and with a strange melancholy. It was a voice that made Caleb feel both terribly sad and not a little ashamed that he could suppose this strange little man was anything much more than that; except perhaps achingly lonely. He could not fathom why he should consider such a thing, for he seemed to have no great difficulty in sweeping women off their feet and yet he realised that was the aura Defane had always carried around with him. It was a great loneliness, as if there was some separation between him and the rest of humanity.

Could that drive a man to hang outside a bedroom window, fifty feet above the ground? Caleb fought down the urge to ask him. It was, after all, ridiculous. It had been a dream, a trick of the shadows, his old childhood bogeyman. Nothing more.

Defane had already taken a step out into the street and was touching his hat in farewell when Caleb's attention was brought sharply back into focus, and he caught Defane's arm and pulled him hastily back into the doorway.

"Well, if you want me to stay, you only have to ask!" Defane declared, suddenly grinning broadly.

"'tis Harriet's father, I don't want him to see me," Caleb hissed, peering around the doorway to peer at Brindley standing outside the door of the shop, talking to someone out of sight inside. Given the hour and the disgruntled gesticulating that accompanied his words, Caleb could only assume that someone was Harriet.

"I do hope she takes after her mother," Defane noted dryly, leaning back against the opposite side of the doorway, padding down his waistcoat till he found his snuff box.

Caleb ignored the jibe and stepped back fully into the doorway, clutching the dress box across his midriff.

"So, you will sneak a few hours with your sweetheart whilst the brutish father is away?"

"No, he has some weekly Society meeting, he will not return until morning."

"Society?" Defane chuckled, between snorts of snuff, "surely he is not a Fellow of the Royal Society?"

"No," Caleb sighed, "not *the* Society. Another one."

"Is there some grand society of musty old booksellers that I am not aware of?"

"The Society for..." Caleb frowned and drummed his fingers against the wall behind him as he struggled to recall the name, "...the Reformation of Manners."

"Oh dear," Defane said, wrinkling his nose in disgust, "that bunch of hair-suited sanctimonious killjoys. I would have thought that lot would have considered staying awake past nine o'clock to be some heinous variety of sin worthy of a vigorous bout of self-flagellation."

"Well, he goes once or twice a week and stays out all night," Caleb said with a shrug, peering back around the corner to see that Brindley had started to waddle down Duck Lane towards Little Britain, "I suppose the world does need an awful lot of saving; what with all us sinners about."

Defane stepped out of the doorway and watched Brindley, before glancing at Caleb with a Devilish glint in his eye, "Why don't we follow him?"

"Why *should* we follow him?"

"Aren't you just a little bit curious to see where he's going?"

"Not particularly," Caleb sighed, "the thought of a clutch of old women huddling in some dreary drawing room, sipping tea and working themselves into a frenzy at the wickedness of the world does not really pique my curiosity."

"How do you know that's where he *is* going?" Defane continued, the enthusiasm for his idea clearly growing by the second, "that is only what he has told his daughter, after all."

"Where do you think he goes?" Caleb asked, eyeing the slight Frenchman suspiciously.

Defane gave an exaggerated shrug and held out his hands, "How should I know? Perhaps he has a fancy woman? Perhaps he is an opium fiend? We all have secrets, after all."

"Even if he does have some dark secret, why should I care? It keeps him out of my way on a regular basis."

"So young, so naive," Defane sighed disappointedly, "Knowledge is power, my friend. Knowledge is power!"

Caleb's eyes lingered on Brindley's dwindling figure. It was a bit peculiar, he thought, the way the man spent so much time away from the shop. He had thought much the same himself on several occasions, but it was only now Defane had expressed it aloud that any real curiosity had welled up inside him.

"Come on," Defane insisted, those cold deep eyes suddenly wide and alive with mischief once more, "it will be tremendous fun. I promise you, there is nothing like a bit of skulduggery to build up one's thirst."

"Harriet's expecting me…"

"Oh tosh," Defane declared, waving his hand about before his nose, "this will take no time at all... and who knows where it might lead?"

Caleb stared into those strange, compelling eyes, still not entirely convinced.

"Come," Defane whispered, wrapping fingers purposefully around Caleb's elbow, "the quarry is almost away! Let us give chase. If he is just sipping tea with crones and zealots, then it will have cost you no time at all, but if... if it is something else... why, then you will have the brute, have him in the palm of your hand, in your power... and if he is in your power then his daughter will be all the more so."

Caleb found his feet were taking him in Brindley's wake. He glanced briefly at the darkened bookshop as they passed, there was a glow of candlelight in an upstairs window, but he found he could not divert his attention away from Defane's eyes for long enough to see if Harriet stood by the window awaiting his arrival.

"We shall have some fun tonight," Defane was whispering, not so very far from his ear, "and your lovely will still enjoy her pretty gift when you go to her. Oh yes, very grateful I'm sure she will be. Ever so grateful..."

And so they hurried down Duck Lane behind Brindley the bookseller, Caleb suddenly curious beyond all reason to know where he went, all thoughts of Harriet slipping from his mind. She would wait for him, after all, where else was she going to go? Defane was right, she'd be happy to see him whenever he turned up. All the dark thoughts and doubts he harboured about Defane slipped from a mind that had become desperate to know what secrets Harriet's boorish, domineering father might have.

If Caleb had chosen to glance behind him then he might have noticed the figures that slipped out of a doorway further back along the street than his own lurking place had been. His first thought would no doubt have been they were cutpurses or some similar variety of ne'er-do-well intent on no good, though any meaningful examination, even in the shadowy half-light that enveloped Duck Lane, would have quickly discouraged that idea for the cut of their clothes was rather too fine for those out and about on the business of roguery.

If he'd been asked later why he hadn't noticed he was being followed he no doubt would have replied he was far too intent upon his own pursuit of Brindley to notice much else, and he would have believed those words to be as true as any he had ever uttered. However, in reality, it was the strange eyes of Louis Defane that utterly consumed his attention.

*

Caleb had sat in numerous taverns during his travels and listened to many tales recounted over mugs of ale and wine, he had invariably found the liquor to be easier to swallow than many of the stories told for entertainment and the hope the listener would stand another round in order to hear more.

Given the continual need for the Kings and Princes of Europe to raise substantial armies to defend themselves from being butchered by one another (or, preferably, get their butchering in first), there was never a shortage of soldiers or ex-soldiers in any given tavern. Therefore, a lot of the stories Caleb had heard revolved around war. How the teller came to be missing some body part or another was a particular favourite and usually involved some questionable act of bravery or humorous ill-fortune, as were those surrounding looting, pillaging, drinking vast quantities of liberated booze and the raping of various unfortunate peasant girls. These were generally considered to constitute the upside of military life.

The downside, of course, was the slaughter, brutality, fear, butchery and the horror of seeing your friends die in various unpleasant ways. These were the events that occasionally interspersed the months of boredom, rubbish food, wet clothes and sore feet that inevitably occurred as soldiers were marched hither and thither around Europe in search of whichever bunch of foreigners/usurpers/heretics/infidels their Lord had decided were in the most pressing need of killing.

Caleb generally found this kind of talk hugely depressing and would make his excuses to get away at the first opportunity, unless the individual was in possession of loot or back pay that required redistributing into his purse via the card table course, and even then only if the fellow didn't appear to be one of those types that might take violent offence at seeing his hard-won coin going to a professional coward, who always tried to ensure there was, as an absolute minimum, one sizeable country between himself and any on-going war.

That said, there was one type of military tale that had always intrigued him. Often, he'd dismissed them as pure fancy, but some were told with such heartfelt conviction that he had to suspect either the individual had missed out on a far less bloodthirsty career by not going on the stage, or there was, at least, some truth to them. These were the tales that revolved around charismatic leaders, be they distinguished Lords or common sergeants, who could inspire acts of absurd courage in their men.

Caleb could not envisage any man foolish enough to lead a charge against a breach defended by overwhelming odds to be worthy of following to near certain death, particularly as all you were offered in return was a life of wormy biscuits, erratic pay and the possibility of leaving the army with fewer body parts than when you joined it. Yet, time and again, he watched scarred, battle hardened old rogues who had lived through appalling hardship grow dewy-eyed as the spoke of Captain This or Sergeant That, whose charisma, oratory and leadership had inspired their men to acts that no sane man would ever do for so little purpose or reward. To follow them where their better judgement screamed at them not to go, when common sense warned them to turn back and when the basic human sense of survival was pointing at a nice deep crater they could go and hide in until it was safe.

As Caleb let the stink of the river mix with the shit filled streets of Wapping in his nostrils, he thought the little Frenchman must have similar powers to those charismatic soldiers, for not one part of him wanted to be here, but he felt compelled to follow Defane all the same. Whenever he'd felt the urge to voice an objection and suggest they turn back, Defane had turned those big mesmerizing eyes of his upon him. He would say something that seemed both reassuring and undeniable, some compelling reason why they should be following Brindley the Book into the slums east of London and Caleb would sit back for a moment and be reassured. After a while, however, he would not be able to exactly remember what Defane's words had been. They seemed hazy and not quite in focus, as if they were a distant church spire on a hot summer's day, shimmering and obscure in the heat. Then the process would be repeated

Brindley had hailed a hackney carriage at the top of Duck Lane and Caleb had assumed then that their pursuit would be short-lived, but another had turned into Little Britain almost immediately. Defane had given the driver instructions to follow the first at a distance and he would double the driver's fee if he didn't lose him.

Being after dark the roads were no longer choked with commercial traffic, but there were still a fair number of carriages and coaches around. Almost all were heading in the opposite direction; into London.

Caleb had not been unduly concerned by their progress as he sat opposite Defane, still clutching Harriet's gift while they rattled along Cheapside and Lombard Street. He could well imagine that Brindley would be visiting the home of some righteous City guildsman, lawyer or financier, but when they continued along Fenchurch Street and then cut down The Minories towards The Tower of

London he became more perplexed. "Where can he be going?" he had murmured.

"We will find out soon enough," Defane had replied. Unlike Caleb, he was not continually glancing out of the carriage to see where they were. Instead, he sat and stared at Caleb with a slightly bemused expression on his face, one you might reserve for a particularly precocious child that you could not help but find endearing.

They had slowed to pass through the tangle of narrow streets that clustered around the Tower, before trundling along through Wapping, which followed the course of the river and was lined with timber and coal yards, warehouses and wharves to service the ships that lined the river bank. On the landward side of the road, taverns and brothels catered to the sailors and dockers while further back dark little alleys and passages led into the warren of slums that provided homes for their families.

It seemed a highly unlikely neighboured for any kind of Society to hold a meeting, Caleb thought, other than a Society for cut-throats and other assorted rascally types of course. He tried to voice his concerns that this was not the kind of neighbourhood a gentleman should be in after dark; the Frenchman had just uttered a few of his hard to remember reassurances and Caleb had duly settled back to stare out at the ship's lanterns and the sailors who huddled around them, guarding the ships against the attentions of mudlarks and other thieves.

Caleb found he was not so familiar with this area, his father had always considered it to be a particularly unpleasant and Godless quarter best avoided as it was infested with intoxicated sailors and foulmouthed blasphemous dockers. His only experience of the place as a child had been sheepishly standing outside makeshift cock or dog fighting pits while his father had tried to press leaflets proclaiming the wickedness of gambling into the hands of the generally illiterate and perplexed punters. Later he had attended a few himself, as much to infuriate his old man as for any love of the sport. After twenty years of absence and the constant rebuilding of the generally slapdash and makeshift buildings, he was soon no longer sure quite where they were when the carriage finally lurched to a stop.

Defane promptly leapt from the carriage and Caleb reluctantly followed him, careful not to drop his dress box on the ground, although it was now too dark to inspect closely what was beneath his feet, he was fairly confident he was standing in several varieties of unpleasantness.

Brindley's coach had disgorged its passenger half way along a side street that run up from the river towards, Caleb guessed, Shadwell, where he vaguely recalled there had been a glassworks and numerous rope makers. Given there had been no slump in the demand for rope or glass in the last twenty years, he assumed they were still there. Their own coach driver had pulled up at the top of the road, and Caleb nervously glanced at a handful of men huddled around a brazier at the entrance to a wharf that currently berthed three sloops. A carriage in these parts only signified two things to the locals; firstly, that the people getting out of it had money, and secondly, they were either lost or unusually stupid. The fact one of the men getting out was clutching an intriguingly large box, in Caleb's eyes, made him an, even more, tempting target for any locals looking to supplement their incomes with a bit of routine knife work.

Caleb pulled his cloak a little tighter around his shoulders, for the temperature had dropped noticeably and a few hazy tendrils of mist had crept up from the river to diffuse the lanterns that burned upon the nearby ships.

Defane was asking the coach driver to wait for them, which the driver graciously agreed to, in return for another doubling of their agreed price, plus the same for the return journey. Defane tried to haggle, just to show good form, but as the driver held all the best cards he soon settled. Once a price was agreed the coachman added he'd only wait twenty minutes.

"Plenty of time," Defane had replied with a grin. Caleb wished he were as confident. He really did not want to be stuck out here with no means of returning to civilization. Caleb noticed the driver glancing at the men on the wharf who were now openly staring at them. The driver gave them a wide toothless grin and flipped back his long coat to reveal a pair of particularly fearsome and well-used looking pistols. The men nodded and returned to warming their hands over the brazier.

The fact the driver had felt the need to display his firepower to the locals reassured Caleb not one little bit, especially as all he had to defend himself with was one rusty sword and a large dress box. Given his limited skill with a blade and the fact that carrying a sword was considered the mark of a gentleman (which in these parts was akin to carrying around a large sign saying "I Have Lots of Money, Please Rob Me) the dress box would probably be more useful.

Caleb was about to enquire how much the driver would be prepared to charge for the loan of one of his pistols, but Defane was already marching purposefully down the road, ushering him to follow. Cursing himself for not having the courage of his cowardice and just awaiting Defane's return from the relative safety of the carriage, Caleb hurried after the Frenchman. Brindley's carriage was already turning out of the opposite end of the street by the time he had matched his stride, but of Brindley himself, there was no sign.

"Where did he go?" Caleb hissed, is if speaking too loudly might awaken the local rogues and bring them scurrying from whatever dark crevices they were currently waiting to pounce from.

"You're really not cut out for skulduggery, are you?"

"Not when it comes to following fat booksellers around cut-throat infested slums, no," Caleb admitted.

"Luckily, whilst you concerned yourself with the business of worrying about the various rough looking fellows hereabouts taking an interest in our good selves, I was focused, like a bird of prey some might go as far to say, upon our quarry, the Fat Bookseller! I noted he disappeared into yonder grubby looking building," Defane indicated a nondescript pile that sat between a timber yard and a row of particularly miserable looking hovels roughly at the mid-point of the road. It was clearly old, and the structure had been subject to numerous expansions, renovations and ramshackle general repairs to ensure it continued to defy gravity. In fact, it had been altered so many times that to Caleb's eyes it now resembled a collection of variously sized wooden boxes that had been thrown up into the air and allowed to fall back to earth and collect together in a vaguely building-like shape

"Being somewhat of an expert in such matters," Defane added, "I can say with no small authority that the Fat Bookseller was acting with sufficient shiftiness for me to suspect he is engaged in either some act of general no-good or vile debauchery."

"Vile debauchery?"

"Oh, I do hope so; 'tis so much more fun than general no-gooding."

"How do you propose we find out?" Caleb asked. Noting the windows bore only grease paper panes or a stained rag curtain he was on the verge of suggesting they try to peek inside. Defane, however, had other ideas.

"We go in and ask."

"Ask? What if it's... general no-gooding!"

"That should not present a problem as you are no doubt aware I am blessed with the quickest of wits and my tongue will be able to extract us from most difficulties."

"And if that doesn't work?"

Defane grinned boyishly, "Then I suggest you throw away that box, you should be able to run much faster without it."

"Hmmpff..."

Caleb had expected the front door to be bolted, and they would be turned away by some rough looking fellow once they failed to produce whatever code word was required to gain entry to the place. However, he was disappointed to discover the door was neither locked nor guarded and thus he had no cause, other than common sense, not to follow Defane further.

The door opened into a single large room, occupied by perhaps two dozen or so men in various stages of drunkenness ranging from the mildly intoxicated to the completely comatose, but no fat bookseller. They had to step over one of the comatose ones to enter the room as he had either passed out across the doorway or he'd been moved there to block any draught that might find its way under the ill-fitting door. The drunk lay face down on a bare floor that had been scattered with sawdust to soak up various spilt fluids, both alcoholic and bodily.

A few of the men sat together, but most appeared to be solitary creatures. A few of the more sober ones looked up from the barrels and crates that acted as rudimentary furniture as Caleb gingerly followed Defane over the human draught excluder, but they showed no appreciable interest in either of them and their minds soon returned to whatever miserable place they had been before.

A fireplace smouldered half-heartedly on one wall, and the only actual piece of furniture, a rocking chair, sat beside it, occupied by one of the few men in the place who did not appear to be glassy eyed with booze. The heavy-set man was rocking gently back and forth as he observed them disdainfully from behind a knotted unkempt beard of biblical proportions while his thick, gnarled hands took comfort from an ancient blunderbuss that sat across his lap. Caleb assumed he was responsible for keeping order though a blunderbuss did seem a little excessive given most of the patrons were barely capable of standing.

A couple of old doors had been lain upon some barrels to form a long table and a middle-aged man in a tatty ill-fitting periwig and an apron that appeared to be welded to his portly body by the countless stains that had eaten into the fabric. He tended bar and was pouring clear liquid from one of half a dozen earthenware bottles of various sizes before him into a filthy shot glass.

On seeing them, the barman smiled warmly, which immediately put Caleb on his guard as London barmen tended to work hard creating an air of cold contempt and general disregard for their customers.

"Evening gents," the barman said with a wet and welcoming smile, once they had negotiated a path across the room without tripping over any of his customers or slipping on anything they'd managed to spill or deposit on the floor.

This was the point where he'd expected Defane's plan to fall flat on its face as he couldn't think of any plausible thing they could say to explain why two well-dressed Gentleman had wandered into a seedy Wapping gin house. He was only thankful Defane had decided not to dress in his usual foppish attire, else Caleb would have given up any hope of them getting out alive. However, the barman came to their rescue by adding, "You here for Mrs Crisp's I take it then gents?" The rather salacious wink he used to punctuate the sentence made Caleb feel vaguely queasy.

"Oh yes, old friends of Mrs Crisp's we are," Defane said confidently.

"Of course you are," the barman chuckled. At least Caleb thought it was a chuckle. The yellowish phlegm that momentarily bubbled up between his lips suggested it might have been something else entirely.

After he'd spat a thick and yellow gob onto the floor, he nodded to the dirty little glasses that lined the bar, "You want a little gin first?" he asked, eyes brightening, "I can make you drunk for a ha'penny or dead drunk for a penny!"

Caleb shuddered and wondered what a shilling would do for him. "We're fine thank you," he piped up quickly, just in case Defane was actually considering drinking any of the Devil's brew. The poor wretches here couldn't afford tavern prices and would come to drinking kens like this because they sold cheap liquor. What they were drinking was undoubtedly alcoholic, but what else had been added to speed the distillation process could run through anything from human urine to sulphuric acid, and they were just the things Caleb knew about.

"Suit yourselves gents, cost you more upstairs, but I guess you don't come to see Mrs Crisp for the drinking," he chuckled and hacked up more phlegm. "Up the stairs you go gents, they'll be happy to see you, always happy to see gents with presents they is," he nodded at the dressmaker's box Caleb still carried and gave him a slow sticky wink.

Defane nodded his thanks and led Caleb to a door at the back of the room that opened on to a dilapidated staircase climbing up into the gloom.

"I think we've seen enough," Caleb whispered once they had shut the door on the gin shop.

"I hardly think so," Defane grinned, "are you not intrigued by this place?"

"Intrigued? 'tis clearly a brothel of some kind, I think we know Brindley's secret now and why he stays out all night. I would not wish to venture outside this place without a coach waiting for me and ours will not dally much longer!"

"Nonsense!" Defane proclaimed, "We have ages yet, besides the driver will wait for his fare back to London. We need to see the manner of the Fat Booksellers depravity," adding with a wink, "you never know; it might be one I haven't tried yet!"

With that Defane bounded up the stairs. Once more, his better judgement crying out unheeded, Caleb followed him.

*

Although the gin shop on the ground floor catered for the dregs of London, the upstairs inhabited an entirely different world. At the top of the stairs, a pair of rough-featured men looked them over and insisted on looking in Caleb's box, but had found nothing remarkable in the fact a man should turn up here with a dress under his arm. He had balked when they had demanded a guinea merely to enter, but Defane had paid for both of them before he could

A Bad Man's Song

complain and they had waved them through into a drawing room that was as tastefully and expensively decorated as downstairs had been cheap and dilapidated.

The floor was lushly carpeted while the crude wooden walls were hidden behind fine hangings and silk damask drapes. The mahogany furniture was well-made and expensive; the high-backed chairs and sofas were luxuriantly and deeply upholstered with velvet. Several men and women floated about, music could be heard coming from elsewhere in the building. Several doors led off the room, which was clearly only a starting point for the establishment. It appeared to be as upmarket as any brothel Caleb had ever visited, and he had visited quite a few.

A boy in his early teens drifted by, dressed in an immaculate scarlet footman's livery, a tray of champagne glasses perfectly balanced upon his palm. Defane casually helped himself to two glasses, passing one to Caleb while sipping his own.

"Very decent," he declared, after emptying the glass in one and flicking the rim with his finger, "good crystal too."

Caleb sipped his own more modestly, but found he had to agree, "Louis, why is this place hiding in Wapping rather than operating in the West End like any other respectable upmarket brothel?"

"Fascinating, isn't it?" Defane grinned, "Perhaps we should forget about that coach. Your fat little bookseller isn't such a bad judge of an evening's entertainment. There must be more money in books than I'd supposed."

"Quite," Caleb muttered, he'd come to much the same conclusion himself while poor Harriet was working all the hours God sent, her apparently penniless God-fearing father was spending a fortune here.

Before he could speculate further a small woman with a wig almost half as high as the rest of her body, tottered towards them; she was probably well into her fifties though her powder was so thick it was difficult to be entirely certain. She curtseyed a greeting, and although her face had long since sailed from ports named pretty or cute, her cleavage still provided a remarkable vista.

"Mrs Crisp, I presume," Defane said, sweeping up her hand to plant a kiss upon it as he slipped effortlessly into charming libertine mode.

"Indeed," she smiled, revealing a set of only marginally blackened teeth, "I'm afraid you have the advantage of me, Sirs, I believe you are new to my little establishment."

"You are quite correct, this is our first visit. We have heard many good things about it and had to come almost as soon as our ship arrived in London."

"Oh my," Mrs Crisp tittered, "I did not know our fame had spread so wide. Or should I say *infamy!*"

"Infamy only in the eyes of the small-minded and bigoted."

"I could not have phrased it better myself."

"Please forgive my wretched manners," Defane said, suddenly aghast, "our long journey has robbed me of my senses while your beauty and that of your House have only fuddled my mind further. Please let me introduce-"

Mrs Crisp cut him short with a sharp snap of her fan, "Though your flattery is most welcome and much appreciated, you should know that there are no names here. We are all friends, but it is best that the only name people here know is mine."

"As you wish," Defane said with a bow.

Mrs Crisp smiled and turned her eyes to Caleb, fanning herself slowly in a manner that would have been considered demure in a woman half her age, "I see your quiet friend has brought a gift?"

"'tis just a dress," Caleb blurted out.

"How lovely!" Mrs Crisp declared before Caleb could go on, "Is it for one of my lovely ladies?"

"Erm.... not exactly," Caleb admitted, shuffling from one foot to the other.

"Aaah," Mrs Crisp smiled, placing a hand gently on Caleb's forearm, "all are welcome here, there is no need to worry, I'm sure you will make lots of lovely new friends. Just settle your bill before you leave. Enjoy! Enjoy!"

"Strange woman," Caleb muttered once Mrs Crisp had wandered off to chat with some of her other customers.

Defane could only look at him and smirk.

"What?" Caleb demanded.

"Have you not yet worked out what this place is yet?"

"'tis a brothel Louis," he replied, in an exaggeratedly measured tone.

"Have you looked at Mrs Crisp's ladies closely?"

Caleb had to admit that the unexpected splendour of the place had so aback taken him he hadn't given his usual degree of attention to the whores within it. Defane nodded towards two girls sitting upon a double backed couch who were observing them closely from behind their fans, which only partially concealed their whispers and giggles. They were heavily powdered and rouged. At first, Caleb thought their movements rather affected, like young girls who had secretly dressed up in their older sister's corsets and gowns in order to play at being grown up.

It was only when one of them lowered her fan to smile encouragingly at him that he realised it wasn't just their affectations that made them seem rather odd.

He glanced at the grinning Defane, "Oh God..."

Defane nodded in confirmation of his fears, "Indeed my friend, we seem to have found ourselves in London's most exclusive Molly House..."

Caleb looked back as the two young boys, so elaborately and expensively dressed as women, rose and started to walk over to them their hips swaying exaggeratedly.

"...and I do believe Mrs Crisp thinks you've brought that gown so that you can dress up and entertain her clients too."

Chapter Three
Lady Henrietta's Cakes

St James' Square, London - 1687

Henrietta Bourness, Duchess of Pevansea, sat on the cushioned window seat of the library, an open book face down on her lap. Her attention was focused on events out on St James' Square, from where a babble of angry voices drifted up through the window. She seemed unaware that he'd entered the room. The low winter sun had made a halo of the gentle blonde curls her maids had so artfully bundled upon the Duchess' head that morning while her pale skin seemed to almost glow in the flattering light. Her wide grey-blue eyes were looking intently at something out of Daniel's sight, and he fervently hoped it would keep her attention so he might stare at her just a little longer, for as much as he delighted in looking at her, even he did not think her so beautiful she was worth getting horse whipped for; which he'd been earnestly warned by the other servants was the Duke's favoured method of disciplining his staff.

No guests were expected or social functions planned that afternoon, so the Duchess wore an informal loose day gown, though even if she had been wearing nothing but flea-infested sackcloth Daniel would still have found her indescribably beautiful.

"You can put the tray on the table," she said softly without looking at him, summoning him into the room with the faintest twitch of her fingers. Daniel cursed silently as he hurried across the room, partly because it curtailed his staring, but mostly because she'd probably been quite aware that he had been standing in the doorway gawking. She was the kind of woman who didn't ever actually need to look directly at you to know exactly what you were doing, Daniel reminded himself darkly.

He placed the Duchess' tea and cakes on the small table beside her favourite window seat, (she had a great fondness for cakes) and once satisfied the tray was secure Daniel straightened up and waited for further instructions. In his limited dealings with the nobility, he had found it was always better to await instruction rather than make assumptions. It might seem reasonable to assume the Duchess would like her tea poured before her servant retreated from the room. However, Daniel was not so foolish as to believe he ever knew what any nob might actually want. It had been something of a surprise to be given the tray to carry up to the Duchess, and he was informed directly that it was a great honour for a boy who'd been in the household for so short a time to bring the Duchess her afternoon tea. Daniel, however, thought of it not so much as a privilege but more a marvellous opportunity for furtive staring and lustful appreciation of his employer.

"The mob is about again," she said finally, still looking out of the window.

"Ma'am?"

"On their way to Parliament I dear say, they appear to have two effigies to burn today. I assume it is the Pope *and* King James; however, it is difficult to be entirely certain," she glanced at him and smiled briefly, "they are exceedingly poor effigies and really could be quite *anybody*. You would think they would get better at making effigies, would you not Daniel, given they burn them so regularly?"

The Duchess' tone was so light and warm she could have been addressing an old friend rather than a servant. Daniel was caught so off guard he only just managed to mumble something that might have been "Yes Ma'am," but just as easily could be a sign that he had swallowed a small bone and was desperately trying not to be so rude as to spoil the Duchess' enjoyment of her cakes by choking to death on her carpet.

"Are you unwell, Daniel?" she asked, eyes widening a little, favouring him with another smile, which was nearly all Daniel could take. Daniel considered Lady Henrietta to possess the prettiest smile in Christendom and to receive two in such quick succession was almost enough to make his head spin. The fact that she actually remembered his name made this a singularly memorable day indeed and he was already looking forward to lying in bed in the darkness and recalling those smiles in every possible detail.

Despite being nearly thirty, she still had almost all her teeth, which made her smiles all the more radiant. To Daniel, it seemed an impossibly old age for a woman still to look so beautiful, but then she had never spent eighteen hours a day cleaning, cooking and hurling buckets of shit out of her home, like most of the thirty-year-old women he knew.

"Very well Ma'am, thank you for asking," Daniel managed to reply in something approaching a normal voice.

"Very glad to hear it," she said, "you may pour my tea now."

"Yes, Ma'am."

Tea, being both fashionable and in extremely limited supply thanks to the monopoly enjoyed by the East India Company, was so ridiculously expensive that even people as wealthy as the Duchess of Pevansea only drank a weak infusion from shallow porcelain saucers. The precious leaves themselves were kept under lock and key, and at a price of around £1 a pound even the used leaves could be sold for a tidy sum, which Daniel guessed was why some of the more senior staff had looked upon him so coldly when he'd been given the job. Servants tended to guard their perks jealously.

He managed to neither spill any of the precious brew nor rattle any of the equally expensive china despite the nervousness he felt at being so close to Henrietta. However, when he straightened up, he found her eyes had returned to the window, and she had not been paying him any particular attention.

She accepted the saucer in her well-manicured hands, and he felt a tingling rush of excitement when her fingers briefly touched his own. Not for the first time, he wondered what it would be like to do more than brush fingertips with her, but he knew that was a line of thought he could only pursue when alone and definitely when everybody else was asleep.

"'tis the tide of history sweeping by my window," she sighed, finally turning her back on the scene outside.

"Ma'am?" Daniel found himself asking again.

"Everybody seems most concerned with getting rid of our King James; it is the talk of the town now that James looks to have gotten himself an heir. *Apparently*."

Given the turmoil and loss of life the country had suffered in removing James' father from the throne (and then his head from his shoulders) Parliament, the nobility and the London mob had just about been prepared to tolerate the closet Catholic James II on the throne. The general opinion was that he was an evil that could be lived with until he had the good grace to die, allowing the crown to pass to his daughter, the staunchly Protestant Mary.

Rumours were sweeping London, however, that the Queen was with child, which, closet Catholics and the happy couple aside, nobody was much pleased about. Despite the voices of reason quietly insisting James was too far eaten away by syphilis to have fathered anything, the prospect of the King establishing a Catholic dynasty through a son to rule England was too much for many to stomach.

Hence the current bout of effigy burning on Parliament Green.

Daniel was somewhat stumped as to what to say, given that there was nothing in his training or experience to help him master the tricky art of *having a conversation with a Duchess*. In the end, he opted for the safe option.

"Yes, Ma'am."

"Do you follow politics at all Daniel?" Henrietta asked, observing him closely as she sipped her tea.

"Not particularly Ma'am," Daniel admitted, though decided it prudent not to add this was primarily due to the fact what little spare time he had was devoted exclusively to more pressing matters; such as drinking ale and staring lustfully at the serving girls working in the *Rose & Crown*.

"Pity," Henrietta sighed, swapping tea for cake, "I find it all rather fascinating, though it is terribly difficult to keep abreast of events, let alone the rumours and gossip. I understand London is awash with libels and handbills debating the matter of King James."

"I believe so, Ma'am," Daniel chipped in when he realised the Duchess had paused in expectation of a reply, "the King has lost much support since the Declaration of Indulgence."

"It would appear so," Henrietta nodded, "'twas a folly to think Catholics and nonconformists can be made happy bedfellows."

James had issued the Declaration of Indulgence when he had lost the support of High Church Tories after he attempted to relax the Penal Laws on dissenters. He had sought to build alliances with those outside the Anglican

Church, by passing laws allowing the freedom of worship. However, rather than a piece of high-minded idealism, many saw the declaration as a way of allowing Catholics overtly back into positions of power, whilst most non-conformists hated James as a matter of principle, the fact that he had passed a law which allowed them to do that which they already did, and generally thought was of no business of the state in the first place, had won him few plaudits.

If Daniel was still speaking to his father, he didn't doubt he would be in his usual state of spit and fury if anybody had the poor sense to mention the name of James Stuart in his earshot.

"The problem is Daniel, my husband has no time for such scurrilous publications and would not approve of any of his household reading them. Let alone me. I was hoping perhaps you could do me a small favour?"

"Of course, Ma'am!" Daniel piped up, in a voice that sounded a mite more enthusiastic than was probably required. Given the disproportionate amount of time he spent daydreaming about Henrietta, he would gladly have trampled over his fellow servants broken, dying bodies to perform any service he could for her.

"I would greatly appreciate it if you could obtain diverse examples of these pamphlets and bring them to me, the more scurrilous, the better," she smiled a knowing little smile, "it will be our little secret, eh Daniel?"

"I won't tell a soul Ma'am, I will get some for you immediately," Daniel blathered.

Henrietta dusted a few crumbs away from the corner of her mouth, before leaning forward slightly to ask, "You can read a little, can't you Daniel?"

This provoked competing emotions in Daniel, the first being simple lust. Although the Duchess' dress was far more modestly cut than the serving girls down the *Rose and Crown*, who were the other current chief sources of sexual frustration for Daniel, Henrietta's impressive cleavage was still amply displayed. Given the angle provided as he stood by his seated mistress, even the slightest movement forward entailed Daniel was treated to the kind of spectacle that made him, even more, grateful that he had been given eyes to see with. Though it would have been nice if the Creator had perhaps put a little more thought into the practicalities this caused certain other parts of his anatomy.

The other thing that was engorged by the Duchess at that moment was his pride, which had become both inflated by Henrietta's interest in him and dented by the fact she had to ask whether he knew how to read; a combination that resulted in a bolder reply than he would have otherwise dared.

"Yes Ma'am, I can read and write..." he said, raising his chin and puffing up his chest a little, "...English, Latin, French, and Classical Hebrew... Spanish and Italian too, though not so well."

"Anything else?"

"I'm well versed in Mathematics, philosophy, history, literature. Mainly."

"And the Bible? You've studied your scriptures I take it?"

"Yes," Daniel smiled thinly, "I spent a lot of time on those."

The Duchess of Pevansea raised the thin, perfect arch of her right eyebrow, before taking another delicate mouthful of cake. As he waited for her reply, Daniel felt the droplets of sweat that had been accumulating under his wig begin trickling down the back of his neck. He took the opportunity her pause provided to fret as to whether he had been overly bold.

"My, my," the Duchess said eventually, once she'd disposed of that particular slice of cake, "what an educated boy you are Daniel. How old are you, exactly?"

"Nineteen Ma'am."

"Pray tell me then, with all this education you've received, why you have not been apprenticed to a trade where you could put all this scholarship to some use. Or perhaps it is of some benefit when you are polishing brasses and scrubbing floors?"

"'twas a financial matter Ma'am... my family could not afford to buy me an apprenticeship."

"I see, and you could find no one else to sponsor you?"

Daniel shook his head, deciding there was no need to explain to the Duchess that, by then, his father had long since alienated pretty much everyone he knew and that no one wanted to waste their money on the son of a man even the local Quakers and Barkers thought too radical.

In the Absence of Light

"Pity, 'tis such a shame to see talent go to waste," the Duchess paused as she leaned forward to select her next piece of cake and in doing so helped generate even more sweat beneath Daniel's wig. "Perhaps I can act as your benefactor?" She suggested looking up him, her fingers hovering over the cakes; her attention ensuring Daniel had to force his eyes to look anywhere, but the one place he truly wanted to look.

"Ma'am?"

Henrietta smiled and settled herself back into the window seat, the lucky piece of cake chosen now resting upon the small china plate on her lap, "Perhaps I can improve your station a little Daniel; my husband leaves most of the affairs of our households to me. You are clearly an intelligent and educated young man. It seems a waste that you should be toiling away as a junior footman. Perhaps we can make your duties more... cerebral?"

"I don't quite follow Ma'am?"

"Instead of just collecting libels and handbills for me, I think I would like you to read them as well... then we can discuss them. Debate them even."

Debate?

That sounded alarmingly like conversation to Daniel's ears. Even his wildest fantasies about Lady Henrietta hadn't stretched to *that* kind of thing.

"You do not need to look so horrified," Henrietta chided, "is the prospect of spending a little time with me *so* appalling. Perhaps you do prefer polishing your brass?"

"Not at all Ma'am... of course not," Daniel blustered, "I'm just a little surprised that you... would..."

The Duchess laughed, it was a sweet, gentle little melody that Daniel had heard only infrequently before and never so intimately. It made him sweat even more profusely, and he could feel his shirt plastering to his skin beneath the heavy footman's jacket he wore.

"Then I will explain matters in order to save you any further confusion," Henrietta said, still smiling sweetly she placed her cake to one side, "I have the misfortune of being an unconventional woman married to a *decidedly* conventional man. Please do not take this as a criticism of His Grace, for I love him dearly and he is an admirable man. However, he is quite strongly of the opinion that a woman's life should revolve around an axis of conformity. In other words, it is my job to be pretty, feminine, charming, produce babies, run the household, support my husband at all times and cater to his whims; my spare time should be spent exclusively upon womanly pastimes, such as music, poetry, embroidery and idle chatter. All these things I do to the best of my ability, and I believe I have achieved success, to a greater or lesser degree, in all of them. However, that is not enough to keep me amused. I wish to know more of the world that passes by outside my window. Unfortunately, my husband and his friends believe the matters of the day should be discussed only between themselves. Be it in their drawing rooms after dinner or at one of their infernal clubs; either way, I am excluded by the misfortune of my sex. I could discuss these matters with my lady friends..." Henrietta sighed deeply,

"...and though they keep me most excellently informed as to precisely who is currently seducing whom, I would have more chance of discussing politics and matters of state with one of my husband's hounds."

She rose gracefully to her feet, gently running her hands down the folds of her skirts as she moved. She was tall for a woman, only an inch or two shorter than Daniel, and striking too; the work of her corsets cunningly improving even that which she had been blessed with.

"This leaves me seeking other companions, who will not raise suspicions."

"Suspicions Ma'am?"

"Well, if I were to be meeting a gentleman of Quality on a clandestine basis, then I am sure people - my lady friends certainly - would jump *entirely* to the wrong conclusion. That is the beauty of servants Daniel, the Quality tend not to notice them very much. I believe my husband thinks of his staff as holding a position equidistant between his furniture and his dogs when it comes to social standing."

She moved around the table slowly, though each step was so gracefully taken Daniel would not have laid a bet against her being on wheels beneath the long skirts of her dress. The room suddenly seemed very quiet and only the swinging of the pendulum in the library's grandfather clock and the swish of silk as the Duchess circled him competed with the hard pounding of his own heart.

"Does that answer your question, Daniel?"

"Yes Ma'am," Daniel replied, unsure whether etiquette demanded his eyes should attempt to follow her or stare blankly ahead, though the dilemma was resolved when she moved behind him, out of eye swivelling range, "I'm very flattered... I'll do my very best to be... erm... *interesting.*"

Henrietta giggled from somewhere that was both behind him and alarmingly close to his left ear. It was a girlish little sound, unlike the refined and elegant laughter that he had always previously heard her make, "I am sure of it."

She moved back into his vision and stood before him, clasping her hands daintily before her as she looked him up and down, before fixing her gaze upon his. Daniel found this doubly uncomfortable as he was unused to women in general and Duchess' in particular looking at him so boldly. His sweat production was duly ratcheted up another notch.

"You know," she said, "you look particularly sweet when you blush, it quite matches your uniform. Perhaps I should insist all my staff flushes so furiously in my presence."

Under such an onslaught of familiarity and bold staring Daniel found his tongue had instigated a divorce from the rest of his body, he feared any attempt at speech would result only in some guttural and incomprehensible moaning noise. Instead, he laughed nervously, which he immediately considered being vastly too familiar and stifled it with a broad smile. The type of smile he suspected would stand him in good stead for any position of village idiot that he might need to apply for, once the Duke had horsewhipped and dismissed him in disgrace.

The Duchess, however, did not appear unduly troubled by his behaviour; instead, she cocked her head ever so slightly to one side and said seriously, "You have a lovely smile, Daniel, I'm sure it will break many hearts. Use it more often."

"Yes Ma'am," Daniel replied, doing as he was told.

Henrietta laughed, "You may go now, Daniel. From today, you shall bring me tea and cake every afternoon... along with whatever libels are circulating on the street you think may be of interest to me."

"Yes Ma'am, very good Ma'am," Daniel replied, both relieved and saddened to be leaving Henrietta's company. Though given the sweat cascading down his body he was in danger of staining the finely woven carpet he was standing on if he had been required to stay much longer.

Henrietta Bourness, Duchess of Pevansea, returned to her seat without further ado where she went about the serious business of selecting another fancy from the various temptations on offer. As he let himself out of the library, Daniel allowed himself one last lingering look at Henrietta poised over the cake tray, her lips slightly pursed as she considered the merits of the French macaroons over the lemon tarts.

He couldn't quite shake the feeling that he had something in common with the cakes on the tray, laid out as they were so carefully for the Duchess' pleasure.

Chapter Four

The Dance of Delights

Mrs Crisp's Molly House, Wapping - 1708

"Later my beauties, later!" Defane cried blowing extravagant kisses at the two young molly boys as he pushed the still dumbstruck Caleb into another room, which, in addition to the same expensive furnishings and decorations as the previous room, boasted a large bronze statue of a naked and athletic young man. The classical perfection of the statue, however, was somewhat sullied by its most prominent and impressive feature being used as an impromptu hat stand.

A much older and fatter specimen of masculinity was using the statue to lean against. A lithe and effeminate young man dressed in only a loose-fitting silk shirt stared intently at him over the rim of a champagne glass whilst he hunted for a way to get his hand between the older man's belt and his prodigious stomach.

"Well I never," Caleb said, his relief that the two mollies had not pursued them was somewhat undermined by the way the fat old man next to the statue smiled and raised his glass in their direction, indicating they should feel free to assist his young friend whenever they wanted.

Caleb managed a polite smile of apology.

Defane only smirked and helped himself to another glass of champagne from a passing serving boy, who differed from the one in the first room only in so much as he wore nothing but scented body oil. They stood for a moment as patrons moved to and from various rooms. Some were respectably attired men of all ages, some were young men dressed as women with varying degree of conviction, disturbingly there were a couple he wasn't entirely sure *weren't* women while others were dressed somewhere between the two. Anywhere else, they would just have been ridiculed as dandified French fops, though the exaggerated femininity of their movements and affectations indicated that their dress was more to do with their sexuality than mere fashion. Which of these were Mrs Crisp's "girls" and which ones were patrons Caleb could only guess, and he was coming to the conclusion the line between the two was somewhat blurred.

"We should be going," he eventually said.

"We have still to find the Fat Bookseller," Defane protested downing the champagne in one again.

"I think we can safely guess what his secret is now."

"Not at all," Defane shook his head, "we do not know his particular fancy at all; is it young boys, athletic youths or more mature men. Perhaps he enjoys dressing up and playing the lady?"

A truly awful vision of Brindley the Book bewigged and powdered, his corpulent bulk forced into a corset and performing sexual favours for various gentlemen momentarily flickered behind Caleb's eyes.

"I believe that really is more than I care to know."

Defane slipped his arm through Caleb's and whispered in his ear, "Do not fret, I will protect you from all these ghastly sodomites. I promise none of them will get hold of your pretty little arse!"

"How kind," Caleb said dryly, pulling himself free.

"You should try to discard the last vestiges of that unfortunate Puritan upbringing of yours, my friend," Defane sighed wearily, "you should not so quickly dismiss the pleasures offered by a pretty lad." When he noticed Caleb eyeing him cautiously, he flashed him a mischievous smile. "As you are neither pretty nor a lad, you may rest easy. Though I much prefer the comforts and curves of the female form if you live long enough, you end up trying most things at least once."

"Given that you are ten years my junior you must have packed a lot into your time."

Defane only smiled a strange little smile, before turning those eyes of his upon him once more, "You are quite safe from me. My love for you is not *that* kind of love."

Caleb's eyes widened slightly as he recalled discussing Defane's proclamation of love the night before with Harriet. He'd been standing by the window, looking out into the street. Had Defane been outside then? Had he somehow found a perch on the wall of the building to listen in to their conversations? If he had been staring into the bedroom during the small hours, was it such a leap to think he had been out there for the entire night?

Before he could consider the matter further Defane had begun to talk again, "Words mean different things to different people Caleb, I say I love you, and I mean I want your companionship, friendship, camaraderie. You say you *like* Harriet, but you mean you want her body and her sex."

Caleb snorted, "I know what I mean-"

Defane waved down his words, "Not allowing yourself to use that one particular little word to acknowledge your feelings about people, is decidedly different from not actually *having* those feelings. We are the same in many ways, but that is one of our big differences. I believe I love everybody, whilst you believe you love nobody at all," he smiled rather sadly; "I dare say we are both wrong."

"This is the strangest of places to have such a conversation, Louis. Though you never seem to struggle to be able to find interesting new ways to disturb me."

"Another time perhaps," Defane smiled, before nodding towards one of the entrances to the room, "besides, I believe we have run our quarry to ground."

Caleb looked up to see a flushed Brindley emerge from a room dabbing his brow with a lace handkerchief. The flush, however, drained rapidly away once he caught sight of Caleb.

"Go talk to him, strike your bargain!" Defane insisted.

"What bargain?" Caleb hissed.

"That the Fat Bookseller allows you to freely spend time with the girl you love and in return you ensure he does not end up being target practice for the mob in the Royal Exchange pillories!"

Whilst Caleb was deciding whether the fact that he didn't actually love Harriet or that blackmail was not really his game at all should be the more pertinent point to protest about, Defane had caught the waist of one of the more convincing "girls" who wandered past and whisked her off to the far corner of the room.

Lacking any coherent idea of how to address the father of the woman he was clandestinely seeing, who he had just bumped into in a male brothel, Caleb decided boldness was a better strategy than nonchalance, "Well, well Mr Brindley what manner of pamphlets are we buying today, I wonder?"

"I had thought you more of a ladies' man, Mr Cade?" Brindley managed to reply when he'd regained a measure of composure.

"And you a more Godly one, Sir."

Brindley smiled coldly, "I suppose neither of us can cast too many stones given our surroundings."

"Are you really a member of the Society for the Reformation of Manners? Or is that just the cover you use to slip away for a night's debauching here?"

Brindley's eyes widened in alarm, and he grabbed Caleb's arm as he hissed in a low voice, "Do not mention *them* here, it makes these people very nervous."

"As the Society would no doubt want everybody here hanging from a Tyburn rope that does not overly surprise me. Please unhand me; I don't take kindly to being manhandled."

Brindley snorted, and released his grip, "I never liked you, Cade, but I suppose we have something in common. You go and enjoy your evening, and I'll do the same."

The bookseller turned to go, but was stayed by Caleb's voice, "Unlike you, I'm not here to sodomise boys."

"Oh no? Tell me, what brings you to this particular Molly House then?" Brindley sneered.

Caleb smiled evenly, "I was just curious where you went so often, leaving your daughter alone to mind your shop and run your home on the few pennies you give her. Now, of course, I can see where all your coins go; a far more important expenditure than your daughter, obviously."

"What business is Harriet of yours?" Brindley spluttered indignantly, the colour returning to his face and more besides.

Caleb felt an unfamiliar cold anger building inside him, he had not intended to confront Brindley when he had reluctantly followed Defane into this place, but now he found himself unable to suppress his words. Perhaps it was the fact that the bookseller reminded him vaguely of his own father, save for the northern accent and being twice his body weight of course. Both men had righteously intoned the words of God to cover their own sins, which in both men had been the neglect of their families in one manner or another.

"Your daughter and I have become... *quite friendly,*" Caleb smiled, almost enjoying the way Brindley's features flicked between horror and despair.

"How dare you! Sneak around behind my back-"

"Perhaps if you spent more time with Harriet and less in such establishments as this, you would be aware of what was occurring under your own roof."

Brindley took half a step forward, eyes wide and angry while his nostrils flared as he sucked in air. Caleb almost expected him to start stamping the floor with his feet, like an angry bull poised to charge,

"Have you dishonoured my daughter, Sir?" he demanded.

"Dishonoured?" Caleb laughed, "'tis not I who dishonour her Mr Brindley, not I at all."

"If you ever set eyes on my daughter again," Brindley said, his voice quivering in time with his jowls, "I will kill you; with my own bare hands, I swear it!"

Caleb shook his head, "You are in no position to make threats Mr Brindley! All it takes is a word in the right ear and the best you could hope for is a session in the pillory followed by a few years in Newgate..." he leaned forward till he was close enough to feel the furious heat radiating from Brindley's flushed face, "and if you're really unlucky, you'll end up dancing a merry jig at the end of a Tyburn rope."

"Don't threaten me," Brindley spat back, "there are powerful people here. We look after our own."

"That would be why you meet behind the façade of a Wapping gin house then?" Caleb shook his head, "We both know it is always the unimportant fellow who falls the furthest when secrets are revealed, and important men face disgrace; and you, Mr Brindley, are a very unimportant fellow indeed."

"You should be very careful about whom you threaten, sir," Brindley retorted though some of the conviction had ebbed from his voice.

"I am making no threats Mr Brindley, I am sure we can come to some, mutually acceptable understanding."

Brindley shook his head and looked at the floor, "From the first I took you for a money grabber and a chancer. I thought you were some dirty philanderer or dowry grabber with an eye for a plain girl with a little money. It never occurred to me that you'd just be using her to get at me. How'd you find out about me? You must have known before you even got on that coach?"

When Caleb tried to answer, Brindley simply waved him down, "What does it matter how you did it, you are just a low blackmailer rather than a dowry thief, 'tis unimportant what type of villainy it is you pursue. How much do you want, to leave my daughter and me in peace?"

Egged on by Defane's words Caleb had been working on the assumption that there was some faint and noble purpose behind this confrontation with Brindley, that he could use what he now knew to help Harriet, freeing her from the lonely servitude her father had inflicted upon her. However, he had not had the time to create anything so defined as a plan, and it had been purely his anger and dislike of her father that had drawn him in so far. Despite the life he had led, he had never been a particularly calculating man, he tended to follow his instincts when opportunities unexpectedly presented themselves, but the narrow borders of his own self-interest had always confined those instincts. Now that he was, at least as far as he considered, acting to benefit another, matters seemed entirely more confusing.

The simple offer of money was far more straightforward.

He did not love Harriet after all, why should he treat her any different from all those other women he had profited from? In many ways, this was better, for she would not be aware of his deceit. She would not wake one morning to find her bed and her jewellery box equally empty and the man she loved revealed as nought but a liar and a cheat. Only her father would know the truth, and as he could not think less of Caleb than he already did, what did it matter?

The indecision that held his tongue clearly played across his face, for Brindley stared at him strangely, before mumbling in a low voice, "Dear God man, please tell me that it is only *money* you want?"

Before Caleb could speak, Brindley gripped his arm and hustled him into the room from which he had just emerged; evidently the finer points of extortion were better discussed in private.

Caleb had expected the room to be some discreet little corner where Mrs Crisp's patrons could come to indulge their pleasures away from prying eyes, furnished with a bed or a couch or maybe some more esoteric paraphernalia. Instead, the room was a rather sober-looking office, sporting shelves of books and a large imposing desk. Only the paintings of half-naked young men that adorned the wainscoted walls suggested this was anything other than the study of some respected man of finance or commerce.

Brindley poured himself a brandy from a decanter on the desk while Caleb lingered by the door. He wasn't overly offended not to be offered one.

"I love your daughter, Mr Brindley," Caleb heard himself saying, hating himself for the lie while comforted by the familiarity of it, the way it slipped over his tongue, like a well-worn and favoured glove might fit his hand.

"Do not tell me that you have come for her hand?" Brindley asked, slowly and evenly, his back still turned, "I don't know who you are, but it is clear you are an educated man, a man with some money, perhaps a background of Quality. Perhaps not. If I knew you were merely some vagrant chancer, I do believe I would have you killed, but it is a far more dangerous game to take the life of a man who may have... *background*. You are lucky I know nothing about you."

"You must be a particularly dangerous bookseller to have killers ready to answer your beck and call."

"There has never been a shortage of men prepared to kill for a few coins," Brindley replied. "The men downstairs, in the gin house, are not the drunken sops they appear to be. Well, not all at least. They take money to keep this place safe and will have few qualms about accepting more to undertake... other tasks." He turned his heavyset frame back towards Caleb, perching himself on the edge of the desk as he sloshed the remainder of his drink about the bottom of the glass.

"I love my daughter very much," Brindley said eventually though his words were quietly spoken they were uttered with conviction, "and just as I know my love for her is deep and pure, I know you have no feelings for her at all."

"Is it so impossible that a man might love Harriet?"

"A man like you?" Brindley scoffed, "all easy charm and empty promises, a quick smile and a glint in the eye that would make every little whore in the street swoon for you? I know your type well enough... I see it every day. I know well enough why my girl might fall for you, but why would a man like you fall in love with my plain little Harriet? Why when you could have your pick?"

"You have an uncommonly low opinion of Harriet."

"No, Cade, I hold her in the highest regard. That's why I keep her safe, away from the users and abusers. Away from heartbreak, pain, and suffering, I keep her safe with the books she loves. Keep her safe where no one will hurt her. I give her the things that will make her truly happy when she has put the last of her foolish girlish thoughts to one side."

Caleb laughed dryly, "She is lonely and afraid. The only person that is hurting her is you. She deserves a life. She deserves a little happiness. All she is now is your servant, bound to you through blood and obligation."

"You do not know us. We are happy," Brindley muttered darkly, his words spat out on his hot wet brandy-tinged breath.

"Your wife ran away with another man. Broke your heart," Caleb said softly, "'tis easy enough to see you're afraid some man will do the same to Harriet, so you lock her in an ivory tower, or rather a tower of books. You shut the door to the world and the chance of harm... as well as any chance of happiness. You don't have the right to do that."

"Of course, I have the right!" Brindley roared, "I am her father!" He slammed his empty glass down on the table beside him. Caleb thought the stocky bookseller was going to launch himself at him, but the fire burned in his eyes for only a second or two before subsiding into sadness and shadow. When he spoke again the words were so soft and quiet they were almost drowned out by the sounds of music and laughter that drifted in from the rooms behind the door.

"My wife did not run away because she fell in love with another man, she run away because she found out what I am," he lifted a hand briefly towards the paintings that hung on the walls, "that I had *unnatural* tastes. It was not my heart that was broken, but hers. When she found out what I was, she did not run into the arms of another man, she run into the arms of Old Father Thames and his embrace was the last she ever knew. That was the coffin-maker I told Harriet about; that foul stinking river." He looked darkly at Caleb, "I will not let Harriet suffer as her mother did. Men are weak, pathetic creatures, slaves to their lust, subject always to their cravings. Believe me, I know that better than most. Whatever those desires are, be they women, or gambling, or liquor or pretty young boys, one day, eventually, any love they might have for my Harriet will fade as ink left in the sun when held against the searing light of their wants. I will not let her wake one day to find that the man she loves is as weak and pathetic as I am... or is as much of a liar as you are."

Brindley walked slowly around the desk and eased himself into the chair with a deep sigh and cracking joints. He pulled a key from his jacket and, after fumbling with the lock, opened a drawer. Caleb half expected him to brandish a pistol. Instead, he produced two fist-sized bags which he tossed casually onto the floor at Caleb's feet, where they landed with the comforting thud of hard currency.

"Take it," Brindley said.

"Yours?"

"Partly," Brindley admitted, "I learned long ago that there is far more money in buggery than books."

Caleb snorted, "So beneath your respectable bookseller façade and your moralising pamphlets you're just a whoremaster, pimping butt-boys to the Quality."

"Business and pleasure," Brindley shrugged, "who says they don't go together, eh?"

"So, while your beloved daughter works her fingers to the bone cleaning your home because you claim you can't afford a maid, you live in decadent splendour here?"

"If people thought me rich," he replied evenly, "then, even more, men like you would crawl out of the woodwork claiming to love my daughter."

"How selfless of you," Caleb spat, pulled by the conflicting of feelings of disgust for Brindley's hypocrisy and the temptation of the money that lay, heavy and alluring and easy at his feet.

In the Absence of Light

"Take it, we both know you do not love my Harriet " Brindley urged again as if reading Caleb's mind, "part of the reason I built this place was so that men could have somewhere to come and be their true selves. So, within these walls, let us both be what we truly are."

Caleb was still staring long and hard at the money when he heard Brindley add, "However, before you go, tell me, what exactly *are* you carrying around in that box?"

*

Of course, the coach was gone. They had lingered far too long in Mrs Crisp's and the coachman had decided the risk of hanging around far outweighed the prospect of their money; if he had waited at all.

"Damn it," Caleb cursed, raising his eyes towards a clearly disinterested heaven.

"So, how was the Fat Bookseller?" Defane asked, tapping out a generous measure of snuff onto the back of his glove.

"The coach is gone, Louis?" Caleb pointed out the rather obvious fact to his companion.

Defane shrugged, put his nostril to the back of his hand and took a short, sharp snort, followed by a shudder.

"I said-"

"My faculties are working most efficiently, I both noticed our coach has gone and heard you telling me the coach has gone." Defane cut him off, with a snap of the snuffbox's lid. "I know the coach has gone."

"How many cut-throats do you think there are between us and our lodgings?" Caleb insisted, feeling a familiar rising panic wash over the melancholy his meeting with Brindley had induced.

"Hundreds... at least," Defane admitted.

"You don't seem unduly concerned that we are stranded in Wapping, the hour is late and murderers abound at every corner!"

Defane adopted a fencing pose; holding out his cane as if it were a blade and made a few dramatic thrusts at various imaginary cutthroats, "Do not worry, dear boy, I am an excellent blades man. If any rabble bothers us, rest assured I will put them to flight in short order."

"Well, if I were a villainous cove looking to stave heads and cut throat's in return for a gentleman's purse I am sure the sight of you twirling your cane around would give me second thoughts."

"Such sarcasm," Defane sighed, "Come let us walk back to London, the night will clear our lungs."

"Walk?" Caleb asked incredulously, "even the locals don't walk here after dark - save for the heavily armed ones anyway. And its miles back to London!"

"You'll be perfectly safe!" Defane assured him confidently, walking up the street purposefully enough for Caleb to have to scurry after him for fear of being left alone.

"Why don't we just wait?" Caleb suggested once he'd managed to match Defane's stride, "Carriages must come her regularly to drop off customers at the molly house?"

"I don't think the men who go there use just any old carriage. They all looked wealthy enough to have their own."

"Then let us wait inside... Mrs Crisp can send a boy out to get a carriage for us."

Defane laughed, "I think Mrs Crisp's boys are far too valuable to her to send out alone at night. I'm sure they have work to perform anyway."

Caleb trudged on in miserable silence, realising there was little he could say or do to deter Defane. During their time in Mrs Crisp's the light mist had hardened into something more menacing. Faintly luminous, it hung thickly in the air shrouding the surrounding buildings in eerie shades while muting all tone and colour from the evening. The mist was tinged sulphurous yellow, a by-product of thousands of sea-coal fires, and it carried the damp, fetid stinks of London into their mouths and nostrils as if the city were some great ailing beast and the mist its foul and rotting breath.

It took them only a few minutes to reach the end of the narrow road that was home to the molly house and Defane promptly turned left into a broader thoroughfare, which Defane surprised Caleb by confidently identifying as Upper Shadwell, "We simply follow Upper Shadwell, which in time becomes Ratcliff High Way and then Upper Smithfield; a simple straight line which will deliver us to The Tower in no time at all!"

"You seem well acquainted with these mean little highways?"

Defane smiled smugly, "All of London is my playground..."

Over the centuries the city had thrown out a spindly arm of buildings eastwards from the Tower of London around the wharves and docks that serviced the ships that made the city one of the major trading ports in the world. A continuous line of generally cheap ramshackle development that had slowly amalgamated the old communities of Wapping, Shadwell and Limehouse into one wretched whole.

They were on the margins of London here. The buildings petered out north of Upper Shadwell, and through the mist Caleb could vaguely make out fields beyond the houses and glassworks on the opposite side of the road. It was a diverse landscape of orchards, market gardens, rubbish dumps, tented camps of itinerant workers, pastures and brick kilns, mixed with lanes so narrow and poorly marked they didn't even warrant a name, though some would no doubt take you to the villages that lay to the north, like Mile End and Stepney.

Satisfied Defane was right; Caleb tried not to think just how long it might take them to walk back to the centre of London and how many cutpurses and highwaymen they were likely to run into along the way. At least it was easy to navigate a route. Initially, there would be a few fields visible to their right though these would soon be consumed by the tangled network of lanes and alleys that housed the wretches of the miserable parishes that ringed The City of London. The river, however, would always be on their left. Although several hundred yards of houses, shops, taverns, brothels warehouses, storage yards and assorted light industry shielded it from view, the simple expedient of turning your nose to the south confirmed the location of the river. The stink was noticeably worse in that direction. The tide was low, and the mist carried the stench from the latest deposits of shit that approximately three-quarters of a million Londoners had made the previous day. The waste had found its way into the Thames up river via the Fleet ditch, the city's various other open sewers and kennels and a large proportion of it now sat on the exposed river mud waiting for the next high tide to pick it up and continue it on its journey towards the North Sea.

Defane filled the silence with a jauntily tuneless whistle that Caleb found so irritating he was almost relieved when the Frenchman asked him again how his meeting with Brindley had gone.

"We came to an understanding," Caleb said finally.

"Did you take his money?"

"What makes you think he offered me money?"

"Through fear that you might send him to the magistrates," Defane replied with a shrug, "a man generally does one of three things when you threaten to ruin him; he does what you want, he offers you money or he tries to kill you. You don't appear to have been the subject of attempted murder, which rules out one possibility, though you seem quite miserable, which suggests he didn't give you what you asked for. This leaves money."

"Don't you think the fact I'm am walking through the slums of London, at night, in the cold, through a foul stinking fog, unable to even see what varieties of shit I am walking through might, just, account for me seeming a mite miserable."

"No," Defane said assuredly, "'tis another type of misery that hangs about you altogether. Tell me about it, it will make our stroll pass all the quicker."

The sound of approaching hooves and the clatter of wheels interrupted Caleb, he turned hoping it might be a carriage they could flag down, but it was only a night soil man's wagon that appeared out of the fog, heading into London for a busy evening of shit collecting. Given the stench that inevitably accompanied the unenviable job of emptying the cesspits and shit-vaults of the well to do, the soil-men worked only at night. Leaving before dawn to either sell what they'd collected to market gardeners as fertilizer or simply dumping it in the Fleet or in roadside ditches outside of London, where it acted as a kind of pungent signpost to inform visitors they were entering the outskirts of one of the greatest cities on Earth.

The soil-man watched them with an expression that was both bemused and wary. Bemused to find two gentlemen abroad in this part of town at night, wary because it was not unknown for young beaux's to give soil-men a good beating for the temerity of exposing their genteel senses to so much excrement.

"You want to see if we can get a ride?" Defane asked, only half-jokingly.

As night-soil men were probably the foulest smelling men in London, an accolade for which there were numerous worthy candidates, the prospect of riding on a night-soil wagon, even an empty one, was arguably even less appealing than being robbed and beaten, Caleb just offered his friend the thinnest of disdainful smiles.

As the wagon trundled by, leaving a quite remarkably pungent aroma in its wake, Caleb took the opportunity to look back along Upper Shadwell. The fog seemed to be thickening by the minute, but he momentarily thought he could make out men moving in the shadows, however the gloom consumed any figures before he could fully focus on them.

There were still a few souls abroad though they either moved with enough purpose to suggest they were concentrating solely on getting somewhere else as quickly as possible, or so shambolically that Caleb doubted they even knew where they were. Neither seemed much of a threat though Caleb eyed them warily anyway and did not relax until they were long lost to the dark and the fog. He tried not to think about his dead brother, walking the streets on a night not so very dissimilar to this one (if you replaced the cold, foul fog with cold, foul rain). He tried not to wonder if he had seen the men who had killed him, dismissing them as harmless and dropping his guard before they kicked the life from his body for a few pennies.

"You were going to tell me why the Fat Bookseller has left you so long-faced and sorry looking?"

Caleb took a deep breath in exasperation, which given the effect the recently departed night-soil wagon and the shit tainted fog had on the local air quality, was somewhat ill advised. Once his eyes had stopped watering he simply stared ahead into the shifting murk for several minutes and was mildly startled by the sound of his own voice when he found himself finally speaking.

"I had hoped to make her life better."

"Because you love her?" Defane replied, his tone only marginally mocking.

Caleb shook his head, "No, 'tis not so simple."

"Explain it to me then?"

"I wanted to make her life better... because I have made so many others worse."

"Sadly, 'tis the lot of a heartbreaker to break hearts."

Again, Caleb shook his head, "'tis more than just a fickle nature and a wandering eye... but that is the past and I have no care to recount it. I think I came back to London to start afresh, to come back and be a different man, the man I might have been if things had happened differently."

"Ah," Defane said knowingly, eyes darting sideways at Caleb, "'tis redemption you seek?"

"I thought I could change... when I met Harriet, instead of just an opportunity, I wanted to do some little good. Make her happy. She has become a grand project, of sorts."

Now it was Defane who shook his head, "And you intend to spend the rest of your life on this project eh? To marry her and devote yourself to her? To produce strapping sons and doe-eyed daughters? To forsake all excess; wine, cards, wanton women and all other craven pleasures?"

"Well... not exactly."

"Then what?"

"She is so sad, I have met so many women like her and have done nothing but use their sadness for my own purposes..."

"So, your grand project amounts to providing access to your britches, before moving on to the next woman you meet whose life requires improving?" Defane asked sceptically, "which, to me, sounds little different from what you were doing before, save now you claim to be rogering her for her benefit, rather than your own. Quite the martyr."

"My plan appears flawed," Caleb admitted, "I have thought much the same myself, how could I actually improve things for her. I know how to make her happy, 'tis not a difficult thing, but I do not know how to love her..." he sighed, "...then when we followed Brindley here, everything became suddenly clear. I could use what we found out about him for Harriet's benefit..."

"A charitable kind of blackmail," Defane offered.

"If you like, I wanted to tell him how wonderful his daughter is, how she deserves to find the things she truly desires, how she deserves better than to be so deceived and used as a servant. That he should set her free, give her money and help find a suitable husband."

"I suspect there is a "but" heaving itself over the horizon?"

Caleb nodded miserably, "Brindley saw through me clearly enough, saw that which even I did not fully realise until he offered me the money; I am purely villainous, there is no good in me at all. I exist solely to use others."

"Come now Caleb," Defane said softly, "don't be so hard upon yourself."

"Don't you see?" Caleb pleaded, "I've travelled all this way, for two decades and God alone knows how many thousands of miles. Lately, I thought I'd always been coming home. I thought that there had been some purpose to it all, that I had travelled and seen and experienced things that other men never had the opportunity to enjoy. I thought I could leave all my ills upon the road behind me by coming back to London, where all things began. I thought there was some purpose to my journey, and that maybe Harriet was that purpose. Despite all the wrongs I've done, I thought I could still be a good man."

Caleb curled his fists around the bags of coins that weighed down his coat pockets, "but I know better now."

"What did you do with your gift?" Defane asked, "I noticed you never brought it out of Mrs Crisp's."

"I was so excited by the thought of giving her that dress," Caleb replied, "Can you imagine? Like some young knave taking a bunch of daisies he'd plucked from the roadside to woo a milkmaid. I have given countless women innumerable gifts over the years. However, they would be more accurately referred to as investments. This one I gave for other reasons. I was so looking forward to seeing her face... I gave it to her father, I told him everyone deserved a little happiness, even Harriet and that if he gave her the dress and told her that he loved her, it would be a small step towards that goal."

"What did the Fat Bookseller say?"

"That he would think about it... more likely he will just give it to one of his Molly boys."

Defane unexpectedly slapped Caleb's back and grinned, "He offered you temptation... you succumbed, 'tis no sin."

"You haven't read your Bible for a while, have you?" Caleb asked miserably.

Defane simply laughed.

"So why did I come back to London? If I am to be the same wretched man I have always been, why did I not simply keep on following the road. Why did I come home?"

"Because it is not your past you are running away from, 'tis your future."

Caleb arched an enquiring eyebrow.

"Good man or bad, you can be whatever you choose; whether it be the earthy pleasures we both crave or some higher form of achievement, 'tis not really so difficult. What you cannot change is your mortality. That is what you truly fear, that is what keeps you awake in the dark, not that you feel you bear responsibility for the deaths of others. Your mortality beckons Caleb, the easy days of youth are lost to you now. You've already reached your mountain top and seen the glorious panorama of creation; you're passing down into the valley now, the dark Valley of Shadows where only bitterness and the eternal cold awaits."

Caleb realised they had stopped walking, and Defane had turned to stand squarely before him, his eyes bright and extraordinary once more, they seemed to make the mist that floated before them glow and crackle with strange energies.

"You do not wish to change because you believe you are a bad man, you want to change because you fear the bent-backed old man you sometimes see in the looking-glass, the one that hides behind your face, the Caleb-yet-to-come. You fear that old man for he will not be able to indulge the pleasures you still crave, still yearn for. Better by far to change now and fool yourself that you no longer want to woo that pretty young girl, rather than admit that you have become too old and ugly for her to notice you at all. Better to fool yourself that you no longer want to drink till dawn, rather than admit your body protests too much and craves only sleep, better to fool yourself that you do not want to gamble insane amounts of money rather than admit you need the coins to buy coal to warm your feeble, broken old body."

Like the mist that swirled around them, Defane's voice was soft and insidious, the words finding their way inside Caleb's skull as much through his pores as his ears. An aural miasma that clouded his thoughts as efficiently as the fog obscured his vision.

"Look at the glass Caleb," Defane whispered, nodding towards a plate glass shop window they were standing before, "look at it and tell me what you see."

A distant part of Caleb's mind, perhaps the part where the memory of his long-dead brother lived, thought it was odd to find such an expensive piece of glass fronting a shop in such a poor and decrepit parish, but that familiar voice was far, far away.

The darkness in the shop beyond had turned the window into a looking-glass, and though Defane's image was somehow blurred and indistinct (a flaw in the glass no doubt) he saw himself reflected perfectly, backlit by the faintly glowing mist.

"Just me..." Caleb whispered, for the image was familiar enough. Tall and well groomed, he carried no excess fat, the road had seen to that while foreign suns had darkened his skin beyond the norm for an Englishman. He looked younger than his years; his hair was long and dark and tied back in a short ponytail. He'd disdained wigs ever since his days with Lady Henrietta, despite their practicality. His face was unremarkable, and always had been, it was only his smile that transformed it into something else. The smile and the wicked glint he could summon to his eye, they were the gifts that had allowed him to break so many hearts.

"Look closer," Defane whispered. Caleb was mildly surprised to feel the Frenchman's breath on his ear, his lips almost caressing his skin as he spoke, for the reflection showed him standing much further away, but that didn't really seem to matter at all and he did as Defane suggested and stared closely at his own face.

Years ago he had thought himself immortal. The young would forever be so, and the old had forever been so. Now time was doing its work; carving, thinning and altering his features slowly and subtly; changing new and young into old and used. Sometimes when he glanced at his reflection, he glimpsed the boy he had once been, the next time he looked he caught sight of the old man yet to come.

Boy and man and wizened old codger, all hidden in the same face, but all there to see if you cared to look hard enough. Without his bidding, the old man stepped forward from the others a little and he could see the debris time would leave in its wake. The lines around his eyes and mouth deepened and widened, his cheeks sagged inwards as his skin drooped and fell away from his face, falling to handles of loose flesh around his throat and neck. Liver spots and broken veins blemished his skin further, becoming as translucent as the mist before his eyes, barely concealing the skull beneath. His eyes became cloudy, and rheumy, the glint and shimmer of them diluted by pain and weariness, his hair receded to a few wispy strands of white twine hanging limply around ears that seemed to have grown as large and prominent as handles on the side of a jug. And then there was his smile, his beautiful, heart-breaking smile as Harriet had called it, now it was nought but a grimace that revealed the broken and blackened ruins of what had once been his teeth, thin, pale lips curled into something that would flutter no more hearts.

"What I will become..." Caleb heard himself say.

"Look closely, is this not the ghost that truly haunts you, more so than your brother or Isabella. This is your ghost, not from the past, but the future. Would a woman as beautiful as Isabella ever want to kiss those thin, cracked old lips? Would she want those wizened crocked hands on her firm young body? Would she want that thick bloated, pale tongue slurping at her teats? Do you think, eh? Do you think?"

That same distant voice that had queried what such a grandiose piece of glass was doing in this slum sent up another yell of alarm. He had only ever told Harriet about Isabella; Defane could only have known of her if he had been outside that window, somehow, hanging from the roof like a bloated human bat listening to their conversation. However, that particular voice was now even further away than before. The fog that lay damp against his skin had seemingly seeped into his mind so that his own thoughts were as murky and distorted as the buildings on the opposite side of the road.

"No..." he whispered hoarsely, "...never,"

"You see," Defane's silken seductive voice whispered in his ear, his breath no warmer than the cold fog, "if you have your beauty, your youth, your *vitality,* then all things become possible, be they good or ill. That broken old man will never seduce a beautiful woman, nor will he put right the wrongs in the life of a plain one. All will be impossible for none will look beyond this old leathery creature; none will know how beautiful you were, and you are beautiful Caleb, you know that you are beautiful, don't you?"

"Yes..." Caleb let the word drop from his lips slowly and thickly, like honey from a spoon, but the only reply was Defane's sudden and urgent grip upon his arm, Caleb pulled his eyes away from the reflection to see him staring pointedly into the dark shadows of fog that covered the road behind them.

"We are followed," he spat.

"Followed?" Caleb asked, his thoughts rushing back into his head, like a half-drowned man popping unexpectedly to the surface to grab a desperate breath of air.

"Always we are followed," Defane said sadly, moving forward briskly in the opposite direction, his fingers like iron clamps on Caleb's arm, *"always..."*

"Cut-purses?" Caleb asked, looking over his shoulder as more familiar ghosts crowded out thoughts of the old man Defane had somehow conjured in the glass.

Defane half dragged him along the road. There were no street lanterns here, and only the occasional faint glow crept from beneath the doors and shuttered windows they passed. The fog swirled behind them, thicker than ever now, there could have been figures moving, just beyond the reach of his eyes, but he could not be sure. For a moment, he was reminded of the Venetian mist that had lain upon the canals the night he had seduced Isabella, but that had been a softer, kinder mist than this sulphurous brew, and her touch upon his arm as they had walked through it had been far gentler than Defane's.

"Of a kind," Defane grinned, flashing him a wide smile, "but there is no need to fear. I am faster, stronger, smarter than they can ever imagine..." his eyes widened, like wrecker's beacons in the fog, summoning ships to their doom, "...I'm a different manner of beast entirely. Come let us run!"

With his arm held in the strongest of grips, Caleb had no alternative but to match Defane's stride as they hurtled forward into the blinding fog, after a moment Defane jerked him to the left and Caleb found himself sprinting down some mean little alley at a breakneck pace.

He was dimly aware of dark broken down buildings leaning over him on either side. There were images of startled faces as they rushed by, of forms huddled in doorways, of feral dogs barking wildly, of glassless windows shielded from the cold, foul fog by shabby soiled rags, of babies crying unheeded from darkened homes and everywhere the stink. The stink of the fog, the stink of countless unseen unwashed bodies huddled out of sight in their cold dank hovels, the stink of gin and stale piss, of shit and waste rotting in the kennel that run down the centre of the lane. Waiting for the next rains to come and wash it all down to the river.

Caleb felt his boots splash through unseen pools of God alone knew what, the spray wetting his britches. They run on, his chest tightening as he fought for his breath, drawing in soggy lungfuls of wet fetid air. Sucking the foulness down inside him so that he could match Defane's insane pace; trusting him, somehow, to see what was before them, dodging left or right, as the Frenchman indicated, for Caleb could see nothing clearly, nothing bar the fog and the night.

They sped past blurred muted shapes; an overturned barrel here, a broken hand cart there. What might have a pile of old rags or a body lying face down in the sewer that had to be hurdled; but above it all a noise, a clicking snickering, wet, wild noise. Alien and vaguely obscene. It took Caleb some time to realise it was not the voice of the fog chattering away to itself like a Bedlam inmate entertaining the crowds, but Defane laughing and yelping as they run, like a young boy on the most exciting day of his life. His wig had gone, and the bristles of his white hair were slick with damp, at first, Caleb thought it was sweat, but it was just the fog condensing on his hair, for the man was not panting at all.

Finally, mercifully they stopped, without noise or warning and Caleb staggered into some wretched doorway, his legs near giving away, grateful only that the door could bear his weight and he didn't tumble into whatever squalor lay on the other side.

He doubled over and retched, spewing forth a little extra unpleasantness onto the ground, when he'd finished his mouth was full of acid and bile that, frankly, was an improvement upon the taste of the air.

When he'd finally composed himself a little, he found Defane grinning wildly, leaning forward to rest a hand on either side of the doorway as if he were trying to push the whole building over. He straightened up a little until he was on a level with Defane's eyes, beautiful and cold in the mist. He could almost feel himself tumbling helplessly and endlessly into their depths. Forever tormented, forever denied because he would never lose himself entirely within their beauty.

"We escaped them..." Defane breathed, his pale cheeks not even slightly flushed from his exertions.

"You... nearly... lost... me... too..." Caleb managed to pant, the taste of the night on his tongue making him want to retch again, but he dared not bend over for then he would lose sight of those wonderful eyes, "where... are... we?"

"Safe in the dark," Defane smiled.

Many questions crowded and jostled at the periphery of Caleb's senses, but only one was urgent enough to force its way through the mob and into his mouth, "What do you want of me?"

"Want?" Defane asked, "I want nothing my friend, I want *for* nothing; nothing that I cannot easily find. No, you see, I have this gift Caleb, this beautiful gift. I come to you to share it so that we may be together always; friends eternal."

"I don't understand," Caleb whispered.

Defane reached out and gently swept back a lock of Caleb's dark hair that had fallen loose during their flight, "Understanding will come later... you will have time aplenty for that. All you need to know is that I can slay your dragons. That old bent-backed man will never ruin your life, for he will never come to be. You shall be young, like me, forever."

"Madness."

"You know that I am not like other men, don't you? The other night in Liselot's apartment I tried to show you what I truly am, but you run from me, from what I offered. There is nowhere to run now Caleb..."

And he changed.

Like a conjurer passing his hand over a coin and transforming it into a flower. There was no process, no mechanics to it, one moment he was the Defane he knew the next he was something altered, something different; neither human nor beast, just... something other. Caleb remembered that night well enough, remembered fearing what he might see if he had turned around, what monstrosity Defane might truly be, but this was not what he had envisaged.

Defane's face had lengthened and thinned, each angle was sharper and more defined than before; his skin even paler than before. So pale it was difficult to be sure where his face finished and the fog began. His skin seemed to be carved from fresh snow. All the colour had leached from it. Only his lips retained any pigment, and even there it held only the faintest possible blush of roses, but beneath the skin the faint blue lines of his veins could be seen, as Caleb looked closer he swore he could even see the blood moving through them, like rivulets of liquid water trickling beneath ice.

Defane's eyes, however, were still vivid, even more so than he'd ever seen before, as if every previous time he had noticed their beauty he had, in fact, been glimpsing them through cheap, fire-blackened glass. Now he could see their true glory. They were so large and round, almost impossibly so. Rings of blue ice cracked with fissures of grey that seemed to move; swirling in slow eddies, clouds dancing endlessly to the silent music of time, orbiting the deep black pits of his pupils; dark, abyssal, eternal.

They had seen such things, he suddenly knew. So many things.

"Am I so terrible?" Defane asked, moving closer, his nose almost touching Caleb's.

"No..." Caleb managed to reply.

"I am still human," Defane breathed, "I still need to be loved." As he spoke Caleb noticed his teeth had changed too. They were so white and long, his canine's grown to the length of fangs. They seemed incongruously bestial when set against the fey beauty of the rest of Defane's face, so Caleb paid them no heed, concentrating instead only on those eyes that loomed ever larger as he moved inexorably closer.

Defane was speaking, something soft and alluring, something that made his heart race and his head spin as he spoke of wondrous things, Caleb knew this, though he could not quite bring those words into focus, they simply washed over him and left every nerve in his body a-tingle. He felt Defane's fingers brushing his cheek and then his breath. Both were cold and alien, but not at all unpleasant for they numbed him; they took away his thoughts and his fears. Isabella and his brother were gone; he saw no faceless women or twisted trees behind his eyes. He saw no houses burning in the snow. He felt no fear for being here in this dark slum, he knew no cutthroat could touch him and that he was safe. He would not die in the dark and the filth like his brother, like the real Caleb.

Was that who Defane truly was with his pale skin and white hair, his features of carved snow and eyes of ice? Had Jack Frost found him at last and could he cleanse him, would all the poison within him wither and die in such a cold embrace, could the ice of Defane's touch preserve him forever? Is that what he'd meant, was that the eternity he was offering?

"Do you love me now?" Defane asked, the words cutting through what currently passed for thoughts in Caleb's head.

"Yes…" Caleb replied without hesitation, knowing in that moment he did, and that he would do anything he asked of him for he was just a man while Defane was something more.

He was the King of the Winter.

"Then we will exchange gifts and be bound forever," he whispered, "you will die once and be reborn; never to die again. We will live the life eternal, and all pleasure will be ours. Is that what you want Caleb, is that what you want?"

"Yes," Caleb mumbled, "oh yes."

Defane raised his hand to his mouth, smiling all the time he bit deeply into his palm until dark, thick blood bubbled over his white skin. "Drink from me," he whispered, "as you did before, drink from me and be strong."

Caleb moved without thought or reason as if in a dream, throwing back his head and opening his mouth as Defane held out his bloody hand. He slowly made a fist and squeezed it until the blood fell upon Caleb's tongue it thick salty drops.

"Drink from me then," Defane repeated, "swallow me and take me inside you."

Caleb's throat moved without thought, and he swallowed; his mouth filled with rich, coppery blood, but there were other tastes too, sweeter and darker and more vibrant than mere blood; things that should not be there, strange, powerful things. Magics that moved worlds and woke the dead. He became impatient for more; his tongue licking eagerly at Defane's bloody fist, wishing the meagre droplets of his blood would become a torrent under which he could drown.

Defane laughed dark and knowing, his hand slipping behind Caleb's head, his blood wetting his hair. "You shall have more my love, much more when I bring you back to the world. For now you must give yourself to me, you must come to me," Caleb felt Defane pull him close and envelope him in his cold embrace, "let us dance the dance of delights."

Caleb closed his eyes for he could not see Defane's anymore, and so no longer felt the need to keep them open. Instead, he savoured the coolness of his skin, the lightness of his touch. His lips caressed Caleb's neck, for a moment his tongue making soft wet circles. Then an instant of sharp, hot pain followed by a pleasure so intense and pure it brought forth tears of joy from Caleb's troubled and bitter heart.

"I am yours..." Caleb heard himself mutter, and the world seemed to move, carrying him elsewhere. He could feel the pressure of Defane's lips against his neck, feeling them working, sucking, drawing out his lifeblood, he could feel moist heat contrasting with the Winter King's coldness. He reached out and braced himself against the doorway, for his knees felt weak and he knew if he opened his eyes the world would be spinning madly about them, but that was not important. All that mattered was that he was enraptured, without reservation or contradiction, and in that moment, he knew truly, for the first time in his life, what it felt to actually be in love.

Distantly he could hear guttural snarls, the noises of beasts, it was like nothing he'd entirely heard before and found it hard to imagine it could be Defane, the urbane and charming King of the Winter. He felt him moving against him, hands clawing at his clothes, face moving in a frenzy over his neck, unable to contain himself, all pretence of humanity had been lost. It didn't matter. This was worth dying for.

Defane made a new noise. A strange gurgling sound and as Caleb felt his body stiffen the ecstasy faded; his eyes snapping open as Defane stepped away from him. Without his embrace, Caleb's legs buckled, and he slid down the door.

From the ground he focused on Defane, who stood over him, staring wide-eyed at the sword blade that had erupted through his chest, spraying a fountain of blood out over Caleb and the doorway. Some word formed on Defane's darkly smeared lips, but before he could fully give it form the light faded from his extraordinary eyes which became, in an instant, flat and cold and unremarkable. As he crumpled to the ground Caleb knew he would never know what his strange friend was trying to say; he was dead before his body hit the ground.

Caleb was consumed with a sudden and terrible sense of loss, the pain of his fear, inadequacies and regrets rushing back into the void of his mind far outweighed the pain in his wounded neck and the weakness in his legs. He felt something incredible had been snatched from his grasp and in that instant a broiling rage consumed him. Though his vision was blurred, he could see shadowy forms in the alley, one of which was drawing his sword from Defane's lifeless body.

"You must cut off the head," a voice was saying, "just to be sure."

"No!" Caleb raged, rising shakily to his feet he fumbled for his sword, which he managed to draw halfway

from its scabbard before something large and fist-shaped smashed into his face.

For the second time that night all his cares vanished..

Chapter Five
A Room Above a Shop

St James' Square, London - 1688

"Tell me, Daniel, do you have a sweetheart?"

Daniel looked up from the collection of pamphlets and libels that lay upon his lap. He blinked several times while he tried to work out whether he had misheard the Duchess; it was not the kind of question that readily followed from a reading of a libel decrying the crypto-papist machinations of King James II in particular and the debauched Godless nature of the Stuart family in general.

"I'm sorry ma'am?"

Giving Lady Henrietta's penchant for abruptly diverting the course of what passed for conversation between them, he had decided early on in their peculiar relationship it was probably best to be entirely sure he knew what she was talking about before replying. He felt this was particularly important as he spent most of their time together engulfed in a mind-fuddling haze of pained longing, perpetual surprise and diluted terror; which wasn't a state of mind that generally lent itself to the accurate following of conversations.

Lady Henrietta smiled, which was something that generally didn't help his concentration as she returned her tea to the table beside her, "I asked if you had a sweetheart, Daniel?"

"No ma'am," he replied, shifting uneasily. The sofa upon which Henrietta reclined and he perched felt unnaturally comfortable to a boy used to resting his backside against nothing more yielding than good English oak. Despite her insistence that he sat at her side while they read the latest libels he had collected from the streets, the wrongness of it all ensured he never allowed more than half an arse cheek to sink into the decadently soft upholstery. It also meant he would be able to spring to his feet should anyone unexpectedly enter the library and glimpse the dreadful impropriety of the Duchess' footman.

He still feared this whole strange business was likely to end in a horse whipping.

"A handsome young fellow like you, pray tell, why ever not?"

Daniel lowered his eyes and blushed, which he suspected was the Duchess' intention.

"I have little time for such things ma'am," he replied weakly

"Do we really work you so terribly hard?"

"I need to save my money if I am to find myself a wife."

"How very practical of you, do you have any inkling whom the lucky recipient of you diligent saving will be yet?"

"No," he said carefully, ensuring he did not look directly at Lady Henrietta lest she might see the truth of the matter. Since he had been tasked with bringing the latest libels to the Duchess his interest in other women had wilted and died; he didn't even bat an eyelid in the direction of the barmaids at the *Rose and Crown* anymore.

"Still," she sighed "I suppose you must have some enjoyments in the meantime while you save your money and await the right young lady?"

"I'm sorry ma'am?" Daniel found himself frowning again.

"Men are such coarse beasts, I'm sure you must... *sate your needs?*"

Daniel bounced uncomfortably from one arse cheek to the other, "I was not brought up that way, ma'am," he explained.

"Ah yes, your father is quite the puritan, I believe?"

Daniel was so surprised he managed to look up at Henrietta and hold her gaze for a moment.

"You think I give positions in my household to just anyone Daniel? I employ men with a talent for sniffing things out; I simply have to know about those I allow close to my family. It takes a little more than a few false references to fool me."

So that was it, she'd found him out; perhaps Uncle Jonathan was not so terribly clever after all. He felt a hollow disappointment settle upon him. Not so much for the fact he would be dismissed, at the very least, and would have to return to casual labouring and the company of rogues and ne'er-do-wells like Crispy Pete, but that he would never be able to lay his longing eyes on Lady Henrietta again.

"I'm... very sorry ma'am," he managed to mutter thickly, quite unable to raise his eyes from the floor.

"Oh, we cannot help whom our parents are Daniel. My own father, for instance, was mostly a *complete* shit."

Daniel's eyes widened, he had never before heard anyone so genteel use such coarse language.

"I meant the references, Ma'am, I intended no harm...I know-"

"Ssssh!" Henrietta ordered, leaning forward to place a soft and extensively manicured hand upon his. This had the effect of shrivelling his tongue and evaporating every last drop of saliva from his mouth, her twinkling grey-blue eyes seemed impossibly close to his own though he concluded that might be due to the fact that his own were near popping out of his head.

"I know your background Daniel, I know your father is a zealot, I also know you are not. I see no wrong in a man trying to better himself. You are a good lad Daniel; I believed that from the moment I saw you, that is why I instructed Greaves to employ you. As I would have done even if you had come with no references at all."

"That would have been improper."

Henrietta chuckled, "Yes it would have been rather, wouldn't it?" She smiled at him and made no move to draw back; her perfume, which he usually found utterly intoxicating at ten paces, made his head swim. He had never entirely gotten used to being close to someone who smelt of something other than stale sweat.

She raised her hand to his face and gently brushed her fingers along his cheek, which was much akin to lighting a trail of gunpowder that sparked and fizzed down his body towards a great keg of the stuff that was concealed somewhere just below the libels on his lap.

"My lady?" He managed to croak.

Henrietta withdrew her hand and sat back though her gaze remained unwavering. "Do you think me pretty?"

Daniel was taken aback. He looked down at the libel he had been reading to her earlier and found to his surprise that he had crumpled it into a tight little ball. He swallowed and tried to straighten out the paper. It was much easier to talk about the King.

"You are very... striking Ma'am."

"Striking?" Henrietta repeated, a pencil thin eyebrow rising a good inch higher, "you make me sound like a grand piece of architecture, or perhaps a horse. Is that how you see me, Daniel? As a horse?"

"No," he mumbled into his lap, "you are very beautiful."

"Beautiful?" Henrietta smiled, "now that is a far more flattering word."

"Do you wish me to flatter you, my lady?"

Henrietta laughed, "Oh my dear Daniel, I have flattery aplenty. I have no need of more."

"Then I do not quite understand?"

Henrietta rose gracefully to her feet. When Daniel moved to do the same she indicated he should remain seated with a wave of her hand. He watched her walk across the library in that wonderfully effortless way she had of moving, following the swish of her skirts and imagining them brushing against the smooth flesh of her legs beneath. It struck him that he had never been seated while she stood before.

She opened the draw of an ornate writing desk and pulled out a small flat box. She was smiling faintly as she returned to stand before him, which felt strange for several reasons, though mainly because her chest was almost exactly at the same height as his eyes.

Henrietta flicked open a brass catch and lifted up the box's lid to reveal a delicate silver necklace from which hung a cluster of precious stones set into the petals of a silver flower.

"What do you think of it?"

Daniel's experience of jewellery was as long and intimate as his dealings with the aristocracy, but it looked pretty expensive to his untrained eye, "It looks pretty expensive," he ventured.

"Yes, I believe it is. I'm advised the jewels are diamonds though I have not had that confirmed. Would you put it on for me, please?"

Daniel's eyes rose from the necklace to look up at his mistress, "I don't really think it would suit me, Ma'am," he replied earnestly.

Henrietta stifled a smile, "Would you put it on *me*, please?"

"Oh!" Daniel said, shooting to his feet so rapidly Henrietta had to step back hastily to prevent him sending the necklace flying from her hands.

He could feel her eyes on him as he carefully lifted the necklace from the velvet-lined box, it weighed less than he expected. He was quite pleased his hands were only slightly shaking as he undid the clasp. Henrietta's lips had curled into a faint little smile as she casually tossed the empty box onto the sofa before turning around; her eyes lingering on him until she was looking back over her shoulder.

"Be careful Daniel, 'tis quite delicate as well as ridiculously expensive. 'tis best handled gently. Just like a Duchess, in fact..."

She turned her head towards the window, whilst lifting the intricate curls of blonde hair that hung so artfully around her neck. Her skin was like porcelain; pale, smooth and unblemished. Her scent curled around them, pulling him closer.

Biting his lip, he looped the necklace over Henrietta's head as carefully as a hunter unarming a particularly devilish trap. The touch of her skin set his fingertips tingling; it was impossibly smooth, impossibly perfect. He wondered how it would feel against his lips.

The clasp was tiny, and he would have had difficulty closing it at the first attempt even if he had not been trying to hang it around the neck of the woman he considered to be the most beautiful in the world. Still, he found that if he focused solely on that small metal mechanism, at the exclusion of every other sense, it only took half a dozen attempts to find the hook and close the clasp.

"There," he said finally, taking a step back to watch entranced as she let her curls tumble back over the flawless white skin of her neck.

Henrietta walked across the library to stand in front of a large and ornate looking-glass hung above the mantle of the fireplace. She raised her chin as she inspected herself, running a finger gently back and forth along the chain of the necklace.

"Do you like it?" She asked, turning around to find Daniel still rooted to the spot, his hands clamped firmly behind his back in a vain attempt to stop them shaking.

"'tis... very pretty Ma'am," Daniel managed to offer with a shrug.

"For something so expensive I would expect a *little* more gushing enthusiasm, Daniel. Does it not enhance my beauty?"

"There is no embellishment in the world that can do that, you are entirely beautiful as you are; 'tis not possible for anyone to be more so," the words tumbled from his lips before he could consider them. By the time they reached his ears, he was already blushing furiously and he returned his gaze to the sanctuary of his feet.

Henrietta regarded him from across the room, her finger still working on the chain as she cocked her head slightly to one side, "You grow bolder Daniel, perhaps deep down inside you are not so meek after all. A natural born flatterer methinks?"

"I mean no offence Ma'am," Daniel said quickly, his panicking heart increasing its beat.

"It was not a complaint."

"I thought you wanted no flattery?"

"I said I did not *need* any more flattery Daniel, which is not quite the same."

"I see," Daniel said with a nod, despite the fact he didn't see at all.

"The man who gave me this," she said, indicating the necklace "is a great flatterer, but not a discreet one. If I were to accept this... pretty thing, I doubt it would be long before every saloon gossip between here and Paris knew about it and all those wagging tongues will have him bedding me regardless of whether he actually had or not."

Daniel frowned, "Why would people gossip about a man giving his wife a necklace?"

Henrietta laughed, "Oh Daniel. It was not the Duke who gave me the necklace, it was a suitor. A young beau whose beauty is only sullied by the fact he is far too aware of it."

"A suitor?" Daniel repeated, trying to work out what he had missed.

"Sadly, for him, both my preference and my station requires the exact opposite," she let her hand slip sadly away from the necklace before turning her back on Daniel once more and lifting her hair,

"Take it off for me please Daniel?" she asked, her eyes finding his through the looking-glass.

Daniel looked down and hurried over to do as he was bid, quickly wiping the sweat from his palms as he did. He felt her eyes on him as he unclasped the necklace. His actions were slow and deliberate. Partly because he did not want to drop the precious little thing, but mostly so he could savour the closeness of her, from the way the hem of her skirts brushed against his feet to the stray curls of honey blonde hair that floated just beyond the end of his nose, teasing and beckoning him to come closer still.

He wanted to touch her and taste her and do things he could not even find names for, but instead he stepped back and let the necklace nestle in the palm of his hand, for he knew he was walking a dangerous line. Lady Henrietta, should she so wish, could destroy an ordinary man like him in so many different ways it did not bear thinking of. He could not touch her, he could not speak out of turn to her, and he certainly could not kiss her. He could do nothing. Perhaps that was the point; perhaps she just enjoyed the torture of it.

When he offered her the necklace, she shook her head, "I need it taken back from whence it came. Can I trust you to do that? Can I trust you to be discreet?"

"Of course, Ma'am," he said without hesitation. The silver trinket he held in his hand was worth more than a humble footman would probably earn in his life. If he were a man with the morals of Crispy Pete, the thought of disappearing with the necklace would have been the only one in his head, but Daniel was far too besotted with Henrietta for him to give any shrift to such base notions as thievery.

"I can trust you, can't I Daniel?" Henrietta asked earnestly, wrapping her two hands around the one Daniel was holding the necklace with, "it would be nice to have someone I can trust."

"I would do anything you ask of me..." Daniel replied, his eyes quite wide and hopeless, "...and would never tell a soul."

"Good Daniel," she beamed radiantly, "very good…"

*

Due to the social imposition of visiting relatives, nearly a week went by before Daniel had another opportunity to serve the Duchess her afternoon tea alone. It was without a doubt the longest week in Daniel's young life. It was not that he was denied the chance to see her, for he spent an inordinate amount of time waiting on the Duchess, sadly they were all in the presence of her husband and their guests. Hour after tedious hour of serving food and clearing away plates, pouring drinks and refilling glasses as quickly as their guests could empty them, disposing of their pipe ash and emptying their overflowing piss pots.

They would chatter and gossip, of this and that, but it was like the distant drone of insects to Daniel's ears. His thoughts and each and every one of his senses revolved solely around Henrietta; the sound of her laughter caressing his ears, the faint hint of her perfume teasing his nose, the lacy frills of her cuffs brushing his hand as he poured her wine, the musky taste of her in the air as he stooped to listen to her requests and the sight of her. Oh, the gloriously breath-taking sight of her.

She turned Daniel's eyes into traitors to his own mind, for no matter how hard he tried to look elsewhere, to stare blankly into space lest his perfidious eyes betray him to the world, he forever found himself staring at her. He expected to be brought to his senses by the harsh voice of the Duke at any moment, probably followed by his fist for having the unspeakable temerity to stare so lustfully at his wife. He feared being dragged through the house, his scarlet footman's tunic torn from his back before he was unceremoniously thrown out into the street, or, more likely, dragged to the nearest open sewer which would provide a more suitable target to hurl him at. Perhaps the Duke would order the other servants to give him a good beating for his trouble, or possibly the hounds would be set on him.

Each time such dark fancies crept into his mind he forced his eyes away from her, but like small boys intent on mischief and naughtiness, they would tip toe back to her as soon as his attention wandered and again he would be lost.

However, despite his fears, no reprimand came from his employer or warning from a fellow servant. It was as if he was invisible, unseen and unwanted until there was a plate to carry away or a glass to refill. So long as he did not break etiquette in any way, such as by ladling the soup from the wrong side, spilling wine over the fancy clothes of the Duke's guests or trying to rip the Duchess' bodice open at the dining table, nobody paid him any heed whatsoever.

After the Duke and Duchess had finished entertaining and their guests managed to take themselves off to their rooms, though the Duke's hospitality and extensive wine cellar ensured a few only made it to their beds slumped between a pair of hefty servants, Daniel would eventually retire to his little room in the attic. Each night he stared into the darkness; listening to the soft noises that gently sullied the stillness of the night; the snores of the two other footmen he shared the room with, the creak of distant floorboards, the scratching of a rat or the distant howling of feral dogs. He would curl into a ball, squeezing his hands into tight fists, his toes curling and digging into the flat straw mattress, his eyes screwed shut as he screamed silently. All of his frustrated, unfulfilled lust would rack his body until he felt hot salty tears squeezing out onto his skin from behind his eyelids.

He wanted her with such a desire he thought his lust might consume him utterly, sending him spiralling into some dreadful insanity, for he knew if he attempted to lay even the briefest gentlest caress upon her, it would be the ruin of him.

He did not know what she wanted of him, why she treated him with such impropriety. In his most unguarded moments, he thought of her as a friend. Perhaps that was all she desired, perhaps she was just lonely and unhappy? It did not take a long study of the Duke of Pevansea to picture how that might be.

The Duke was far older than her. Four decades earlier he had been a dashing young cavalier, the third son of a respectable but modest landed family he had joined the army and served as a Captain of Horse noted for his dark good looks, bravery and charisma. Those days, however, were long past and now he looked every part the canny and craggy old politician that he was.

The passage of time may have rewarded him with wealth, title, influence and a stunningly beautiful young wife, but that journey had also left his face cold and gaunt, sculpted by the pain he endured from the wounds that had nearly taken his life when he had fought for the Crown during the Civil War. He sat beneath the flowing curls of his long full-bottomed brown wig, his spare frame as immaculately and fashionably dressed as any man in his sixties could be, his polite and appropriate smiles rarely touching the slate coloured eyes that sat between heavy sagging bags and thin hooded lids, viewing the world with coolly calculated disdain.

As with any collection of individuals forced to spend hours on end in each other's company, there were any number of gossips and wag-tongues eager to recount the details of the Duke's life to a newcomer like Daniel. Some things he dismissed as speculation and fancy on the basis that Peers of the Realm rarely discussed their innermost thoughts and feelings with half-witted scullery maids, but from the various accounts he could draw the bare bones of a tale he was fairly certain was accurate.

Henrietta was the second wife of John Bourness, the Duke of Pevansea; his first had been the daughter of a minor French Baron he had wed during Charles II's exile in France. Having chosen to remain loyal to the Crown after the execution of Charles I, rather than accepting the rule of Cromwell's Commonwealth, he had fled England and joined the dead King's sons, Charles and James, in France. Like most of the Royalists in exile, he had little in the way of money, coupled with the poor health he had endured after his injuries; he had not been considered a particularly desirable match for any Lady of quality or wealth. He had eventually wed Margarit, a French woman of good breeding, but modest means, little dowry and plain looks. She had helped him to convalesce after he had been struck down by fever whilst travelling in France and her father had been prepared to gamble a few gold coins on the chance the young Englishman might make something of himself one day.

Despite the constant pain from the injuries he'd suffered at the debacle of the Battle of Naseby, which had turned him into a man of sour disposition and little apparent humour, he'd proved popular with the flamboyant and fun-loving young King in exile and quickly made a name for himself at court. He'd stood out from most of the other courtiers by means of the fact he was neither a lickspittle brown-noser nor an incompetent fop.

Such a thing was a rarity amongst the King's surviving advisors, whose wise counsel had been such a resounding success that his father had ended up losing his head outside Westminster Hall one cold January morning in 1649. John Bourness rapidly found himself rewarded with the delegation of a number of the minor matters of the exiled state that were too trifling for the King to interrupt his womanising, gambling and drinking for.

His standing rose fast and far enough that some nine years later, when Oliver Cromwell eventually had the good grace to die and leave his ineffectual son Richard to inherit the mantle of Lord Protector, John Bourness had been one the King's trusted advisors who had travelled covertly to England to persuade Parliament that after a decade of government by Puritanical killjoys, England would be far better off being ruled by a young playboy who was only able to keep his hands off the ladies of court long enough to create some truly stupendous gambling debts.

Somewhat surprisingly, Parliament had agreed.

Once restored to the throne, Charles II had wasted no time in dealing with the most pressing matters of state, which chiefly involved arranging due retribution for those responsible for the execution of his father – an execution that Daniel's own father had watched as a young man and remembered so fondly – and rewarding those who'd helped him return to his rightful place on the throne of England.

Thus, John Bourness had been granted a shiny new Dukedom which included several estates whose previous owner had been one of the gentlemen who had so carelessly signed the death warrant of Charles' father a decade earlier and was, therefore, one of the first to be dispatched off for a premature meeting with his maker by the new King.

The Duke had been a close friend and advisor to Charles during his reign, eventually rising to a seat on the Privy Council, a role he had continued when the heirless Charles had died and been succeeded by his younger brother James, the Duke of York. He had remained close to the new king despite the fact that James was generally considered to be a fool who could only have managed to plonk his backside upon the English throne as part of some tasteless divine joke. Most people had come to this conclusion due to a combination of three rumours that were largely considered to be indisputable facts by most of his subjects. Firstly, the wanton whoring of his younger days had left him riddled and half insane with syphilis, secondly, he was a Catholic in all but name, and thirdly he was an incompetent buffoon.

Buffoonery and the clap, along with incest and madness, were not generally considered being sufficient reason amongst European royalty to deny someone their divine birthright, and in some European principalities, it appeared to be almost compulsory. However, as the Duke of York, he had plummeted to rare depths of unpopularity. Fairly or not he was blamed either directly or indirectly for most of the calamities that afflicted his brother's reign. However, it was his leadership of the Navy that had taken his unpopularity to levels of derision that even his father had not been able to achieve.

The Duke of York's stewardship had coincided with the second and third Anglo-Dutch wars, a series of naval engagements fought by the English to usurp the Dutch Republic's position as the world's leading trading nation. Cromwell's England had been fought to a stalemate in the first war in the 1650's, but a decade later there was a mood in the country that there was unfinished business with the Dutch. Leading the call for war was the Lord High Admiral (James, Duke of York), seemingly for no greater reason than the desire to do something during the week other than whoring and watching his brother rule the country. Another leading proponent of the war was the Royal African Company, who hoped a victory would allow them to take over the Dutch East India Company's valuable overseas possessions. By one of those strange coincidences that historically abound in matters of politics, the head of the Royal African Company happened to be one James, Duke of York. He no doubt expected the wheeze would not only transform him from a figure of mild ridicule to a populist hero and make him exceedingly rich into the bargain.

As a result, two costly wars were fought between England and the Netherlands, which culminated in the destruction of the Duke of York's entire fleet at the hands of the Dutch after they had rather unsportingly sailed up the Thames at night and fired the English fleet whilst it lay at anchor, effectively ending the war and handing England a crushing defeat. To lose any war was galling, but to lose an entire fleet and tens of thousands of sailors in a dispute nobody actually understood to, of all people, the Dutch, was a national shame. Defeat to a country that England had historically considered so insignificant that they had never even bothered to give the inhabitants their own name, simply referring to them as "*the Deutch*" and grouping them with the numerous Germanic principalities and city states of Northern Europe

The celebrations when James succeeded his brother were, to say the least, muted. If he had simply been a syphilitic buffoon then England, who had reaped the benefits of centuries of close inbreeding amongst the royal houses of Europe as much as any country, could have tolerated him. The fact that he was a *Catholic* was simply one piece of baggage too many.

Only the fact that the English had no stomach for another bloody and disastrous civil war had allowed James to keep his backside on the throne, as well as his head on his shoulders for the last few years. However, dark rumours of plots and machinations were sweeping London, the King was to be exposed as a Catholic and deposed, James was about to dismiss parliament, the army was against James, the King was recruiting Irish regiments and French mercenaries to maintain the throne. Amongst all these rumours the Duke of Pevansea sat at James' shoulder, whispering in his ear.

The position of junior footman generally allowed little time free for idle speculation; however, Daniel found his utter inability to sleep for more than a few fitful hours since he had become the Duchess' confidant, runner of discreet errands and gossip monger allowed plenty of time to mull all manner of things over in his mind. Most of these, obviously, involved parts of the Duchess' anatomy, but when he could force his mind onto other matters, he thought of the Duke in those years after the restoration. A suddenly rich and powerful man, with title, lands, a grand house in the country, the ear of the King (when those ears weren't wedged between the breasts of his latest favourite concubine anyway), who, despite all that good fortune, found himself married to a barren wife. Even by the most kindly accounts, Margarit had aged quickly into a dried old prune of a woman who generally displayed an expression and a temperament akin to a particularly mangy, decrepit and toothless donkey being roughly herded off towards the slaughter house.

What would a man do to get himself the kind of wife his wealth and station demanded? One who might be able to give him an heir for his new-found title and fortune?

Margarit had conveniently died of smallpox ten years ago; the grief-stricken Duke managed somehow to overcome the loss and found a pretty young wife to replace her. Three months after burying Margarit in his local parish church the eighteen-year-old Henrietta had met him at the altar of the same church to take her place as the Duchess of Pevansea. In the intervening ten years, she had given the Duke two children, Richard and Anne.

Had it really been smallpox? Daniel conjured all manner of dark plots as to how the Duke had done away with poor Margarit in order to replace her with the beautiful Henrietta. A man who had served three Kings and helped maintain such an unpopular man as James on the throne was surely capable of anything and powerful enough to get away with it. Perhaps that was why Henrietta was befriending him, perhaps she had found out what had happened to her predecessor and feared for her own life. Perhaps she suspected the Duke was lining up a younger woman to replace her. Perhaps smallpox was in the air again? Daniel imagined the black-hearted Duke scheming in some darkened room, probably consulting with witches as to the most suitable poisons and curses for the doing away of unwanted wives. The more he thought about it, the more likely it seemed that one of the most powerful men in England would be consulting with witches.

He looked the sort.

This was where Daniel's fancies usually drifted off in the direction of how he would uncover the Duke's fiendish plans, reveal him as a murderer, who had probably done all manner of other black deeds and intended to do away with the King. After much heroism and daring, the evil Duke would be thwarted and carted off to the Tower for a well-earned beheading. A grateful King James would obviously bestow the Dukedom to Daniel by way of thanks from a grateful nation and Henrietta would throw herself upon him, declaring him her hero, one true love and she would acutely like to marry him thank you very much.

As with most fancies, there were several glaring discrepancies in Daniel's daydreaming, the most obvious being the fact that around fifteen years elapsed between John Bourness attaining a Dukedom and Margarit's death, which was rather a long time to plot the demise of your suddenly surplus to requirements wife. Still, Daniel was in no mind to let such doubts soil his contempt and hatred of the Duke.

The fact that the Duchess spent the dinner parties he endured laughing gaily and generally presented a happy and contented countenance was another irritating fly in his ointment, but he could easily put that down to the importance the aristocracy generally placed in showing good form at all times. Underneath all her gaiety and good fortune, he just knew she must be as miserable as sin, and he was prepared to do just about anything to deliver her the happiness she deserved; climb mountains, cross deserts, swim seas, whatever it took. He'd even run a blade through the black heart of the vile old Duke if that was what it took, for Daniel loved his Duchess quite hopelessly.

*

Daniel found Lady Henrietta in the drawing room, pulling on her gloves as she inspected her appearance in the looking glass.

"Ah, Daniel there you are. I have need of your assistance in averting a terrible calamity."

"A calamity, Ma'am?"

"A *terrible* calamity Daniel; the Lord Mayor's ball is barely a month away and my wardrobe is scandalously unfashionable. I fear I will disgrace my husband in front of society by turning up dressed like some pauperly country maid. However, all is not lost as I have received word that the latest designs from Paris have just arrived in town. We must make haste if I am to keep that vulgar Lady Ambrose in her place," she continued to fix her gloves as she spoke, but paused to turn to look at him as she concluded, "I'll have need of your broad arms to carry all my new dresses, Daniel, I hope you are feeling strong?"

"Of course, Ma'am," Daniel replied.

His pulse had raced from the moment Lady Henrietta had called for him; when he'd found her alone, his heart had tossed off its hat and coat and begun a mad sprint around his chest. She smiled, warmly he thought, and after he had closed the door he had fervently hoped for some little familiarity, some confidence perhaps, something to suggest he meant more to her than someone who just fetched and carried. Although her eyes sparkled in the morning sunlight that flooded the room, her tone was as proper as one would expect from a mistress addressing her servant.

As the morning was crisp and bright, Henrietta declared she had no need for her carriage. Once they'd left the house, Daniel had summoned a sedan chair at her bequest. Although the weather was dry, the shit filled streets of London were no place for a lady to drag the hems of her expensive silk skirts, even if they were in last season's style or colour.

Daniel had no real understanding of fashion having been brought up in a house of Puritan thrift; out of both necessity and dogma, new clothes were only purchased when old ones could no longer be repaired. It seemed both frivolous and absurd that rich people would waste vast amounts of money replacing perfectly good clothes just because someone in Paris (which generally seemed to be to blame for all this fashion malarkey) started wearing a dress with a slightly longer collar or shorter cuffs. It seemed to be no more than a ruse to separate people from their money, but as the likes of the Duchess had no apparent shortage of money he supposed it wasn't something she had to worry about. He was just grateful ordinary people like he would never have to concern themselves with such nonsense.

Once the Duchess and her billowing skirts had been stuffed into the box of the sedan, Daniel passed on an address in Piccadilly to the bearers, who doffed their hats respectfully before lifting their load. Daniel trotted dutifully alongside, keeping a sharp eye for any riff-raff who might make a grab for the Duchess' jewels.

Despite their load, the bearers trotted at a fair pace, dodging between traffic where they could, barging pedestrians out of the way when they couldn't. The Duchess raised the screen at her window after a few minutes and looked at Daniel from behind the fan she used to waft away the ripe smells of the street from her nostrils.

"You returned that small gift without incident?"

"Yes ma'am," Daniel nodded, trying not to pant. Life off the streets had softened him up.

"Did the gentleman make any comment?"

Daniel considered his reply for a moment, "He appeared disappointed, Ma'am."

"One should hope so," she said, smiling faintly, before settling back into her seat and pulling the blind back down.

Save for a delay caused by a spilled load of bricks on Charing Cross Road, they arrived in Piccadilly in good time, and Daniel paid the bearers their fare plus a tip generous enough to induce a veritable plague of hat doffing, forelock tugging and toothless smiles.

Daniel had expected Henrietta to head straight for the fashionable shops, but instead, she produced a key and entered a nondescript door between a haberdasher and a milliner. She looked over her shoulder and indicated he should follow her inside. He stifled his puzzlement as he followed her up a steep and narrow staircase; the view was enough to push *any* thought from his mind.

At the top of the stairs, the Duchess produced another key which she used to open one of the doors on the landing and ushered him inside with a casual flick of her gloved hand. A short, unadorned corridor led into a modestly furnished drawing room that looked over Piccadilly. The room was simply decorated while the furniture was straightforward and sturdy, lacking the baroque flourishes, cartouches, scrolls and gilding that characterised everything back at St James' Square. It was the kind of unassuming unfussy furniture Daniel's father would probably have bought, had he not been such a parsimonious old skinflint.

"Are we... visiting Ma'am?" Daniel enquired, his puzzlement flooding back as soon as he'd lost sight of Henrietta's swaying hips.

"No, Daniel, there is no one here but us. This is my home or, at least, one of them."

"But, it's above... *a shop*?"

"Oh dear, you have been with us less than a year and we have already turned you into a snob Daniel!" Henrietta laughed, turning her back to him to indicate he should remove her fur lined cape and coat.

Daniel hurried to help her as he always did when an opportunity to draw as close as possible to her presented itself, "I'm afraid I don't really understand Ma'am?" he asked, once he had slipped the cape and coat from her shoulders and hung them on a stand in the corner of the room.

"'tis quite chilly," she glanced at the cold fireplace, "why don't you warm the room, Daniel."

"Of course, Ma'am!" Daniel said, cursing himself for putting his own foolish questions before his mistress' comfort. The coal scuttle was full, and he quickly had a fine fire going. Once he was satisfied he straightened up upon his knees and looked around for further instruction, he found the Duchess had settled herself into a large straight back wooden chair, the kind a medieval baron might have inspected a grand banquet from once upon a time. She wore a fabulous flowing dress of jade green silk, trimmed and embroidered with snow white thread. She had worn a short jacket of similarly coloured velvet, but had removed it while he had worked the fire to reveal the daringly low cut of the dress, adorned with only a necklace of fabulously large pearls; he was close enough to see faint goosebumps dimpling her chest.

With a slightly trembling hand, he threw a few more pieces of coal on the fire.

She reclined in the chair as far as the constrictions of her corsetry allowed, she still wore her long kid leather gloves and her hands were folded demurely among the rumpled layers of her skirts that bunched in her lap.

"Why don't you take off your coat and that silly wig Daniel," she said after a moment or two longer spent watching him frankly.

"The wig?" Daniel touched the horsehair periwig that adorned his head, the thing had itched hellishly when he had first had to wear it as part of his footman's uniform, but he had become so used to it that he now noticed it no more than his own hair.

"I wish to see you without it; I have never liked the wretched things. They are quite ridiculous. Don't you think?"

"Quite ridiculous," Daniel found himself agreeing as he slid the grey powdered wig from his head, to reveal the dark stubble of his own shaved scalp.

"You should grow your own hair again, 'tis far more agreeable."

"The rules of the house," Daniel shrugged.

"Not of *this* house, now take off your jacket and sit down," she indicated an equally baronial chair opposite her own. Daniel did as he was instructed, before tentatively lowering himself into the chair. The wood was smooth and cold through the thin cotton of his shirt; it fitted the contours of his body as if he had been using it for centuries, gently wearing it into shape.

"I have a confession to make," Henrietta announced conspiratorially once he was settled, "I am not a Duchess at all."

"You're not?" Daniel asked; he was pretty sure nobody had mentioned that to him before.

"Well, *technically* I am a Duchess," Henrietta admitted, conceding the point with a slight wrinkle of the nose, "I am married to a Duke after all, but I was not born to the aristocracy. I am just an unsophisticated country girl, a parson's daughter, in fact, and I consider this..." she waved a gloved hand about her, "...to be my real home. These are the things I grew up with in my little parsonage. After my father died, I had them brought to London, and the Duke was kind enough to find me a little apartment where I might come and feel comfortable, surrounded by the simple things of my childhood."

"Would it not have been more convenient to have these things at St James' Square Ma'am?"

"They are old and unfashionable; they would not sit happily amongst all of that gilt and extravagance. Besides, I like the solitude, the peace to do as I wish," she stared at him boldly, "the privacy to do as I wish."

"I see," Daniel said, as usual, he didn't actually see at all, but thought it better not to make it too obvious, "do you wish me to read to you here instead of the Duke's library?"

"Perhaps..." Henrietta looked towards a heavy oak dresser which was almost large enough for the Navy to have built a warship out of, upon which rested a decanter and several crystal glasses, "...will you fetch me a drink please Daniel."

"'tis whiskey ma'am?" Daniel queried with a frown after leaping across the room to pour a small measure.

"Yes Daniel, I know. Please do not be so prudent with your measures and pour one for yourself too."

Daniel did not know which suggestion shocked him the most; that the Duchess drank whiskey, that she wished him to drink some with her or that he'd stumbled upon the shocking secret that she was the kind of woman who consumed hard liquor before noon. His father had several words to describe such women; none of which would be fit for a Duchess' ears.

Once he'd returned to his seat, he stared uncertainly at the glass in his hand, before confessing, "I don't really like whiskey, my lady."

"Nonsense," Henrietta chided from behind the rim of her own glass, "you simply do not know how to drink it correctly."

Daniel's eyes flicked between his mistress and the unwanted drink before taking a quick gulp. "It seems a straightforward enough task," he concluded with a grimace.

"The trick is not to rush the drink," Henrietta advised, swirling the whiskey around the glass several times before raising it towards her lips, "the taste needs to be savoured, it should linger on the tongue, it's complicated flavours permeating the senses..." she sipped the drink,

"...before you swallow and allow it to slip slowly down your throat..." she emphasised her words by running a finger along her throat, across her chest and down to her stomach, "...firing your blood as it slides down to your belly..."

Daniel wordlessly did as she suggested; it was still like swallowing hot ash, but out of politeness he tried not to pull so much of a face this time.

"See?"

"Much better, Ma'am."

"There is no need to call me Ma'am here, my friends call me Hetty."

"Am I your friend, Ma'am?"

"I would like that."

Daniel sipped a little more of his drink, "Why?"

"Why not?"

"Because you are a Duchess and I am a footman."

"I am a parson's daughter, and you are the son of a..."

"Teacher."

"Then we are not so very different, are we?"

Daniel looked at her exquisite silk dress, expensive jewels and artfully crafted hair. "I suppose not."

Henrietta looked towards the window, "There is a whole world out there Daniel, I used to be able to come and go as I pleased in my little village. I am grateful for my good fortune, but the company of Lords and Ladies can be very tiresome. Sometimes I yearn for the company of people more like myself." She turned back to face the room, "Tell me more about yourself, Daniel."

"There is not much to tell."

"Tell me about your father; he has fallen on hard times I understand?"

"He lives within the Rules of the Fleet," Daniel admitted quietly.

"Debtors prison; an unfortunate place to find oneself I would imagine."

Daniel shrugged, "He has always thought of money as something sinful, perhaps he will be happier without any."

"You do not seem overly concerned?"

Daniel turned away from her bright inspecting eyes, confused by everything, "We are not close."

"A family feud; how fascinating. Tell me more?"

"I thought you had people to ask questions?"

"They can only learn so much. Tell me what happened; I am your friend after all."

He looked up to see if he was being teased, but her expression was earnest enough.

"I do not like to talk about it."

"Tell me. Please."

Daniel stared into his drink awhile, "He killed my brother."

"My God," Henrietta exclaimed, eyes widening.

He was going to add that he hadn't actually killed Caleb himself, but the words faded from his tongue. Why should he? It was true enough in its way. It would take too long to explain to her what a monster that man was, and however he explained the bald facts they would never fully convey the truth; they would just sound hollow and trite. This was easier, better.

"They argued. My father was always free with his fists, Caleb, my brother, was getting too big to push around. He reacted, they fought. He died. Simple really." No actual lie there, Daniel thought coldly, "I was twelve years old and he died in my arms."

"Were you close?"

Daniel nodded. "Not a day goes by that I do not miss him," that at least, was the complete truth. He downed the remainder of the whiskey in one, even though he was not able to stifle his grimace this time. His thoughts must have carried him away for a moment, which was not unusual when the memory of Caleb suddenly confronted him, for the next thing he noticed was the Duchess tipping more whiskey into the empty glass that he cradled in both his hands.

"It will solve nothing, *but...*" she said with a shrug, before topping up her own glass. To be served by a Duchess, what a particularly strange day this was turning out to be. "Tell me about your brother?" Henrietta asked softly, lowering herself back into her chair.

"He was my best friend; clever, honest, talented, touched by God people said," Daniel twitched his shoulders, "for all the good it did him." He rose hesitantly, propelled by an idea he was unsure he should follow though he found his feet moving across the room all the same. He picked up his jacket, and from an inside pocket he withdrew a small pouch of soft leather bound with twine. He carefully opened it and handed it to the Duchess, "'tis all I have left of him."

Henrietta placed her drink on the arm of her chair before accepting the pouch; carefully she opened it and found inside a sheaf of folded paper which she opened to reveal the charcoal sketch of a young boy.

"Your brother?" she asked, her eyes rising to look up at Daniel after she had studied the drawing.

"No, that boy is me. Caleb drew it... he was always drawing things."

"He was very talented, this is remarkable. How old was he when he drew this?"

"Just sixteen."

"You were right," Henrietta sighed, "he was touched by God."

"I still remember the day he drew it; we were sitting by London Bridge, watching the boatmen shoot the starlings. I usually teased him about everything, but when he showed me that drawing I could find nothing to ridicule. I told him that it was wonderful... he blushed and thought I was mocking him," Daniel's voice trailed off thickly.

"And you have no more of his drawings?"

Daniel shook his head, "My father burned them all... he thought them profane."

"I would have liked to have seen them," Henrietta said, still staring at the sketch.

"So would I," Daniel carefully accepted the drawing back from Henrietta and returned it to the safety of the pouch. "I still see him sometimes..." he smiled and shook his head, "not for real... I'm not mad. After he died, I thought that if I could remember hard enough, concentrate long enough, then his memory would have enough substance for me to believe that he was not entirely gone. Ever since, I've found it a comfort to imagine him with me so that I can talk to him, ask for his advice. He was always the sensible one. I was always the fool, getting into trouble."

"Can you see him now?"

Daniel smiled shyly and looked towards the window, that was where he would be, where the light was best, working with paper and charcoal, head down, eyes darting up to peer through hanging tendrils of hair for a moment while his hand paused in mid-air. Still as a statue until he was ready to draw some more. Still dressed in his baggy threadbare clothes, fingers still blackened by ink and charcoal; still sixteen, forever sixteen.

"I can imagine him if I try really hard," it wasn't true of course, Caleb's memory had taken on a life of its own; coming and going of his own accord, but he wasn't going to tell Henrietta that. He wasn't going to tell anybody that as even to his own ears that sounded dangerously close to insanity.

"Tell me what you can see."

"He is standing by the window, in the good light with his charcoal and paper. He would very much like to draw you."

"And why would he like to draw me?"

Daniel looked at her as boldly as he had looked at anyone in his life, "Because he always loved to draw extraordinary things..."

"You flatter me again," she said, her eyes flicking momentarily away from him, the slight rose flush at her checks not entirely due to the soft dusting of rouge upon her skin.

"You embolden me... *Hetty*," he pronounced her name slowly in much the same way she had advised him to drink whiskey; though it warmed his blood in a similar fashion, he found its taste was much more to his liking.

They regarded each other in silence for a while, Daniel rejoicing in the simple pleasure of staring at her openly, swimming in her beauty until he found a smile had cracked his face.

"Ah, that smile again," Henrietta murmured, "betwixt that devilish smile and those mischievous, sparkling eyes I believe you will break many hearts."

"Including yours?"

"Oh, I have no heart to break Daniel; when a young girl agrees to marry an old man in return for money, comfort and security, such a troublesome thing as a heart would be nought but a burden. The very idea of it would be an impediment to her contentment."

"And you are content?"

"Why ever should I not be?"

Daniel looked about him, "You find the need to surround yourself with the things of your childhood. You encourage rich young suitors. You treat your servants... *oddly*."

"Do you judge me?"

"No, my lady," Daniel replied evenly.

"One should hope not," Henrietta raised one gloved finger, "and incidentally, I do not encourage rich young suitors. They assume because I am, apparently, quite beautiful and am married to an old man, I would wish to take a lover."

"So, you return their gifts."

"Indeed, I do, even the lovely ones," Henrietta smiled, "I have a weakness for jewellery that the Duke is happy to indulge, even so it can be hard to turn away such pretty things."

"I can imagine."

"You are not such a shy boy after all, are you?"

"I used to make people laugh, I was a joker..." Daniel shrugged, "...after my brother died I changed, I turned myself away from the world."

"Why?"

Because playing the fool led to my brother dying, Daniel thought, but replied with only a shrug and a faraway look that would have been seen as insolence if Henrietta had looked upon him only as a servant. As it was, she was sensitive enough to realise it was a subject Daniel did not want to discuss. Instead, they talked of other things, mainly their childhoods.

It turned out that Henrietta had been right to suggest they were not so very different. Their fathers were both strictly devout men and stern disciplinarians though her father had been a by the letters Anglican scornful of zealous non-conformists such as Daniel's father. They had both endured difficult relationships with their fathers though Henrietta had never fallen to actually hating hers in the way Daniel did and she had come to a reconciliation with him in his later years to the degree she could now recount his beatings with something almost akin to fondness.

Her father had been a long-time friend of John Bourness, and if he'd had any reservations when his recently bereaved old friend had asked for the hand of his youngest, and prettiest, daughter, he had kept them to himself. Perhaps the fact that the parson had a great fondness for money and position, which had resulted in him spending much of his life unsuccessfully scrabbling for both, had convinced him his daughter's best interests would be served by moving to the Duke's grand house and his equally grand bed.

They talked of small inconsequential things, each made the other laugh a little and smile a lot, and for a time, Daniel could almost forget that Henrietta was both a Duchess and breathtakingly beautiful.

It was only when the light at the window began to fade did it dawn on Daniel that they had spent most of the day talking.

"We must go," she said, following his eyes to the window, "questions will be asked if I am not home before dark."

"I wouldn't want the Duke to worry," Daniel said, hurriedly standing.

Henrietta smiled ruefully, "I was thinking of the household, the Duke is much taken with matters of state currently; he is at home so rarely I doubt he even notices me, let alone worries for me."

"I notice you," Daniel said simply.

"I know you do," Henrietta replied, rising to her feet.

They stood facing each other, eyes locked and ghosts of smiles dusting their mouths. "So, we are friends then?" Daniel asked.

"In these rooms, we are the best of friends... outside, things must appear as they all always have."

"I understand... my lady."

She smiled, so radiantly Daniel could almost feel himself melting inside, "We must be gone, but like all friends when they take leave of each other, you may kiss me. Just this once."

If her smile made him melt, her words had the reverse effect, and he groaned mentally, he had lain awake each night driven halfway to madness and back by the thought of simply laying his lips on hers. He had always thought if such an unlikely event were ever to occur his heart might as well stop beating when their lips parted for he could never possibly be so happy again; whatever life might offer him afterwards would be but a pale and laughable mockery of that one moment of utter perfection.

Now, here she stood before him, eyes wide and expectant, lips fractionally parted, head tilted upwards; surely as beautiful a sight as any man had laid eyes on in all of creation... and he could not do it. Partly for fear that it would not be as wondrously beautiful as he had always fantasised, but mainly because he knew all too well if he kissed those perfect lips months of lust and frustration would come surging out of him, like a flash flood tumbling down a mountainside, all froth and fury.

He feared he would not be able to contain himself. He envisaged himself throwing her to the floor and ripping her expensive dress to shreds as he clawed at her, desperate to reach the soft sweet flesh beneath; like a bear with a bee hive he would crack her open and take what he wanted, regardless of how fiercely he was stung.

More by instinct than reason he reached out and took hold of her still gloved hand, the kid leather was incredibly soft and warmed by the flesh within. Her hands were small though her fingers long in comparison; artistic, sensual fingers. He lifted her hand to his lips and bowed gently as he placed the softest of kisses upon it; the leather had been infused with jasmine so that the lady might find relief from the noxious fumes and miasmas of the city, the scent filled his nostrils and curled into his mouth. All the time his eyes held Henrietta's. As wide and blue as the vaults of heaven they returned his gaze with amusement and no little pleasure, Daniel thought.

"My lady," he said, straightening up as he regretfully allowed her hand to slip from his, her fingers sliding through his like silken ropes.

"That was not... entirely what I meant," she smiled, raising the hand he had kissed to her own lips.

"I know... but I have dreamed of such a moment for too long to let it pass. I have endured the sight of a hundred rich men greeting you so, from the dashing young beaux to the corpulent old dodderers. I have watched merchants, princes, bishops and ambassadors salivate upon your hand; I envied each and every one of them. Not their wealth or their power, their fashionable clothes or their full bellies, just the fact that they could lay their lips upon your glove and I, who adore you utterly, could not.

Now I am their equal in every regard that truly matters to me."

"My my Daniel..." the Duchess whispered through a smile, "...now you have found a tongue there is no stopping you at all."

She took a quick step forward and placed a hand on each of his shoulders, she was but a few inches shorter than he, but he felt her weight upon him as she reached up and placed the briefest caress of a kiss upon his cheek. Before he had the time truly to appreciate the moment it was gone, and she had taken a hasty step backwards. In truth, it was no more of a kiss than a sister might bestow upon her little brother, but Daniel could feel his skin tingling where her lips had momentarily rested, and the memory of her breasts briefly pushing against his chest would make sleep a stranger for an awfully long time.

With that, she breezed past him to wait by the coat stand. Daniel hurried after her, and if he took a little longer in helping her into her coat and cape than usual, she did not comment upon it or anything else. She simply stood in silence looking a fraction more flushed than she'd ever done before when a servant helped her with her coat.

Chapter Six

The Workshop of Curiosities

Lincoln's Inn Fields, London – 1708

"Ah," a voice declared, "I do believe you may not have killed him after all!"

"Pity," a second voice muttered from somewhere even further away.

Although Caleb wanted to keep his eyes closed a little longer, he found it impossible as his nostrils were suddenly filled with a foul sulphurous stench, which forced his eyelids apart by means of the tears that instantly welled up behind them.

"A-ha! Splendid!" Through watery eyes, Caleb made out the rotund figure of a portly man leaning over him. The man straightened up and carefully fixed a stopper onto a small vial before secreting it into one of the pockets of a shapeless frock coat.

"Mr Cade, I am so very pleased to see you're not dead."

"I'm not entirely sure I can share that sentiment," Caleb managed to reply, gingerly touching his face to ensure everything was roughly where it should be, "death can't possibly feel this bad."

"Yes, so sorry about that, but cheer up I don't think there is any permanent damage."

Caleb tried to look around him, but the room's oil lamps were bright enough to bring forth further tears. He closed his eyes and sank back into the chair upon which he was seated. "What happened to me?"

"You don't... ahem, recall?"

Caleb tried to shake his head, but that hurt too much. He felt a welcome damp coolness as a wet towel was gently laid across his forehead.

"Perhaps you should just rest; we can talk in the morning."

"I was with Louis..." Caleb managed to say, his words trailing off as his memories began hazily to return, "...oh God, we were attacked, robbers, I think they killed my friend!"

"Now, now," the voice said gently as Caleb felt hands firmly pushing back into the chair, "let's not get too excited, eh?"

"Did you chase the rogues off? Is Louis dead?"

"Well-"

"Actually," the other voice added, drawing closer, "*we* killed him."

Caleb drew a hand across his watery eyes; he decided it was time to start paying attention. With some difficulty, Caleb forced his protesting eyes to look at the nearer of the two men. His voice had seemed vaguely familiar, and as he blinked his vision back into focus, he recognised the portly frame of Dr Samuel Rothery.

Caleb fought down a rising sense of panic, thoughts of his brother's death came rushing back to him, he had always carried a vague fear that one day he too would suffer the same fate and although this pair seemed an unlikely company of footpads, by their own admission they were murderers. Caleb's eyes flicked nervously from one man to the other.

He didn't recognise the second man, who stood motionless at Rothery's shoulder; there was nothing about his appearance that suggested he would ever want to either.

A tall, imposing figure he carried his years easily upon a heavy muscular frame that would shame most men thirty years his junior. He wore an unfussy dark grey suit of immaculate press and skilful trim, his shirt and britches were dizzyingly white, which was no mean feat in the muddy shit filled streets of London. Upon his head sat a functional wig, powdered white with wheat starch. He had the air of a man who paid the utmost attention to his appearance, without ever descending into foppery.

There was something terribly cold and distant about the man's face as if he had seen all that a man might be capable of, both magnificent and terrible, and had been neither impressed nor troubled by any of it. It was an air of disdain that seeped out of his eyes to settle upon a face that was dominated by a prominent hooked nose which must have been broken several times during his life. He wore a neat little beard upon his chin that once would have been jet black but time had faded to grey. Deep lines were etched into his leathery skin, darkened by years under a sun much fiercer than the one that shone upon England

"You killed him?" Caleb asked, his eyes finally settling upon the old Doctor, who at least did not look like he wanted to pull a blade across his throat.

"Louis Defane was not all what he appeared to be," Rothery said quietly.

"I would have said he was far more than he appeared to be," the hook-nosed man corrected, his voice deep and authoritative.

"Yes, yes," Rothery replied dismissively, his tone causing a ripple of annoyance to flicker over his companion's features, "what is the last thing you remember Mr Cade?"

"Someone hitting me."

"That would have been me," hook-nose said.

"I never would have guessed."

"Yes, yes gentlemen... I meant before that?"

Caleb opened his mouth to speak, but no words came. What had they been doing? His memories were hazy. More than just hazy, in fact, they came to him as a strange mixture of a dream and the recollection of a story that he might once have read, rather than the clearly defined memories of events that had occurred just a few hours before.

"Take your time," Rothery encouraged, retreating to sit in another chair.

"We have all night," hook-nose added, still standing ruler straight.

Caleb looked around hoping the normality of the room might help him anchor the memories that spun out of reach around his mind. They sat by a comfortingly crackling fire, most of the walls of the room were lined with book laden shelves. Not the mouldy dog-eared books of Harriet's shop, nor the pristine leather bound volumes of Henrietta's library, these were expensive books that someone read on a regular basis, perhaps at the mighty oak desk that sat behind the chair into which Rothery had just eased himself.

The thought of Harriet brought some of his memories sharply back into focus; waiting outside her shop, Defane turning up and persuading him to follow her father, the molly house... he felt a vague stab of guilt as he recalled taking Brindley's money, but it was like a pinprick compared to the throbbing in his head. Unconsciously his hand brushed against the coat he still wore, the heavy bulges of coin filled purses, at least, reassuring him Rothery and his friend weren't thieves.

"I remember... running," Caleb muttered eventually, ill-formed recollections danced about him, grey indistinct shapes and forms that had rushed by them as they had fled headlong into the fog infested alleys that spread through the ghastly hovels which hugged the riverbank to the east of London.

"You nearly got away from us," Rothery admitted.

"Lucky my boys got a nose for sodomites," hook-nose spat.

"You murdered Defane because you thought him a sodomite?"

"That would be a perfectly good reason in itself," he sneered, "but if that were all we were interested in, you would have been killed too."

"Lazziard, *please*," Rothery insisted, "you are really not helping. A little *shush* might help matters."

The big man looked at his companion darkly; he clearly wasn't used to being spoken to so dismissively. A retort hovered upon his lips for a moment, but it died into a sigh and a thin, forced smile that revealed the blackened ruins of his teeth. It was not a pretty sight. He moved slowly across the room and poured himself a brandy from a decanter that sat upon the desk behind Rothery; he kept his back turned towards them as he drank.

"Now, Mr Cade, what else do you remember?"

Caleb sighed, "I remember running through the fog... the next thing I recall is the tip of a sword sticking out of Defane's chest."

"Nothing in between?"

"Just..." Caleb laughed weakly.

"What else?"

"Just his eyes, Defane's eyes, they were..."

"Captivating?"

"I was going to say the whole world, it was like nothing else existed but his eyes and everything that happened, everything that I did, said and thought somehow... tumbled into them. Does that sound ridiculous?"

"Not at all, dear boy," Rothery said earnestly, leaning forward slightly, "you do know he wasn't entirely human, don't you?"

"What do you mean?" Caleb replied with a weak laugh that fooled no one at all. He couldn't recall what had happened with Defane a few hours ago, but he remembered there was plenty of strangeness about the man.

"You've seen a doorway that leads to a darker world Mr Cade," Dr Rothery said, his words becoming slow and measured, "a world where all the realities and certainties we take for granted are without value. A world where man does not have dominion over the beasts, but one where we are simply prey. Cattle reared by the things of the night, cattle to be feasted upon and slaughtered as they see fit. Do you want to step through that door and see the world in its true colours?"

Behind Rothery's chair, Caleb noticed the room's sole window was shuttered and barred. He could imagine beyond that stout oak the darkness pushing hard against the barrier; a hungry feral creature, eager to consume the light of the room and all those that sought its feeble sanctuary.

Caleb nodded, not trusting his voice to speak.

"When you were a child," Dr Rothery began after a long pause, "were you told stories to entertain you?"

Caleb nodded again, "My brother often made up stories when I was very young."

"Fairy stories, yes; tales of dragons, damsels in distress, and knights of old in shining armour. That kind of thing?"

Caleb nodded again.

"And monsters too, dark, dreadful creatures that hide in the shadow places, always hungry to eat up young children; especially ones who had been naughty?"

Caleb nodded, he felt Jack Frost's name forming on his lips but fought down the urge to give it the breath of life.

"The thing is Mr Cade; some of those monsters are real though the part about them only eating naughty children is a fallacy. They will eat most anyone they care to."

"Do these "monsters" have names, Doctor?"

"Many, but I prefer the term vampire..."

"And Louis Defane was one of these... *creatures*?"

"We have been trailing him for some time, which is fortunate for you as he would have drained your body of blood and discarded your corpse for the rats to deal with had we not intervened."

"This is preposterous!" Caleb tried to stand up, but the room began to swim so alarmingly he had no choice but to slump back into his chair. He was clearly in the hands of madmen, and he had not the strength even to walk to the door, let alone fashion some manner of escape.

"Is it really?" Rothery asked.

Caleb found he had been rubbing his neck without realising it, when he drew his fingers away he found they were tacky with partially dried blood.

The memory of pain overwhelmed him. Not the kind of pain he felt from Lazziard's fist, not the throbbing and aching of his head, but an altogether different kind; sharp and instant and all consuming. A pain so great it teetered on the brink of pleasure and left him yearning for something he could not describe once the memory had slithered away from him.

Rothery fumbled with his coat and produced an unadorned looking glass that he handed to Caleb, "Examine your neck."

Caleb felt reluctant to do anything these men wanted, but given he felt too weak to even argue he did as the Doctor urged. The collar of his shirt was stained dark with blood while his neck was smeared with more. Gingerly he touched his skin, but there was no pain, not even any soreness. Partially obscured by the blood, he found two small marks, no more than scabs really, they looked like wounds that had been inflicted weeks earlier and were all but healed though he swore he'd never seen them before.

"The wounds these creatures inflict heal almost instantly; it is one of the ways they conceal their foul handiwork."

"More likely the blood is Defane's and the marks are just spots."

Lazziard laughed richly from the corner of the room.

"Murderers and madmen," Caleb spat, letting the mirror slip from his fingers, his eyes once more darting about the room.

"Sodomite." Lazziard retorted.

"Gentleman, *please*," Rothery sighed, "this is getting us nowhere."

"Do you mean to kill me too?"

Lazziard revealed his blackened teeth in a manner that suggested he would like to do nothing more, but the

Doctor shook his head emphatically, "I understand this is a terrible ordeal for you and I am sure most men would think us lunatics-"

"Most men *do* consider us lunatics," Lazziard corrected the Doctor again.

"Quite, but the fact of the matter is, my dear boy, we mean you no harm," Rothery smiled. It was the kind of smile, Caleb assumed, he reserved for patients whom he intended to hack some body part from. "We have gone to a great deal of trouble to save your immortal soul, not to mention considerable inconvenience to our plans. Why would we do that just to kill you afterwards?"

"Because you are lunatics?"

Before Rothery could reply a slight man hurried into the room, his head bobbing frantically in time with each step.

"Cade!" Richard Rentwin exclaimed, "How good to see you awake again. I knew you were a fellow with a thick head."

"Getting thicker all the time," Caleb managed to force a smile, "please tell me you're not one of these lunatic... *vampire hunters*, are you?"

"Vampire hunters? No, nothing so barbaric, we are a Society, with rules and a constitution," Rentwin said, tugging the lapels of his jacket, "I am the treasurer!"

"*The Society for the Investigation, Comprehension and Restraint of Vampiric Creatures and their Demonic Behaviours*," Rothery beamed, "at you service."

"I thought *The Society for the Eradication of Vampires* was a better name," Lazziard chipped in, "but I was outvoted."

"And your rules and constitution allow for murder and kidnapping?" Caleb demanded.

When Rentwin looked at his companions in mild bemusement, Rothery explained, "The poor fellow is still a little confused; his senses have not quite-"

"'tis not I who has taken leave of my senses, Doctor!" Caleb snapped, "I saw Louis Defane murdered in front of me, by your own confession you have admitted responsibility and by way of an explanation you have offered me some ridiculous fairy tale about vampires. I'll admit Defane was a strange little chap, but he wasn't a monster. I hope you realise you will all hang for this!"

Caleb felt his bubble of righteous anger deflate somewhat when his words were met with only mocking laughter from Lazziard, who was continuing to help himself to the brandy at a steady rate of knots.

"You cannot be hanged for murdering a beast, particularly when that beast was a man-eater," Lazziard barked.

"I see..." Rothery jumped in before Caleb could respond, "...that you require a little more evidence."

"I require a *lot* more evidence."

"Splendid!" the old doctor beamed, "then you must come take the grand tour of my workshop of curiosities!"

*

He had followed Rothery down into his workshop with some reluctance. Partly due the room spinning so alarmingly when he'd risen to his feet that the Doctor had to summon his manservant Scaife to half carry him down the stairs, but mainly because he feared they intended to finish him off in some particularly ghastly fashion and bury his remains in the cellar.

Perhaps he had acted a little rashly when he'd accused them of murder before threatening to see them hang.

As it was, by the time he'd been half-dragged and half-carried down several flights of stairs he decided a quick end might be a mercy compared to enduring any more of the devil's trying to chisel their way out of his head.

"Here we are," the Doctor beamed, unhelpfully slapping Caleb's back before pushing open a door to reveal a large windowless room lit by an inordinate number of lanterns, "my domain!"

"Very impressive," Caleb muttered as he slumped into a chair Rentwin dragged over for him, "must cost you a fortune in whale oil."

"Yes, it does rather," Rothery agreed, "but I must have illumination for my work and windows are a little... inconvenient in my line of investigation."

"It would disturb the neighbours greatly if they happened to look in at an inopportune moment," Lazziard explained.

"That will be all, thank you, Scaife," Rothery said, waving away his servant.

In the Absence of Light

Scaife, a tall bald man of imposing build and discouraging features, nodded and shuffled from the room without a word.

By the time the door clicked shut Caleb had recovered enough of his senses to pay more attention to his surroundings. The workshop was a clutter of all manner of things, as if Rothery had tried to cram all the knowledge of the world into the confines of one small room.

Shelves lined every wall, some piled with books, loose stacks of papers, rolled up charts and parchments, others held bottles, jars, vials and containers of varying sizes. Many of the vessels were opaque, though some were clear enough to display their contents. In most cases they held a nondescript powder or liquid, in a few dried leaves or roots, but one particular shelf held only jars containing fluids in which floated preserved... *things*. Caleb didn't look too closely, but they appeared to be body parts and internal organs.

The possibility that the vampire hunters were actually planning something worse than just burying him flitted across his mind.

Quickly his eyes moved on; other shelves held small boxes and crates, while chests and barrels were stacked neatly along the far wall. Scattered around the workshop were numerous pieces of machinery in various states of dismantlement, some appeared to be clock workings, others were less obviously apparent; levers, weights, gears and pulleys heaped in seemingly random piles. Along the far wall the shelves held glass boxes containing stuffed birds and small animals, many so moth-eaten they were probably older than Rothery himself.

In one corner what appeared to be a small furnace sat squat and ugly, its small blackened door hung open, the glowing embers inside throwing a soft orange light across the floor.

Three large tables filled the centre of the room. Two were covered with open books, sheets of paper, notebooks and writing materials strewn around assorted paraphernalia; jars, bells, tubes, vials, extinguished candles, earthenware vessels, bellows, numerous scales and weights, magnifying lenses, countless bowls and beakers containing various liquids, powders and dark tar-like residues. The third was covered with a sheet, underneath which appeared to be something shaped not entirely unlike a body.

A young man was hunched over the end of the shroud covered table. He'd been furiously writing in a leather-bound ledger when they'd entered, his wide restless eyes flicking between each of them, quickly followed by the rest of his head like a small rodent sniffing the air for danger before venturing from the safety of its burrow. His bulging eyes gave the impression that during his childhood some prankster had given the back of his head such a hearty whack with a large plank of wood that his eyeballs had been permanently forced from their sockets.

His hair was long, unkempt and hung greasily about a pale, thin face coloured only by a smattering of pimples and yellow heads that huddled around the sides of his nostrils and forehead. He wore a loose-fitting shirt that might once have been white but was now stained with various substances, the most identifiable of which were the yellow-brown patches around his armpits.

"Mr Cade, my I introduce my assistant and apprentice, Archibald Jute," Rothery said with a sweep of his hand that was so extravagant his fingers caught a tall glass tube filled with a black viscous substance and set it wobbling upon its base.

Rothery grabbed it quickly with both hands, "Ho! Really wouldn't want to knock *that* over!"

"My pleasure," Caleb managed to say, not wanting to dwell on what was in the vessel exactly.

"We have met actually," Jute replied, hurrying over to pump his hand a little too enthusiastically, "though I doubt you would remember the fact given that you were unconscious at the time. I'm glad we are able to save you from that creature."

"Don't expect too much in the way of thanks," Lazziard muttered.

Caleb ignored them both and turned his attention back to the shroud, "I take it that is your evidence?"

"Indeed," Rothery nodded, "do you think you are up to standing again, it will make things easier to see."

"Of course," Caleb managed a nod, accepting Rentwin and Jute's assistance in getting back to his feet.

Although it was only a few short steps to the table, by the time he reached it he needed to rest both his hands upon its thick scoured wooden edge. He really did not feel at all well.

"Is that Defane?" he managed to ask eventually.

Rothery nodded, "Yes my boy, it certainly is. If you will kindly do the honours, Archie."

Jute hurried around to the other side of the table and begun pulling the shroud away. Caleb could feel Rothery, Rentwin and Lazziard surrounding him, far too close for his comfort. They seemed to be breathing all his air for he found himself gasping slightly with each breath he took. The workshop was stiflingly hot, and the air heavy, stale and strangely metallic as if so many chemicals and compounds had been burned down here that some extraordinary alchemical process had caused the air to become more solid.

"Is this some kind... of joke?" Caleb asked eventually after Jute had finally hauled away the shroud.

"No," Lazziard boomed from somewhere behind him, "this *is* Louis Defane."

Although the corpse was dressed in the same uncharacteristically sober clothes Defane had been wearing and it bore the same short white hair his friend wore beneath his usually flamboyant wigs there was no other similarity. The shrivelled, desiccated figure that lay before him had clearly been pulled from some tomb where it must have lain undisturbed for centuries. The thing's skin was like dark scorched parchment and even as he watched it seemed to be crumbling away in patches to expose the white bone beneath.

"This is something from a crypt!" hissed Caleb.

"Quite so," Lazziard retorted.

"If this is Defane you must have hit me hard enough to knock me senseless for a very long time. What year is it, by the way?"

"Cade, I assure you this is Louis Defane," Rothery insisted, carefully he reached out and pulled back the thing's withered lips, Caleb couldn't help but wince as the skin audibly cracked and come away in the Doctor's hand to reveal the teeth beneath. They were vividly white against the darkened skin, and two sharp inhuman fangs were evident where the canine teeth should be.

"Note the fangs?" Rothery pointed out, "They can be withdrawn inside the jaw to give the vampire's teeth a human appearance, but as he was feeding at the moment of death, they are still fully released. You will see the fangs are somewhat darker than the otherwise perfect teeth?"

"Yes," agreed Caleb quietly.

"That would be because your blood is still smeared over them. The reason you have to grip the table so firmly my friend is not due to the force with which Captain Lazziard hit you, but to the amount of your blood that now resides inside this creature."

"How can this be Defane?"

Rothery brushed the powdered remains of the corpse's lips from his hands, "These creatures live for centuries, perhaps they are even immortal, we do not know for certain, but if one is killed, and, believe me dear boy, that is not an altogether easy feat to achieve, they decay with incredible rapidity. 'tis as if once the essence of life is removed, whatever force that preserves them through the centuries dissipates instantly, leaving behind something more becoming to the creature's true age."

"That is one theory," Lazziard offered.

"There are others?"

"Indeed," Rothery nodded, "another is that this is how they actually do look, and it is only through some trick, some magic or glamour that they appear as they do. We have much anecdotal evidence that vampiric creatures can cast illusions and conjure apparitions to make people see things that do not exist. Have you had any such experiences in Defane's company?"

"One or two," Caleb admitted, wondering what he would have seen that night if he'd turned around when Defane had asked him to, instead of those startlingly beautiful eyes, would Defane have looked back at him with the dark, shrivelled prunes that now sat sightlessly in his skull,

Rothery placed a gentle hand upon his shoulder, "Look upon him for the last time dear boy, by morning there will be nothing left but dust lying on that table. I have tried to preserve them before, but nothing works; alcohol, vinegar, salt, ice, all the things that might preserve once living flesh, be it man or beast, has no effect whatsoever on them. We mean you no harm, if we had not intervened he would have killed you, to him you were just a beast of the field, prey to hunt and slaughter, do not think of him in human terms, because that is the exact thing he was not."

"He was my friend," Caleb said softly, staring at the things chest and the bloody wound where the sword had erupted after running through its heart. The blood looked fresh on the fabric, but the skin beneath was just blistered parchment hanging from exposed ribs. It wore Defane's clothes, its fingers, the bones already poking through the skin in places, wore his rings. How could they have faked such a thing? How?

"You will see in time that he was not that at all."

"What do you want of me?"

"Only to know what happened between the two of you, vampires are intelligent, dangerous creatures, they are aware that there are people who know of their existence. It is almost impossible for one of us to get close enough to study them. That was what we were trying to do that evening you stumbled across us in the coffee house, but you presented us with an opportunity. Rentwin knew you were unaware of Defane's true nature and that we could keep in contact with you. We had hoped Defane might take you under his wing, they do that you know, groom a human before they feast on them. Perhaps the blood tastes better if it is taken from someone they know. You will need to take a few days here to recover, and during that time I would like you to recount all that has happened to you since you met Defane, however irrelevant it seems to you, it may prove a vital clue that will significantly assist our work. Everything you have done, everywhere you went, everyone you met, can you do that for me Caleb? Can you do that?"

Caleb closed his eyes and let out a long breath which slowly formed into a single anguished word.

"Liselot..."

Chapter Seven

The Courtesan

Southwark, London, 1708

She was even prettier at close quarters.

Defane had found space on the bench behind the young courtesan, a few feet to her left, giving them the opportunity to study her profile discreetly while they awaited the next bout. She was very young, no more than eighteen or nineteen at most. Her young skin was lightly powered to a fashionable paleness, coloured only by patches of rouge on her cheeks to simulate a faint feminine blush and her red lips, which occasionally flickered into a half-hearted smile as her companion bestowed some laboured witticism or another.

The girl had an intriguing mouth, Caleb thought. Her bottom lip was noticeably fuller, giving her a pleasing pout, it also appeared slightly crooked and he wished the buffoon she was with would find the wit to say something genuinely amusing so that he might examine the contours of her smile. Caleb suspected it would be a wickedly enticing one.

Instead, he settled for the ample consolation of her cleavage, which was so deep and fulsome it appeared to be on the point of exploding from the confines of the pale green silk dress that framed it all so pleasingly. The gallery's steps gave him an almost perfect angle to enjoy the spectacle.

"Who is our lady's companion?" Caleb whispered, dragging his eyes away for a moment.

"Sir Charles Massingham," Defane replied, noting Caleb's blank expression he added, "he is something significant in the Navy Office, as well as being the member of Parliament for some godforsaken collection of cowsheds and inbreds too far north of London to be much noticed by anybody."

"He must be very rich," Caleb noted, for the man had taken ugliness to a quite unnecessary extreme. Not all the powder and beauty spots in the world could disguise his pudding belly, bulbous nose, sagging folds of overindulged flesh and spectacular collection of warts. "No doubt that expensive looking silver necklace and those large pearl earrings that decorate her so prettily have helped her enormously in coping with her beau's appearance?"

"His wealth is only exceeded by his appetite for pretty young girls, a quite terrible old letch in fact; a buck fitch, I believe, is the local term?" Defane replied, "He is also quite corrupt, by all accounts, it is only his connections at court that have kept him in office and allowed him to indulge his one unqualified talent, which is keeping that bulging snout of his snuffling deeply into the trough of government finance."

"I am beginning to suspect you are a terrible gossip, Louis."

Defane airily waved away the comment, "One simply likes to be well informed, it is an unavoidable hazard that if one is diligent enough to keep one's ear pressed closely to the ground, the lobe will occasionally pick up a little dirt."

Caleb smiled, more at Defane's boyish expression of pleasure at his own word play than at the Frenchman's wit, and returned his attention to Massingham's little companion. He must be paying well for her favours; she was pretty enough to attract a fair number of wealthy young beaux who would be happy to shower her with gifts in return for her pleasures. Still, it was not for him to judge her choices, perhaps she was smart enough to know the career of a courtesan lasted only as long as their beauty and so indulged the highest bidder accordingly, whatever his looks. Many a lovely girl had not appreciated that simple fact, believing their prettiness to be eternal they squandered their money almost as soon as it filled their purse. When their looks faded they had nothing left to fall back on, their former suitors rejecting them in favour of younger, fresher game and their lives became an inevitable spiral of despair that ended in destitution, working the slums of St Giles as pox-ridden hackney drabs for a penny trick or a couple of shots of gin.

Whatever Massingham was paying, it was obviously not enough for her to feel she needed to conceal her tedium, for behind the torpid swish of her silk fan the courtesan's eyes moved listlessly across the old theatre, dull and flat, as if vainly searching for something that might offer a little diversion from Massingham's company. The old letch regained her attention however as he leaned close and squeezed her knee, while his lips whispered wetly against her ear. Judging by the eager bulge of his eyes and the lascivious smile that split his face, he was not asking her about the weather.

She half turned towards the old man and breathed a reply through the luxuriant tresses of his wig before shooing his hand away with a light swish of her fan. Massingham rocked with laughter, his fleshy jowls trembling with delight as he roared in her ear. The courtesan smiled demurely before checking the delicate powdered curls of her own intricately sculpted wig, ensuring they had not been displaced by Massingham's fetid breath and flying spittle.

"And what of our little courtesan, do you know anything of her?"

"A little," Defane returned his attention to the stage, his hands folded over the head of the cane he had planted firmly between his splayed feet. "Her name is Liselot Van Schalkwyk, daughter of a Dutch merchant. Her family was once quite wealthy by all accounts; indeed her grandfather was a supporter of William of Orange and helped to finance the fleet that brought William across the Channel to depose that Catholic buffoon James Stuart whose arse you English had carelessly allowed to rest upon your throne."

"Sadly, Liselot's father did not inherit either the talent for making money that so many of our Dutch cousins enjoy or maintaining the family's friends in high places. From almost the instant Van Schalkwyk got his hands on the purse strings the family fortune was frittered away on high living and some rather unfortunate overseas investments, leaving the Van Schalkwyk business teetering on the verge of bankruptcy. Consumed by his failure he tried to find inspiration in the bottom of gin bottles, which, no doubt, led him to a final desperate attempt to regain the Van Schalkwyk fortune; the card tables of Amsterdam."

"Unfortunately, he was even poorer at cards than he was at business. Faced with destitution with her father or a dowry-less marriage to some clerk or shopkeeper, little Liselot came to London to make her own way in the world," Defane concluded.

"As a courtesan?"

Defane shrugged, "I do not know if that was her attention on arrival in London, but there are few paths open to independently minded women that require a maiden's knees to stay together; however I understand she is *very* good at what she does."

"Tell me more?" Caleb demanded.

"I'm far too much of a gentleman to recount such ribald gossip... besides, if you had a little more ambition you might have found out for yourself."

Further discussion was curtailed as the crowd roared to herald the arrival of Bob Figg and Pretty Jim.

"Let us hope this is more of a spectacle than the last shoddy affair!"

Rapturous applause greeted Figg as he climbed onto the stage, acknowledging the adulation of the mob by pounding a clenched fist against his heart as the Master of Ceremonies introduced him as a "true son of Southwark and a defender of the Faith!" He was a tall brute of a man, with shoulders as broad as a door lintel. He had pulled his thinning hair back into a tar stiffened queue tied in a short bow, naval fashion. He carried himself with a confidence that bordered on arrogance and a manner that suggested he was used to winning.

"He looks impressive," Caleb muttered, "are you sure this Irish lad is good?"

Defane merely smiled, his eyes flicking between the stage and the figure of Massingham who had pulled himself unsteadily to his feet in order to clap and encourage Bob Figg in the manner of a drunken peasant.

"Did I mention he also hates Catholics with a rare passion?" Defane added as Pretty Jim joined Figg on the stage and the cheers turned to a cacophony of hisses and catcalls as he was introduced as "Pretty Jim O'Conner, Champion of all the Irish!"

"It would appear he is not the only one," Caleb noted.

The Irishman matched Figg for height if not breadth, but he had at least ten years on his opponent and his fresh-faced good looks, unmarred by a broken nose or old scars, spoke of either a man with little experience of the brawl, or one who was an exceptionally good fighter indeed. His body was taut and lean, with nothing to spare. He positively glowed with good health, which made Caleb suspect he was new to London.

A sea of fists were being waved at the Irishman while the Master of Ceremonies description of Pretty Jim as "The Papist Prize Fighter" only managed to whip up the mob's fury further.

"My man Figg will break that pretty little Broganeer clean in two," Massingham bellowed as he juddered back onto his bench, loud enough for Liselot to wince behind her fan.

Defane leaned across Caleb to call to Massingham, "Would you care to wager the matter, Sir?"

Massingham's head swiveled in their direction, his eyes narrowing to podgy slits as he peered quizzically at Defane "What say you?" He bawled, his primary mode of communication appeared to lay somewhere between a shout and a belch, a habit he'd probably picked up in parliament, Caleb assumed.

"You seem most certain of the local boy's victory; would you care to take a small side bet on the matter?"

Massingham snorted, "Sir, I think you know little of the art of fisticuffs if you believe that papist whelp has any chance against Bad Bob Figg, it would be little more than theft to take your money."

"£50 says the Irish will bring Figg's arse to anchor on the canvas..." Massingham's eyes widened at the size of the bet while Liselot, who had been staring disinterestedly into the middle distance, froze her fan in mid-stroke and threw Defane a brief sideways glance "...in the first three minutes of the fight."

Massingham laughed loudly, "Either you jest with me, or you have more money than sense."

"I am quite serious," Defane insisted, "of course if the bet is too rich for you..."

Before Massingham could answer, Liselot giggled behind her fan, "How little you know! Charlie is one of the richest men in London, such a trifling little bet is *utterly* beneath him," her English was perfect, though her accent was pronounced enough to reveal her continental origins; deep and smoky, Caleb couldn't help but imagine how it would sound if whispered softly in his ear, the only sound to break the still darkness of the night after all passion was spent...

Sir Charles flustered a little at her boast, but before he could reply, she flashed a sudden smile at Defane that was even more dazzling and intoxicating than Caleb had imagined. "You'll have to wager at least £100 for it to be worth Charlie's time and effort," her eyes widened suggestively as she asked Defane, "Is your purse big enough to satisfy us, Sir?"

"It is deep and wide enough for *all* pleasures, Ma'am" Defane replied, almost slyly.

"Steady on!" Massingham declared, staring aghast at the little courtesan, but Liselot smiled sweetly at him before leaning close and whispering something behind her fan. Her voice was far too low for Caleb to make out her words above the clamour of the crowd, but judging by the way the old letch's eyes bulged and face flushed beneath his powder he assumed Liselot was explaining *exactly* how grateful she would be if he took Defane's bet. No doubt, she expected to take the winnings for herself, on top of whatever gifts Massingham had already plied the courtesan with for her company.

While she worked her wiles on Massingham, Caleb turned incredulously towards his new friend, he had made some insane bets during his life, but at least he could blame those on drink, Defane did not have even that meagre excuse for such folly for barely a drop had passed his lips. "Louis, what are you doing? This is insane, you cannot be so sure-"

"It would seem the lady is in the mood for wagering," Massingham announced after clearing his throat and giving Liselot's knee another playful squeeze, "will you take my hand on the matter?"

"With pleasure," Defane beamed, ignoring Caleb's protestations, even when he clutched at the Frenchman's arm. "Life is nothing without risk... you know that already I believe?" Defane carefully pulled his arm away from Caleb's grasp before nimbly clambering down onto the bench below and squeezing next to Liselot. He leant across the courtesan to take the wager, his small hand engulfed in Massingham's fleshy grip.

"Sir Charles Massingham," the portly man said with a nod.

"Louis Defane..." he indicated Caleb, who still sat on the bench behind, "and my good friend Mr Caleb Cade."

Caleb nodded a greeting; Massingham moved his voluminous bewigged head in a barely perceptible nod, while Liselot offered even less by way of acknowledgement. Unlike Defane, he had done nothing to indicate he was of sufficient worth to be of any note to her. Caleb felt the faint damp hand of disappointment settle upon him as it always did whenever a beautiful woman took no interest in him whatsoever. He quickly shook the feeling aside however, intrigued as to Defane's game. Did he seriously think he could bed this mercenary wench based on his flamboyant betting alone. Moreover, just how much was Defane worth if he was prepared to risk the princely sum of £100 on top of the sizeable bet he had already placed with Barrel Jones?

"And may I ask the name of your delightful companion?" Defane was asking Massingham, tilting his hat slightly back upon his head in order to cut a more rakish figure for Liselot's benefit.

"Forgive my manners," Massingham said, in the cold manner of a father who suspected sharks were circling his daughter, "may I present Miss Liselot Van Schalkwyk."

"What an absolute delight it is..." Defane murmured throatily as he took Liselot's gloved hand and raised it gently to his lips, "to meet another stranger from a foreign land in this great, but lonely, city."

He is so smooth his arse is in danger of slipping off the bench, Caleb thought sourly.

Liselot smiled her crooked, enticing little smile that Caleb was sure would make her a fortune one day (if it hadn't already). "It is always a pleasure to meet a gentleman, wherever one finds one self," she purred as Defane let her hand slip reluctantly from his.

"I suspect there is something of the French about you, Mr Defane," Massingham interrupted with a sniff.

"Indeed Sir Charles, my parents were Huguenots who fled to London many years ago to escape persecution by the papists."

"Ah!" Massingham nodded; obviously relieved he hadn't made the mistake of inadvertently shaking hands with a Catholic, "I presume your family has found prosperity among the decent God-fearing people of London."

"God has smiled upon me," Defane replied, his mouth curling into a strange little half-smile.

"That won't go on for much longer if you keep backing papists, eh Sir?" Massingham guffawed, pleased at his own wit.

"We are happy to take Spanish gold on the high seas, and use Irish workers on our lands and in our mines," Defane demurred, "I'm sure the Lord will not object to a little more wealth finding its way into a good Protestant purse on the back of Catholic labour."

Massingham seemed unconvinced, but any further debate was cut short by the master of ceremonies winding up his oratory with some even handed comments about Ireland being Europe's urinal, before retreating into the cheering mob and leaving the fighters to circle each other, apparently eager for the contest to begin.

"Inside three minutes, you say?" Massingham checked, fumbling with his pocket watch.

Defane nodded, "If Pretty Jim wins in three minutes and a single second the money will be yours, Sir."

Massingham nodded, settled back and examined his watch as the fight began. Around them gentlemen rose to their feet to cheer on Figg, their behaviour only marginally more refined than the crowd gathered below. As the two men circled each other warily, the mob appeared to be in a good mood, the disappointment of the previous fight already forgotten as they hurled their insults at the Irishman; one well-prepared wag had even produced a crude effigy of the Pope which he was waving good-naturedly about his head from the end of a noose.

Roared on by the crowd Figg launched a series of murderous right hooks at Pretty Jim's torso. Caleb winced, but the young Irishman nimbly dodged the blows with ease and flashed a toothy grin in his opponent's direction.

Figg scowled and came forwards again, powerful arms trying to club Pretty Jim to the canvas; once more the younger man danced away, his broad smile clearly infuriating the local hero.

"The bog-trotter is light on his feet, I'll give him that, but he can't run away all night," Massingham scoffed, glancing at Liselot he added, "I think we will be dinning royally at Mr Defane's expense tonight, my dear."

Though Caleb had always loved the thrill of a good wager he'd never had much appetite for violence. Rather than watching the fight, he found his eyes drawn to the three figures below him; Defane motionless, hands once more resting on his cane, Massingham shifting uncomfortably from one inflated buttock to the next as his attention moved from fight to timepiece and back again, and the lovely Liselot, all fashionable disdain behind her ever-moving fan, though her eyes remained fixed and fascinated on the contest below.

In fact, he became so engrossed, particularly in the pale smooth line of Liselot's neck, that he entirely missed Figg's clubbing blow that Pretty Jim had clearly anticipated. Deftly ducking inside his opponent's reach he delivered an uppercut of such force that the Englishman's feet left the floor before his twitching body crumpled to the canvas a good yard away from the grinning Irishman.

The sudden gasps of the crowd brought Caleb's

attention back to the fight. Only Massingham's strangled cry of, "Good grief!" broke the stunned silence that fell around them.

Defane glanced casually over his shoulder and gave Caleb a slow theatrical wink.

*

They retreated to the back of the gallery when the mob turned ugly.

By the time Bob Figg had been dragged unceremoniously from the stage, the shocked silence had turned to anger at the Irishman's unsporting behaviour. Obviously someone had forgotten to tell him that he had only been invited to take part on the proviso he took a good beating. A hail of assorted missiles, ranging from the obligatory rotten vegetables to the effigy of the Pope, forced Pretty Jim to flee the stage. The magnitude of the crowd's displeasure was demonstrated by the Pope's demise escalating from a good natured hanging to a more symbolic burning, before it was hurled at the only obvious Catholic in the building. Once the Irishman had made it to safety the mob turned their wrath towards their betters perched on the gallery above them.

Defane grabbed Liselot's hand and unceremoniously pulled her over the benches towards the back of the gallery. Any reluctance Liselot might have had at being manhandled evaporated as a mouldy potato narrowly missed her elaborately decorated wig. Given that the long silken skirts of her hooped dress were not the most practical design for clambering over benches Caleb positioned himself to take her other arm, and between them they half carried half dragged the girl out of missile range.

There was space enough at the rear of the gallery to accommodate a small bar and the ladies and more refined gentlemen quickly gathered along its length. Spirits were hastily fortified with a stiffening brandy or two while the more hot-headed bucks returned the missiles thrown at them by the mob, along with the occasional empty bottle, whose impact on the masses below was no doubt sharpened when accompanied by the cutting wit of the young gentlemen.

"Why thank you," Liselot managed to pant, a slight flush visible beneath her layers of powder, "the rabble are most volatile this evening."

"Once the Irishman was out of sight," Defane mused, "the mob vented its anger on the next best thing after a papist."

"Which is?" Liselot asked, deploying her fan once more.

"Anyone dressed better than they are," Defane sighed sadly, brushing some minute speck of dust from his lapel, "which means I am in some considerable danger."

"Poor thing," Liselot declared, "I must make sure Charlie sees you are both kept safe."

"There is no need to fret," Defane said reassuringly, "besides as you can see from Mr Cade's sartorial performance tonight, he is in no danger whatsoever!"

Liselot laughed softly, covering her mouth with a gloved hand as her eyes darted between Caleb and Defane. Caleb forced an indulgent smile in return.

Defane patted Caleb's arm playfully before he produced a bottle of brandy from somewhere and pressed a glass into Liselot's hand, which he generously filled, "Seriously, I am sorry you had to face such an ordeal, this is no place for such a refined young lady."

Liselot smiled demurely before downing the glass in one and holding it out for a refill, "Sir Charles does have a fondness for the rougher things in life."

"That must be quite a tribulation for you," Defane smiled, pouring more brandy into her glass. Feeling in as much need as the young courtesan for a little fortification Caleb looked around in vain for a glass of his own. Sadly the remaining glassware appeared to have been requisitioned as ammunition by their gallant defenders out on the edge of the gallery.

"Er, where is Sir Charles?" Caleb asked, realising a spare glass was not the only thing missing.

"I do hope he hasn't vanished with my winnings," Defane grinned, taking a swig straight from the bottle."

"No," Liselot sighed, her chest heaving majestically with the gesture, "I believe he has other matters on his mind just at the moment." She nodded back down the gallery, to where the Honourable Member of Parliament for some remote corner of Lancashire was hurling, what appeared to be, a blackened turnip at the mob below.

"Swine!" Sir Charles bellowed down at some unseen target.

"He seems to be quite enjoying himself," Caleb noted, accepting Defane's offer of the bottle.

"Charlie has never been particularly enamoured with

the London mob," Liselot admitted, "I think it is because they always throw shit at his coach." Caleb took a long hard swig from the bottle as he wondered if he'd ever heard the word shit pronounced so beautifully.

Defane tutted loudly, "A man should never hold a grudge; it is most unseemly; Cade would you be so kind as to rescue Sir Charles for us. I wouldn't want some particularly heavy vegetable to strike his head and rob me of my winnings, I would go myself, but I am just too captivated by this delightful creature."

Liselot snapped open her fan to cool her brow and conceal her smile.

"My pleasure," Caleb said, giving Defane a long knowing look that said he thought the Frenchman still had no chance of getting between Liselot's legs.

Caleb hurried down to retrieve the old reprobate, not because of any great concern for his safety, but to minimise the time Defane would be alone to work upon Liselot. Caleb had never liked losing a bet, whatever it was and whatever the stake. It was one of his very few principles

He trotted quickly down the steps of the gallery towards Sir Charles, who was busily berating some hapless steward who had the temerity to try to stop the Honourable Member from using the theatre's better glassware for ammunition.

Before he could intervene Caleb felt someone grab his coat and yank him backwards with enough force for him to lose his balance and totter on the edge of one step.

"Dr Rothery!" Caleb exclaimed, trying to regain his composure.

"Are you well?" Rothery asked urgently, his brow creased in concern beneath his lop-sided periwig.

"The entertainment has proved a little more riotous than I expected," Caleb managed a thin smile, and glanced at the Doctor's ink stained fingers that now tightly clutched his lapels, "but I have managed to survive the mob so far."

Rothery peered above his spectacles for a moment, his mouth slightly agape. Just when Caleb was about to repeat himself the Doctor blinked and nodded vigorously in understanding.

"Ah, no! I meant your health. Have you been unwell?" The Doctor tilted his head to one side, causing his wig to slide perceptibly across his scalp, like the side of a mountain slowly gaining momentum as it slid towards some unsuspecting valley below, "Anything... *odd* been troubling you?"

Apart from being accosted by the odd quack, you mean? Caleb pushed the thought aside and smiled warmly, "No, I'm quite well; if you're looking for business-"

"No! No! Dear boy!" The Doctor cried, waving podgy ink-stained fingers beneath Caleb's nose, "Not so mercenary! Just enquiring... you look a little... pale?"

"I believe that's the fashion?"

Rothery stared at him for a second or two; so intent was his gaze that it seemed the Doctor's entire body went quite rigid, every bodily function frozen in place while his mind turned over Caleb's words as if they were some devilish puzzle that required his entire attention to solve.

Without warning, he grasped Caleb's hand between both of his and pumped it vigorously, "Good to see you again dear fellow," he murmured before raising it up to his face to examine. For a moment, he thought the eccentric old fellow was going to kiss it, but instead Rothery let Caleb's hand slip from his grasp. His face cracked into a smile, and he laughed heartily enough to send his wig jigging back up the slope of his forehead, "Yes you seem quite well," he said, expression flowing back into his momentarily slack features.

"As I said," Caleb replied, shuffling awkwardly from one foot to the other, but Rothery just continued to peer at him. Caleb was about to make his excuses when the Doctor was struck on the shoulder by a rotting vegetable of indeterminable type.

"My, my!" Rothery exclaimed, brushing off scraps of putrefied vegetable from amongst the assorted clutter that already soiled his black shapeless coat, "I didn't realise this prize-fighting game was such a dangerous sport for the spectator."

"You know how volatile the mob can be," Caleb muttered, nervously glancing over his shoulder in case anything more dangerous might be coming their way.

"Volatile, yes..." Rothery moved his great head in what might have been a nod of agreement or a shudder; his movements being so exaggerated and random it was hard for Caleb to be entirely sure, "Perhaps it would be best to take my leave, such rowdiness is certainly not my thing. If you do fall ill Mr Cade, please feel free to call on me. I have residence in Lincoln's Inn Fields..."

"You sound as if you expect me to fall ill; you're not looking for some ghastly plague are you?" Caleb demanded, his eyes widening in alarm; the plague was one of the great fears of the age, and in the overcrowded filthy streets of London all manner of horrid diseases could spread like wild fire. The only way of protecting yourself from a wretched death was to get out of the city for the relative safety of the countryside as soon as a new outbreak appeared. This option of course was only available to the rich, who would pay handsomely to be forewarned of impending contagion. Was this the Doctor's game?

Rothery laughed again, "No, nothing like that dear boy, nothing like that."

Caleb remembered the strange weakness that had left him bed-ridden, but quickly dismissed any connection to what the Doctor must be looking for, if he had been suffering some variety of plague he would never have risen from Defane's bed.

"Must be off!" Rothery announced, in the manner of a man who had just remembered he should be somewhere else. Once more Caleb's hand was engulfed in the old Doctor's flesh and shaken vigorously before he turned and hurried up the stairs.

"Nice to see you again!" Caleb called after him.

Caleb watched as Rothery struggled to the top of the stairs where he lingered to mop his brow with a grubby handkerchief. He stood panting and resting on his cane, to all intents a fat old man regaining his breath amidst the hurly burly of younger men rushing back and forth. However, for all his apparent discomfort, it seemed to Caleb his small dark eyes lingered long and hard upon the figures of Defane and Liselot standing in the shadows at the back of the gallery, the courtesan pressed close against the Huguenot, head tilted upwards, eyes wide and attentive, stretching up to speak softly into Defane's ear.

She is so beautiful...

Caleb sighed, all thought of the Doctor, and anything else, slipping from his mind. Unnoticed he simply stood, his chest tightening as he watched her, feasting upon the sight of her beauty until another vegetable splattered by his foot and brought his attention back into focus. He blinked and looked around him before remembering his task. He hurried down the stairs to find Massingham; the quicker he could drag him away, the quicker he could get back to Liselot and prevent Defane from working whatever magic he expected to weave.

Sir Charles stood by the gallery rail like a corpulent emperor looking down upon a besieging barbarian horde that was threatening to visit rape and ruin upon his civilisation; which was probably pretty much how Massingham *did* view the situation.

He seemed in no particular mood to retreat as he glowered down at the mob, his face flushed with a combination of excitement and indignation, "Look at the filthy laggards!" Massingham growled as Caleb joined him, pointing down at the milling crowd. The audience had thinned a little, but a fair few remained intent on breaking whatever came to hand. Stewards were cracking heads and trying to regain some kind of order, but the mob seemed in no mood to be dispersed. Caleb guessed only a call out of the militia would finally bring them to heal.

"They are in a foul mood," Caleb agreed soberly,

watching the blackened remains of the pope being whirled around on the end of its smouldering noose above the baying heads of one particularly vociferous knot of the crowd.

"Surely, we are enduring the end of all days," Massingham announced with a melodramatic sigh, "when the masses lose respect for their betters all that is left is chaos."

Caleb thought King Charles I probably thought much the same when his inferiors decided to lop his head off sixty years earlier, but decided it was probably not the wisest quip to make as Massingham had the look of a Royalist about him. "I believe your companion is a little troubled by all this dreadful brutality," Caleb said instead, nodding towards the back of the gallery, where Liselot could be seen bravely coping with her distress by giggling flirtatiously with Defane, "perhaps she would be more at ease if you were closer at hand to protect her honour from the mob?"

The bluster fell from Massingham like the wind from unexpectedly becalmed sails, his face softening as he spoke, "The poor creature, what a terrible boor I've been! Abandoning her in this arena of brutes!" Sir Charles hastily dusted down his billowing scarlet coat as he turned towards the stairs, the mob forgotten. "Isn't she a prize?"

"A great beauty," Caleb agreed.

"I do quite love her, you know," Sir Charles blurted out in a voice that for an instant belonged to a man forty years his junior, struck down with love for the very first time. He stared longingly up at Liselot and Caleb was quite sure Defane's presence at her side was utterly unnoticed by him, let alone the playful look in her eyes and the way she leaned far closer towards the diminutive Frenchman than was entirely necessary for the mere act of conversation.

"Any man would," Caleb replied after an awkward moment's silence.

Liselot's attention returned immediately to Massingham once the old man reappeared at her side, flushed enough by his exertions for some of his powder to have washed down his face in small chalky rivulets.

"Forgive me my dear!" He boomed. "Those rascals fair raised my blood."

"You should not fret so," Liselot purred, leaning into Massingham's vast belly to add in an audible whisper, "after all, is that not my job?"

Massingham laughed hard and lewdly, "Am I not the luckiest man alive gentlemen?"

"Indeed, and so long as your wife remains away from London I'm sure you will remain in that happy condition," Defane replied with a knowing smile and a wink, before adding, "alive that is!"

Caleb wasn't sure whether the old man was going to laugh or hit Defane for his jest; in the end he did both, slapping the Frenchman heartily on the back as he belched another laugh. "You're a capital fellow, Sir!"

"For a Frenchman," Caleb added ruefully.

"Nobody is perfect," Massingham conceded, before he turned to Liselot and added with uncharacteristic gentleness, "well, almost nobody..."

"*Charlie...*" Liselot sighed with a demure little flutter of her fan.

Any further banter was cut off by a raucous cheer from the mob below and the acrid smell of fire; they appeared to have tired of pope burning and had progressed to firing parts of the old theatre itself.

"Perhaps it is time to depart," Sir Charles offered, protectively seizing Liselot's elbow.

"Those savages have quite ruined my evening Charlie; I was so enjoying myself," Liselot pouted, "perhaps we could continue elsewhere?"

"Of course, my dear. I will just need to arrange to settle my debt to this good gentleman."

Defane shook his finger theatrically, "I will hear nothing of the sort Sir Charles, and I would be no sort of a gentleman if I did not give you the opportunity to win your money back."

"Very decent of you," Massingham replied with an approving nod, "perhaps-"

"Cards!" Liselot chipped in before he could finish, "let us play cards, I do so love a little flutter. Tell me you play, Mr Defane? Mr Cade?"

"I have been known to study the history of the four kings, from time to time," Defane conceded.

"Then it is agreed," Liselot snapped her fan shut, "we can show these good gentlemen our hospitality at the card table, safe from these scoundrels!"

"Well-"

"Besides, the streets will be swarming with vermin looking to crack heads from here to the other side of London Bridge, our new friends will be much safer in your coach, will they not Charlie?" Liselot declared, staring pointedly at Massingham, the rigid set of her jaw suggesting the matter was decided.

Massingham sighed in mock exasperation before leading the way, "Gentleman, if you will be so kind as to follow me, my carriage will soon have us away from this place, and it's wretched denizens!"

"This will be such fun!" Liselot declared, clapping her small hands softly together in delight before taking Massingham's arm. She glanced back over her bare shoulder to shoot Defane a look that was both smouldering and knowing.

"I quite like cards too..." Caleb muttered faintly to Defane as they began to trail in the couple's wake, but the Frenchman said nothing in return for he was far too busy concentrating on the delicious curve of Liselot's waist.

Caleb was beginning to wish he hadn't taken Defane's wager...

Chapter Eight
The Fields of Venus

Piccadilly, London - 1688

Nobody seemed to pay much notice of the fact that the Duchess was doing an awful lot of shopping, nor that she would always take the same young footman to assist her, or even that her face often had a rosy flush not usually associated with cold London winters. The Duke, for one, certainly did not, as his visits to St James' Square were both fleeting and infrequent. As Henrietta had forecast, he had little time even to notice his wife, let alone discern any change in her.

The Duke would be gone for days at a time, occasionally weeks might pass before he appeared on the doorstep. When he was in the house, he was usually cosseted away in his study with various men who would turn up unannounced. Whatever was discussed no one thought they were social calls for the men never took more than cold meat and wine for sustenance before they were off again, often via the servant's entrance.

Inevitably there was much gossiping as to the nature of the Duke's business amongst the household, much of it centred on how the loyal Duke would keep his Catholic king seated upon a Protestant throne.

Daniel, however, no longer cared one hoot what the Duke did, so long as he continued to do it. The less the Duke was at home, the easier it was for Henrietta and he to spend time together, either over afternoon tea in the library or, better still, in her Piccadilly apartment.

In the three weeks following their first "shopping trip" they'd returned five times, and, as at the end of their first visit, the Duchess had Daniel carry a number of boxes containing fabulously expensive dresses, hats and shoes he'd found stacked neatly in a closet back to St James' Square.

"Who buys all these for you?" Daniel had asked.

The Duchess had smiled enigmatically, "I have people," was all she would give by way of an explanation.

Throughout February, they sat in front of that roaring fire and talked; they would eat uncomplicated meals of bread and cheese while she vainly continued to try and teach him the finer points of whiskey drinking. When he'd finally confessed he preferred beer she had sent him out to buy a crate. One of Daniel's abiding memories of Henrietta would be of her sitting by that fire in all her finery, as straight-backed and refined as any lady of quality, swigging beer from the bottle like a common doxy and descending into fits of giggles when she'd been surprised by a loud and decidedly unladylike beer burp.

They talked about any and everything, save why she wanted to spend so much time with him. Daniel thought he was being seduced, but as he'd never been seduced before he was still wary of jumping to unwarranted conclusions. Whenever he'd tried broaching the subject, she'd smile and moved the conversation on.

So Daniel continued with the game though he had no idea exactly what kind of game they were playing. She would favour him with a little intimacy on each visit to Piccadilly, usually just before they returned to the real world and had to leave their friendship locked in the rooms behind them. It amounted to little but was enough to send his mind and body reeling with lust and confusion; a kiss upon the cheek here, a squeeze of the hand there. One time she asked if she might run her fingers through the hair she had asked he let grow, he had come so close to throwing her to the floor as she toyed with the bristles of his hair he'd had to walk away, explaining he needed to relieve himself outside.

He had rushed out into the back yard to stand in the dirty grey snow, shivering through his thin cotton shirt, his cock in his hand as he stared at the yellow crystalline patches were other residents had previously used the back wall to relieve themselves. He had no need of a piss, but he thought the freezing air might drive the lust out of him. Only when his manhood had shrivelled to a small grey-blue worm did he feel it proper for him to return.

February had almost given way to March when Henrietta took him shopping again, something that filled his heart with both excitement and dread, for, despite the regularity of the event, he feared his lust would get the better of him before long.

He was somewhat surprised when he followed Henrietta into the drawing room, his wig already in his hands, to find a large copper bath, filled with steaming milky white water, sitting in the middle of the room.

Although he was caught between asking either "How did that get here?" or "What is that for?" he ended up saying nothing and simply stared at the bath as if it were some strange mystical beast that had wandered into the room and started munching at the dried flowers that decorated the table.

"I left instructions," the Duchess offered, by way of explanation.

"Who with?"

"You don't think *I* clean this place, do you?"

"Well, no."

"I have a girl... she is very loyal, a Jewess, but very trustworthy all the same. I asked her to have a bath prepared today... a fire too."

Daniel had been too taken with the bath to notice the fire was crackling away merrily. He looked at the big copper bath once more.

"She must be quite a strong girl..."

"She copes," Henrietta smiled.

"May I ask what it's for Ma'am?" Sometimes it took a little time for Daniel to leave his footman persona at the door.

"Certainly Daniel, 'tis a contraption for bathing in."

"Oh," It took only the briefest calculation for Daniel to conclude it must be for either Henrietta or himself, "Who is it for?"

"How often do you bathe Daniel?"

"Household rules are very specific, all servants must go to the bathhouse once a month," he recited earnestly, "regardless."

"How often do I bathe Daniel?"

He knew the answer to that; her maids were constantly carping about their mistress' unnatural fondness for soap every time they had to carry buckets of hot water up to the Duchess' bath.

"Frequently."

"Then who do you suppose the bath is for?"

Daniel brightened considerably as the Duchess was perversely fond of bathing it was obvious who the bath was for. A thought that made him hurriedly cross his hands in front of him, "For you!"

Henrietta sighed, "Try again."

"*Me?*"

"You have many virtues Daniel; you are well educated, intelligent, mildly amusing and far too good-looking for your own good. However, these are all attributes best enjoyed upwind of you."

"*Mildly* amusing?"

"I know bathing is a chore, and if I could not afford to have servants running around for me then I probably not bother much with it either and make do with a basin of tepid water and a flannel. However, I have been cursed with an exceptionally keen sense of smell and ask that you indulge my sensibilities a little."

Daniel managed a nod and helped the Duchess out of her cape and furs. He noted she was wearing the same jade green dress she had worn the first time they had come to Piccadilly, which he thought was mildly odd as she rarely wore the same dress out of doors more than once. However, the business of the bath was too pressing for his mind to linger on other matters.

"Come now," she said handing her jacket to Daniel.

He stared blankly as she removed her gloves and

when he made no move to do anything much she clapped her hands sharply, "Off with your clothes and into the bath before the water gets cold!"

"Strip off?"

"There's little point in bathing whilst fully dressed; do not worry you have nothing I haven't seen before." Daniel reluctantly removed his jacket, before moving awkwardly from foot to foot and staring at the bath as if it were some terrible instrument of torture.

Henrietta sighed, "Do not fret; I will spare your blushes. See I will stand here by the window, my back to you, observing the traffic in Piccadilly and note all the grubby and sooty-faced plebs going about their business in the inclement weather, I don't doubt most of those fellows would be only too happy to warm their chilly bones in a delightful hot bath. I do hope you're stripping off Daniel? I have no intention of standing here for more than a few minutes, if you are not in the water by then, I will just have to suffer the sight of your terrible nakedness regardless."

She played with the hem of the curtain for a moment, before adding, "I do hope my sensibilities will be able to withstand the sight. I'm sure you wouldn't want me fainting, would you?"

"Not at all," Daniel replied, amid sounds of rustling fabric and hurried grunts.

"Getting rather bored with this view now," Henrietta

muttered through pursed lips, "all I can see are carriages clattering by and a few hardy souls trudging through that dreadful grey snow."

"Nearly there!"

"Too boring!" Henrietta declared turning back into the room as soon as she heard a splash, finding Daniel hunched forward in the tub, his arms thrust forward into the still sloshing bath water.

"Why's the water all funny an' white?" Daniel asked, peering down into the bath.

"'tis just rose water salts, they will make you smell adorable and hide your embarrassment in the water's milky depths," Henrietta explained. As she walked slowly towards the bath she removed the detachable frilly lace cuffs that covered most of her lower arm from the sleeves of her dress, tossing them casually to one side.

"What are you doing?" Daniel asked suspiciously.

"You need a wash, and I am certainly not going to trust you to do it for yourself."

"You're going t-"

"What's the matter Daniel, have you never been scrubbed raw by a Duchess before?"

"Not recently," he gulped.

She hitched up her skirts so she could kneel beside the tub, no mean feat in itself given the acres of silk involved, before resting both arms on the rim of the bath as she smiled at him, "Then you're in for a treat..." She placed a silky warm hand against his palpitating chest and pushed him gently backwards,

"Relax," she insisted, "enjoy the indulgence."

He smiled thinly and allowed himself to be eased backwards until the nape of his neck rested on the highest part of the bath's rim; next she placed his arms on each side of the bath.

"Does that not feel divine?" She asked.

Daniel managed a nod, but only after glancing down at the bathwater to ensure nothing that might alarm a Duchess was poking out of the water.

Henrietta produced a bar of soap and begun to rub it gently into his chest, working the lather outwards in slow, ever increasing, circles.

"Close your eyes," she whispered. Not looking at Henrietta was something he had found particularly hard to do from the moment he had seen her, but he managed to do as she bid.

His heart was hammering in his chest, its beat echoing so hard he wondered if the bathwater might be rippling to its rhythm. Her hands moved the soap across his body, along his arms, around his neck, always slowly, always gently. The fragrance of rose water and soap mixing in his nostrils with Henrietta's own heady scents and perfumes, his sense enthralled by her closeness. The world was silent save for the mellow lap of warm water on skin and Henrietta's breath, as quiet as a sigh on the wing, but in the dark world behind his eyelids he could hear it clearly enough, as clearly as he knew she studied his face while she worked.

Down beneath the water his cock ached urgently, but the pain just seemed like another pleasure, another sense being teased along with all the others as she slid the soap across his wet skin time and again until finally she replaced it with a soft flannel, which she continually wetted to work away the soap.

He felt her hand come to rest atop his head, "Slip under the water for a second, I need to wet your hair."

When he half opened his eyes, he found her beautiful face looming over him,

"I promise not to drown you."

Daniel closed his eyes again, took a deep breath and allowed her to push him gently beneath the water. For an instant, he was cut off from the world, all he could feel around him was the warm caress of the water, the sound of his heart was a thousand times louder in his ears and he wondered if it were possible for a man to die from excitement. Before he had time to ponder that particular question he came back up spluttering slightly, the rhythm of his heart replaced by the sweeter melody of Henrietta's giggling.

She wiped his face dry with a towel and told him to keep his head back. For a few seconds her hands were gone, and he yearned for their touch from the instant they broke contact with his skin. After a few unbearable moments, her fingers returned, working through the short thick bristles of his hair.

"What's that?"

"Just a little oil to clean your hair," she murmured, her voice seemed far far away.

"Do I have enough to trouble with?"

"It will help it grow, and the scent is quite intoxicating."

"I see..."

Her fingers worked at his scalp, not as gently as she had washed his skin, but it soothed him all the same. It was as if the oil and the soap were somehow washing away more than just dirt and sweat, but years of solitude and anger too, though he knew that was just nonsense of course. It was her hands that were doing that.

"Perfect," he heard her murmur, and from the way her breath played across his forehead he could tell her lips hovered only a fraction above his skin, she breathed deeply to take in the richly scented oil.

Eventually, her fingers slid from her his hair and he heard movement, he cracked his eyelids open a fraction once more and found her kneeling at the foot of the bath.

Smiling at him she dipped a hand into the water and eased one of his feet out.

"You don't have to," he said, sitting up a little. It somehow seemed too disrespectful to allow her to wash his feet.

"I want to," she insisted, ignoring his protests, lifting one foot after the other, diligently cleaning between each toe, sliding the wet soap up along his calves.

"I'm sure I shall never feel so clean again," he said, unable to help himself from smiling after she let his leg slide back into the water.

Henrietta moved to the midsection of the bath, "Oh, I haven't *quite* finished yet."

"You haven't?" Daniel licked his lips nervously.

"Not quite," without taking her eyes from his, she slid her hands into the water and he felt her moving the soap slowly up and down the inside of his thighs.

"How does that feel?" she asked innocently.

Daniel could manage no more than a flickering smile by way of a reply.

"I love the smell of clean skin," she explained softly, "and there is one place on a man I do so like to be clean... ah, here we are. My my Daniel, what an outstanding young fellow you are..."

Daniel was now far beyond any rational kind of thought, let alone conversation and all he could do was let the shudder that her touch provoked course through his body, sending fat droplets of milky bathwater splashing on to both the floor and the Duchess' dress.

At first, she worked the soap along his shaft and around his balls, even lifting his pelvis slightly so she could rub between his buttocks, each movement resulting in a little more of the bath water finding its way to the floor.

After a few minutes considerate cleaning, the Duchess exclaimed, "I do appear to have dropped the soap," she stared at Daniel, her chin resting on the edge of the bath, "perhaps you've had enough now anyway?"

"No!" Daniel managed to cry hoarsely.

"Oh, you'd like me to continue?" She grinned, slowly running her hand once up and down his shaft, "like this?"

"Hetty... *please.*"

"If I'd known this was all I had to do to get you to use my name I would have done it ages ago," she gave an exaggerated sigh, "well if I *must...*"

Her hand worked teasingly, squeezing so firmly he gasped a little, before moving up and down vigorously enough to make him gasp a lot more. His hands gripped the side of the bath as his body rocked in time with the movement of her hand.

"Oh God," he gasped as she went from slow to fast to slow again.

"Do not take the Lord's name Daniel, 'tis a sin you

know."

"Is this not a... sin?" he managed, through gritted teeth.

"Of course, 'tis *wickedly* sinful." She smiled at him in a way that, even if his mind still had been able to form coherent thoughts, he could not even begin to describe. Later, when he had been able to think about it, he realised her expression had been a mirror to his own feelings. She had looked how he felt. He had looked at her beautiful, perfect face and witnessed raw animal lust, which was probably why he'd shot his seed the moment she had smiled at him so.

"'tis like a breaching whale!" Henrietta exclaimed, her hand splashing in the water as she vigorously pumped him. Daniel cried out, shuddered, cried out some more, thrust his hips so high his pelvis was lifted clean out of the bath, before slumping back into the water with a final almighty shudder, which left both floor and Duchess sodden.

They looked at each other a good long while, both panting, both smiling, her hand still wrapped around his shaft, thumb and forefinger occasionally squeezing the head as if to make sure all was spent.

"My dear boy," she smiled, finally letting him slip from her fingers. She dried her hands on a towel before flicking away a few loosened curls that had strayed across her eyes, "how long have you been saving all that up?"

"All my life," Daniel grinned.

"Have you never...?"

"Well, no one has ever done it *for* me."

"Now that *is* a sin... the sin of wastefulness. I will have to make sure we put a stop to that."

"Why do you want me?" Daniel asked, shaking his head in amazement. Never could he have dared to believe this might happen to him. It scared him and excited him, thrilled and confused him in equal measures.

"Why?" Henrietta rose gingerly to her feet, flattening down the damp and ruffled skirts of her dress. "There is no why, other than the simple fact that I want you; I wanted this to happen from the moment I saw you. 'tis a terrible thing, but I have become very used to getting exactly what I want..."

"I was not complaining."

"One hopes not." Henrietta opened up a large towel that had been warming in front of the fire, "the water will be getting cold, best we get you dry..."

Daniel stood up slowly and stood before her, sloshing in the water, his hands cupped discreetly in front of him. Henrietta glanced down over the towel, looked back up and cocked an eyebrow; "*Really?*"

Gingerly he stepped out of the tub and allowed Henrietta to wrap the towel around him, which was of a finer cut and material than any shirt he'd ever owned.

"What now?"

"We get you dry lest you catch a chill."

"You sound like my mother."

"What a strange house you must have grown up in."

She led him to stand before the fire, for no sooner than had he stepped from the bath than goose bumps had formed upon is chest and arms. He stood in its glow for a few minutes, savouring the feel of the towel and Henrietta's hands.

"I'm dry now," he muttered finally, a few minutes later.

"Then we best get you dressed."

"Do I have to?"

Henrietta pursed her lips, "Not if you don't want to."

"I was hoping..." Daniel cocked his head and looked at her with imploring eyes.

"'tis better to travel in certainty than hope," she replied carefully, taking a small step back from him, "if there is something you want, you should ask for it."

"You have seen me naked, touched me naked," he shrugged, "'tis only fair that I should enjoy the same intimacy."

"Well I suppose..." she sighed theatrically, "...I did say that under this roof we are friends, equals if you like, in which case it would be poor form to deny your request." She turned her back on him, indicating the clasp on the back of her dress, "you may do as you please..."

Daniel let the towel slip from his shoulders and reached out to touch her, how many nights had he lain awake torturing himself with this impossibility? He sucked in air through his teeth as he slowly bit his lower lip; he ached to explore every part of her.

Rather than struggle with the fastenings of her dress he turned her gently around to face him again so that he could stare into her eyes, his hands resting lightly on her shoulders. He drank in her beauty before letting his hands follow where his eyes had led; he run a finger along her shoulder and across her collarbone, lightly stroking the soft nape of her neck, the hollow of her throat, her small rounded chin. He let his finger trace the path of her jaw, feel the sweep of her high sharp-cut cheek bones and the elegant downy arches of her eyebrows. His finger slid along her ruler straight nose that ended in the slightest of upturns, and down into the gentle indent of her philtrum. He sketched the outline of her sensual lips, committing each curve and texture to memory.

He felt her breath, hot and moist upon his skin as her lips parted; without thinking he pushed his finger gently into her mouth, having no thought how she might react. Her teeth pressed down upon for a moment as she looked up at him, her pupils so large the irises were just the faintest rings of blue-grey marble at the periphery of a darkness so complete they seemed to draw the very daylight from the air around them. She smiled and released his finger, letting him push inside to feel her tongue and explore the warm flesh within. She made an O of her lips and sucked his finger as he withdrew it, making a small wet popping sound as it came out.

He brushed her cheeks and felt the silky grains of powder she had dusted herself with that morning embed themselves in whorls of his fingerprints. He imagined her sitting before her looking-glass, perhaps with her maids fussing around her, what had she been thinking when she had sat there; had she thought she must make herself beautiful for him? For her Daniel? For the man she was to take as her lover? He shivered ever so slightly.

He moved both his hands up to caress the ringlets of her hair, entwining them in his fingers, pulling them straight and then watching as entranced as a child captivated by his first snowfall as they sprung back into place. He sank his fingers into the body of her hair, a downy tangle of curls held in place by a multitude of clasps and pins, each ringlet that fell around her face and neck doing so only through design and choice.

How long did it take to arrange her hair so artfully, he wondered as he pulled the first silver pin slowly out; her nostrils flared slightly and she took half a step backwards. He did know whether it was because she feared being able to duplicate it when they left or she was simply overly fond of the style and did not want her carefully prepared appearance altered. He found he did not much care either way.

He stared at her boldly and raised his eyebrows a fraction.

After a moment, she smiled and stepped forward, lowering her eyes for an instant as she murmured, "You may do whatever you wish…"

He slowly discarded one pin after another, with each one removed the great structure of her hair trembled and sagged a little more; a grand edifice where one support after the next was systematically knocked away until, inevitably, the whole structure tumbled down around her face, an avalanche of rich blonde curls, so long and wild they obscured most of her face, leaving only one half covered eye and a crooked smile peeking out of the mess.

Daniel removed the last of the clasps before running the long blonde strands between his fingers, from scalp to shoulders. He leant in and buried his face in the curls, breathing in the scent of sweet jasmine, he felt her hand momentarily flat against his naked chest, but it fell away as he stepped back a little. He stroked the hair away from her face, so its beauty was simply framed in those long tumbling locks that fell to the top of her cleavage.

He had never seen her hair so loose, it always had

been conjured into one design or another, all, of course, quite lovely, but now she took away what little breath remained within him. He could feel her hands twitching to inspect her hair, to flatten out any imperfections, rearrange the wayward strands. Daniel reached down and held them in his own; he did not want a single hair moved for in the chaotic imperfection of her tangled and collapsed hair he had found a beauty he could compare to nothing in all the world.

"You are beautiful," he said, the words were inadequate; he needed to say something, but lacked the vocabulary to express all that he felt and saw.

She lowered her eyes and smiled, shyly. Like the daughter of a country parson might. Without the artifice of her elaborate coiffure, she was no longer the haughty Duchess, she was just a woman, just the woman he loved.

Eventually, he let his hands slip from hers, and placed them gently upon her waist, so small and tight within the confines of her corset. He traced the concave line that run from her hips to her breast, fingering the stiff whalebone ribbing of the corset through the jade green silk of her dress, feeling the way it constricted and confined her. He felt the silken embroidery on the front of the dress and traced it with his fingers before returning to the perfect curves of her figure, unable to resist the way his hands slid, naturally, over them. His hand wandered lower until it was engulfed in the flowing layers of silk that formed her skirts, billowing out from her to emphasise the smallness of her waist and the curve of her figure even further. His hand moved lazily across the material, which shimmered and rippled at his touch; if he could ever climb high enough to reach a cloud, he thought fancifully, it would surely feel much the same. A softness he could tumble into and be removed from all the cares of the world.

He found himself bending in towards her until his forehead touched Henrietta's dishevelled curls. He felt her breath again, hot and quick, upon his skin. All the time his hands worked through those acres of silk his eyes were locked upon the inviting cleft of her breasts; a valley so deep and awe-inspiring he felt his head swim as if he were tottering on the very edge of some abyssal drop.

Gently his hands found her hips, and he turned her slowly around, he felt her eyes upon him, for a moment her lips were as close to his as it was possible to be without touching, close enough for him to taste her breath on the air. Despite the dreadful desire he felt to kiss her, he turned her away. He had dreamed of this for so long, played out a thousand ways to touch her, but this had always been what he wanted most, the desire that had fuelled his lust beyond all others. The simple freedom to touch her, to be allowed to explore her, to slowly run his hands over all those places only his eyes had been able to linger upon, let alone all those mysteries where even his eyes, up to now, had been excluded; for to know her completely was to understand perfection.

His dreams had been tortured by her beauty and the things he yearned to do to her. That such loveliness could raise so many base ugly thoughts and desires within him was something Daniel had not cared to think of too deeply, though they disturbed him distantly, like a fly on the far side of the room, its nuisance did not merit breaking from the task at hand.

He felt her skirts swish against his legs as she turned, the hems rustling over the rug upon the only sound in the universe other than the din being made by his heart.

Once her back was turned, he pulled her as close to him as the hoops upon which her skirts hung allowed. His hands moved slowly up from her hips, pressed flat against her stomach, again feeling the taut whalebone ribs mirroring her body until his hands rested beneath her breasts. Gently he squeezed them through the fabric of her dress and the rigid confines of her corset. She made a small noise. Although no great cry it was a strange little sound, the like of which Daniel had never heard before; part moan, part sigh, both sounds mixed with something else that he could not quantify, but it reminded him vaguely of the noise a small trapped animal might make, desperate and hopelessly ensnared. Unsure of what it meant he released his hold but instantly found Henrietta pushing his hands back.

He needed no more encouragement; he felt the dams of his restraint struggling to hold back the engorged flood of his desires. Where before his hands had moved slowly, they became ever more urgent as he squeezed and teased, first from beneath and through the satin and whalebone that separated skin from skin, then from above, feeling the firm warmth of her cleavage, exposed by the cut of her dress, forced up by the design of her corset.

She was pushing back against him and felt the hoops of her dress buckling for he had no intention to step away.

His heart felt like it was climbing up his chest; a manic and frenzied lunatic, bouncing from one side of his throat to the other as it clawed its way towards the daylight. His hands had taken on a life of their own too, for he found that they had moved to the back of her dress and were desperately scrabbling to unhitch the hooks that fastened it. So desperate was he to reach the prize within he heard the silk rip several times, but it registered only distantly and Henrietta made no complaint, if anything she seemed as eager as he to be free of the garments that separated their bodies.

Her clothes may have been both beautiful and expensive, but they had been designed by the whims of fashion rather than practicality or ease of removal. Daniel's long rehearsed exploration of Henrietta became a series of clumsy fumbles as they worked together to free her first of the dress and its long skirts, then the wooden rigging of hoops below upon which they had hung and billowed away from her so stylishly. Her petticoats were fair torn from her body before Daniel enclosed her in his arms from behind, without the multitude of skirts, petticoats and scaffolding to separate them he gasped when Henrietta pushed her now exposed behind back into his groin again. He buried his face into her hair to stifle his cries as his hands gripped her hips and encouraged her to push backwards.

"Rid me of this thing…" Henrietta pleaded, indicating the white embroidered corset that, along with the silken stockings tied at the thigh, were all that she still wore.

The corset had been tightly tied and not being a garment designed with haste in mind it took Daniel several attempts to unravel the mysteries of its workings. By the time it eventually loosened enough for Henrietta to wriggle free of its grasp she had swivelled to turn in his arms and he was utterly lost in the heat and passion of her kisses.

*

Maybe he wasn't even awake.

Or if he was, then it was just the remnants of dreams taking the harsh, sharp edges off the world that made him feel that he was floating.

He opened his eyes, which was generally as good a way as any to confirm that you were awake, and stared into the glowing embers of the fire. The faint heat of its breath was clearly playing across his face while its smell and the faint acrid tang of burnt coal on the air helped convince him that he probably *was* awake.

Daniel thought he should turn to look and make sure Henrietta actually was beside him, but he decided that wouldn't truly reassure him that he wasn't dreaming for he didn't consider the sight of her naked body, which he could feel pressed up against him well enough, to be entirely trustworthy evidence that he had returned to the *real* world.

They lay entwined together in front of the fire, snuggled between soft furs that added to the fire's warmth. When he had breathlessly suggested the bedroom, Henrietta had, eventually, mumbled that if she had wanted a soft bed she would have stayed at home. After his passion had been spent on the floor, he had fetched furs and spread them before the fire so they could lay in its crackling glow, kissing softly and constantly, stopping only occasionally to murmur sweet words to each other.

The memories came flooding back to him and chased the last pretence of dreams from his mind. Carefully he turned his head and found his face buried in a mass of flowing blonde curls; it really wasn't a dream.

He kissed the top of her head, gently enough not to wake her for he could hear the slight wet sound of her breathing against his chest and knew she slept soundly. He closed his eyes again for a little while, between her perfect skin and the thick, luxuriant fur he had never felt such decadent comfort. He breathed deeply, the soap and lavender from his own skin mixed with Henrietta's perfume and the other, earthier, smells they had created between them.

He wanted her again, he realised, an old familiar ache returning to his groin though it did not feel so much like torture anymore. Instead, he returned his gaze to the fire; he would let her sleep, he felt so at ease he almost wished that he could lie like this forever; as if in some fairy tale eternally guarding his sleeping Princess.

How could life, that had for so long been a slow cold procession of various miseries, suddenly taste so sweet? Everything was simple while they laid like this, the world and its worries a faint and insubstantial thing that lived somewhere beyond the distant walls of the little Piccadilly apartment, so far away he could barely hear its rumbling over the soft whisper of Henrietta's breath.

Had Caleb ever felt anything like this?

He found himself thinking as if his mind wanted to return him to darker and more familiar themes All those months he'd spent dreaming about Maggie, studying her face, drawing her time and again as it was the only way he could express his feelings. Had he been tortured in the same way Daniel had been until this day, tormented by a desire he could not fulfil?

If Caleb had lived, then perhaps, one day, he might have had a day like this, but that had never come to pass. He'd lost his life before he could ever lose himself in the perfect softness of a woman.

Daniel had never known for sure what Maggie had felt about his brother, she had shed tears at his funeral and for weeks afterwards. The local women would exchange sad knowing looks whenever she went by, for a while at least, but Daniel had been still a young boy lost in his own grief and people didn't speak to young boys about broken hearts and lost loves.

All the same, deep down, he'd believed she felt as he did. Daniel had liked the idea that she grieved for his brother, it seemed to lessen his own pain, only a fraction maybe, but it was the only thing that did. He fancied it was a burden they could share together, that if two people could keep him in their head, then Caleb would be twice as alive as if it were only one. He didn't believe anyone else *really* grieved for Caleb, no one else cried for him. His father certainly did not, for his mother it was just one more misery to bear on top of all the others that would eventually drag her down to her own grave a year later while Jacob had been too little to understand.

No, as the weeks became months only Daniel and Maggie kept Caleb alive, even if they never spoke of him. He could see it in her eyes and in the sad little smile she gave him from time to time. Occasionally, she would stop whatever she was doing to bid him good day. When he nodded and moved on he could always feel her eyes on him as if they were trying to sculpt and rearrange his features until they were more like Caleb's.

When Maggie had married a shipwright and moved to Deptford a few years later, Daniel had felt a vague sense of betrayal as if she would only grieve a little longer than perhaps, somehow, Caleb would escape from Jack's Kingdom and find a way back to them. But she was a woman by then, and the memories of a moon-faced boy she had once played with as a child and had flirted with in the first flushes of her womanhood had faded like drawings left in the sun by then.

The shipwright had turned out to have a fondness for hard drinking and the company of harlots; Maggie had given birth to one stillborn child and died herself six months later. The Bills of Mortality recorded it as consumption, but back in her old neighbourhood the doorstep gossips, who eighteen months earlier had nodded sagely that Maggie had found herself a good match, concluded it was from a heart broken by the loss of her child and the misfortune of being married to a pig of a man who they all had known was a decidedly bad sort of a fellow. If only Maggie had listened to them.

Perhaps it had not been just Caleb's life that had been taken that wet night back in 1680, for had he lived maybe he would have wed his Maggie, maybe he would have become a lauded artist and she wouldn't have died in a chilly Deptford hovel.

The thought acted as a small dark cloud on the edge of Daniel's bright blue sky; familiar feelings of guilt and loss began to gnaw away at him. Not a day went by, however good or bad, that his brother did not feature somewhere in his thoughts. He wished Caleb was here so he could have someone to talk to about all that had happened to him. But Caleb was long gone, and there was nobody else he could tell, so cut off had he become from what was left of his family and his few friends. It had been a slow process of isolation that started the day Caleb died and continued throughout the intervening years without him consciously realising he was doing it, a process that had only gathered pace after he had moved into St James' Square and fallen so dreadfully in love with his mistress.

Although his brother was long dead, he had worked so hard to keep his memory alive he sometimes wondered if he actually had managed to summon him back from the grave. When Daniel turned to look at the window, he was not in the least surprised to see the figure of a sixteen-year-old boy standing next to it, just as he'd described him to Henrietta earlier, engrossed in his drawing, as always. Eventually, he looked up when he realised Daniel was watching him and wanted to talk. Carefully he put his paper and charcoal to one side, crossed his arms and sighed heavily. He'd always sighed heavily when he felt the need to impart some advice to his brother as if it somehow gave his words more gravitas.

"'tis a great folly Daniel," the memory of his brother said earnestly, "no good will come of it."

Daniel shrugged, "I know... but she's beautiful and clever and funny and-"

"Married?"

"Well... yes."

"She is married today, and she will be married tomorrow. Where will you be?"

"Wherever she wants me to be."

"'tis bad enough you have fallen in love with a married woman, but a *duchess?* Have you even begun to count the number of ways in which that is an extraordinarily bad idea?" The memory of Caleb rolled his eyes theatrically skyward in the search for the divine confirmation that his brother was a most extraordinary kind of idiot, as he often did when Daniel was refusing to listen to his wisdom. Eventually, though, a smile crept across his face, as slow as a thief working his way across loose boards, "she is beautiful though."

"Who would have thought it, me with such a beauty!" Daniel agreed eagerly. "You couldn't imagine how good she makes me feel, how good *she* feels!"

"No," the memory of his brother said, both his smile and his form slowly fading away, "I can't imagine that at all..."

Daniel felt a small hard knot in his throat and wished for the millionth time that it was more than just his memory speaking to him.

"You were muttering," Henrietta's voice floated lazily up from somewhere within the mass of blonde curls upon his chest.

"Was I?" Daniel replied, wincing that he had let his imagined conversation with his dead brother seep out of his head. Like being caught wearing your mother's best dress, it was one of those things that rarely came across well when you tried to explain it to someone.

"Either that or you snore in quite a peculiar fashion."

"I was just dozing. Sorry, I didn't mean to wake you."

Two sparkling blue eyes emerged to stare at him, "I quite like men who talk in their sleep," Henrietta declared suddenly, as if she'd just decided the matter after some considerable thought, "They tend to have fewer secrets."

"I don't have any," Daniel replied earnestly, before sighing, "or rather I never used to."

"I do hope you're not fretting about this... your muttering wasn't some prayer for forgiveness, was it?"

"I'm more worried about the Duke than God."

Henrietta rose slightly, resting on one arm so she could look him squarely in the eye, "You have nothing to fear from my husband."

Daniel paused, partly because he wanted to choose his words carefully, but mainly because in the warm and flattering glow of the dying fire she was unutterably beautiful. The ability to look at Henrietta in those particularly breath-taking moments and attempt any other task that involved conscious effort was one he had not quite yet managed to master.

"I am not greatly experienced in these matters," he eventually offered, "but I believe few men take kindly to being cuckolded, and the Duke has a reputation for..."

Henrietta raised an eyebrow.

"...*sternness.*"

"My beautiful Danny..." Henrietta caressed his cheek, "you don't believe all those horrid stories about John horsewhipping the servants, do you?"

"Well..."

"Don't be so foolish," she scolded, "he has an austere countenance I grant you, but that is largely due to the fact he is in constant pain from his old wounds. They have never entirely healed even after all these years, coupled with the seriousness with which he takes the important matters of state that are entrusted to his care. Beneath the façade he presents to the world, there is a very kindly old man. I can assure you that he has never horsewhipped a servant... or anybody else for that matter."

"He hasn't?"

"Of course not! He has a man to do that sort of thing for him."

"Oh."

Henrietta leaned forward and brushed her lips against his.

"That was a joke."

"Really? About which bit?"

"You have nothing to fear... unless you don't stop bellyaching and make love to me again of course. In which case I may have to whip you myself."

Daniel smiled; it was the kind of offer that would wash the cares from any man's mind. He curled a hand around her hip and pulled her towards him, it was only as he teetered upon the brink of her kisses, beyond which all realisations would have been utterly lost, did it occur to him how dark it had become.

"'tis night!" he uttered with a start, pulling away from her lips to turn and stare dumbly at the gloom pushing at the room's windows.

"Nearly," she sighed, pursing her lips as she took the opportunity to examine Daniel's right ear, which bobbed agitatedly just beyond the tip of her nose.

Daniel sat up, the furs tumbling away as he did so, how had they ever been here so long? Surely it had been only a few hours.

"I'm cold," Henrietta huffed.

"But... 'tis dark? People will worry when you don't come home. The Duke will be informed!"

"You're thinking about horsewhips again, aren't you?"

"At the very least," Daniel admitted.

"Do not worry about His Grace."

"How can you be so sure!"

"Because I act with my husband's blessing."

"You... *what?*"

Henrietta pulled him back down into her embrace and hurriedly piled the furs back over them.

"I see I am going to have to explain all this, am I not? There was a time when a Duchess could jump merrily into bed with her servants and not have to explain anything at all. They would simply have been *grateful*, 'tis a sorry state this world of ours has come to when servants become so uppity after they've been seduced."

"I'm not exactly ungrateful."

"One would hope not..." she kissed him slowly for a

while, before pulling away and turning onto her side. "Obviously, none of what I am about to tell you leaves this room."

"I assumed nothing at all would leave this room."

Henrietta nodded before continuing, "When I married I was but seventeen and my husband was nearly forty years my senior. I had known him since I was a little girl and knew him to be a kind, if distant, old man who would from time to time drop by to debate theology and politics, along with local gossip, with my father. He was never a man I harboured any desires for. I was barely old enough to harbour a desire for anybody. When he came to ask for my hand, I was utterly flabbergasted. When I'd recovered from my shock, he explained his reasons for asking, he spoke so plainly it bordered on the verge of bluntness, but that is his manner in most regards."

"His first wife had died childless after a long and otherwise happy marriage; he was an ageing man with no heir. That would have been a sadness he could have endured if it were not for the fact that his title, estates, money and property, all of which he obtained from virtually nothing by means of his wit, courage and loyalty to the Crown, would pass to one of his brother's sons, all of whom he detests thoroughly. They are a lazy assortment of wastrels and drunks who would no doubt enjoy themselves merrily on such an inheritance and leave nothing after them but debts and the ruination of my husband's good name."

"He told me he was an old man and did not expect to live for more than a few years; all he wished for in those few years, other than to serve his King and his country, was to produce an heir worthy of inheriting all that he had achieved in his life."

"Obviously, he needed a new wife to accomplish this and one that was young, fit and healthy was most likely to give him the heir he craved; he felt he had no time to woo eligible aristocratic daughters, to negotiate dowries and undertake all the traditional formalities of finding a wife. So, he came to me."

She smiled ruefully.

"He was very matter of fact about it. He said he knew I could have no feelings for him, but that he was truly fond of me. If I could stand the small unpleasantness of producing him an heir, I would be rich for life; I would be comfortable and have no worries. I would only have to endure him for a few years. Once he had died, I would be responsible for his considerable wealth until such time our son came into his inheritance."

"How romantic," Daniel muttered, playing with her hair.

"Love, usually, has little to do with marriage, and I have always been a practical girl," she shrugged, "I trusted that he was no ogre, and the only alternative was to marry some lowly parson or squire. My father had no dowry with which to attract desirable husbands and here was one of the richest men in England offering to share everything he had with me in return for..." she shrugged, "...it honestly wasn't such a terrible thing."

"And yet here we are?"

"The only thing that my husband has ever said to me that turned out not to be true was his prediction that he would not live much longer, and I know that was no deception. He is constantly in pain; I believe part of him craves death for it will be the only thing that can ever release him from it. Over a decade has passed and he shows no sign of going to the Almighty. I have given him two children, and he has lived long enough to see them grow, it is unlikely he will live till they are adults, but with John, you can never be too sure."

"He came to me one day, almost apologetic that he had not died as he had promised. He said he was an old man and no longer had the desires of his youth. He thought it cruel that he should keep me to himself when he was unable to fulfil all the duties of a husband. He gave me permission to find what he could not give me elsewhere, all he asked is that I am discreet and bring no dishonour to the family name."

"So, my beautiful Danny, I have been discreet. I do

not turn to the gaudy young braggarts and beaux who see an old man's young wife and think it would be a great conquest to bed her, before crowing their triumphs on the Fields of Venus to all and sundry in every coffee house, tavern and brothel in London. Instead, I have found you, whom I trust not ruin my name or bring shame to my husband."

She kissed him softly, "And we shall take some pleasure from each other in this terrible world, and no harm shall come to me, or thee or to John."

"But-" he tried to ask.

"Sssh, my darling."

"But you will still be missed surely?"

Henrietta giggled, "Do not worry, I sent word my Aunt has fallen ill and I have gone to visit her. You have accompanied me."

"And how long is she likely to be ill?"

"Oh... for quite some time I fear," Henrietta grinned, gently drawing her nails along the inside of Daniel's thigh.

"You... arranged all this beforehand?"

"Of course, I did say I was a practical girl remember."

"But, what if I had not wanted this?"

"Oh Daniel, you do make me laugh..."

He still had questions aplenty, but they were soon dissolved upon the caress of her lips.

Chapter Nine
The Nature of the Beast
The Strand, London - 1708

Liselot looked both beautiful and happy; which were characteristics he had never previously associated with the dead.

"We found her last night," Dr Rothery said quietly.

"Like this?"

"We covered her with the sheet for the sake of her modesty, but otherwise yes."

She lay naked upon a large ornately carved four poster bed which, save for the heavy drapes that hung by the windows, was the sole remaining object in Liselot's bedroom. No pictures hung on the walls, no rugs or carpets covered the floorboards, there was no night stand, no washing basin, no looking-glass. The room had been stripped clean of possessions, just like the rest of the apartment. Caleb crouched down and looked under the bed; there wasn't even a chamber pot.

Defane had literally left her without a pot to piss in.

"Are you feeling faint again?" Rothery asked, still gripping the sheet he had pulled back to reveal Liselot's corpse.

"No..." Caleb shook his head as he straightened up. In fact, he had been feeling faint all day, but he was trying not to admit it. He had insisted Rothery bring him to Liselot's apartment immediately, but had compromised and agreed to wait until daylight so that he could rest and eat some beef stew the Doctor swore would help restore his blood.

Hesitantly, he reached out and placed a hand gently upon Liselot's forehead, the cold, clammy touch of her skin confirming that there was no life left within her. He quickly drew away his fingers.

Caleb remembered the night they had met her and how fascinated he had been by her pouting slightly crooked lips and the way they cracked into a wickedly enticing smile; now she would wear that smile for eternity for she had died with the memory of it upon her lips. Her eyes were closed and her arms splayed out on either side of her body. She looked as if she had just slumped back onto her pillows after being released from the longest and most passionate kiss of her life.

Her skin was ashen; no powder could make her

any paler. Other than her short blonde hair the only colour to be seen on her body was on her lips, which were darkly stained. He stared at them for a while and wondered why she had painted them rusty brown until he realised it was the same colour as the dark splatters over the pillows. His hand involuntarily moved to his neck, he'd washed the smeared blood from his own skin, but still wore the same soiled shirt from the night before.

Liselot's neck bore no mark other than two faint red blotches that mirrored the position and angle of the scabs he'd seen on his own neck, though when he'd woke after a few restless hours in one of Dr Rothery's guest rooms he'd found that they had reduced to no more than slight welts, which he expected to fade to marks like Liselot's before evening. Only a few faint smears of blood could be seen on her skin and the image of Defane's tongue flicking over her neck eager for every last drop of her blood came unbidden into his mind.

Despite himself, Caleb felt his knees buckle and he sat hurriedly upon the edge of the bed for fear he would hit the floor otherwise.

"Such a waste," Rothery sighed sadly, placing the sheet back over Liselot's face.

"I don't understand," Caleb said eventually in a small voice, "Defane... he said he loved Liselot and I both. He said the three of us would be together for centuries... I didn't understand what he meant at the time when he said we would see empires rise and fall. Why say that and then kill us both? Or at least try to."

"Words are just a tool people use to get what they want," William Lazziard growled, "actions are a far better guide to someone's true intentions; be they man or monster."

Caleb looked up at the broad-shouldered man, who had stood brooding with his arms folded staring out of the window from the moment he had entered the room and pulled the heavy curtains open. Was it that simple? God alone knew how true that was of Caleb Cade, was that all Defane had been doing too, offering him a false promise so that he could take what he wanted, but the false promise of what? Immortality? Caleb let out a long sigh, he hadn't a clue what Defane's motivations had been when he was alive; he had even less now that he was a pile of dust.

"What do you want me to do?" Caleb said finally, turning his attention back to Dr Rothery.

The Doctor smiled kindly, "Nothing too awful my dear boy as I said last night you spent a considerable amount of time in the company of a vampiric creature, all I ask is that you recount your recollections to us. We will transcribe your account and add it to our archive. Are you happy to do this for us?"

Caleb nodded.

"So, you accept we are not lunatics and murderers then?" Lazziard asked.

"You're not lunatics."

Lazziard turned slowly from the window, "but you still think we "murdered" your vampire friend, even though you know he killed this poor girl and would have done the same to you if we had not intervened?"

"I... liked him, for all his faults."

Lazziard laughed, "Are you so forgiving of all your friends or just the ones you sodomise?"

"What?"

"You forget we have been following this monster for some time, we are quite aware you both visited what is reputed to be one of the most notorious molly houses in London. Or are you going to tell me that you were just sheltering there from the inclement weather; and to think you threatened us with a Tyburn noose!"

If Caleb had been less exhausted and Lazziard less frightening, he might have been insulted enough to lose his temper. As it was he just shook his head and muttered "Idiot," which was probably just as well for the word had barely escaped his lips before Lazziard had crossed the room hauled him to his feet and was pressing his hooked nose hard against his own.

"Do you want to say that again?" he spat, his eyes wide and wildly bright.

"Put him down William, *please*," Rothery sighed as he brushed some detritus off the shoulder of his coat.

"Should have let that thing suck you dry," Lazziard muttered contemptuously, releasing Caleb with a sneer before returning to stare out of the window.

"I'm afraid William isn't used to people being disrespectful, 'tis all that naval discipline, eh?"

Lazziard only grunted and continued to wipe his hands on a handkerchief he'd pulled from his jacket. When Caleb had been formally introduced to Captain William Lazziard of Her Highness' Navy, he'd asked why he wasn't in uniform.

"I'm between commissions," Lazziard had replied.

It had perhaps not been Caleb's most diplomatic response when he'd said, "I would have thought, as England is at war, that all of her Captains would be in service."

"So would I," had been Lazziard's only response, along with a darkly withering look that suggested further questioning would not be welcome.

"You said you found her last night?" Caleb asked, straightening his jacket and moving to place the bed and Dr Rothery between himself and Lazziard just in case he said something else to upset the Captain.

"Our boys had not seen her for some days, I gave word the next time Defane left here they should try to contact the young lady, we knew she was at risk and intended to move to prevent the vampire hurting either her or you. Sadly, we acted too slowly. When news reached us that she was dead, we knew we needed to extract you from danger."

"And this was your plan from the outset?"

Rothery shook his head vigorously enough to set his wig sliding about his scalp, "No, it was our intention to take the vampire alive."

"Alive?"

"As you have seen, we are limited in what we can learn from a vampiric corpse as they decay so rapidly; which is somewhat inconvenient when one wishes in engage in the application of curiosity."

"In other words, there is only so much you can learn from a pile of dust," Lazziard translated.

"Quite," Rothery smiled, "the military mind tends to take a more direct approach to things than one trained in the ways of natural philosophy."

"This is why I prefer just to kill the monsters, 'tis simpler."

"Only by understanding one's foe can one ever hope to enjoy complete triumph."

Caleb got the impression the two men were warming up for an old and familiar argument which he was not much interested in hearing, "How did you intend to capture

Defane?" he interjected.

"Oh, we have been perfecting a strategy for quite some time, every detail has been worked out in minutiae; I had every hope of it succeeding splendidly."

"It involved lots of men, cudgels and chains," Lazziard explained.

"Ah, that incisive military mind again," Rothery grinned, "anyway, that is quite enough chat, you're looking almost as pale as that poor girl, 'tis best we get you back to bed for some rest and more beef stew. I'll hear no arguing," he added holding up a finger before Caleb could protest he'd rather go back to his lodgings.

"What should we do with Liselot?"

"I will inform the Parish, one of the Seekers of the Dead will have to invent some suitable cause of death for the Bills of Mortality.

"It does not seem right just to leave her here."

"There is nothing we can do for the child, she will not rise now."

"Rise?"

"Become vampiric."

Caleb looked at the shrouded form, "How would she become a vampire, she's dead?"

"That is a prerequisite of the vampire Mr Cade, for a human being to cast off their mortality and become vampiric they must first die. From what I've been able to learn it appears the vampire must drain the victim's blood until the point of death and then ensure the unfortunate ingests an amount of vampiric blood, a few hours after death the unfortunate will be resurrected in vampiric form; in a kind of ghastly undeath if you like."

"And be immortal?"

A memory flashed behind Caleb's eyes, an image of an old and withered version of himself many years hence, floating before his reflection in the fog of a plate glass window on a street where there should be no plate glass windows.

"Mr Cade, are you feeling unwell again?"

"No, just the flash of memory."

"From your time with Defane?"

"Yes."

"What exactly was it?" Rothery demanded, instantly producing a notebook.

Caleb bit his lower lip, "No... 'tis gone, just something in the fog..."

"Never mind," Rothery sighed, "I'm sure your memories will return, and when they do they will be most useful."

"Perhaps we should send word to Sir Charles," Caleb said shaking away the memory.

"Sir Charles?"

Caleb looked up, "Sir Charles Massingham, Liselot

was his... *ward*."

"I doubt he will be able to help," Rothery replied.

"Why ever not? He may have been an old rascal, but I believe he does truly love her."

"Charles Massingham was found dead in his bed three days ago," Lazziard said, moving away from the window, stuffing his handkerchief back into his pocket.

"Dead? How?"

"Your guess is probably as good as any, the Bills of Mortality recorded it simply as "passing peaceably during sleep," but as those old crones are only ever looking for the plague, it could have been anything."

"Defane?"

Dr Rothery shrugged, "I'm afraid we do not move in high enough circles to gain access to the body of a Member of Parliament, it is possible, but we will probably never know for sure. He was old; it could have been any of a number of things that killed him."

"Such as a broken heart," Caleb whispered, looking down at Liselot's shrouded body a final time.

*

"'tis locked," Lazziard decided after a brief but violent rattle of the heavy wooden door.

"Perhaps we should knock?" Caleb ventured.

"Are you expecting someone to be home?" the Captain

returned, glancing over his shoulder to stare pointedly at Caleb.

"I haven't the faintest idea."

"Did you ever see anyone other than Defane here?" Rothery asked, looking from one man to the other as he leant against his cane.

"No."

"And as we have never seen anyone but Defane enter or leave, I think it is safe to assume Mr Defane had a singularly small household."

"In which case..." Lazziard grunted, planting a hefty kick against the door's lock.

Caleb looked about him wondering if he should mention the lock picking tools he had stitched into the lining of his coat. He quickly decided it best to say nothing. The house was set well back from the road by a short drive and was screened by what may once have been a carefully trimmed hedge, but was now a veritable thicket; the chances of anyone noticing their forced entry were slim. When this old Tudor pile had been built some two centuries earlier the area around Tottenham Court Road had been countryside, now London was slowly enveloping it, Inns and timber yards had been built close to the old house. Fashionable streets and Squares were being laid a few hundred yards to the south.

He glanced up at the dark windows that looked

sightlessly out from their rotting frames; when he'd left here with Defane it had been evening and he had paid little attention to the building, he hadn't realised just how much of a crumbling wreck the place actually was. He felt tired and drawn though the few hours he had rested once they'd returned from Liselot's apartment had restored a little of his strength. When he had heard the two men were going to inspect Defane's house, he had insisted he come along in the hope it might cast a little more light on the life of his erstwhile friend.

"Are you coming in or are you waiting for an invitation to cross the threshold?" Lazziard asked, wiping dust from his hands. The door had looked solid enough to Caleb, but it had taken only a couple of kicks to splinter the frame around the lock and a further shoulder charge to barge it open. Caleb didn't know whether the ease with which it had given way was a testament to the weakness of the door or the strength of Captain Lazziard.

He decided he shouldn't antagonise the man just in case the door really was as solid as it looked.

"Is it how you remember?" Rothery asked after they'd entered and stood in a fair-sized hall that contained a large staircase, a few closed doors and a lot of dust.

"I don't recall it being so dusty," Caleb replied, poking the toe of his boot at the thin layer of dust that covered the worn floorboards, "but otherwise, yes."

"How much of the house did you see?" Rothery pulled a handkerchief out to stifle a sneeze.

"Very little, I awoke in a large bedroom, I was exhausted from the worst hangover of my life, we talked a little, I dozed again until Defane woke me in order to give me something to eat, I slept again, right through the day. When I awoke it was night, and I was much refreshed, my clothes were on the bed. I dressed, Defane came into the room, we talked and then we walked down these stairs and out of the house."

"There was nothing else the two of you got up to during your stay then?" Lazziard asked, opening one of the side doors and sticking his head into the gloom inside.

"Such as?"

"Oh, I don't know," Lazziard mused after finding nothing of interest and returning to the hall, "a friendly game of chess perhaps?"

"No," Caleb answered coldly, "we did nothing else."

"I'm sure," Lazziard flashed him a brief black-toothed little grin.

"I suggest we explore the ground floor first then move through the upper stories," Rothery announced, heading along the hallway without waiting for objections.

"It would be quicker if we split up?" Lazziard called after him.

"Best not; in my experience one never quite knows

what one might find in situations like this."

Caleb shrugged and indicated Lazziard could go ahead of him.

"After you," Lazziard insisted, "I prefer to keep you where I can see you."

Once they found the shutters on all of the windows were nailed shut they explored the ground floor as methodically as the gloomy light and Lazziard's continuous stream of insidious comments and innuendos allowed; however, each room was deserted save for the occasional rat that scurried away from the echoing creaks of their boots upon the floorboards.

Like the entrance hall, not a scrap of furniture or a piece of decoration was to be found anywhere. The dust lay even thicker away from the entrance hall, covering the floors in thick grey carpets that were undisturbed save for the tiny tracks of mice and rats.

"Nobody has been in here for decades," Lazziard announced as they entered yet another dark and empty room, his tone weighed down by boredom.

"Best part of a century I would wager," Rothery replied, sniffing air that was heavy with the musty stink of rot.

"Do you know anything about this place?" Caleb asked from the doorway, reluctant to tiptoe through the gloom of another deserted room.

"Indeed!" Rothery exclaimed, "Mr Rentwin has been diligently looking through the parish records for us. He's rather good at that sort of thing."

"What did he find out?"

"Haven't the foggiest idea, been too busy to read his report," Rothery began patting down his shapeless coat, "rather remiss of me I suppose, but what with all the excitement I plain forgot, ah here we go." The Doctor produced a crumpled sheaf of folded paper from one of his pockets. "Ah," he muttered, peering at the letter, "'tis far too dark in here to actually read it."

"Let me cast some light upon it then Doctor," Lazziard offered, tugging the window shutters which came away almost immediately with a wet splintering crack.

The room looked out upon what was once probably quite a pleasant garden at the rear of the house but was now a tangled thicket of briars, weeds and wild rose bushes which pressed up to the very window itself. Thanks to the vegetation and the dirt encrusted glass the room was only marginally brighter than before though Caleb still fancied he heard a multitude of things scurrying away from the unfamiliar daylight into the darker corners.

"Splendid!" Rothery beamed, repositioning himself by the window and holding the letter at arm's length, "now what has dear Rentwin unearthed for us, eh?"

Caleb wandered across the room, drawn to the

meagre light of the window, which illuminated the room just enough to reveal the damp stained ceiling and peeling discoloured plaster.

"My Dearest Dr Rothery blah blah... yes, yes Rentwin very good... hmmm... parish records most excellently maintained eh? I'm jolly glad to hear it..."

"Well?" Lazziard sighed.

Rothery held up a hand for silence while he scanned the rest of the letter, his forehead creased like ripples in the sand before he finally looked up at his companions, "According to Rentwin's investigations this house is the property of the Lansdowne family and has been since it was built in 1525."

"So where are the Lansdownes now?" Lazziard asked, looking about the house that appeared to be slowly disintegrating about their ears.

"Well, the last birth Rentwin could find recorded in the parish register is for one Percy Lansdowne, who was born in the year of our Lord 1618 and appears to have been the only child of John and Rebecca Lansdowne to survive to adulthood."

"And when did he die?" Caleb asked uneasily.

Rothery shook his head, "There is no record of his death, which is not entirely sinister, many men went to unrecorded graves during the Civil War; however, Rentwin found one later record, in 1639 registering the marriage of

Percy Lansdowne to one Mary Hughes of Oxford."

"Nothing else after that?"

"No, nothing at all. No children were born or christened to the family and there is no record of Mary's death either."

"Parish records are not always entirely reliable."

"True enough Cade, but Rentwin comments several times as to the diligence of these particular record keepers. He made enquiries regarding this property in the area; though it is still referred to locally as the Lansdowne House, he could find no one who has ever had any dealings with the owners."

"Given that they've probably been dead for the past sixty years that's hardly surprising," Lazziard muttered.

"Whoever they were they must have been rich, given the size of this place," Caleb speculated, looking around the crumbling room and wondering what it must have looked like when Percy and Mary had lived here, "Defane told me that he was looking after the house for the owners."

"It would appear the Lansdowne's made a poor choice of house sitter," Lazziard muttered.

"According to Rentwin, the family owned quite a bit of land in Oxfordshire, as well as a number of breweries in Southwark."

"I've never heard of them."

"Like many breweries, they didn't survive the

Interregnum, no doubt one of the many reasons Londoners decided they wanted their King back once Cromwell died. Rentwin is continuing to make enquiries as to the land the family owned."

"All sold a long time ago," Caleb muttered, adding with a shrug when the other two men looked at him, "I would guess."

"Of course, Louis Defane could have been Percy Lansdowne," Rothery speculated, "he could have suffered a vampiric rising sometime after 1639 and changed his name to avoid suspicion as to his longevity."

"No," Caleb said adamantly.

"Why not?" Rothery asked, stuffing Rentwin's letter back into his coat.

"This is what Defane did to Liselot Van Schalkwyk," Caleb said, gesturing at the empty room around him with a sweep of his hand, "he was a cuckoo, I even accused him of such a thing once not realising just how accurate my accusation was. He found a way into someone's heart and home and then he stripped them both bare for the things he wanted. No doubt the land went the same way as all the furniture and fittings that once filled this house. His expensive tastes had to be paid for somehow; this is how he did it, besides... I think he was a lot older than ninety."

"And why do you believe that?"

"If you'd looked into his eyes the way I did, you'd

realise just how much they must have seen."

For once Lazziard had no retort, and they continued their exploration of the house; finding nothing of note until they stumbled into the room Caleb had awoken in the last time he'd been in the house. It was noticeably cleaner than the rest of the house and strangely the shutters here allowed more sunlight to creep past them than in most of the others they'd come across. The large dishevelled bed, the heavy old-fashioned chair in the corner and the huge old clock were all familiar to Caleb, as was the shuddering *clunk-tock* sound the clock made.

"Fascinating!" the Doctor declared, hurrying over to investigate no sooner than he'd clapped eyes on the clock's worn walnut façade and towering battlements.

"Something interesting?" Lazziard asked, pulling open the shutters to illuminate the dust motes that danced lazily in the sunlight.

"This is quite ancient," Rothery muttered, pulling open the door of contraption to examine its workings, "I'm not sure I've seen a mechanism quite like this before."

"I was referring to matters of *vampiric* interest Doctor," Lazziard rolled his eyes in exasperation, "not the fascinating world of clockworks."

"Well, you never know..." Rothery's voice echoed from deep inside the bowels of the machine.

Lazziard shook his head and leant against the wall by

the window, crossing his arms he turned his attention to the bed, "I take it this is the room you awoke in?"

Caleb nodded, eyeing the clock suspiciously. It made so many ghastly mechanical noises he feared the Doctor might be in some peril inside the wretched thing.

"Were the pillows so blood-stained when you were here?"

Caleb's attention turned back to the bed, where dark splatters, much like the ones they'd seen about Liselot's corpse could be seen on the faded sheets.

"No..., I don't think so."

"So, either Defane brought other victims here, or you are singularly unobservant about your own life blood."

"We know he had the power to confuse and deceive," Rothery interjected, emerging reluctantly from the innards of the clock and waving away cobwebs from his face.

"Remind me to tell you about his prowess at cards some time," Caleb said weakly, unable to pull his eyes from the stains. Could Defane have fed from him whilst he'd been here? Fed from him and then used his strange gifts to ensure Caleb didn't even see the bloodstains that surrounded him. Before he could fully digest that thought, Lazziard threw another question at him.

"What did you eat?"

"Eat?" Caleb muttered, not really paying attention.

"You said Defane gave you something to eat after you

woke?"

"Er... yes, just some soup. He said it would make me feel better."

"Did it?"

"Well yes, eventually. I fell asleep again, when I awoke it was dark, and the malaise I had felt before had entirely passed. In fact, I was so refreshed we spent the whole night drinking and..." his eyes flicked between Lazziard and Rothery "...carousing."

"I'm sure you did."

"Why do you ask?" Caleb sighed, ignoring Lazziard's innuendo again.

The Captain walked across the room, stooped down and lifted a tray that contained a shallow china bowl which had been pushed under the bed.

"Well, I was wondering how the vampire might have prepared a nice warm bowl of soup for you, given the kitchens were as empty as the rest of the house and so thickly laid with dust I doubt it has been disturbed since that usurper Cromwell got ideas above his station?"

Doctor Rothery hurried past Caleb to peer at the soup bowl with as much interest as he had moments before with the clockworks, "Do you recall what kind of soup it was perchance?"

"It was..." Caleb started assuredly before realising he couldn't recall much about it at all, other than it had been dark and lukewarm, "...some kind of... meat broth," he finished weakly.

Lazziard and Rothery were both staring pointedly at him over the rim of the bowl they had been examining closely.

"It looks like bl-"

"Well, there's no point speculating eh!" Rothery quickly cut off the Captain as he deposited the bowl into the small black bag he carried. "Let us examine this room a bit more closely than the others eh? This seems to be the part of the house the vampire used most frequently, given the furniture and the lack of dust."

Lazziard grinned unpleasantly before they turned their attentions to searching the rest of the room. Between them they found nothing of interest and Caleb was grateful to move on, closing the door behind him to shut off the mournful *clunk-tock* of the clock.

Lazziard opened the opposite door across the corridor, which swung open upon a dark and profound blackness. In every other room, some small sliver of grey light had managed to penetrate the shutters, but this room was utterly dark. Even opening the door upon it seemed to have had little effect in shifting the blackness, as if the dark was itself some beast that had taken up residence in the room and had no great fancy to move on.

The three men stood silently on the threshold of the

room, sensing it was not as empty as the others they'd visited.

"I don't suppose you have a lantern in that bag of yours Doctor?" Lazziard asked.

"Very remiss of me," Rothery tutted, "I should have anticipated a vampire might keep his abode dark."

"Not to worry, I'll find the window," Lazziard shrugged and plunged into the darkness, he did not entirely disappear, but became indistinct as the shadows partially consumed him. His footsteps echoed about the room, the old boards groaning balefully in protest at his footsteps.

"Found it, 'tis well boarded and hidden behind a thick curtain!" Lazziard's voice boomed back after a series of low guttural noises came from the far side of the room, followed by a few choice curses and the crack of protesting wood as the Captain finally managed to gain some purchase and prized away whatever had been nailed across the window.

The window was directly facing the sun and the light that streamed in made Caleb wince as it flooded into the room for the first time in decades.

"Oh, my!" Rothery exclaimed.

An enormous silk draped four poster bed dominated the room; it seemed to Caleb to be roughly the same size as the entire bedroom he'd shared with his brothers when he'd been a boy. Lazziard had only managed to pull open one of the shutters and the light it let in fell directly upon the bed and the figure that lay upon it. Caleb thought the figure's head would snap round to stare darkly at them before demanding to know who had disturbed its slumber, but that was just a moment's foolish fancy for the figure had not moved in decades.

"I know the vampire was not one for keeping his house clean," Lazziard growled, "but you would have thought he'd have thrown *that* out."

Caleb and Rothery moved to the side of the bed and looked down into the sightless eyes of the skeleton, which lay with its hands folded serenely over its stomach, its head propped up on a mountain of moth-eaten and half rotten pillows; a few wisps of dark hair still splaying out from the skull to spread across linen that had turned to the colour of brittle sun-baked parchment. No blanket covered the figure, and the sheet beneath was stained dark and half eaten away, at least on that side of the bed. Covering the side nearest to the window a new silk sheet had been laid and fresh pillows that still bore the impression of a head were piled next to the rotting heap that propped up the skeleton's skull. Caleb rested a hand upon one of the thick wooden posts of the bed, his weight shifting the bed enough to dislodge a gentle flurry of dust from the faded silken drapes.

What appeared to be scraps of paper lay scattered all around the skeleton, deep enough in places to hide the rotten sheet beneath, without thinking Caleb scooped one up and crumpled it between his thumb and forefinger.

"Dried rose petals..."

"You note the dark discoloration beneath the skeleton, like dried liquid stains," Rothery was asking. Caleb nodded letting the dust of the rose petal fall from his fingers. "She died here, and her body putrefied upon this bed, many, many years ago."

"She?"

"Mary Landsdowne," Lazziard said.

"How can you be so sure?" Caleb asked, glancing up to find Lazziard wasn't looking at the body, but at the wall it faced, the light revealing a large portrait of a woman which was hung upon it. Next to the painting a single wrought iron candlestick stood as tall as Lazziard's shoulder, discoloured wax tumbled from its rim to touch the floor; a frozen waterfall that had formed from decade's worth of candles lit one after the next.

"It says so here," he replied, peering at something written on the frame, "*Mrs Mary Landsdowne, 1641.*"

"So, we know what happened to poor Mary then," Rothery sighed, bending over to sweep aside some of the dark, brittle strands of Mary's hair to reveal darker splatters upon the pillows beneath her, "do these marks look familiar?" They had faded and merged into the rotten fabric as her body had decayed into it, but Caleb recognised the spots well enough.

"Blood splatters," he said quietly, "just like Liselot's."

"And no doubt that would have been the fate of her corpse too," Lazziard said returning to the opposite side of the bed, "to be some grisly trophy to vampiric lust, denied a decent Christian burial and left to rot for his amusement, her soul forever lost to heaven."

"My love is so great, it breaks all that I hold dear..."

"I'm sorry Cade, what was that?" Rothery asked, looking up from the skeleton, but Caleb ignored him, moving instead to stand beneath Mary's portrait. He thought he might see some similarity to Liselot, something that had caused Defane to repeat what he had clearly done sixty odd years ago, but if she did bear any similarity the artist had not captured it. She had been beautiful to be sure, but it was a dark, striking, confident beauty that stared out of the picture, her attention focussed on some distant point behind his shoulder, not the soft, demure fragility that had hallmarked little Liselot.

"Something Defane said to me once, I did not understand his meaning at the time, but now..." he shook his head sadly, "the sheet next to the corpse is fresh, the pillows new and recently slept upon. He spent sixty plus years sleeping next to the corpse of a woman he killed, scattering rose petals over her bones and staring at her picture in the flicking light of a thousand candles he lit one after the other," Caleb said softly, not looking back at his companions, "lust, violence, hunger do not explain such a thing, only love can drive a man to such madness. Could you imagine such a thing? What it must feel like to still be in love with someone you killed a lifetime ago."

"It would be a torture," Lazziard replied distantly, "it would haunt and torment a man, it would burn like hellfire itself, it would strip a man of his humanity and sear away his very soul. If he had one to start with of course; wherein lies the flaw in your argument Cade. Vampires like Defane don't have a soul and, therefore, are incapable of so noble an emotion as love. Like a fool who sees human characteristics in his favourite hound, you continue to make the mistake of thinking him a man, he was not; he was a monster who killed this poor woman, he did the same thing to Miss Van Schalkwyk and God alone knows how many others in between. He would have done the same to you too had we not intervened; forgive me if I am boring you with my repetition of this point, but you seem so obstinate in your refusal to understand it." Caleb heard Lazziard's footsteps pounding behind him until the Captain was close enough for his breath to play against Caleb's ear.

"Accept it," Lazziard hissed angrily, "he never loved *you* either..."

Caleb looked around, but the Captain had already marched out of the room.

Rothery shrugged, "Although it is not usually apparent, sometimes I do believe William possess the soul of a poet."

Caleb snorted a laugh, "He hides it very well, I must say."

The Doctor nodded, "He hides it so well even he doesn't know he has it."

With that, the Doctor turned his attention back to Mary's remains while Caleb continued to stare at her portrait.

He had loved a woman once, loved her so much every fibre of his being ached when he was away from her. In the end, his love too had brought only death, and it had haunted him ever since, but unlike Defane he had never repeated the mistake.

But then again, he'd never slept with Henrietta's corpse either.

*

"He fed me his own blood?"

"Yes."

"From a soup bowl?"

"It would appear so."

"With a silver spoon?"

"Would you have preferred it in a mug?" Lazziard growled from across the room.

Ignoring the jibe, Caleb continued to stare at the

shallow blood smeared china bowl that sat in the centre of Dr Rothery's vast paper strewn oak desk. The Doctor's study was silent for a while, save for the faint scratching of Archibald Jute's quill.

"You seem... a little bemused?" Rothery ventured.

Caleb managed to drag his eyes away from the bowl, "Apart from feeling faintly nauseous, I was under the impression that vampire's drunk human blood, I didn't realise they served it to unexpected house guests in their best china!"

Rothery smiled thinly, "We know the wounds they inflict heal unnaturally fast, even on a corpse. I have a theory, of sorts, that the vampire's blood is some manner of curative and that its ingestion allows a part of the vampiric essence to be transferred to the recipient."

"Do you mean that... *I'm* a vampire?" Caleb nervously glancing at Lazziard, the Captain already seemed keen to lop off his head just for the hell of it; he didn't want to give him any more motivation.

"No, no, not at all, you would need to have died first for that to have occurred," Rothery beamed reassuringly. "The malady that confined you to Defane's bed was due to the blood you had lost to the vampire, for whatever reason Defane fed you a little of his own blood, passing on just enough of the vampiric essence to speed your recovery."

"I don't understand, why would Defane drink my

blood only to replace it with some of his own?"

"For some reason, he wanted to keep you alive for a while, I don't suppose it was for your wit or company; perhaps you have an unusual flavour," Lazziard offered, "you know what a strange palate those Frenchies have."

"William, we digress," Rothery said sternly, holding up a hand before Caleb could retort, "Mr Cade has had a particularly tiring day, and we greatly appreciate the assistance he has offered us. I am sure he is eager for his bed, so the sooner we can finish this session of documentation, the sooner we can all retire."

"What do you mean by *vampiric essence*?" Caleb asked, looking from Rothery to Lazziard and back again.

Rothery sighed and eased himself up from his chair, "As I said, it is late perhaps we should continue our discussions tomorrow when our old bodies, and young Archie's writing hand, are better rested."

"*Please...* just a moment."

The Doctor glanced at Lazziard who twitched his shoulders by way of a reply, "As I said, 'tis only a theory..."

"You are not usually so reticent in discussing your theories Doctor, is this something... secret?"

"Secret!" Rothery guffawed, "not at all."

"Well then... what is the vampiric essence?"

"The supposed soul of a vampire," Lazziard said darkly when the Doctor remained silent.

Rothery sighed again before reluctantly lowering himself back into his chair, "The vampiric essence is what I believe changes mortal men into vampires, it is their power, their strength, the very core of their being. It heals them, makes them stronger, faster, agiler than us. It is what makes them immortal. It resides, in part, within their blood and by passing on that blood to a mortal they pass on the essence; a little will heal and restore, a lot will kill and induce a vampiric rising. There is much that we still do not know, but it is one of the goals of our Society to find the source of the vampiric essence."

"The source?"

"As these creatures are immortal it is my conjecture that they cannot have enough of the essence to last forever, it must, therefore, be replenished from somewhere. I believe that the vampiric body grows some manner of organ to produce the essence, a reservoir if you like, from which to restock that which the vampire uses to heal its own body or pass on to make others of its foul kind."

"And why is it so important to find this source?"

Rothery leaned forward his eyes suddenly bright and excited, "Because if we can locate such an organ, we can remove it. We can bestow upon these creatures the greatest gift possible; we will be able to restore their humanity, return unto them their immortal soul!"

Caleb's eyes flicked around the other men in the

room; Jute was sitting quietly, his quill no longer moving, hanging upon the Doctor's words. Rentwin sat by the fire, a Bible unopened in his lap nodding slowly in agreement as he silently watched their discussion. Lazziard, however, was staring up at the ceiling, a distant, disinterested expression set upon his face.

"And I thought you simply wanted to kill vampires Captain?"

Lazziard's eyes swivelled languidly in Caleb's direction, "Oh, I can aspire to loftier principles too Cade; I am not a complete savage you know. Of course, if we cannot find the vampiric essence it will be necessary to have an *alternative* plan."

"And that is where you come in?"

Lazziard flashed him one of his humourless black-toothed smiles.

"Doctor, I don't quite understand. Why should a vampire welcome their immortal soul back in return for their actual immortality? Might they not consider that a poor bargain?"

"Well, I suppose they would if you put it like that."

"The Devil has blinded them with his trickery," Rentwin interjected, his head suddenly twitching more violently than ever, "they are consumed by His foulness and will no doubt fight tooth and claw to retain the vampiric essence, but I am sure once their soul has been restored, they will thank us greatly for returning them to God's glory."

"Even if they die in the process," Lazziard added coldly.

*

He'd been exhausted, as profoundly tired as he'd ever felt in his life, every part of his body felt as heavy as if he'd had lead weights sewn into all of his clothes, but sleep still had not come.

Instead, he had lain upon the bed in one of Rothery's guest rooms, staring at the faint shadows the single candle he was too afraid to blow out cast upon the ceiling. He'd listened to the silence that was punctuated by only the occasional tortured squeak of an un-oiled wheel as a night-soil man's wagon clattered by on the road outside, that and the constant rhythm and pulse of the blood that pounded in his ears.

Eventually, he had risen, taking the single candle before heading downstairs almost without thought. He'd half expected to see Rothery's man Scaife come looming out of the darkness beyond the reach of the candlelight, for, in his long, tired features, he had the look of a soul rarely troubled by sleep. However, Caleb found his way down to the Doctor's workshop of curiosities without interruption.

He had stood in front of the door for a good long while, telling himself he was better off going back to bed and awaiting the first birdsong of dawn, however, his hand had resolutely remained upon the cold worn door handle. He was still telling himself the same thing when he eventually found the courage to open the door, which he was mildly surprised to find unlocked.

The windowless room was utterly dark, and he took a firmer grip upon the candlestick as he stepped inside. The workshop was unchanged from his last visit, save the lanterns were now dark and cold, the air inside tasted heavy and stale in his mouth, tainted as it was by burnt metal and strange chemistries.

The candlelight pushed the darkness back, but only a little and he crossed the room in small hesitant steps that he told himself was for fear of stumbling in the gloom. The shroud had been placed back over Defane's remains, and after he had carefully set down the candle, Caleb gripped one end of it, feeling the coarseness of cheap linen between his fingers. Gently he pulled the sheet back, almost expecting to see Defane lying on the table, propped up on one elbow and resplendent in some particularly garish wig, a mischievous grin on his face, he would tip Caleb a wink and laugh shrilly that he'd fallen so perfectly for his little wheeze. Vampires indeed!

But that was just Caleb's fancy whispering hopefully into his ear, and there was little in the pile of dust that could be remembered as a man, let alone his friend. When he'd been shown the remains the previous night it had looked like a corpse that had been pulled from a centuries-closed tomb, but now it was hard to believe that what lay on the table had ever even been a man.

It seemed to Caleb that someone had sculpted the shape of a man from the wet sand of a beach before dressing it in a suit of sober clothes, but the tide had not washed back in, and the sand had dried in the heat of the sun, slowly losing form and substance as it crumbled and dissolved. A sandman returning to just a pile of powdery dry sand.

Caleb stared at Defane's face, which was nought but a pile of grey dust that only tenuously retained the form of a skull, two dark depressions marking where his beautiful eyes had been the most obvious surviving feature. Caleb could have bent down and blown upon the face, and it would have dissolved completely under his breath.

"What were you?" Caleb heard himself ask, his voice much louder than he'd expected, "Just a man, or some other manner of beast after all?"

The sandman remained silent, the shadowy pits of his eyes expressionless.

"You were right, after all, I think," Caleb continued quietly, "we were just the same, both tortured by the memories of women we'd loved. Women our love had killed. Forever apart from our fellows, always searching for something that could not be regained; twenty years I kept moving and followed the road though it brought me no peace, twenty years of chasing pleasures to salve my pain. I can't imagine what doing that for centuries would do to a man's mind."

He gently reached out and rested his fingers upon the dust that spilt out of the sleeve of the sandman's coat.

"They think you a monster Louis, and they killed you for it. They were right too, probably, but I cannot find it in me to hate you, even if you did mean to kill me. You loved a woman so intensely you curled up to sleep next to her bones for decades. Was she the only one I wonder; was Mary Lansdowne the first? Was she the one who broke your heart, or was she just one of many. Are there a score of forgotten bedrooms scattered across London, shuttered and barred from the world and its sun, rooms where time has stopped and the bones of someone you loved patiently await your return, await your caress? I carry my bones too, Louis, the only difference being mine are all in my head. Did you keep them to remember lost loves or just to torture yourself with? I've never been quite sure why I carry mine; perhaps we both just needed something to fill the holes in the parts of us that are broken."

Caleb felt the dust of what once had been the vampire's long sensuous fingers crumble beneath his touch.

"I don't understand Louis; I don't understand why you tried to kill me."

"He wasn't trying to kill you."

Caleb raised his eyes from Defane's dusty corpse; a figure was leaning against the far wall where the shadows were deepest. He could barely tell where shadow ended and figure begun. It was as if some acclaimed artist had painted the memory of a sixteen-year-old boy onto a canvas of night with from a palette of shadows and candlelight.

"I thought you had left me, it has been a long while brother."

"I can never leave you, Daniel, you know that, I live only in your memories, so long as you remember me then I will have some manner of breath in my imaginary body."

"Do not call me Daniel; he is as dead as you are."

The figure shrugged, "It gets confusing if we both use the same name, and it was mine first, after all."

Caleb sighed, "You are just my imagination, my invisible friend; the brother I lost and keep alive through my memories. You'll do as you're told."

"Of course," the memory of his brother might have grinned boyishly out of the shadows.

"Why do you think he didn't want to kill me?"

The figure had started to sketch something preserved in one of Dr Rothery's bell jars, "Fascinating place this workshop of curiosities, eh?"

"Do you remember more about the night Defane died than I do?" Caleb insisted.

"Of course."

"How does that work exactly, given you are only a figment of my imagination?"

The memory of his brother shrugged, "'tis your mind Daniel, if you don't know how it works how do you expect me to?"

"Never mind," Caleb sighed, "just tell me."

"He was your friend, he didn't want to kill you; he wanted to live a life eternal with you. That was what he offered you last night in the fog; that is what you cannot fully remember. He showed you the future, he conjured an illusion to show you the old bent-backed man you would one day become; then he offered you an alternative. Immortality."

"Yet, strangely, he tried to kill me," Caleb replied sceptically.

"For a vampire to rise, a man must die."

"But Liselot died and did not rise."

"No, but perhaps Defane did not intend to kill her either."

"You mean it was an accident?"

The memory of his brother swept smoky tendrils of hair from his shadowy eyes, "It was *always* an accident Daniel; that was his curse; he was achingly lonely yet could not make another like himself."

"I don't understand."

"Can you imagine him living for centuries, surrounded by mortals, everybody he fell in love with would wither and die before his eyes, yet he remained untouched by time; whenever he met someone he loved he tried to make them like himself so that he would be spared that torment."

"But Liselot died, Mary died, I would have died!"

"My love is so great it breaks all that I hold dear..." his brother conjured Defane's words from the darkness, "he told us it all in that one sentence little Daniel."

Caleb fell to silence, staring at Defane's crumbling skull in the wan candlelight.

"He was a tormented soul, he could not make others like him, could not pass on the vampiric essence, as Dr Rothery would have it, not in sufficient quantities to make a mortal rise as a vampire anyway, thereby denying him a friend or lover eternal. Leaving him alone – forever."

"But he kept trying."

"Because if he accepted he could never make someone he loved like himself, he would have to accept he would be forever cursed to be alone. So he kept trying."

"And as a penance for that sin, he kept the bones of the friends and lovers he'd killed close, keeping a part of them alive."

"As you keep part of me alive."

"Perhaps," Caleb muttered, staring at the insubstantial form of his long-dead brother. Once his memory had been so sharp and clear it had been hard to believe he had not actually been standing before him. Through all those years he had remained with him, his one friend and companion, they would talk long into the night as once they had when they'd been boys sharing a blanket to keep the chill of a London winter from their bones. Or he would find some quiet shady nook in a tavern and sup ale while the memory of his brother drew the other patrons. Sometimes they would talk about his adventures, sometimes they would sit in companionable silence, but it was always a comfort to be with him.

But that had been decades ago; now his memory was an insubstantial thing. He'd been only a child when his brother had died. Now all his mind could invoke was an ephemeral suggestion of the boy he had loved, something that hugged the shadows, something conjured of smoke and grease smeared looking-glasses, something that was only really a boy if you looked at it out of the corner of your eye; something as tenuous and wispy as mist before a breeze or a ghost before the dawn.

Time had reduced them both.

"I loved you," Caleb said, staring at the figure, willing it to be more real, trying to summon the memory as strongly as he had once been able to. Trying to place back the flesh that had once knitted the bones that lay under that awful tree in Tindell's burying ground, to bring his brother back from Jack's Kingdom.

"You still do," the figure said sadly, fading slowly back into the shadows.

"Wait!" Caleb cried, "I don't know what to do!"

"Avoid the dark and bitter places," the voice said faintly.

Caleb called out again, his voice echoing amongst the shadows, but the memory of his brother was gone and he was alone once more. After a while he realised he had been gripping the table edge furiously enough to make his knuckles ache, he let out a shuddering sob, and when he looked down he saw his tears had fallen in fat salty drops upon the dust of Defane's hand.

He watched the tears darken the powdery ash, but nothing else happened, his sadness had no power over anything but himself.

Tears were just tears.

*

Caleb was so lost in thoughts about Defane that he did not see the figure standing in the hall until he had stumbled into it; provoking firstly a yelp of surprise, followed swiftly by one of alarm as he lost his grip on the candlestick and it crashed to the floor. He had seen enough in the instant that the candlestick tumbled from his hand to recognise the figure was female and assumed she was a maid up and about for early chores. Deciding that she wasn't likely to do him much harm and that the Doctor might be slightly put out if he managed to burn his home to the ground, he ignored the woman and scrambled to recover the still burning candle before any serious damage was done.

"That is a particularly expensive rug," a softly Scottish voice said from somewhere above him after he'd retrieved the candle and was busy brushing down a few singed fibres.

"Then it is fortunate there is no harm done," Caleb replied, glancing up; the woman had made no move to step backwards and stood over him in a manner that was, quite frankly, rather insolent for a servant.

"I believe I am a more suitable judge of what harm has been done, particularly in cases when strange men are found creeping furtively around one's house in the wee small hours."

"If I had been either furtive or creeping, I would not have run into you and dropped this candle on the Doctor's expensive rug," Caleb snapped back, paying more attention to the rug than the maid, "as it was I was making haste back to my room, hence our unfortunate collision. You need not fear Miss, I am no thief."

Caleb heard a rustle of clothing as she crossed her arms and continued to stare down at him, "Actually I consider all men to be thieves."

"Is that so?" Caleb sighed, satisfied no real damage had been done and climbing back to his feet.

"Aye," she retorted, "just as you believe all women to be whores."

Caleb blinked in surprise at her words as he found himself staring into a pair of vivid green eyes that sparkled mischievously in the candlelight. The young woman was almost as tall as he was and she stared at him candidly; she wore a dark cape and bonnet that framed a pale and striking heart-shaped face, the thin, elegant arches of her eyebrows were raised in expectation of his reply.

"I can't imagine what I've done to give you such a low opinion of me."

"Men with a habit for skulking are usually the most debased and crude examples of the species, I find."

"Well, best I not keep you from your chores, the hour is late and all this *skulking* has fair tired me out," Caleb replied with a resigned sigh.

"Will you not be gentleman enough to hold the candle for me whilst I remove my cape and bonnet?" she asked her tone softening as she smiled sweetly.

"You are a bold young thing," Caleb replied, despite his tiredness he found he was rooted to the spot; there was something about the way her lips curled slowly and precisely around each word that he found quite sensual. It was not a beautiful mouth, for her lips were too thin and too pale, but there was something about the shape of it that held the attention, something vaguely carnal and intriguing.

"For one of such a lowly station, you mean?" She moved to a looking glass by the hall's coat stand, and Caleb found himself following her despite himself, candlestick outstretched, "I take you do not associate boldness with one who makes a living from scrubbing floors, turning down sheets or... warming beds?"

"There is nothing wrong with warming beds," Caleb watched her intently as she unlaced and removed her bonnet to unleash an avalanche of fiery red curls. He supposed it was poor form to make hay with the Doctor's maid, but she was fetching enough and the warmth of her body would dispel Defane and his other demons awhile. It had long been both Caleb's philosophy and his fancy that any trouble could be forgotten in the comforts of a woman's body.

"Indeed Sir," she turned back to face him after running her hands through her hair, "it can be the most rewarding of chores."

"'tis very early to start work."

"I have much to do... is there something you require

of me; something to make your stay... more comfortable?"

Caleb smiled and raised the candle a little as she moved half a step towards him. Her eyes really were the most vivid green, smoky emerald rings orbiting the wide dark chasms of her pupils. He found himself suddenly aroused and eager for the feel of her. Perhaps she thought him a rich house guest who might bestow a few gifts on her if she were easy with her favours, but Caleb didn't care about her motives, carefully he reached out and begun to untie the front of her cape with his free hand, when she made no move to step away he pulled more urgently at the fastenings. All the time she regarded him boldly, eyes fixed on his, her thin lips pulled into a half smile that was full of encouragement and promise.

The candlelight danced about them as his other hand worked ever more frantically until the cape came loose and he pulled it from her shoulders, none to gently. His hand froze as he saw the sparkling necklace that tumbled down towards heavy cleavage framed by a vibrant red silk gown.

"You are not the Doctor's maid, are you?" Caleb said quietly, raising his gaze from her chest.

She shook her head, pursing her lips to make a sad little face.

Caleb took a step backwards, "I am sorry Miss, given the hour I thought you were a servant arriving for work."

"I am returning from a night on the town... somewhat

late."

"The streets are no place for a lady at this time," Caleb said, partly in surprise and partly to cover his own lewdness.

Her eyes widened in amusement and she laughed from somewhere deep in her throat, "I was able to navigate London's streets without a moment's trouble, yet as soon as I crossed the threshold of my own home I am accosted by some rogue in a gentleman's garb!"

"Hardly accosted Miss!"

"But you fair ripped my cape from my weak, trembling and undefended body!" she protested, a gloved hand splayed across her chest as she glanced at the crumpled cape at her feet.

"I was only helping you remove your heavy cape as any gentleman might assist a pretty young lady; there is no crime in that."

"Indeed, Sir there is not, but you did not take me for a young lady, you took me for some strumpet of a maid, a foolish girl who might be swept off her feet into a scoundrel's bed in return for a few meagre flatteries and the possibility of something better than a life of scrubbing and cleaning."

"You say it as if I was doing something wrong?"

"Wrong? Not at all, 'tis only your nature. As I said earlier, I am well aware you look upon all women as whores."

"You have made your point, Miss…"

"Alyssa, Alyssa Rothery."

"A relative of Dr Rothery?"

"His much loved only daughter."

"Oh."

"He is *very* protective of me by the way; he would be quite upset if he heard of your behaviour, he might be so angry as to have a wee word with his man Mr Scaife, who is equally protective. He's a strange man Mr Scaife, I believe he used to be in the Army where he was called upon to undertake any number of black deeds; a man best not to upset." Alyssa spoke with a jaunty smile upon her face, but her eyes held his firmly enough to suggest she might not be being entirely flippant.

"Well then," Caleb said, leaning against the wall, "it would be best you said nothing about it."

"It would, but you know what we prattling young girls can be like…" she fluttered her eyelids a few times to emphasise her innocence.

"And I will say nothing of you creeping home in the small hours."

Alyssa smiled brightly, "Sadly when one has to suffer the attentions of an overprotective father, it can sometimes be difficult to enjoy assignations with particular gentleman friends."

"'tis fortunate I can be discreet then."

Alyssa leaned against the wall too, still regarding Caleb boldly, "Agreed, so long as you show me the courtesy of introducing yourself."

"Caleb Cade, I am... a friend of your father's."

"You do not need to explain your presence Mr Cade; I am quite used to my father bringing home all manner of oddities, waifs, vagabonds and ne'er-do-wells."

"And which category do I fit into?"

"I will need to make further observations before I can be sure," she smiled radiantly before kissing him quickly and inappropriately on the cheek, "but that will have to wait for another night."

"I know you're not the maid," Caleb said before he could stop himself as she scooped up her cape and turned away from him, "but my bed is rather cold..."

"A ne'er-do-well," she smiled, walking backwards from him, a crooked grin splitting her face, "I'm definitely thinking ne'er-do-well..." with that Alyssa turned and ran up the shadowy stairs in quick, graceful strides, leaving behind only the echo of her throaty laughter.

Chapter Ten

J'entends Ton Coeur

The Babbington Estate, Essex -1688

"How do you feel now?"

Although her face was slightly flushed Henrietta's breathing was far easier than his; the Duchess had warned Daniel he would need to use a firm hand to show her who was in control, however, it was advice he'd been struggling to follow.

"Sore," Daniel complained, squirming as he sought a more comfortable position. His mock scowl suddenly dissolved into to a cry of alarm, leaving Henrietta trying to stifle her laughter as he lurched away from her. Martha had spotted a particularly enticing clump of foliage and had decided neither the wailing young man on her back or the steep grassy bank that separated her from it were going to impede her gluttony.

By the time Henrietta had wheeled her own horse

around and followed Daniel down the bank, Martha had already buried her face into the grass and was munching happily, despite Daniel's best efforts to pull her away with the reins.

"You're not a natural born horseman are you, my dear?" Henrietta giggled, pulling up alongside him and letting her own, apparently far better behaved mount, join in with Martha's feast.

"Never had much call to ride them in Smithfield; however, I'm highly skilled at jumping out of the way of both their hooves and their shit."

They spent a good long while smiling at each other before she leaned over and kissed him lightly on the lips. For perhaps the hundredth time that day Daniel stopped himself from telling Henrietta that he loved her.

Henrietta pulled away with Martha's reins in her hand, yanking them forcefully enough to drag the reluctant animal from her meal and leading them both back up the bank.

"A *firm* hand," she repeated pointedly, before returning the reins to Daniel.

"I know," he sighed, patting the back of Martha's neck, "I just don't want to hurt her."

"Strength is required when riding a horse Daniel, 'tis only a lady that responds to gentleness…"

With that, she headed off along the edge of the woods

leaving him with no alternative but to persuade the ever-hungry Martha to follow suit. Though the horse was reluctant to leave the vegetation in peace, she eventually waddled after Henrietta and fell in step behind her mount, Blythe.

Despite the natural wariness of horses that most Londoners quickly developed as a means of avoiding being trampled to death on the city's chaotic streets, coupled with Martha's natural preference for eating over moving, Daniel found that he was rather enjoying himself. The afternoon sun was warm and although the air was sticky with moist summer heat they were skirting the edge of woodland and mostly rode in the comforting shade.

Daniel had initially found it unnerving to live in a place that lacked the constant noise, stink and random violence of London, however, he found he was slowly adjusting to the countryside. He'd even become accustomed to his spit not being black anymore.

Along with most of the Quality, every year the Duke of Pevansea moved his household out of London before the summer heat made the city air too fetid and heavy with disease-ridden miasmas. However, this year the Duke had insisted his wife and children moved to his country seat at Babbington on the Essex-Suffolk borders early to ensure their safety, for London had become increasingly volatile as the unrest concerning the King grew.

The Duke's caution had proved justified for the following month the Queen had produced a male heir for her husband, James Francis. Rumours had swept the city that the boy was a changeling, smuggled into the Queen's chamber in a bedpan to replace (depending on which rumour you preferred) her stillborn son/healthy daughter/cloven-hoofed offspring of the Devil, in order to ensure that King James had a Catholic heir to succeed him in preference to his fervently Protestant eldest daughter Mary, the wife of William of Orange-Nassau.

The mob were, apparently, most unhappy.

However, London seemed a distant land to Daniel, who felt so far removed from the business of Kings and Parliaments here that even the dark mutterings of a new Civil War that emanated bleakly from the other servants when they gathered around the kitchen table to eat did little to darken his mood. He had found life on the estate to be almost blissful, for the Duke spent even less time here than he had in St James' Square and at some point, he wasn't entirely sure when, he had been promoted from humble footman to the Duchess' semi-official "companion."

He was certain that every member of the household, apart from Henrietta's two young children, knew exactly what his duties actually entailed, but while he had initially feared for their lack of discretion regarding the Duchess' honour, everybody seemed quite content to turn the blindest of eyes to their relationship.

Daniel put this down to the fact most of the staff at Babbington, be they those that maintained the House throughout the year or those that had travelled up from the London residence, were exceedingly loyal to the Duchess. Henrietta not only treated all of her staff with great kindness but also ensured they were paid as well as any servant in London. Now it was a thought he rarely dwelled on, for, like virtually all his other thoughts and concerns, it had been entirely submerged by his happiness, his desire for Henrietta and the fact he was quite, quite hopelessly in love with her.

His infatuation for her had grown into something far more after his desire had been consummated in those little rooms in Piccadilly; now he ached to be even momentarily separated from her and each second he spent with her in the company of others, when for the sake of form and honour he had, at least, to attempt to convey the deceit that he was no more than her servant, was the most dreadful of tortures, for it meant he was unable to hold her hand or her eyes, to kiss her or stroke her hair, to slide his hand around her slim waist and make her laugh at his foolishness; in fact all the gestures and actions he used to express the feelings he could not use simple words to announce.

She had not forbidden him to speak of his love; it had never been discussed, but from the occasional flash of alarm he saw in her blue-grey eyes whenever he had sailed close enough to that particular word, he knew it was not permitted. It was the one Rubicon he was not allowed to cross, the one territory upon which he could not trespass.

She was young and beautiful, and her husband was old and absent. Daniel was her solace and her companion, he fulfilled the needs her husband could not, but it was not love, it could not be love, for she was a Duchess and the confines of status and society could only be stretched so far. They had no real future; that he knew, though it was a thought he pushed from his mind at every opportunity, even when the memory of his brother came to speak to him about it in the quiet, lonely hours of the night when he was separated from her.

This moment in time would be all that they could ever have together, there would never be anything else, to speak of love was to suggest something more, and that was a lie neither of them was prepared to utter. Daniel knew that well enough, but it did not stop the words burning his lips for the want of saying them.

He had unguarded moments, particularly when they were with her children, when his fancy would whisper impossible things. Initially, he had been particularly wary around young Richard and Anne, for children knew no such thing as discretion and he feared they might catch him acting inappropriately around Henrietta and mention it to their father (he had never entirely lost his fear of the Duke's rumoured fondness for the horse whip), but it was a needless fear for both children had taken to him without question. Of course, he was just another servant, but they were both sweet children and most of the household indulged them terribly, so it was not a particularly strange thing for him to play with them in the gardens to the rear of Babbington House, and when Henrietta and her children laughed at his tomfoolery, life was all the sweeter.

Neither child appeared to have inherited their father's stern aloofness, and Daniel could see much of Henrietta in both of them, Richard had her quick, intelligent eyes and easy smile while Anne already shared her mother's prettiness and, if, by God's grace, she lived to see adulthood she would be a great beauty, Daniel didn't doubt that around the turn of the century, most of the richest and most eligible bachelors in England (if not Europe) would be making tracks to Babbington.

Despite himself, sometimes, he fancied that Richard and Anne were his children and Henrietta his wife. He knew it was an idle, impossible and almost hurtful dream, but the Duke was old, and Richard was many years from his majority, Henrietta would be the guardian of the estate until her son was old enough, they could be together, a family of sorts, it would be-

He never finished the thought, because it was a thing that could never come to pass. Whenever his mind wandered in that direction, he would look up and see the memory of his brother sitting nearby, perhaps in the boughs of a tree, his legs dangling in the air while he shook his head sadly at Daniel's foolishness.

So, he lived for the moment and tried not to ponder the things that might come to pass.

There was an abandoned cottage on the edge of the estate, more a ruin than a building; it was where their rides were usually interrupted for an hour or two and Martha was left to plough through the vegetation in peace. They would eat a simple picnic of bread, cheese and summer fruits, they would talk freely, hold hands, kiss each other and finally make love on horse warmed blankets, their scents mixing with the rich, moist smells of the woods that were slowly reclaiming the cottage.

He had watched the seasons slowly melt into each other during these rides, seen the fresh green buds of spring ripen and swell, flowers burst and fruit ripen. Distant crops had grown until the fields became swaying seas of sun-kissed wheat and barley. As they rode, he watched the distant figures of peasants toiling in the sun to bring in the harvest. Life was good, the world was good. Every single thing was good, but he knew it couldn't last;

happiness was like the seasons. Eventually Jack Frost would come again and all things would wither.

It was the way the world worked.

*

Beyond Babbington time passed, momentous events unfolded as the great and the good jostled for position to rule the Kingdom according to their beliefs. Great changes were afoot, but at Babbington things had adopted a more predictable rhythm as Daniel's life became a pendulum swinging between the idyllic hours when he was alone with Henrietta and the painfully slow and agonising ones when he was not.

The household would normally return to London around the time winter's breath first started to touch the autumn breeze and Babbington would be closed up until the spring, but the Duke sent word that Henrietta and the children were to remain there until further notice. There was talk of William of Orange raising an army in the Low Countries to oust King James from the throne; a Catholic England allied with France and Spain would be too much of a threat to the Protestant states of Northern Europe to contemplate and England too much of a prize for the ambitious William to resist.

There would be war, the servants whispered despondently. Once more the young men of England would be asked to shed the blood of their brothers on English soil, this time, not over the supremacy of King or Parliament, but over God, which had always been the most terrible of things to fight over for nothing could provoke good men to do evil deeds like a dispute over religion; all knew the tales of the great atrocities that had been endured across the Channel as Protestant and Catholic armies inflicted terror and slaughter upon their foes in the pursuit of their own particular version of righteousness. Despite being Dutch, many would rally to William's Protestant flag while the King was busy raising an army of Irish and French mercenaries to defend his throne.

Daniel knew he should have been scared, for he had no wish to die for either his foolish King or his cold-hearted God, but as a young man he would be expected to choose a side and fight for it; contempt for a coward was one of the few principles shared by Protestants and Catholics alike.

As the days grew shorter and the leaves upon the trees turned to gold under Jack Frost's breath, Henrietta and Daniel's rides became less frequent, and their relationship more chaste. Henrietta would not allow him to come to her bed; she considered such an act too brazen and too much of an insult to her husband. So they spent their time more in the manner they had at the beginning of their relationship, talking together in the big house's library. Often, they would speak in French or Latin for, as a parson's daughter, Henrietta had learned only the rudiments of those tongues whilst Daniel, thanks to a natural leaning and his father's constant and demanding tutelage, enjoyed a rare fluency. They would talk about history, art, literature, philosophy and religion; though Daniel was careful to hide the fact his heart had forever been hardened to God by his brother's death. The conversations would be long and meandering affairs that filled the ever-colder days and were only interrupted by long and frequent kisses that took every care he had and locked them away in a dark and distant place.

News eventually came that the inevitable had happened and William had landed an army unopposed in Devon and was marching on London; Henrietta became distracted and fretful, keeping her children close at hand. Daniel did what he could to lift her mood, but she was reluctant to discuss her fears with him, though he could guess them well enough for the Duke was a close ally of the King and if James were to lose his throne the new regime might not treat those it saw as its enemies with any kindness, not even their children.

The Duchess' mood was echoed throughout the household as all fretted over which side they should choose, the King their master served or the usurper who shared their faith. Dark rumours of what terrors James' Irish mercenaries might inflict on good Protestant folk made many of the younger men question whether they should answer William's call for the able-bodied men of England to rally to his flag.

Arguments and even fights broke out amongst the hotter heads; Daniel could only wonder what was happening on the streets of London, whose populace had never needed much of an excuse to resort to violence. Tales of armed men galloping along the road to London were passed from servant to servant as they gathered in tight febrile knots and with each telling the numbers grew from tens to hundreds to thousands, fiery-eyed Irish brigands set on putting down the London mob on King James' command some claimed, Yorkshire men rallying to William's call others insisted.

Henrietta grew paler with worry as each new rumour flitted across the threshold of her home, and as he had done with the libels and pamphlets of London, Daniel dutifully brought each one to her, even the ones that he knew made her heartsick with worry for her husband and children. Occasionally a letter would come from the Duke, and she would retreat to her study where even Daniel was forbidden from disturbing her while she poured over the contents. Sometimes she would emerge with her mood lightened and her worries eased. Other times her brow would be creased with concern and she would find consolation only in the company of Richard and Anne, who were bright enough to know trouble was abroad, but were far too young to realise how events unfolding hundreds of miles away might affect their young lives.

Daniel never asked what the Duke wrote, he offered what comfort he could, but the concerns of great politics were not his so instead he tried to make her laugh and forget her cares a while, which he did with diminishing results as the days inexorably passed and the first snows of winter coated the estate. They'd be no war till spring, the wise old men who'd fought in the Civil War announced, winter was Jack Frost's realm and no place for men to be making war.

Henrietta broke out arms for the men to carry all the same, they would offer little protection against soldiers of course, but on the heels of war, all manner of rogues and brigands followed, and it was her responsibility to protect Babbington as best she could.

Despite her fears, Henrietta never forgot who she was, even though she may have been born a parson's daughter, she was a Duchess now, and she was responsible for all under her care until her husband returned. She hid her worries as best she could from all bar Daniel. She carried herself as a noblewoman was expected to and all drew strength from her courage. Babbington would be a grand prize for a marauding army, but no one run away, their sense of duty and their love for their young Duchess ensured they stayed.

In adversity, Daniel found he loved her even more, for she hid her fears well behind her strength and her duty, where others would have been consumed by them. Only with Daniel did she let her mask slip; in the end, she needed that which only he could give her and she eventually called him to her bedchamber despite her reservations about cuckolding her husband under his own roof.

Their lovemaking was more frantic, more needful than it had ever been before and afterwards he would hold her tightly and stroke her hair as she released her fears and cried softly into his chest. If any of the other servants noticed him creeping away from her rooms before the weak winter sun climbed over the estate's horizon, none mentioned it.

It was mid-December when the Duke returned unexpectedly. The sound of hooves on gravel sending most of the household scurrying to the windows as His Grace, John Bourness, Duke of Pevansea arrived in the company of a dozen armed men who none knew, but all recognised by their stern faces and cold eyes to be hardened soldiers.

The children had run into their father's embrace, and Daniel had looked at his feet when Henrietta had quickly followed them. The Duke had whisked his wife away into the study immediately, but the news he bore reached the ears of the household almost as soon it did hers for soldiers were as fond of gossip as servants. Beer and hot soup was pressed into their hands as they warmed themselves around the great kitchen fire and it loosened their tongues in short order.

Daniel had hovered on the fringe of the gaggle of servants that pressed around the soldiers, watching silently as they guzzled down beer and flirted with the maids. He listened to the news, but with less intent than anyone else present for his thoughts were filled with the memory of the way Henrietta had flown to her husband's arms.

There was much muttering amongst the servants as the Captain of the troop recounted events. William's army had reached London virtually unopposed save for a few skirmishes that were considered by these men to be of little importance. Most of James' men had either melted away or pledged allegiance to William rather than fight a Protestant army; the much-rumoured Irish regiments had shown little stomach for a fight and in the end, the King had shown even less, fleeing in panic before the army of his son-in-law. He had tried to gain passage to France but had been recognised by a group of fishermen in Sheerness, who had been singularly unimpressed by their King's behaviour and had handed out something of a beating before passing him over to William's men. All were of the opinion that James Stuart, by the grace of God, King of England, Scotland and Ireland, would meet the same fate as his father and the

London mob would be treated to the spectacle of another King losing his head.

When someone wondered aloud what would become of the Duke (and them) under William's rule, the Captain had taken a large draught of beer before announcing with a reassuring wink that the Duke was a "canny old goat" and they had nothing to worry about. The few cries of indignation at hearing their master so described were quickly drowned out by laughter and a collective sigh of relief.

More kegs of beer were hurriedly produced, and an impromptu celebration begun as the realisation dawned that a new Civil War had been averted, remarkably little blood had been shed, their unpopular Catholic King had been exposed as a coward, and a true Protestant would soon be sitting upon the throne of England again. Daniel, however, had long since slipped away to be alone with his thoughts by the time everybody agreed it had, all in all, been a quite glorious revolution.

*

The Duke, it appeared, was indeed a canny old goat.

Whilst everyone, including Henrietta, had believed him to have been engaged in ensuring his friend James Stuart retained the crowns of England, Scotland and Ireland, he had, in fact, been working to see that King James' daughter Mary and her husband William of Orange replaced him.

Although it might have been considered slightly bad form and more than a little ungrateful, considering all the power and wealth he had accumulated during his life had largely come to him through the patronage of James's brother, King Charles II and latterly James himself, Henrietta had explained to Daniel that, above all else, her husband's loyalty was to England. He was not so blinded by his friendship for James to realise that an openly Catholic king sitting upon the throne of Protestant England would be a disaster that would inevitably lead to another catastrophic civil war that might well rip the Kingdom apart once and for all.

While Charles II had been in all but name a Catholic, he'd been an intelligent enough man to know this to be true, and he'd had the good grace to not formally to convert to Catholicism until his death bed. Everybody might have suspected he was a Catholic, but he had ruled as a Protestant and that had been enough. However, although James shared his brother's taste for women, gambling and drinking he appeared to have missed out on his common sense. When he'd succeeded to the throne it had always been his intention to rule as a Catholic and to set in train a chain of events that would eventually return England to the Church of Rome, if not in his lifetime then certainly in that of his son's.

Almost from the moment of his succession, the Duke

of Pevansea had worked with those plotting to oust James from the throne and install Mary. It was a dangerous game to play and one that would have seen him executed as a traitor if James had caught wind of his treason, but it had worked. The birth of James' son had been the catalyst and now James languished in custody, the Duke had no doubt Parliament would ask Mary to succeed her father; her husband William would not serve as her regent so they would sit upon the throne of England as joint monarchs.

When Daniel had asked Henrietta whether James would be executed, she had shaken her head but would say no more. A few days later news came that James had managed to escape, and, this time, made his way to France unhindered by the fishermen of Sheerness. Perhaps it had been a daring escape, but Daniel got the impression that neither the Duke nor the new Queen to be had wanted to see James die – after all he was her father – and his escape had provided a convenient solution to a potentially messy problem.

The Duke intended to stay a few days at Babbington before returning to London for there remained much work to be done in both Lords and Commons to ensure Parliament decreed that James' flight was an act of abdication and anointed William and Mary as his successors.

Daniel had seen little of the Duke in the last six

months, but it seemed he had aged a decade in that time. Where before he had been spare of frame, now he was gaunt, where before his back had been ruler straight, now there was a slight stoop, the trials of his endeavours (or treasons some would have said) had carved and chiselled new furrows around his eyes while each and every movement he made was that of an old man beset by pain and indescribable tiredness. Only his eyes seemed unchanged, bright and alert they burned with a fierce intelligence that Daniel thought might well make a man's knees turn to jelly if they were to bore upon him with sufficient intent.

Inevitably, with the Duke present, his time with Henrietta became both fleeting and chaste; they exchanged a few words when he served her tea in the afternoon, but there were no smiles, no discreet touches of the hand, no kisses. Daniel had expected her mood to brighten now that the matters of state had been resolved, and the danger of war appeared to have passed, but if anything she seemed, even more, distracted and he often found her staring distantly into space, her mind clearly far away from her body.

He yearned for things to be as they were. For the Duke to return to London and Henrietta to be alone with him, or as close as you could be to being alone when you shared a house with several dozen servants, but he feared even when the Duke left Henrietta would remain changed for the cold bleakness of Jack Frost's realm seemed to have somehow seeped into his lover's heart.

One afternoon when he brought her tea she asked him to sit with her, which he gladly did. They sat in silence for a while, her tea and cakes untouched, until she finally stood and walked to the window to look out over the window at the snow dusted gardens of Babbington. It had turned fiercely cold, and frost still clung to the corners of the window panes, despite himself Daniel wondered whether the King of the Winter might have been peeping into the house looking to see what naughtiness had been going on inside.

"Is... something wrong?" Daniel eventually asked tentatively.

"No," Henrietta whispered sadly, "everything is wonderful."

As she looked back at him, he thought her beauty was almost too terrible to behold in the flat winter light of the window.

"I am with child."

Daniel blinked and found himself thankful that he was sitting down, "How... how is that possible?"

"'tis quite a simple process really Daniel," Henrietta replied with a slight smile, seemingly almost despite herself.

"I know, but I thought... well, there are herbs and

potions..."

"I have never taken the council of a Cunning Woman, 'tis what I wanted."

"But the Duke... he will know the child cannot be his, you have barely seen him these past six months!" Daniel cried in alarm.

Henrietta returned her attention to the window, "The Duke is well pleased," she said quietly.

"The Duke knows?"

"The Duke has always known Daniel."

"That you may take a lover, yes, but..."

Henrietta turned and faced him once more, "I have not been entirely honest with you Daniel, I had intended to dismiss you without explaining matters fully, but I have grown quite fond of you, and your companionship through these last difficult few weeks has been greatly appreciated. I owe you the truth at least."

"What truth? I have always known what is between us, that we can never truly be together. I know that. I have accepted that, I-"

She stilled his voice with a flick of her hand, "The truth Daniel is that this is what my husband and I required, another child. Young Richard is a strong and healthy boy, but one male heir is never enough. The Duke's injuries were more severe than I led you to believe, the wound he received in the Civil War... unmanned him. It is not so much that it is difficult for him to please a woman, it is impossible for him. He cannot father children."

"But Richard and Anne?"

"Are no more his children than this child will be."

"So, who is their father?"

"Fathers," Henrietta corrected, "fine young men Daniel, fine young men like you that the Duke and I chose to produce an heir for him. The fact is Daniel, with no heir all that my husband has achieved would pass to his nephews, who are wastrels to a man, His Grace could not bear the thought of his fortune being squandered on cards and whores by those fools. So this is what we did."

Daniel could think of nothing to say and was only vaguely aware that his mouth was hanging open.

"His Grace thinks you a fine young man Daniel, sound of body and quick of mind. He is confident you have provided him with a strong and healthy son. He is most grateful."

"Is that all I have been?" Daniel asked incredulously as something thick and wretched uncurled heavily in the pit of his stomach, "something for you to breed with? Something for the Duke to service his wife with like the stud he brings in to service his favourite mares?"

"Of course not Daniel," Henrietta insisted, "I am very fond of you."

"Fond? Like the Duke is fond of his horse and hounds,

how do I compare my Lady? Am I rated more highly than Blythe perhaps? And the hunting dogs, where do I rank in comparison, who would be thrown the juiciest scrap from the table I wonder?"

"Daniel, please do not be so... *emotional* this has not really been a burden for you has it? It has not been so terrible a chore? You will be well rewarded for this, we are not so callous as to discard you with no more than a by your leave. We are both extremely grateful."

"That means so very much," he spat.

"Daniel, I really don't approve of your tone, let us not be bitter about this. His Grace and I will be returning to London shortly, now that matters are settled it is vital the Quality are once more to be seen in Town so that all will appreciate that order has been restored, plus, of course, there is a coronation to be planned. You will not be returning with us, I will see you receive a most handsome severance and references that will open the door to any House in England though frankly you are far too bright to be in service, I hope the money will be used wisely to improve your station. We will not speak again, you will not see me again, and if you have any ideas of spreading malicious tales about the parentage of this child, well, let us say, that will be a most foolish thing to do, but I know you are not a fool Daniel."

"Why do I have to leave?" Daniel asked quietly, his

eyes wide and pleading.

"Why, what else can you do? Stay here and watch your child being brought up as another man's, knowing that the child will never know you as anything other than a servant? No, quite impossible... as much as I will miss you."

"But... I love you."

Henrietta sighed deeply, "I know you do and I am truly sorry for that, but what else is to be done? You expect me to run away with you and live as some footman's wife, give up all I have for a life of squalor and want. I am fond of you, but not that fond, nobody could ever be *that* fond of someone."

"I don't care about anything else! Just let me stay, I will say nothing, do nothing to cause you harm or embarrassment, just let me be with you," Daniel choked, the words tumbling over his tears, he hated himself for begging to her, like a favourite dog pleading for a scrap of her affection, but the thought of never seeing her, or holding her, or kissing her again set his heart afire with unspeakable misery.

"I am so very sorry Daniel, but that simply cannot be for you would go mad with the misery of it in the end and even I am not so cruel as to wish that upon you." Her faced softened and she moved closer to him, "I am so very sorry, my sweetheart."

Daniel looked up at her with wet miserable eyes, it was

the closest she had ever come to saying she loved him, and he knew it was the closest she was ever going to get. The tears and loathing came over him in alternating waves. Henrietta stood above him uncertainly, before crouching a little and pulling him to her. Daniel tried to turn away, but it was only a momentary resistance for he could not refuse the comfort of her final caress.

Her hand softly stroked his hair, and he half turned his face away from her for fear she would feel his tears upon her skin. He felt her heart thundering against his ear and wished he could hear some echo of his own pain and loss in its beat.

"*J'entends ton coeur,*" he mumbled finally in a thick and miserable voice.

"And I hear yours, my beautiful Danny," she replied, "I hear yours too..."

...

Chapter Eleven

A Bad Man's Song

Lincoln's Inn Fields, London - 1708

The Doctor had already begun his breakfast of smoked fish by the time Caleb entered the dining room, and he realised with a little surprise that he was quite ravenous.

"I hope you are partial to fish, Mr Cade?" The Doctor boomed as he attacked his breakfast with some gusto, "I find it to be excellent for the brain!"

Caleb took a seat, and Rothery's man Scaife arrived within moments to place a plate with two large smoked herrings before him.

"Sleep well?" Rothery asked between mouthfuls.

Caleb offered a weak smile, "As well as could be expected."

"A hearty breakfast and a good walk on such a fine morning as this will dispel any horrors that still play on your mind."

"Indeed, I was hoping to ask-" Caleb was interrupted by the arrival of a young woman into the dining room. She was in her early twenties, he guessed, tall and graceful she wore a modest cream dress of little embellishment while her long red hair had been arranged without fuss into a simple bun. Alyssa appeared quite ordinary, the vivacious and playful creature he'd briefly met in the hall, with her vaguely wanton smile and sparkling mischievous eyes, was quite transformed into the respectful and dutiful daughter.

"I didn't realise we had a guest, father?" She asked innocently from the doorway, tilting her head slightly to one side as she looked at Caleb.

"My dear, how very remiss of me," the Doctor said rising stiffly, "Mr Cade, may I present my daughter, Miss Alyssa Rothery."

"Delighted," Caleb said rising to bow formally and bestowing his warmest smile.

"'tis a pleasure to meet you," Alyssa replied, holding his eye for a moment before taking a seat at the table.

"My friend here was set upon by a ruffian the other night," Dr Rothery explained, "luckily we managed to chase the rascal off before any harm was done, but I thought it best if Mr Cade spent some time with us until he has quite recovered. He was a little shaken."

"How awful!" Alyssa exclaimed, "you didn't hurt yourself did you father, I do wish-"

"I'm perfectly fine my dear - one hearty blow from my stick and the scoundrel disappeared."

"Dr Rothery was most brave," Caleb confirmed, examining Alyssa carefully as her father gave her an extremely edited version of events. She was unmarried and not without a degree of comeliness. Judging by the size and decoration of the Doctor's house his patients were clearly generous in their reward of his labours. No doubt the old man could provide a handsome dowry for the suitor who took his daughter's hand.

He sighed inwardly at the old familiar whispers of his fancy; the situation fitted him like an old and comfortable glove, it was normality, it was what he did; charm and deceive, plot and calculate. At once, the world seemed normal again. Nothing had changed, no monsters stalked him, no horrors tried to damn his soul; only a tempting young woman and the money that went with her. It was the way his world was made.

Except...

"You are new to London, Mr Cade?" Alyssa was asking, her tone even and polite.

"Not entirely," Caleb replied, returning his thoughts to the matter at hand, "I've travelled extensively, but this is the first time I've been in London for many years."

"I do hope these unpleasantries haven't soured you to the city's charms?"

The girl clearly knew nothing of vampires judging by her father's explanation of events. "I'm afraid cutthroats are not unique to London; wherever men gather wrongdoing will follow."

"That is sadly true," Alyssa agreed.

"Mr Cade is here on business, I believe," Dr Rothery said, steering the conversation gently away from Caleb's encounter with Defane.

Caleb slipped easily into the routine of deceit, explaining how his father needed capital to invest in a venture to mine tin from the hills that made up part of the family estate.

"I wish you every success Mr Cade," Alyssa smiled softly, "you have come such a long way, it must be a burden to be away from your family.

"In truth, I have spent much of my time away from home. I have suffered from wanderlust for many years, much to my father's chagrin. But my father is no longer a young man and it is time to put my travels behind me. I will one day, hopefully many years hence, inherit my father's title and it is time I devoted myself to the estate."

The lies sat comfortably on Caleb's lips, the false tale of his wealth and inheritance had opened many doors for him over the years. He had learned long ago that if one dressed and presented yourself as a gentleman people would tend to believe whatever unlikely tale you chose to weave, despite the fact that the wealthy were just as prone to lying, cheating and deceiving as the poor.

"'tis a father's lot to worry about the paths their children choose to follow," The Doctor sighed glancing at his daughter as he pushed his plate gently away from him.

"I fear my father believes I am a terribly troublesome child Mr Cade," Alyssa smiled softly at her father.

Caleb's eyes lingered upon Alyssa once more. It was a scene he'd played so many times before, and, as always, he wondered what she would be like in bed, how easily she might succumb to his charms, how delicious the conquest might be. But this time, other thoughts crowded into his mind. What it would be like to take her in his arms and lower his mouth to her long graceful neck? How would her soft skin feel against his lips? What the sensation of sinking his teeth into her yielding skin would be like? How joyous would be the moment when the skin burst and her hot, sweet, young blood spurted into his mouth? How she would moan with pleasure as she pushed herself hard against him, her breasts against his chest as she yearned for him to drink from her until she embraced oblivion.

"Why Miss Rothery," Caleb smiled, "I can't believe you would be any trouble at all...."

*

Caleb took the Doctor's advice, but a brisk walk through the teaming congested streets did little to ease his troubles; particularly the disturbing images that Alyssa had provoked at the breakfast table. Not only had the thought of ripping open her neck with his teeth been one that had returned again and again while he talked to the girl, he'd found it incredibly arousing. So much so that he hadn't been able to leave the table until Alyssa had excused herself after thirty minutes of bothering her fish disinterestedly with a fork. When she'd leaned closer to him to whisper conspiratorially that she hated fish he'd had to fight a terrible urge to grip her by the hair and pull her neck towards his teeth.

He'd almost seen the blood spurt over the crisp white linen of the table cloth.

Even just thinking about it again made him pull up and place a hand against a wall to steady himself; it took several deep breaths of pungent London air to chase the thought away.

Although Caleb was well acquainted with all his many vices and weaknesses, he'd never been a violent man and certainly not towards women; this sudden desire shocked him profoundly.

"The vampiric essence..." he hissed, once he had stopped shaking. That could be the only answer; some part of Defane had leached into him when the vampire had opened his neck, some minute portion of it, not enough to physically change him, but enough to allow some echo of a

vampire's desires to take root in his soul.

I am not a vampire.

He composed himself and adjusted his coat as a few passers-by eyed him curiously, some possibly out of concern for his well-being, others no doubt ready to make the most of their good fortune if he was about to drop down dead. He was wearing an expensive coat and good boots after all and Londoners hated seeing expensive coats and good boots go to waste.

Caleb moved on again at a brisk and confident pace to demonstrate his good health. Several times he glanced up and squinted into the greasy morning sunlight, but finding it had no effect other than searing diffuse images of the sun on the back of his eyes and giving him a mild headache, he was reassured that he wasn't actually turning into a vampire.

As a further test, he found two pretty young maids on Chancery Lane out on errands and followed them for a while; forcing himself to stare at their necks. His only reaction was a wistful fancy to bed the pair of them together, which he considered being entirely normal and healthy.

He walked a while longer before deciding his mind was probably simply over tired, all this talk of vampires was as much to blame as any vampiric essence, whatever that might be.

What he needed was a strong dose of normality. Something far removed from the strange events that had unfurled around him these last few days, yes, that would be just the ticket. Something to anchor himself back to reality with, something to reconnect him to the normal world.

Or rather someone.

*

There was a green book in the window above the shop, but Caleb entered anyway as he didn't particularly care if Brindley was present or not.

Harriet was immersed in some arcane bookish practice, cataloguing perhaps, when Caleb forced the reluctant shop door to begrudgingly open enough to let him in. When she looked up it was clear several conflicting emotions were fighting to take centre stage; surprise chief among them, but then so were anger, hurt and disappointment.

"I've missed you," Caleb said quietly, surprised to find that he wasn't lying in the slightest; which was almost as disturbing as wanting to rip out Alyssa Rothery's throat.

Harriet blinked and her mouth twitched, but as nothing else followed Caleb decided to press on, "I suppose you are mad at me, if I could have sent word I would have, but th-"

The flat of Harriet's hand on his cheek suggested

maybe he shouldn't have pressed on.

"You're quite upset, I see," Caleb ventured after taking a step backwards to ensure he was out of range.

"I think you should go," Harriet said simply, her hands returning to the more familiar territory of her books as she stared at him with eyes that were noticeably red and puffy.

"I just wanted to apologise."

"Very noble of you, am I to be honoured with an explanation also?"

"Well..." Caleb hesitated, it was one thing to lie to Rothery, but he didn't want to deceive Harriet; he'd found the concept of a relationship with a woman that wasn't built on deceit to be strangely refreshing, but vampires? She'd think he'd become deranged or that he was must mocking her, either way, she'd probably try to hit him again; "...'tis complicated Harriet."

"Oh, I am sure it is! No doubt you have devised some intricate explanation, a string of calamitous events that kept you from my door..." Harriet spat, before adding in a small quavering voice, "...and my bed."

"I have devised nothing," Caleb sighed, the sight of her large watery eyes looking up at him made him want to gather her up in his arms, "I simply cannot tell you."

"You cannot?" Harriet repeated, before biting down on her quivering lip.

"I do not want to lie to you, which is unusual for me as I find it most convenient to lie to people in general and women in particular, but in this instance, the truth sounds too fanciful, too fantastical. You would not believe me, and I have no wish to give you another reason to be angry with me. All I will say is I truly wish I had been able to come to you, for if I had the world would not seem so strange to me as it does now and a man I considered a friend would perhaps still be alive, even though I accept it is probably better he is dead."

Harriet made no move to respond, she simply stood regarding him with uncharacteristic boldness, only her hands moving to find comfort in the solace of the worn bindings of her books. Caleb tried to smile, but when it garnered no response he let it fade.

He wished he had sent Defane away with a flea in his ear and had come to Harriet, how much a life can change in one small decision, in one moment everything becomes different, and no matter how hard you might wish it to be otherwise the world is irrevocably altered.

"How simple I am," Harriet said finally, her voice more composed than before, "that I would take your pretty words and believe them, for I want to believe them, honestly, I do, for nobody wishes to believe themselves to be a fool, 'tis the very worst of revelations and people are prepared to contort their worlds in order to deny that truth from their hearts. I wanted to share my bed with you, give you the most precious thing I have, the *only* thing that I have to give, even though, in doing so, I would be turning my back on much that I hold to be good and true. I am a foolish and lonely woman, and I allowed myself to be ensnared by your charm, to become enraptured by the glamour of a bad man's song. I see more clearly now."

"Harriet, I have told you no lies, in fact, I have told you more truths than..." his hand clawed at the air in exasperation, "...*anyone* I've ever known, I do care for you."

"How cheap are your words, even when you make them trickle so sweetly."

"I am sorry, I understand this was not some frivolous thing; I assure you there was no flippancy on my part, in my actions. I made a decision, a bad one, but it was not taken as a slight upon you. I had every intention of being here, but circumstances dictated otherwise."

"Ah, circumstances dictated, did they?" she snapped, anger rising in her voice as quickly as the flush to her cheeks, "and in what form did these circumstances take? Which pretty doxy was it? Which captivating harlot? Which comely manner of whore did you forsake plain little Harriet's humble favours for?"

Caleb frowned and cocked his head to one side, "Er... what exactly are you talking about Harriet?"

"Oh, such innocence! Such bravado! You have missed

your vocation, Sir; though what is a loss to the theatre lover has no doubt proven to be an immense boon to the brothel keepers of Europe!" Harriet abandoned the protection of her books to stand before him, physically shaking with rage, her hands tightened to hard white-knuckled fists.

"I have never claimed to be an innocent-"

"No, you did not, but nor I did not think you so cruel that you would come into my lonely little world and give me some flicker of happiness! Some hope as to what life might be able to offer beyond dust and books and then on the very night I was to give you my virginity, you snub me in favour of a night spent cavorting with whores!"

"I did not!" Caleb protested.

"Do not lie to me anymore, Father saw you!"

"Your father?"

"He was leafleting outside one of the most notorious bawdy houses in London that night and saw you enter, as bold as brass and twice as drunk. The very night you promised to lay with me!"

Caleb shook his head and smiled thinly in rueful disbelief.

"The bastard."

Harriet hit him, harder than before, and then again, her arms flailing in fury until Caleb managed to catch hold of both her wrists. She writhed and struggled in his grip, trying to kick his shins all the time screaming incomprehensible words of rage in hot spittle-flecked gasps.

"Shall I tell you about your father!" Caleb eventually shouted back, "do you want to know? Do you?"

"Get out!" Harriet sobbed, her foot finally making a hard enough connection with Caleb's shin for him to cry out in pain. He pushed her away with more force than he had intended, she stumbled and lost her footing, falling backwards onto the floor. She simply lay there panting, her hair fallen about her face, her miserable tear-streaked eyes looking up at him.

"Shall I tell you about your father?" Caleb repeated in a calmer tone.

"More lies," she muttered.

"Your father..." where should he begin he wondered; that her father was a sodomite? That he runs a molly house for rich men with a fancy for young boys? Perhaps he should mention her mother didn't run away with an undertaker but threw herself into the Thames? Oh, and he certainly shouldn't miss out on the part about him keeping her in poverty and servitude whilst keeping his own ill-gotten riches a secret.

He ran a hand through his long dark hair and knew there was no point; she would just think him a liar and even if she did believe him then it probably would destroy her.

"I did see your father that night," Caleb finally said

softly, "but it was not as he described it to you."

Harriet said nothing, but, at least, she wasn't trying to batter him to death anymore.

"He had found out I was seeing you, he was not greatly impressed. He paid me money to stop."

"My father has no money."

"That is not *entirely* true," Caleb reached into his coat pocket and pulled out the two purses Brindley had given him.

"I have a fondness for gold and a fear of violent fathers, I took the money, I am ashamed to say," Caleb tossed the purses onto the table where they landed with enough of a heavy metallic clunk to cause a momentary pang of regret somewhere deep down inside him, somewhere close to where his soul used to be he suspected.

"I now wish to return the money."

"Where would my father get such money from?"

"You would need to ask him that Harriet, you will also need to ask him why he wants to keep you here alone and unloved forever. You think it is because you are plain and unbecoming that no man has ever wooed you? Harriet, you are quite lovely, and the fact that you are alone is because your father ensures it. He will pay off any suitor who comes near to you, he does it, not out of meanness or cruelty, but out of a twisted kind of love for a daughter he fears is too good for an unforgiving world that is full of men like me."

Caleb held out his hand to help Harriet back to her feet, she accepted it after a moment's hesitation and allowed herself to be pulled up.

"You look a state," Caleb noted, handing her his handkerchief.

"'tis my normal condition," she sniffed.

"Not at all."

Harriet picked up one of the purses of coins, "How much is there here?"

"I don't know; I never counted it."

"I would have thought in matters of money men would be more precise."

"I was too disgusted with myself."

"I do not know whether I should be more insulted that you forwent my bed for a whore or a bribe. I will need to think upon it for some time." Harriet tossed one of the purses up into the air a few times to test its weight. "If this is a lie 'tis a very expensive one."

"Do you believe me?"

"I don't know," she sighed, "perhaps in part... I think there is more, but I am not sure they are things I truly wish to hear."

"I have lived a bad life Harriet; I have stolen, lied and cheated. I had a fortune once. It should have lasted a lifetime, but I squandered it all in the name of pleasure; for the turn of a card, for the throw of a dice, for a bottle of wine and a whore's delights. In its passing I developed a rich man's taste but no means of making money. No means bar one. I found I had a gift for winning the affections of women, and I have used that gift to live in wealth and comfort. It is not how I intended to live my life, but that is what happened, I am no more than a charmer who woos women for their money; a sharper of hearts if you like. Now I have come home and I want to be different, I want to be who I once was. I have never lied to you Harriet and I never will; I am just weak and foolish and undeserving of your affection."

"Although I have limited experience in the matters," Harriet said, placing the purse back on the table, "you do appear to have a singularly unusual manner of wooing a woman."

"'tis far easier when I simply lie," Caleb admitted with a sigh.

"I cannot trust you, Caleb, I do not know you or understand you and as lonely as my life is I understand it," she indicated the purses on the table, "you should take your money and go..."

"I don't want the money, I want your friendship."

Harriet smiled, "Whatever your reasons, be it money or whores, you have hurt me too badly for that ever to be possible. A woman's virtue might be a trivial thing for a man like you, but it is all I have. I see that now, and if I am to give it to any man then it should be for a man who appreciates its worth and would not be so easily *distracted*," she took a few small steps away from him.

"Please Harriet, I am so sorry..."

"I am sure a part of you thinks you are, and no doubt you will leave accompanied by all manner of regrets, at least until the next woman crosses your path. You say you wish to change, but I do not believe it is in your capacity to change Mr Cade. You would hurt me again, eventually, because you are not capable of loving me, perhaps you are not capable of loving anyone, even yourself."

"I want to change..."

"Wanting is not enough, please leave now... leave me alone to my little life."

"Take the money Harriet, you don't have to give it back to your father, you can use it to build a new life, a better life."

"That would simply be running away, is that not what you did?"

Caleb nodded, not wanting to meet her eye.

"And what was the result of all that running?"

"It just brought me home again... in the end."

"That is all you can offer me, isn't it? A life spent running away, a life without love or purpose or foundation. That would be all your hollow friendship could ever amount to, I think I will stay where I am, thank you very much. Take the money and go, whether it is my father's or not, I think it will always be closer to your heart than any woman will ever manage. Goodbye, Caleb."

He tried to take a step towards her, but she simply turned her back. He hesitated, wishing there was something he could say because he had never intended to hurt her, but what could he say? That he'd fallen under a vampire's glamour? That all she said was false? That his friendship was something of worth? No, she was right; he had nothing to offer her at all.

"Goodbye, Harriet," was all he managed to say. He thought she made some small noise that could have been a stifled sob, but perhaps that was just his fancy. His eyes lingered on the bags of coin for a moment, but he turned sharply and left them where they were for even the sight of them filled him with disgust.

*

He awoke with a strangled cry and remembered.

His heart raced and his body was slick with sweat, but he made no move to open his eyes or shift in his bed. He was too busy clinging to the memory, like a drowning sailor desperately clutching some piece of flotsam that had unexpectedly bobbed up in front of him. Instead, he lay still until he was sure it was not just the remnants of a dream. Sleep fell quickly away from him, and he felt strangely rejuvenated as if he had never truly been awake before.

He remembered.

The promises Defane had made in the moments before he died; the touch of his lips on his skin, the mad beauty of his eyes, the way his face had *shifted*, the sweet intoxicating taste of his blood, the pain as his strange elongated teeth had burst through the yielding skin of his neck, the wet eager noises of the vampire as he'd sucked the life blood from him. He remembered everything, but above all, he remembered the love he'd felt; that momentary all-consuming love that had made the very loss of his life seem an irrelevance in comparison.

It was no more than a vampire's glamour of course; some trick Defane had played in order to drink his blood, in the same way he'd tricked Liselot and Massingham with those cards. Perhaps, but for the first time in twenty years he'd loved somebody; genuinely, utterly and completely. The fact that it was no more real than that which he thought he'd once shared with Henrietta was irrelevant; he had felt it, known it and been consumed by it.

And now that he remembered it, he missed it terribly.

Would it be possible to live an eternity feeling like that? Feeling that love, feeling that pleasure; would his immortal soul be such a price to pay to know such things? He had lived most his life in the dark anyway.

He did not doubt that if the vampire hunters had not

found them, then he would have died, and fifty years hence Defane might still be lying next to his bones in some dusty forgotten room, but what if... what if it *had* worked and Defane had changed him, would he still have felt that love? Would he still feel the pure, undiluted pleasure that had coursed through his veins as Defane had drunk from him?

He felt a vague but very real sense of loss; turning restlessly, he opened his eyes and stared out across the darkened room.

Given that the memory of his brother would often visit him in the small dark hours when he was closest to sleep, he was less inclined to be startled by the sight of a ghostly form standing by his bed than most people.

"Caleb?"

"You think me a mirror?" a woman's voice replied.

"Miss Rothery?"

"There is no need to be so formal," she smiled radiantly in the darkness.

"What are you doing here?"

"I heard you call out; I thought you were in distress?"

"No... it was just a nightmare," Caleb insisted sitting up.

"It must have been a most dreadful nightmare; I am surprised it did not wake the house?"

"I am very sorry, I apologise for waking you."

"I was already awake; I was prowling the house as I

often do in the small hours."

"Another assignment?"

"How improper you are to suggest such a thing."

Without invitation, she crossed the room and sat gently on the edge of his bed. She wore a long billowing white cotton nightdress that would have been a most modest garment if she had bothered to lace up the front of it properly; she reached out and placed her hand against his bare chest, her palm was cool and smooth against his own sticky dream warmed flesh.

"Tell me about your dream?"

"There is nothing to tell, you know the way of dreams. It was one of those that are barely remembered once you wake," Caleb replied uncertainly. Her scent, a heady mixture of rosemary and bergamot was strong enough to dispel the stink of pungent sweat that clung to him.

"Liar," she smiled, "you are drenched in sweat, and your heart beats so fiercely I can almost hear it in the dark. It must have been a most terrible nightmare."

"Perhaps my heart thunders because I find a beautiful young woman is sitting on my bed," this was not entirely a lie; he regularly awoke with an erection even when he was sleeping alone; the combination of her presence, her perfume and her touch made the familiar stirring almost inevitable, but the desires that he felt circling within him were not all familiar ones.

"I assure you, Mr Cade, I am a respectable young woman, who would on no account creep into the bedroom of a man I have barely been introduced to. I think it is probable you are still dreaming."

"If this is but a dream, then I may do as I wish for none of it is real."

"Indeed, that is true, though it would suggest you are a particularly low and lustful beast if your dreams are filled with nothing more than your fancies for whatever particular wee lass has most recently crossed your path."

"'tis fortunate then that you are no more than a dream, for otherwise you would see the truth of me and no doubt be most terribly appalled."

"I saw the truth of you from the moment I laid eyes upon you."

Caleb grinned and reached out to stroke her cheek, "You are cold?"

"'tis the wee hours Mr Cade, the fires are dead and the sun is a distant memory."

"Why don't you let me warm you?"

Gently she pulled down the blankets that still covered Caleb from the waist down.

"Do you always sleep naked?"

"If I had been expecting visitors perhaps I would have dressed more appropriately."

Her eyes slid over his body; although the room

was dark, he thought she could still see well enough. Slowly she lay down with her back to him, pulling the blankets back up to cover them both. Caleb lay behind her, the soft cotton of her nightdress against his still clammy skin. Tentatively he placed a hand on her hip.

"You may hold me," she whispered into the darkness, "but no more."

Caleb did as she bid, his arm snaking around to pull her closer to him, her own fingers found his hand between her heavy breasts and entwined with his.

They lay in silence for a while, Caleb wrestling with his desire as he rested his face in the soft fiery curls that tumbled loosely down her back. His lips were but a few inches from her throat, and for the most fleeting of moments the taste of hot coppery blood filled his mouth and his body ached for the want of it.

"You are aroused?" Alyssa asked, somewhat unnecessarily.

Caleb shifted his hips slightly, "Do not fret my lady; I will not let it come between our new-found friendship."

Alyssa giggled in the darkness, "I knew I would like you."

"You do not know me at all."

"This is when I find men to be at their most attractive, for I have yet to be made aware of all their failings."

"Is that why you remain unmarried?"

"I crawl into the beds of strange men Mr Cade; do you not think *that* may be why I remain unmarried?"

"In my experience, marriage does not entirely forgo the possibility of such practices."

"Perhaps, but contrary to my appearance as a respectable physician's daughter, I am a wild and free spirit. Society might dictate I should be wed, but I have no desire to be any man's chattel. I am sure my behaviour would scandalise polite society, which, I suppose, is why I do my utmost to avoid polite society. I hope you do not think sharing a bed for warmth is so brazen that you must ask my father for my hand in order to protect our honour?"

"I generally never ask for a woman's hand until I've ravished them a few times."

"Well, there will be no ravishing here. Not tonight at least."

"How do you know I am not the manner of man who will simply take what he wants regardless?"

"I do not... which makes this all the more exciting; a little fear once in a while is a good way of reminding yourself that you are still alive."

"'tis a dangerous way of thinking."

"I am in no danger."

"You do not know me..."

"You are a man and, therefore, I know the best way to ensure my safety."

"How so?"

"If you were to try anything I would simply pluck your manhood from your groin like a gnarled old carrot from moist soil."

Caleb winced at the imagery, "I think such a thing would likely see you sent to Bedlam Hospital for the rest of your days."

"We are all lunatics Cade, 'tis only the manner of our asylum that differs."

He thought of all the people sleeping under this roof tonight, himself included, and decided she might have a point. "What would be the manner of your asylum then?"

"Too many questions," she mumbled sleepily, "this house is horribly cold, please just hold me and warm me, let me find a little rest..."

Caleb did as she asked. Despite his arousal and the disturbing vampiric thoughts that flitted around the darker corners of his mind, he found it a comfort simply to lie with her and listen to her slow rhythmic breathing in the darkness. If he had been alone thoughts of Defane and Harriet would have harried sleep away from his mind, but with one arm slung protectively over Alyssa he found sleep soon took him again.

*

The bed was empty when he awoke.

He had slept long and dreamlessly; sharp morning

light was already spearing around the drapes as he sat up in the bed and rubbed the sleep from his eyes. He wondered if Alyssa actually had snuck into his bed during the night. It did seem a particularly unlikely event, perhaps it had just been a dream.

He sat on the edge of the bed awhile, a blanket pulled around his shoulders, and wished his brother would appear for there was so much he wished to talk about, but no matter how hard he had tried the memory of his brother was something he had never been able to conjure at will. From whatever peculiar and distant part of his mind the memory resided in, he came and went as he chose; which was invariably when Caleb least expected it.

Caleb sighed heavily and pulled himself to his feet, he might lie in bed all day, and his brother wouldn't appear. He poured cold water from the jug into the basin by the bed; wincing as he gingerly washed before dressing quickly for the room was chilly. The house about him was silent though his pocket watch told him that it was gone eleven o'clock, which, even by his standards, was slovenly.

For a few minutes, he stood by the window and watched the traffic rattle and clatter outside; he toyed with the idea of going to see Harriet as she was the only other person he felt he could talk to, but quickly pushed the idea aside. He saw little point in going back just to confirm she really did hate him. He'd left no end of woman upset and broken-hearted before and had generally found the wisest course of action in such circumstances was to put as many miles between himself and any heavy objects they might find to hand as quickly as possible. He decided simply staying in the same city as Harriet demonstrated a new degree of maturity and responsibility.

Defane and Harriet, in decidedly different ways, had been the closest he'd had to actual friends in a long time. Oh, he'd spent much of his adult life in the company of libertines and lonely women, but he'd shown something of his true self to both of them in ways he never had in all the time he had been Caleb Cade. He had opened himself and shown what was left of his soul to both the spinster and the vampire. Now, through his actions, one was dead and the other hated him. He was alone again, save for this strange company of vampire hunters. Rothery, Lazziard, Rentwin and Jute, four men he suspected might not be entirely sane.

It was ironic that the only person he could discuss his feelings with would laugh at him if he broached the subject of vampires while those people he could talk about vampires with would probably do the same if he tried to discuss his feelings with them. He considered what Captain Lazziard's reaction might be if he were to mention he'd recalled not only the events leading up to Defane's death but also the fact that he had, in that moment, been utterly in love with the man.

Caleb shuddered and hurried out of the bedroom; he wandered downstairs with no great enthusiasm, particularly when he found Alyssa was not about. The Doctor's study and workshop were deserted and the only person he could find in the house was Scaife, who was busy polishing the Doctor's silverware.

When he'd asked Lazziard about Scaife's silence the Captain had growled over his brandy, "'tis not a matter of choice, he has no tongue."

"Really," Caleb had responded leaning towards the Captain, "how did that happen?"

"I have no idea... apparently, he doesn't like to talk about it!"

Lazziard's roar of laughter had made Caleb wince and sit back sharply to avoid the fetid stink of his breath.

Caleb asked Scaife where everybody else was the mute servant nodded in the general direction of the front door, without looking up from the fork he was working on, to indicate they were out.

"Everybody?"

Scaife paused as if mentally ticking through all the house's possible inhabitants before nodding vigorously.

"Do you know when they are likely to return?"

Scaife shrugged in a manner that might be considered insolent if he'd possessed a tongue, before carefully placing

In the Absence of Light

the fork back with its fellows in order to move on to the spoons.

Assuming he wasn't going to get much joy if he asked for breakfast, Caleb found some bread and cold meats left over in the pantry from the night before. He ate quickly and alone in the kitchen, the occasional distant rattle and clink of cutlery the only reminder that Scaife was still about.

Once he'd finished eating, he wandered back to the Doctor's study and was casting an eye over his book-lined shelves to see if the old man had any manuscripts regarding the not obviously related subjects of vampires and love when a ringing bell indicated someone was at the front door. Carefully replacing a moth-eared book on Carpathian folklore he headed off to the hall in case Scaife had not heard the bell. It was not in his nature to be overly helpful, but he hoped it might be Alyssa returning home.

The Doctor's manservant, however, was already at the door, and Caleb felt a vague sense of disappointment that Scaife did not usher in Rothery's daughter, but a tall fashionably dressed young man. From the cut of his expensive clothes to his heavy full-bottomed wig he was clearly a gentleman of some wealth; the way he carried himself with easy straight-backed confidence suggested he was also a man used to deference.

"I wish to see Dr Rothery if you please," he asked, breezing past the servant, his familiarity indicating that he either was a frequent visitor or that he treated everybody's home as if it were his own.

Scaife shook his head apologetically, but the young man was already halfway down the corridor, causing the servant to scurry after him. The visitor casually discarded his feather plumed hat, kid leather gloves and walking cane in Scaife's direction without a backward glance.

"Do you know if he is likely to return home soon?"

Scaife shook his head even more regretfully and cast his eyes towards the floor in mournful apology as he juggled the young man's expensive looking possessions.

"Dashed pity... don't mind if I wait a bit do you, on the off chance?"

"Can I be of any help?" Caleb offered, stepping into the hall.

The young man turned towards Caleb, noticing him for the first time. Bright, intelligent eyes regarded him in an instant and offered him a shallow bow befitting to a stranger who was of some station in life though that station was clearly considerably less than his own.

"I would be obliged Sir, I was hoping to catch Dr Rothery, but his man seems to be suggesting he is out. My own fault for not making an appointment I suppose, but been so damned busy lately, barely had time to get any cards in."

"Might I be so bold as to enquire whether it

was a...ahem *medical* matter that you wished to see the Doctor about?"

The young man smiled, "I'm in capital health thank you, Sir, no, I am the Doctor's patron in certain matters of natural philosophy. I was simply calling to discuss the Doctor's progress as I was in the area and have an hour to kill before luncheon."

"Would that be in relation to the Society..." Caleb let the words trail off, suddenly not wanting to look like a mad man if the fellow was bankrolling the Doctor's work on gall bladders, cat's rectums or whatever other strange subjects tweaked his formidable curiosity

"Why yes," the young man smiled and brushed past Scaife, "are you aware of the... *specific* nature of the good Doctor's current work?"

"Of late I, have become quite acquainted."

"Splendid!" the young man leaned closer and whispered conspiratorially, "the Doctor sends me regular updates, but I'm dashed if I can understand half the things he writes about."

"He makes little more sense verbally," Caleb agreed.

"Now you have the look of a practical sort of chap, I'd be damned appreciative if you could explain the latest goings on in a manner a fellow might actually understand. I would rather like to see what the good Doctor's spending my money on..."

"We are talking about things of an... *arcane* nature, are we not?"

The young man nodded at Scaife to indicate he would be staying a while before gripping Caleb by the elbow and leading him back into the Doctor's study.

"Quite right," the young man nodded, "best not discuss this vampire business in front of the lower sorts. They might get a bit put out."

"Indeed," Caleb smiled awkwardly and closed the door behind them, wondering what exactly he should be telling this young man.

"I was not aware The Society had any new members?"

"It was a recent development," Caleb admitted, holding out his hand, "it is a pleasure to meet you, Sir, my name is Caleb Cade."

"Quite forgetting my manners," the young man smiled, "'tis a singular honour to meet you, Sir, I am your humble servant, The Duke of Pevansea."

Caleb's smile froze as his stomach fell to some point considerably lower than his feet.

"Richard?" Caleb managed to eventually mutter.

The young Duke's smile flickered into a frown, "Richard died eighteen months ago, in a riding accident, I am his younger brother; Daniel Bourness, the Third Duke of Pevansea... Mr Cade are you alright, you've gone quite pale?"

Chapter Twelve

Love Burns

Babbington House, Essex – 1688

Daniel lay on his bed, alternatively staring into nothing or stuffing a pillow into his mouth to stifle the cries that would alert the rest of the household to his abject misery.

The Duke and Duchess would leave for London in the morning with the children and Daniel would never see her again. She had pressed a letter and a purse into his hand before she had finally sent him away. He had opened neither though he still felt their weight in the pocket of his jacket. He did not want money or references, he wanted to ride with Henrietta in the summer woods again, he wanted to hear her laughter, he wanted to feel her breath playing across his chest as she slept, he wanted to hear her murmur his name as he entered her. He took the memory of every single moment he had spent with her and held it close to him in the darkness, and every last one burned him just a little bit more.

He was utterly lost to her, he would have done anything, accepted any humiliation to stay by her side; he would have been her dog, her pet, he would have sired her children and never looked upon them as his own if only he could stay. If he were allowed only to hold her hand for a single minute every day, he would endure it all, for the prospect of never seeing her again was too much for him to contemplate.

He knew he should have been consumed by rage and hatred, would that not be the reaction of most men if they found their love had been not only unrequited but that they had been used like an animal and discarded when their purpose had been fulfilled? However, no anger would come, he wished earnestly that it would, for surely fury would be preferable to the dreadful melancholy and sickness of spirit he felt now. Instead, he lay and wondered how many hours remained until Henrietta left for London, and what he possibly could do in that time to convince her that he should not be thrown away. That he would give his life to her and expect nothing in return, he was just a rag man without her, an empty, threadbare and pathetic excuse for a human being. She had given him meaning and purpose; the love he felt had given him a life he had never known was possible. He had been so empty and alone before, and he could not bear the prospect of returning to that life for he knew, no matter how long he might live, he would never love another the way he loved Henrietta.

No revelation came, no scheme, no words, no poetry that might move her heart; everything was hollow and worthless. He tossed and turned fitfully upon his thin mattress, still as fully dressed as he had been when he had returned to his room that afternoon and flung himself onto the bed in despair. Eventually, no more tears would come, and he fell to some awful mockery of sleep where words and images came in endlessly repeated dreams though they were as meaningless and nonsensical on the hundredth repetition as they had been on the first. He would bob between sleep and consciousness, vaguely aware that his throat burned from crying while cold sweat bonded his clothes to his skin, but lacking the care to drink water or strip away his sodden uniform he allowed himself to be pulled back to his dreams rather than to rouse himself.

All things were lost to him, bar the pain and misery that manifested itself in taunting nightmares of twisted trees and icicle-haired imps that mocked him with Henrietta's voice; calling him down, down, down into the dark clammy soil where all his brothers and sisters were waiting for him to join them, waiting for him in Jack's Kingdom where he would be punished royally for his naughtiness.

Other, peripheral, voices came too, cries and shouts lost in the darkness. At first distant and insubstantial, like the wind teasing the dry twisted boughs of an ancient tree, but gradually they become louder and more insistent until he felt hands roughly clawing at him and his eyes snapped open fully expecting to see Jack Frost's leering face and cold sly eyes, come at last after all these years to take him away.

"Fire! Wake up you fool, there's a fire!"

Daniel felt warm spittle spray his face as he was pulled unceremoniously upright. He blinked in the gloom before recognising the face that loomed over him as Barnes, one of the senior footmen in the house.

"Fire?" Daniel heard himself ask, quizzically, not entirely sure he had woken up.

"Have you been drinking man?" Barnes snapped, hauling him up, "the damn house is ablaze, you'll burn to a cinder if you stay here!"

Barnes was already heading out of the door as Daniel staggered to his feet to follow him, the stink of smoke alarmingly apparent. He caught up with the older man in the corridor and grabbed him roughly by the elbow.

"The Duchess?"

"Her Grace is safe, I saw her myself outside on the lawn with the young master and Miss Anne, not five minutes ago," with that Barnes pulled himself free and hurried along the corridor, pushing open each door in turn to ensure nobody else remained unaware of the fire.

Daniel stood forlornly watching Barnes disappear around the corner, he should have been relieved that Henrietta was safe, but part of him wanted her to be trapped in the burning building, not because he wished her ill, but so that he could stage some daring rescue, risking life and limb for his love. Surely then she would not be able to discard him?

A spluttering cough interrupted his fancy as he breathed in too much of the ever-thickening smoke, and he quickly hurried after Barnes. Most of the household had already fled to the safety of the gardens at the front of the house; a few were struggling with portraits and other heirlooms that could be saved from the parts of the house furthest from the fire. A ragged chain of men snaked between the ornamental fountains and the house, passing buckets back and forth, but it was clearly a futile endeavour. The entire west wing of the house was ablaze, merry dervishes of flame dancing from the windows while great billowing clouds of smoke funnelled out of the roof, tongues of flame were already appearing between the tiles.

The Duke had taken charge of matters and was furiously waving people out of the house.

"Leave it all to burn!" he cried, forbidding any to return inside to save more of his possessions.

A small collection of furniture, mainly from the grand hall, had been stacked upon the lawn; it looked a sad little pile indeed sitting atop the grey slush of melting snow.

Daniel sought out Henrietta and found her in the shadows far back from the burning house. Young Master Richard on one side, little Miss Anne at the other. With one hand the little girl was fiercely clutching her mother while the other cradled her favourite doll.

"You are well?" He asked breathlessly, not even realising he had traversed the lawn and the milling crowds of servants and soldiers.

"Yes Daniel, we are well," Henrietta replied evenly, she still wore her night dress and a rough horse blanket was all she had to keep the winter's chill from her bones.

"Take my jacket, you will freeze," Daniel said, struggling out of his coat.

"There is no need," she said, her eyes sliding past him to settle on the burning building, "what a terrible thing," she sighed sadly.

"Terrible, yes," Daniel repeated, rooted to the spot, his arm still outstretched offering her his jacket.

"Daniel, your eyes are all red," Anne asked, looking up at him curiously, "have you been crying?"

"'tis just the smoke Miss Anne..." Daniel replied quietly, looking down into the soft slush that sucked at his boots, "...just the smoke."

"Father!" Anne cried as the Duke approached, before asking earnestly "are we vagabonds now we have no home?"

"Do not fear little one, I promise you will not have to sleep in the hedgerows just yet. I will build another house for you, a house as fine and beautiful as you are," the Duke smiled, though his face seemed even more creased and careworn than usual.

"But my dolls are inside, all my pretty things…"

"Ssssh," Henrietta chided, pulling her daughter close as the little girl sniffed back her tears.

"They are only things my dear," the Duke said to the girl who Daniel now knew was not his daughter, "things are not important, but people are and by the grace of God none have died this night so we can give thanks for that at least, eh?"

Anne nodded and gave him a wan sooty smile before Henrietta handed her children over to their matron to take to the outbuildings which would have to serve as a makeshift lodging for them until morning.

Daniel shuffled away in miserable embarrassment as the Duke placed his arm around his wife and comforted her. Henrietta laid her head against his and muttered, "I've lost all my pretty things too John, all my jewels, all my dresses and perfumes. I will miss them terribly."

"They are only things, my darling."

"I can fetch them," Daniel said, without thought.

The Duke and Duchess both looked up at him as if not realising he'd still been standing there.

"Could you?" Henrietta asked, almost hopefully. The warm dancing light of the flames played across her beautiful face, somehow making it seem wild and alien, like a savage before a tribal fire.

"I know they are only baubles, but they mean much to me-"

"I forbid it," the Duke snapped, "look at the house man, all is lost. I'll not see you go to your death for a few trinkets."

Daniel did as the Duke commanded; in the short time they'd been standing there, the fire had rushed along the roof consuming two-thirds of the building. However, the apartments in the east wing where Henrietta's rooms were situated remained untouched.

"The fire has not yet reached Her Grace's apartments," Daniel insisted, "I could get there before the fire, I know the way to her bedchamber well enough."

He saw Henrietta visibly stiffen at the remark, but the Duke was unmoved; "I forbid it," he repeated firmly. His tone was that of a man used to being obeyed without question.

"I have betrayed my friend and my king to save the young men of England from wasting their blood on futile causes; I will not order one of my own servants to his death to retrieve a few trinkets."

"They are not trinkets," Henrietta insisted, her eyes sparkling in the firelight, "they are tokens of your love for me. They mean everything to me."

"I said no."

Her eyes were wide and pleading in the firelight, did she truly want her jewels so badly or did she just want him to die in the house, would that simply be a convenience for her. A loose end, neatly disposed of?

"I thank you for your bravery young man, but it is not required, go help make the outbuildings as comfortable as possible for the children."

He had offered to run into a flaming building to rescue her most prized possessions. What more could he do to let her know he loved her? For a moment, he simply stood and stared at Henrietta, feeling his love for her despite knowing that it was not returned, knowing that he meant nothing to her at all. He also realised that he would never see her again; one way or another.

"Yes, your Grace," he said flatly.

He only vaguely heard the Duke's cry as he found himself sprinting through the melting snow back towards the burning house. Part of him hoped to hear Henrietta call his name too, and if she had he would have obeyed her, for he could refuse her nothing and it would have signified she had some small care for him, but no other voice was raised and he was soon engulfed in the smoke from the burning building.

*

The bed was unkempt, the sheets thrown aside when Henrietta had been abruptly woken, the pillows still bearing the impression of her head. Had she been asleep, he wondered when the servants had come to pound on her door? Or had she been tossing and turning, the memory of their last conversation echoing in her mind as it had in his?

He closed the door behind him, the fire was a little way off, but it would be here soon enough, the stink of smoke already permeated the room, and in the distance, he could hear its tormented roar as it devoured the building.

The room was dark; only the soft light of a winter's moon and the fading glow of the embers in the fireplace illuminated it. Henrietta had left in such a hurry there had been no time to light candles or make preparations, the servants only concern would have been to save the Duchess and in her sleep-muddled panic, she had left all her pretty things behind.

Daniel lit a candle on the mantle from his tinderbox, and then a second from that so that he might see the room a little better; he caught sight of himself in the ornate looking glass that hung above the mantle. His face was grimy with tear-stained soot; the smoke had been thick and cloying in the main hall, the flames already hungrily licking the great oak banisters of the main staircase. They would soon be consumed, cutting off any hope of reaching the main door; not that he had any intention of trying to get out.

One of Henrietta's dresses was draped over the back of a chair; she must have retired without the assistance of her maids who would surely have hung it with the others. It was the same gown she'd worn when he'd seen her that afternoon; when she'd dismissed him... Gently he picked it up and held it to his face, breathing in deeply until he became giddy with Henrietta's scent that still clung to the silk and lace.

He sat on the bed cradling the dress; the memories of just a few nights past when he had snuck like a thief into Henrietta's bedchamber came strong enough for a small pitiful cry to escape his smoke-parched throat. Slowly he toppled onto the bed, placing his head upon the indentation in the pillows so that between bed and dress he was surrounded by the scent of her.

It did not seem a terribly manly way to die, part of him thought, but he did not particularly care; life held nothing for him now. What manner of a man would he become if he continued to draw breath anyway? A broken pitiful thing of use to no one, forever comparing the meagre life he had to endure to the riches he had once enjoyed. Life without Henrietta, without the love he felt for her, would be unbearable, doubly so with the knowledge that it was all a lie. A falsehood woven with kisses and kindness was surely the cruellest deceit of all.

The noise of the fire as it cracked wood and cackled along the corridor outside became steadily louder, the stink of it growing ever more unbearable no matter how hard he pushed his face into the soft scented material of Henrietta's dress.

"So, this is how we shall die is it?"

So startled was Daniel that he physically jerked in shock; looking up from the pillows to see the figure of a boy staring at the door and the smoke that was curling through the gaps around it.

"Oh, 'tis you," Daniel sighed to the memory of his brother before sinking back down into the sweet embrace of the dress once more.

"'tis nice to see you too," the memory of Caleb grinned thinly.

"Like Henrietta's love for me, I know you are not real, so do not expect too much of a welcome."

The figure shrugged and moved to sit on the edge of the bed, grubby ink-stained fingers clutching paper and charcoal as always.

"Is she so great a loss you would rather die than live

without her?"

"Evidently."

"I died," Caleb said sadly, "I have found there is little to recommend it."

"I love her."

"That explains little."

"I was happy!" Daniel cried, "For the only time in my life, I knew what happiness was and I cannot bear the thought of living without it!"

"Happiness is as transient as the daylight little brother, 'tis the nature of the world to turn forever darkly towards the night."

Daniel peered up at the imaginary figure, "That sounds very profound, especially considering you're nought but a figment of my imagination?"

"I am the part of you that does not want to die," the memory of his brother said with a shrug, "besides I find I have little to do these days but think, try to sound profound and advise you not to be stupid."

"You think me a fool?"

"Do you intend to lie there until your flesh burns?"

"Why should I do anything else? I have nothing now."

"You have more than I do little brother. I am already dead remember, do you think there is anything I would not give to have back that which you so casually intend to throw away? I am just an illusion, I have no breath of my own, I will never love, or hurt or laugh or cry; I will never experience anything again. I am gone from the world, I exist only in your mind Daniel; 'tis only the breath of your memories that give me life; 'tis only you that keeps some small fragment of what I once was, what I might have been, alive. Once you die, well, who will remember me then? I will die all over again, only, this time, I will be lost utterly and completely to the darkness."

"Now you're just trying to make me feel bad," Daniel muttered.

"Rescue her pretty things if you must, but don't die for her Daniel. No matter how beautiful she is or how much you think you love her, she is not worth dying for. *Nobody* is worth dying for."

"But I will never be in love again; I will never feel like this again. How can I live like that?"

"Perhaps, perhaps not, but a loveless life is better than an eternity in Jack's Kingdom, believe me."

"What is it like... to be dead?"

"Cold and dark and very, very lonely," the memory of his brother said in a small and distant voice.

Daniel lifted himself up from the embrace of Henrietta's dress to rest upon his elbows and stare carefully at the vision of his dead brother. The soft light from the candles was getting hazy from the smoke stealing into the room, but the sixteen-year-old boy who perched on the edge of his bed, from his faded cotton shirt to his ink-stained fingers, from the hair that hung in his eyes to the curves of his sad little smile, seemed so remarkably real.

"Am I insane?" He asked his brother softly.

"You're lying on a Duchess' bed, cuddling one of her dresses and talking to the imaginary ghost of your dead brother while the house around you burns down around your ears," the memory of his brother looked at him pointedly, "you tell me?"

"Are you truly just my imagination, there are times when you seem too real?"

"Perhaps... perhaps many years ago, some old witch, for reasons best known to herself, tied my soul to yours so that as long as you remain alive part of me will too, guiding and advising you as best I can to keep you from the... the dark and bitter places."

"Is that what happened?"

"No, Daniel, I really am just a figment of your imagination and perhaps you are a lunatic, but all of that will matter little for unless you change your mind about this, and I have to say even by your standards this isn't one of your better ideas, you're going to be dead very soon."

"I miss you."

"I know you do, and, unlike Henrietta, I love you too, but that is not the thing brothers say to each other, is it? 'tis your love that binds my memory to you, Daniel, there is no greater magic than that. Do not shatter it for her..."

Slowly Daniel rose to his feet, letting the dress slip from his hands as he did so, even though the silk felt like a thousand tiny hooks catching and tearing at his skin as it passed through his fingers.

Caleb was right, as usual, he realised. He did not want to die; he just did not want to live without Henrietta, which wasn't the same thing at all.

"Be quick little brother," the memory of his brother hissed urgently as he started to fade into the dark, smoky light.

Heeding his words, Daniel pulled one of the sheets from Henrietta's bed and spread it upon the floor, on top of it he piled whatever he thought might be of value to the Duchess, unceremoniously sweeping her jewellery boxes, perfume bottles, hair brushes, her toilette and hair pins. Only her dresses he discarded for they would have been too bulky. Once he had grabbed all the pretty things he could see, he tied the corners of the sheet together to form a rough bundle.

His eyes were watering from the smoke, and his chest was starting to ache from the effort of breathing. He looked about for the memory of his brother in the hope that he might be able to offer further advice, but Caleb had returned to whatever part of Daniel's mind he spent most of his time.

Daniel hoisted the bundle over his shoulder and stumbled half blindly to the door, which he only needed to open a fraction to know it had taken too long for the memory of his brother to change his mind; the searing heat and smoke that rushed through the open door meant the corridor outside was now impassable. He slammed the door shut again and staggered back across the room, doubled up in pain from racking coughs as he tried to clear the smoke from his lungs.

He found the window more by touch than sight, with a desperate shaking hand he released the catch and pushed it open.

Leaning outwards, he took down great shuddering breaths of cold winter air and wiped away some of the tears from his eyes with his sleeve. The Duchess' apartments looked out upon the rear of the house so that she might enjoy views over the gardens, which had been beautiful in the summer, but looked eerie and otherworldly now it was dusted with snow and frost reflecting the orange glow of the inferno that was engulfing Babbington House. Ice and fire, Daniel thought darkly, truly this must be the way to Jack Frost's domain.

It was clear he had only two choices; stay and be consumed by the fire or jump to the ground. He leaned further out of the window; it seemed an awfully long way down. The room was on the second floor, which meant the drop to the ground was forty to fifty feet, though the ground would be soft with snow and slush.

Without further thought, he threw the bundle of Henrietta's pretty things out of the window and tried not to count how many seconds passed between it leaving his hands and the sound of the dull wet thump from below reaching his ears.

With trembling hands, he hoisted himself onto the window ledge and swung his legs out so that they dangled in the air. He glanced longingly back at the bed and part of him wished he were still curled up upon it, for the life ahead of him now seemed cold and uncertain, but Caleb was right, it would be better than being dead.

The smoke was pouring through the window around him, the fresh air feeding the fire to a greater fury. He could see tongues of flames clawing around the edges of the door. He could wait no longer; carefully he stood up on the window ledge, his toes teetering over the edge.

"I guess a broken neck is better than burning alive," he muttered, jumping into the night.

*

The night sky was crisp and clear though the moon was hazy and discoloured by the smoke that billowed heavenwards

Daniel wondered if his soul might also be floating in

the same direction, before dismissing the idea, partly because he was too sore and wet to be dead, but mainly because if he had broken his neck he was pretty sure his soul would be going in the other direction.

Gingerly he sat up, wincing both at the pain in his back and the wet squelching noise that came as his coat parted company with the cold mud bath he had landed in. The heat from the inferno had turned the snow laden lawn into a quagmire of slush and mud, which had no doubt played some small part in ensuring he had broken nothing of significance.

He found the bundle of the Duchess' pretty things more or less intact; the heavy and sickly scent that hung around the sheet suggesting several of her delicate perfume bottles had fared less well than he had in the fall.

Daniel looked up towards the window he'd jumped from; he supposed he could have flung her dresses out of the window too once it became clear there was no other way out of the building. He shrugged to himself and retreated further into the gardens to escape both the heat of the fire and any stray bit of the building that might topple in his direction.

"I'm sure she will be very grateful," the memory of his brother said from his side once he had retreated a safe distance.

"You could have stayed with me while I got out?"

Daniel muttered, glancing sideways at the shadowy boy next to him.

"You know I've never liked heights," Caleb shrugged.

"Do you think she will be grateful?" Daniel asked hopefully.

"You risked your neck for her... pretty things."

Daniel glanced at the stinking bundle that hung limply from his hands, "I think she will say thank you very much, and walk away."

"She is a Duchess, and you are her servant... what else can she say?"

"She carries my child."

"She carries the *Duke's* child; if you go about saying otherwise that jump from the window will all have been in vain," the memory of his brother drew a ghostly ink-stained finger across his throat to emphasise his point.

"Then what should I do?"

"Take her references and purse of coins and disappear... find somebody else to love."

"How can I do such a thing... she has broken me," Daniel muttered, dropping the bundle into the snow; its pungent aroma had started to make his eyes water again.

"Then you must mend yourself, make yourself a new man."

"And how might I achieve such a wonder precisely?"

Caleb shrugged, "I don't know, I'm just a figment of

your imagination, remember?"

Daniel drew his coat more closely about him. He was grateful Henrietta had not taken it after all, for the cold of the winter's night was seeping into his bones now that he had moved away from the fire.

Suddenly aware it might seem odd for him to be standing in the snow having a conversation with himself Daniel looked sheepishly around; there was nobody to be seen. The entire household must have gathered at the front of the house. Nobody had seen him jump from the window; he supposed they all thought he was dead by now.

He wondered what their reaction would be when he emerged from the shadows, covered in soot, mud and the sickly scent of the Duchess' perfumes.

Idiot, probably.

"You should go back to the others, you will catch your death standing here up to your ankles in snow," Caleb advised, "if you go and die from a chill after all the trouble I've gone to save us, I won't be at all happy."

"I'm already dead," Daniel muttered.

"Oh, you're not still going on about that! I understand she's broken your heart but really-"

"No," Daniel insisted, "I actually am dead. To everyone else in the house, Henrietta, the Duke, the household... Daniel Plunkett is dead. He burned to death in that house."

"No, you're not; you're standing here freezing our

backside off."

"They don't know that."

"So?"

"So, perhaps I deserve more than a reference and a few coins."

"I'm not sure-"

Daniel snatched up the bundle of pretty things from the ground and waved it in the imaginary face of his dead brother, "How much do you think this lot is worth? All those jewels, all that silver and gold. Enough for me to make a fancy new man of myself I'd say."

"Daniel, that's stealing!"

"No, no 'tis not! 'tis payment, 'tis what's due to me, 'tis the going rate for siring a Duchess's child and a broken heart I'd say. They won't miss it; they thought it all lost in the fire anyway!"

"You'll hang if you get caught," Caleb insisted aghast, "and more to the point, I'll get hung too!"

"Oh stop whinging, you're already dead!"

Daniel turned on his heels and begun to run across the gardens towards the woods beyond.

"Where will you go? What will you do?"

"I don't know!" Daniel cried, almost laughing. At last it had come. The anger and the fury over what had happened to him, at how he'd been used and discarded. Gold would never repair what had been broken, but it was some meagre justice, some payment, some recompense.

She had taken the dearest thing he had, now he would take what she held dearest; her gold, her silver, her jewels and her pretty things. He would take them and build a new life with the money he could sell them for. He would never need to bow or scrape before another living soul. He would be a rich man and no one would use him again.

Ever.

Chapter Thirteen
The Things We Leave Behind

Lincoln's Inn Fields, London – 1708

"I'm quite alright... really," Caleb managed to say after a long and awkward pause, "in truth I haven't been feeling quite myself for some time, all this vampire business I suppose."

"Did you know my brother?" Daniel Bourness asked.

Caleb turned away from his son and poured two large brandies from the decanter that sat amid the papers strewn absentmindedly over the Doctor's desk, "Is it too early for you... Your Grace?"

"Generally, I never drink in public before noon, but as I'm not in public just at the moment..."

Like father like son...

Caleb stood with his back turned for as long as he could, pretending to be troubled by the stopper on the decanter while he tried to calm himself and ease the tremor that had sprung into his hand and his throat.

"I hope you like your measures generous?" Caleb asked, eventually turning once he had steadied his nerves a little.

He found the young Duke already settled into the most comfortable chair in the room, his long legs stretched out before him, one booted foot hooked over the other while his abundant wig hung unceremoniously from the back of the chair, revealing his close-cropped hair which was as fair as his mother's had been.

"Capital!" Daniel Bourness beamed, a warm and easy smile lighting his face.

"I find it is always easier to be generous with another man's brandy," Caleb handed the Duke a glass before easing himself into the opposite chair.

"So... why did you think I was Richard?"

"I knew your parents... briefly, when Richard and Anne were very young. I was aware Richard had inherited your father's title, but I had not heard that he had died, I have only recently returned to England after many years abroad. I am still catching up with events it seems."

"You were a friend of my parents?" The Duke leaned forward, his eyes suddenly wide and bright.

Caleb chose his words carefully; he could almost hear the ice cracking beneath his feet.

"I would not be so presumptuous as to say *friends*; I

had the honour to meet your parents several times, our paths crossed at a few social occasions..."

Which was not exactly a lie; he had poured wine for the old Duke's guests numerous times.

"Have we met?"

Caleb shook his head emphatically, "No, the last time I saw the Duke and Duchess was before your birth, Richard and Anne were both very young."

"Strange," the Duke smiled staring at Caleb, "you look vaguely familiar, are you sure we haven't met? I attend so many functions..."

"I doubt it very much; I have been abroad these last twenty years. Unless you have spent time in Europe recently?"

"No, I've never been abroad," the Duke of Pevansea sighed regretfully, "I was going to undertake the grand tour to Italy before joining the army; then Richard went and got himself killed and I found myself a Duke with all of the responsibilities that entails..."

"Richard was a fine boy, I am sorry that I never had the chance to meet him as a man."

Daniel's voice grew faint and sad, "He grew up to be a fine man too, you would have liked him; everybody did. I miss him terribly; I keep thinking he will walk in through the door one day and announce it was all one gigantic jest, and I can go back to wasting the family fortune on cards."

Both the young Duke's words and the expression that flitted across his face were horribly familiar to Caleb.

"I was very close to my elder brother; it was a terrible loss for me when he died. Although I was but a boy when it happened not a day has passed when I haven't thought about him; not a single day..."

"Richard and I were very close too, we both took after our mother far more than our father; so people tell me," the Duke continued to stare at Caleb in a manner he found vaguely unsettling, "What was she like?"

"Oh... I'm sure there is little I can add..."

"*Please...* I was but a babe in arms when she died, I never knew her." Daniel Bourness insisted, "When I was a boy I used to stand in front of her portrait for hours, desperately trying to remember her, trying to imagine how she had looked in the flesh, trying to remember her eyes, her touch, her voice; anything at all. Sometimes I fancied I could hear her singing a lullaby to me, when I lay alone in the darkness for long enough, very faintly and so terribly far away. I can never be sure if it is a memory, a fancy or some lonely ghost singing to me from beyond the veil of our world. That's all I have of her, so whenever I meet someone who knew her, I'm afraid I question them quite mercilessly. I suppose that makes me something of a bore..."

"No," Caleb shook his head, "not at all."

He drained his glass and stood, not so much because

he wanted another but because he did not trust himself to look at his son when he spoke. Part of him so much wanted to tell him the truth, to tell him how much he had loved his mother and that how he was a product of that love. He could see her in him, the shape of his face, the sensual smile, the long straight nose, the fair complexion; only when he looked into the Duke's eyes, dark blue and mischievous, did he see anything of himself.

He recognised them both in this tall, handsome young man, and it broke his heart utterly.

The Duke shook his head at the offer of a refill and Caleb gratefully turned his back on him and slowly poured himself another measure.

She had called him Daniel; she had named their son after him, or least the man he used to be. What did that mean? Had it been through guilt over his death or because she had truly loved him and her rejection had been because of the old Duke, or the fear of scandal or the knowledge they could never truly be together. Had it simply been the right thing to do and she masked the pain she felt by making a stone of her heart to him? What did it mean? He had spent twenty years believing he had meant nothing to the only woman he had ever loved, the only woman who had ever made him happy and whose memory had chased him halfway across Europe. Had he been wrong? Now he would never know, for all he had of her was the locket he wore around his neck and the young man across the room, neither of which could provide him with any answers.

He remembered clearly enough the moment he had heard of Henrietta's death, many months after the event. He had been playing cards in an Antwerp saloon with a couple of arrogant young English gentlemen. He'd assumed they were Jacobites who had fled England in the wake of King James, and he was happy for them to think him a fellow traveller. He was studying them as much to ape the manners of free-spirited young beaux as to take their money when, for reasons he could no longer recall, talk had turned to the latest gossip from England. Their vitriol and spite when it came to those connected with the new court of William and Mary reinforcing his suspicions that they were supporters of the exiled former King James.

They had laughed heartily over Henrietta's death, retribution from God for the Duke of Pevansea's betrayal of King James; Caleb had listened in stony-faced silence as the gossips recounted how she had died a few months after producing a second son for the Duke, a fever brought on by a difficult labour.

"How was the child?" He had asked eventually or, at least, thought he'd asked, for the world had suddenly seemed a strange and distant place far beyond his numb and shaking body.

"A healthy boy," one of the young gentlemen, had

replied, eyeing Caleb strangely over the rim of his wine glass, "unfortunately."

"Did you know the Duchess?" The other enquired, followed by a hefty snort of snuff.

"No, I didn't know her at all" Caleb had whispered, "I just heard she was extremely beautiful…"

"Oh 'tis a tragedy indeed," the first gentleman replied, barely able to contain his laughter "by all accounts England has lost one of her most obliging and comely whores!"

It had been the only time in Caleb's life that he had punched a man in the face.

"She was beautiful…" Caleb said quietly, his hand instinctively feeling for the locket he always wore beneath his shirt.

"I'm sorry?" The Duke asked, "did you say something?"

Caleb returned to his seat, "There really is not much I can tell you, I did not know your mother very well at all… she was uncommonly beautiful, I remember that. She lit up any room she entered and broke every man's heart in it when she left. I don't think your father ever realised how lucky he was…" he let the words drift away, he was saying too much, far, far too much.

"My father loved her very much, he was broken-hearted when she died; they say he never thoroughly recovered from it. My memories of him are of a creased and wrinkled old fellow sitting by the fire staring endlessly into space, slowly shrivelling into something that was no longer quite a man. I've heard it said it was only his hatred of my uncle's family that kept him alive long enough for Richard to reach an age he could inherit the title, for he feared my uncle would do away with both Richard and I if we became his wards."

"You were not close to the old Duke?"

Daniel shrugged, "He was a cold and distant man; there was no cruelty in him, but no love either. I sometimes think he blamed me for mother's death, or blamed himself. I never really knew..."

"I wish there was more I could tell you Your Grace, but it was all an awfully long time ago."

"Of course, but if you do remember anything... even the smallest anecdote or story about my mother, it would be something that would be very precious to me. I would be ever so grateful to hear it," he stared pointedly at Caleb for a moment before adding, "I think you knew her a little better than you say."

He's a smart boy, Caleb thought, keeping his face impassive.

"I will spend some time trying to recall, I would not want to recite half-truths blurred by two decades of..." he lifted his glass apologetically, "...over indulgence."

"I would appreciate it, Mr Cade, though I have to say

you are singularly well preserved, or you were just a boy if you knew my mother, you don't look a day over thirty."

Caleb laughed, "You flatter me, Your Grace, I am somewhat older than that and if I do not look my years it is not for the want of hard living."

"Please, there is no need to call me your grace; all this Duke malarkey doesn't sit easily on my shoulders; as the second son, I never expected the title to be mine. When people say "Your Grace" I still half believe they are referring to my Father or Richard."

"I will try to be a little less formal..."

"My friends call me Danny," the Duke stretched over his hand; "I would like to think you among that number."

"Danny..." Caleb mumbled the word as he accepted his son's hand.

"'tis what my mother called me," he said with an almost apologetic shrug, "she was terribly weak in the months before her death, but they tell me on her good days she liked to sit on the window seat in the library of our residence in St James' Square and hold me, showing me the world as it passed by the window. Her beautiful Danny she used to call me. I wished I could remember."

The young Duke was too caught up in his own words to notice Caleb look sharply away as the memory of Henrietta sitting in that very seat with him came flooding into his mind, sudden and startling enough to make his pulse quicken.

My beautiful Danny...

How many times had she whispered that to him as they had lain together?

Caleb forced his attention back to the present; he had to turn the conversation to other matters, the boy was no fool, it would only be a matter of time before he gave his feelings away if they continued to discuss Henrietta.

"So...Danny, I believed you came here to discuss Dr Rothery's work?"

"Yes, of course," the Duke's eyes snapped back to the present, "you must forgive me rambling about my mother; I almost forgot the business in hand."

"Not at all, though I am curious as to why a Duke would fund such a strange undertaking."

"Oh, 'tis all the rage."

"Really?"

"Natural philosophy, The Royal Society, that sort of malarkey. Anybody who is *anybody* is giving patronage to some venture or another; be it grand mechanical devices, great voyages of discovery and exploration, the secrets of the human body, new improved telescopes for peering further into the heavens, oh the list is nigh on endless. There is great prestige to be gained if *your* fellow invents or discovers something... important. This is an exciting age we live in; men of learning are making momentous progress in all areas of knowledge, but men of learning require men of money to pay for all their... curiosity."

"But vampires?"

"Well, it sounded more interesting than steam pumps or counting engines."

"Though less likely to see a return on your money, or are you simply doing God's work?"

"God? Oh, I doubt he needs me, he is altogether powerful enough to do his own work," the Duke leaned forward, "apart from an interest in matters arcane and occult, this could also make me tremendously rich; or rather, even richer."

"I thought the aristocracy generally turned their noses up at making money, bad form and all?"

"Times are changing," the Duke grinned, "and if you do not change with them, then you will be left behind."

"I still don't quite see how money could be made from this?"

"The vampiric essence!" The young man declared enthusiastically as if that explained everything.

"How do you propose to make money from a vampire's... soul?"

"Why, 'tis the fountain of youth, of course, any man would pay a fortune for that, surely?"

"I don't believe becoming a vampire would be to

everybody's taste."

"Ah, but that's the point! If the good Doctor can locate the vampiric essence it can be distilled, refined, purified into some potion that will imbibe the recipient with the youth and vitality of the vampire, but without the more unfortunate aspects of that sorry condition."

"Skulking in the shadows, drinking Human blood, losing your immortal soul?"

"Yes, that kind of thing... surely the Doctor has discussed this with you?"

"Of course!" Caleb beamed sincerely, wondering if Rothery had lied to the young Duke to get his money or to him to hide the true nature of his studies. Or perhaps he simply told everybody what they wanted to hear, "I just am unsure whether such a thing is possible."

"Oh, the Doctor is quite insistent it can be done, and he is as great an authority on the subject as anybody, perhaps the greatest alive. Saying that, it can be difficult to understand exactly what he's getting up to, his reports can be a little... dense."

"Have you ever seen a vampire, Danny?"

"Why no!"

"Would you like to?"

*

"Doesn't look much of a monster," the Duke sniffed, staring down at the pile of dust that was all that remained of Louis Defane. A suspicious fellow might be tempted to think he was looking at no more than several weeks' worth of detritus collected from the Doctor's fireplaces and spread out over the table in the rough approximation of a man.

"Their remains quickly reduce to dust, which is hampering the Doctor's work somewhat."

"Who was this chap?"

"A friend of mine," Caleb said quietly, his eyes studying his son's profile in the lantern light of the Doctor's workshop. The more he stared at him, the more he could see Henrietta. The somewhat perverse thought flicked through his mind that it was fortunate Henrietta had not given him a daughter, for had Daniel been born a girl she would have been the absolute image of her mother; which would have been even more confusing for Caleb.

"Do you normally choose such peculiar friends?" Danny asked, picking up a few grains of greasy dust and rubbing them thoughtfully between his thumb and forefinger.

"As a rule, I don't have any friends," Caleb admitted with a shrug, "although I knew there was something strange about Defane, I had no inkling as to his true nature, or would have believed it even if I had."

"What a peculiar thing to say."

"Oh, I've never been the sort to believe in monsters, before all this anyway."

Danny smiled, "No, I meant about not having any friends, most people crave company and friendship."

"I travelled around Europe for many years; never settling for long anywhere. Friendships tie you to a place, and the road always beckoned me to keep moving," Caleb glanced away from the intent enquiring eyes of his son, "we must all be true to our nature, however inconvenient it may be."

"And in all those years you never found anywhere you wanted to stay, anyone you wanted to stay with?"

"No," Caleb replied curtly.

I was too busy looking for someone to mend the heart your mother broke...

"You must excuse me, I am cursed with an inquisitive nature; I did not mean to pry."

"There is no offence."

"Good, now this chap Defane, tell me about him?"

"That could be a long story or a very short one, what do you want to know?"

"The Doctor provides me with the cold facts; Samuel is a true son of Apollo. 'tis the mechanics of the world which fascinates him, and although that interests me too I also wish to know who these creatures are as much as what they are. It seems to me perhaps you are better placed than any other member of Rothery's Vampire Society to scratch that particular itch for me. For a man who seeks no friends to claim the friendship of a vampire, then it suggests that vampires must have an extraordinary allure, does it not?"

"I liked him," Caleb admitted, looking at the ashes that had once been Defane's face, "even though his company could be as disturbing as it was amusing."

"Where did you meet him?"

Caleb smiled, "Where I meet most men, over a card table..."

He talked for a long time, long enough for his mouth to become dry and sticky with the peculiar metallic air that pervaded Doctor Rothery's workshop of curiosities. He did not tell the young Duke everything, of course. He did not talk of the whores he and Defane had shared, partly because most of those events were too hazy for him to recall clearly, but mainly it struck him as an inappropriate tale for a father to recount to his son. He did not mention Defane's talk of love or the feelings that had coursed through him when the vampire had taken his blood; he did not want the Duke to think him some manner of sodomite in the way Lazziard did. Instead, he talked of Defane's outrageous attire, their nights of carousing, the strange glamour he had thrown over Liselot and Charles Massingham and how it had eventually led to both their deaths, he told his son of Defane's house and what they'd found in that dusty bedroom, he told Danny how he believed everything Defane had done was through some twisted notion of love and that the vampire had been the loneliest man he had ever met.

"The Doctor has never mentioned that these creatures could be capable of such emotions," the Duke commented when Caleb had finally finished his account, "it makes them seem more... human?"

"Defane was a man once, like you and I, if the Doctor is right, he was changed by another vampire into this form long ago. Is it so impossible to believe that the emotions he carried as a man would not cross over to his new vampiric self in the way his memories and intellect did?"

"Because, in order to know love you require a soul, without it such noble feelings cannot surely be possible?"

"That is Captain Lazziard's contention, I am not so sure. Defane was probably insane, but I don't doubt what he felt was genuine enough."

"So you think him more human than monster?" The Duke indicated Defane's remains with a nod of his head as he wiped the greasy ash from his fingers.

"I think he was more than just a monster; it is too simplistic to think of him in such terms. Whether he was unique amongst vampires in that respect, I cannot assuredly say, given that he is the only vampire I've ever met."

"The only vampire you know you've met," Danny

corrected.

"Perhaps..." Caleb conceded.

The Duke pulled out his pocket watch as Caleb covered Defane's remains once more, "I really must dash," he exclaimed, "It's been fascinating to meet you, I would love to continue our discussions, both about vampires and my mother, but I've got luncheon at one o'clock, a pretty little thing who I really don't want to keep waiting."

"Best not to," Caleb agreed, leading him back up the stairs.

"I find I rather rattle around my place in St James Square, so I leave it to the servants as much as I can. Most evenings I dine at my Club on Shire Lane; please feel free to find me there if you have a care to continue our conversation."

"I would like that," Caleb replied, unsure if he wanted any such thing.

Scaife came scuttling from the shadows and once the Duke was reunited with his coat and cane, he pumped Caleb's hand vigorously once more, "It's been a rare pleasure Mr Cade, really, I am sorry to leave so hastily, but I find pretty women should never be kept waiting too long."

"Anything more than fifteen minutes and they can get rather feisty, in my experience."

The young Duke laughed, tipping his hat before turning for the door, Scaife scurrying ahead to open it for him.

As soon as the door had closed Caleb turned on his heel and returned to the Doctor's study, which looked down upon Lincoln's Inn Field. From the window, he watched as the Duke settled himself in the seat of a bright and freshly lacquered landau carriage that prominently bore the Pevansea coat of arms. As the day was bright and passably warm, the landau's leather top was pulled down so that the Duke might enjoy the sunshine. A driver sat up front and a footman was clambering on to the footplate at the back after ensuring the Duke had made a dignified ascent into his seat.

He must be looking to impress whichever lucky young woman he was lunching with, Caleb thought ruefully.

The driver looked over his shoulder awaiting instruction from the Duke, his whip poised to get the two splendid bay mares harnessed to the carriage moving. The Duke, however, remained silently staring up at the Doctor's house, even though half his face was lost in the shadows of his wide-brimmed hat, the young man's thoughtful expression was plain enough to see. Caleb took half a step back from the window, but the house faced the bright sunshine and he was sure the light reflecting off the window made it effectively opaque. Still, he couldn't shake the idea his son was staring directly at him.

"He's a fine-looking boy," a soft and familiar voice said

from beside him.

"Yes, he is," Caleb muttered softly as the Duke finally waved his driver on and the landau pulled out into the traffic.

"Takes after his mother then?"

Caleb glanced at the indistinct form of his long-dead brother, the sunlight streaming through the window seemed to pass through him, illuminating the shape of a long-haired boy, distinct enough to recognise but hazy, as if it were made of strange filaments of smoke curling slowly within. He seemed so delicate that if Caleb opened the window and let in the breeze, he would be blown entirely away. Perhaps that was all memories were, smoky recollections slowly dissipated by the breath of years.

He found his hand clasping the locket around his neck, and he pulled it free without thought. Carefully he worked the tiny clasp and opened it, the portrait inside was clear enough in the bright sunlight for his throat to catch.

"She called him Daniel..." he whispered, "...did she have feelings for me after all?"

"Guilt perhaps?" The memory of his brother said; his voice clear even if his form was not.

"Maybe," Caleb admitted, letting his finger run over the locks of blonde hair that were curled tightly on the opposite side of the locket. Despite himself, he felt his eyes moisten and hated himself for it.

"Why does it still hurt brother? Twenty years have passed and yet I still weep for her as if it were yesterday; even though there is nothing left of that foolish boy I was bar the pain of her memory. I am an entirely different man, yet still I bleed," his eyes lifted to stare at where the Duke's landau had been parked a few moments before, "how does life still conjure new ways for me to feel this damned pain?"

"Sometimes the living must bear the weight of the dead throughout their lives."

"You, Henrietta, Isabella, Liselot, Defane... I seem to be weighed down by more than my fair share of the dead."

"'tis what happens when you keep moving," the memory of his brother explained, "You cover more ground that way."

"It seems no matter how far I travel the things I left behind have a habit of finding me again; be they the memories of my misdemeanours, the ghosts of my lovers or..."

"Your sons."

"I found I rather liked him."

"As I said, he clearly takes after his mother."

Caleb smiled for a moment, but it quickly passed, "I should not have come home, nothing good can come of me being here. I should have kept moving."

"You met Harriet?"

"And that all worked out rather well, didn't it?"

"She would have been good for you; I don't know why you didn't give her that dress instead of running off with Defane."

"Neither do I."

"Perhaps it is not too late?"

Caleb shrugged, "She hates me now and I am not much used to being hated."

"No, you always managed to move on before they started hating you."

"Since when did you become my conscience?"

The memory of his brother turned his smoky blurred head towards him, "Well, ever since I died, if you hadn't noticed."

"Well, what does my conscience think I should do?"

"Why ask me, you'll do what you normally do regardless?"

"Which is?"

"You'll avoid Harriet, you'll bed Alyssa, thoroughly enjoy yourself until you find some reason to slink off, inevitably leaving some God awful mess in your wake."

Caleb sighed, "I'm getting to too old for that."

"Are you really?"

"What does that mean?"

"Look in the mirror," the memory of his brother swept an arm in the direction of the looking glass that hung over the fireplace, leaving tiny blurred strands of his memory fading in the air.

Caleb scowled but did as he was told.

"What do you see?" The memory of his brother asked, not moving from the window.

"The King of France, obviously."

"Look closer, Danny was right; you don't look your age... *anymore.*"

Caleb was about to dismiss his brother's words, but instead, he found himself frowning and leaning closer to the looking-glass. Despite having lived off his looks for many years, he had never been a particularly vain man and rarely spent time examining himself, but as he looked soberly at his reflection he noticed that the flecks of grey that had begun to sprout around his temples were gone while the crow's feet that had been developing about his eyes had all but faded away. His skin was taut and firm, his teeth whiter and straighter than he entirely remembered.

"How peculiar..."

"The vampiric essence," his brother said softly.

"Huh?"

"You drunk Defane's blood... twice, remember? Perhaps it has had some other effect than your desire to sink your teeth into Alyssa's lovely neck."

"Oh, you know about that?" Caleb, rather absurdly,

noticed he was blushing slightly.

"Of course I know, I'm a figment of *your* imagination remember. I know everything that goes on inside your misbegotten head!"

"Good job the dead tell no tales eh?" Caleb chuckled.

"Very funny... but don't you see what this means?"

"I've got a feeling you're going tell me."

"Danny was right, the elixir of eternal life exists, in a vampire's blood, just by drinking it you have shaved five, maybe ten years off your appearance. If you were to find more, who knows, perhaps you would never age. You would never grow old. We would never die and go to Jack's Kingdom. You would never forget me..."

"Aren't you forgetting the part where I have to become a blood sucking fiend?"

"Look, if the good Doctor can find a way..."

"Never die?"

"Never... and then Jack Frost will have no power to haunt your dreams anymore."

"If you ever stay still, still, still..."

"Ol' Laughing Jack will kill, kill, kill..." the memory of his brother finished Valentine Cade's rhyme from the nightmare that had haunted him since childhood. Caleb shivered despite himself. It was only a nightmare, but it had been with him since the first time he had dreamt it the night after his brother's funeral. Like the memory of his brother itself, the nightmare came less often now and was far less vivid, but it still had the power to terrify him nonetheless and the advice he'd received from the thief they couldn't hang was something he'd been following ever since the night Babbington House burned to the ground.

All his life he had been terrified of death. Terrified of the thought of the cold earth being shovelled on top of him, terrified of the thought of that dreadful old tree's roots wriggling through the soil. Eager to wind around him and bare him inexorably down into Jack's Kingdom with all the other naughty boys to spend eternity in the dark bitter cold. It was nonsense, of course, just the product of a fairy tale and a child's nightmare, and he *knew* it was nonsense... but sometimes during the quietest hours of the night when sleep refused to come, in the absence of light, fairy tales and childish nightmares could still seem real enough to make his heart quicken with fear.

Carefully he ran a finger down the skin of his cheek, it felt smooth and warm, untouched by disease or blemish. What would it be like to be young forever? If he were young and handsome for long enough might it not be possible to meet another Henrietta? Except this time she actually would love him, and he would know happiness again, the kind of happiness he had never found whilst he had been moving along the road for twenty years following Valentine Cade's advice; save for those few seconds when Louis

Defane was sucking his life blood away. How long might it take, another twenty years? Thirty? He saw a sad, bitter smile break out in the looking-glass. Perhaps that was what Louis Defane had told himself during the long years he had slept beside the corpses of those he had loved and killed. That if he waited long enough, lived long enough, then happiness would eventually, inevitably, find him.

How long had Defane waited? Just how many years...

"Vanity is such an unappealing quality in a man," Alyssa Rothery said dryly from the doorway.

Caleb turned away from the looking-glass sheepishly, "And what qualities *do* you find appealing Miss Rothery?" He glanced at the window, but the memory of his brother had faded to nothing though he fancied there was the hint of a knowing smile hanging in the sunlight for a moment.

"None commonly shared by ne'er-do-wells," Alyssa replied evenly, leaning against the door frame rather than entering the room.

"Ne'er-do-well?" Caleb repeated, slowly crossing the library to stand before Alyssa closer than would commonly be considered polite, forcing her to look slightly up at him to meet his gaze. She made no move to retreat. He felt the familiar beasts of lust and desire stirring within him once more, spurring him on to the chase regardless of the consequences, regardless of the knowledge that once sated they would leave no happiness in his soul.

"I will have you know that, in polite circles, I'm more generally regarded as a scoundrel."

"Oh, there lies my mistake then, for my father isn't generally in the habit of bringing home scoundrels," she smiled sweetly, "especially vain ones."

"I can assure you young lady that vain scoundrels are by far the most desirable breed of scoundrel, for we take far more care of our appearance than the more common or garden variety of shabby, unkempt scoundrel that is so familiar on the streets of London."

"You must forgive my naivety, Sir, for I am but a poor wee lass not at all accustomed to the company of such men. Pray tell what sort of behaviour I might expect from a vain scoundrel if one were to find oneself alone with one?"

"Well, all manner of dastardly schemes and ruses designed with the sole purpose of corrupting your soul, so that you might willingly and enthusiastically debase yourself pleasuring the aforementioned scoundrel. That or steal all of your money of course."

"So, might these schemes involve escorting an innocent and uncorrupted girl to the theatre this evening?"

"Of course it would!" Caleb beamed as amused as always by the fact women never believed the bit about him wanting to steal their money, "which girl did you have in mind?"

"Me of course," Alyssa fluttered her eyelashes.

"Oh, my apologies! You confused me with the innocent and uncorrupted part."

"Generally, most men try to flatter me into their beds. I find your approach quite novel Mr Cade."

"I would normally try that approach, but as you've already been in my bed there doesn't seem much point."

"What a rude and uncouth man you are," Alyssa smiled and leaned close enough for her hair to brush against his face, "'tis rather refreshing!"

"I try to please."

"Be ready for seven," she smiled, turning on her heels.

"On one condition," Caleb called after her.

Alyssa paused in the shadowy hallway to look back at him and raise an enquiring eyebrow.

"Given that I am so very vain, please take a care not to look prettier than me; I wouldn't want to think people were looking at you rather than me."

"I will do my best to look singularly dowdy and spinsterish."

"Splendid! By the way, what are we going to see?"

Alyssa shrugged, "Oh I have no idea; 'tis just an excuse. I need some time to decide if I like you enough."

"Enough for what?"

"Why, enough for you to take me down a dark alley and fuck me like a tuppenny whore, of course," she replied with a sweet and dazzling smile, before hitching up her skirts and hurrying off up the stairs, whistling tunelessly.

For once Caleb could not think of a retort.

Chapter Fourteen
A Matter of Commerce

Holborn, London – 1689

"Oh, my dear boy!"

Uncle Jonathan hugged him fiercely. Daniel was suddenly enveloped in his plump arms and pulled in so tightly that his nostrils were filled with that old reassuring scent he'd always associated with his Uncle; the jasmine scented alum that only partially masked the earthier smells of stale tobacco and sweat. For an instant he was a little boy again, his brother was still alive, and Uncle Jonathan was about to produce some sweet sugared treat, which he would push into his nephew's hand with a theatrical wink lest Daniel's father might see.

He hugged his Uncle back and wished fervently he might have only the cares of a small boy once more.

"I thought you dead," Uncle Jonathan half-sobbed when he was finally released, Daniel felt vaguely embarrassed by the tears welling up in the older man's eyes, and he looked politely away as he produced a billowing white handkerchief into which he blew his nose with the ferocity of a bugler.

"I am not..." was all that Daniel could find by way of explanation.

He felt himself led further into his Uncle's study and deposited into a chair before the room's fire. "I will arrange some supper, you look half starv-"

"I am not hungry," Daniel said curtly, his eyes wandering to the flames as his Uncle hovered uncertainly above him. The study was lined with books, and although both the room and the collection were far more modest, they inevitably reminded him of the library in St James' Square.

Eventually, she would come to her favourite window seat. If I waited long enough on the street, I might see her one more time, my child in her belly, but no thought for me in her head or love for me in her heart.

That room was only a mile or so away across London, but even if it had been in Virginia, Henrietta could not have been any further away from him.

"Daniel?"

He let his eyes be pulled reluctantly towards the concerned face of his Uncle.

"Do not worry Uncle," he said quietly, "I am quite

well."

"You've lost weight… you appear much changed?"

"I *am* much changed."

I'm rich, I'm broken-hearted, and I'm dead.

Daniel supposed that would change most men. His hair had grown in the months since Babbington burned to the ground, and it hung lank and dark about his face, which now sported a scruffy half-hearted beard. He hoped he looked different enough.

Uncle Jonathan eased himself into another chair, pulling a slight face with the effort. He certainly had not lost any weight.

"We heard about the fire, they said you died in the blaze… where on God's Earth have you been for all these months?"

"Hiding…" Daniel said simply.

"Hiding? Why?"

"I had nothing better to do." Daniel shrugged, finding that now he sat before his Uncle he had no great wish to talk at all.

After his flight from Babbington, he had slunk about the back roads and byways of Essex for days, his fear of Jack Ketch's rope or a footpad's cudgel far greater than the discomfort brought on by cold and hunger. Eventually, he had buried the greater part of Henrietta's treasure beneath the rotten trunk of a wind-felled oak in Epping Forest before travelling on with the intention of returning to London in some assumed guise, but the sight of the busy roads leading into the capital had unnerved him, every drover and coachman that glanced in his direction sending him into cold seizures of terror. If anyone recognised him, a man who had supposedly burned to death in Babbington House, then the inevitable questions would surely send him first to Newgate prison and then the Tyburn gallows.

Terrified that he would be recognised he had abandoned the London road and found refuge in the East Ham levels, an expanse of marshy grassland interspersed by numerous small rivers, creeks and inlets between the Thames and Epping Forest to the east of London. It was inhabited by enormous flocks of seabirds, a few shepherds and cattlemen, reapers who cut down the plentiful reeds and osiers for basket weavers and those principled souls, eager to facilitate free trade, who helped ship's captains unload some of their cargo before they reached the Pool of London and the Excise men stationed at The Custom House.

In other words, it was the kind of place a thief might find refuge without too many questions being asked.

He had sat in the quietest room of a dilapidated and apparently little used coaching inn. Day after long day had passed, with only the gulls that circled endlessly above the

Levels and the memory of his dead brother for company whilst he tried to decide what he might do with his life and Henrietta's jewellery; what he might do that would not end up with one of Jack Ketch's fine ropes around his neck at any rate.

When no answers came, he had eventually slipped into London on the coat tails of the night to visit the only person he could think of who might.

"I don't understand Daniel, what happened?" Uncle Jonathan pressed again.

"I fell in love," Daniel mumbled as if that would explain everything.

"I thought it must be something serious," Uncle Jonathan sighed and folded his hands across his bulging stomach, "and who exactly brought about this unfortunate malady in you boy?"

Daniel tried to form the words, but nothing came for he feared the bittersweet taste of her name upon his lips would start him crying again and he had become so terribly tired of crying. When his Uncle continued to stare expectantly at him, Daniel pulled a small silver locket from around his neck, which he held out before him.

"With her."

He'd found the locket amongst Henrietta's pretty things; a small silver oval which opened to reveal tiny, but quite perfect, portraits of the Duke and Duchess. He'd found himself unable to bury it with the bulk of the jewellery in Epping Forest, and instead he'd slipped it into his pocket without thinking too much about why he did not want to be parted from her image. Days later, whilst he had sat alone in his room he had taken a knife and carefully prised out the image of the Duke. He found he had no animosity towards the old man, but neither did he want to be reminded of Henrietta's husband either.

Day after day, hour after hour, he had sat and stared at Henrietta's likeness and the thought that this would be as close as he would ever come to seeing her beautiful face again had brought forth tears that came in strong convulsing sobs that seemed to burn his very soul.

Weeks later he had returned to Epping Forest and his treasure hoard. He had told himself that he was simply checking to make sure it was still safe, he didn't think either he or the memory of his brother believed him, but it was as good an excuse as any.

When he'd found everything was as he'd left it, he'd recovered Henrietta's silver hair brushes from the bundle and hastily reburied the remainder. Once he was safely back on the East Ham Levels, he'd carefully pulled every last one of the long blonde fibres of hair he had been able to find from the brushes before delicately curling them where the Duke's image had once sat.

Quite why he had felt the need he had not been able to

fathom, but it provided some manner of comfort for him, albeit of a choking tear stained kind.

His Uncle curiously took the locket and opened it. He stared at it in the palm of his large fleshy hand for a good minute before carefully closing it and returning it to Daniel.

"Oh dear…" he sighed finally.

"You know who she is?"

Uncle Jonathan nodded.

"I fell in love with her…" Daniel muttered, fixing his eyes upon the locket he let dangle from his fingers rather than meeting his Uncle's eyes, "…and I still am, which is the worst of it, for if I could find it in myself to hate her, I am sure I would not feel half so wretched as I do."

"Did she seduce you, boy?"

Daniel nodded, his eyes never leaving the swinging locket.

"And you mistook seduction for love?"

"She never said she loved me, not once. I knew I was just a comfort to her, an entertaining distraction, no more than that…"

"But you wanted more?"

"What man would not? Of course, I knew such things were impossible. I was content to be her discreet *companion*, I-" Daniel raised his eyes towards his Uncle suddenly; "You do not seem overly surprised that the Duchess of Pevansea seduced one of her servants?"

Uncle Jonathan shrugged his big shoulders, "These things are not entirely uncommon... I assume something happened to alter your situation?"

Daniel nodded and returned his eyes to the locket.

"Do not trouble yourself so greatly Daniel, the nobility are a feckless breed that quickly tire of their games..."

"She is with child. With my child."

"Oh."

"Should not a man be happy when he learns he is to be a father for the first time, even if that child will be brought up as another man's?"

"One would suppose."

"But I feel nothing, just emptiness. Henrietta is all I want, and if this wretched child had not come along, perhaps I would still be at her side."

"'tis not the child's fault Daniel..."

"I should hate Henrietta, but I cannot find it in me. Perhaps the pain would be easier to bear if I had anger and hate to act as a salve upon it."

"'tis not Her Grace's fault alone she is with child. I would assume this matter will be no small predicament for her after all."

"You assume wrong Uncle; *Her Grace* is precisely where *Her Grace* wishes to be."

Uncle Jonathan moved forward slightly in his chair, "My dear boy, whatever do you mean?"

He had said too much. If word of the illegitimacy of all of Henrietta's children were to spread it would be the ruin of her, perhaps that was something he should have been shouting from the rooftops, but despite everything he could not bear the thought of causing her pain.

"Nothing," Daniel muttered.

Uncle Jonathan's eyes narrowed slightly, and his face took on a cast Daniel didn't believe he'd ever seen before as if something shrewd and calculating had taken up residence behind Jonathan's plump, friendly features.

"So Lady Henrietta *wanted* to be with child..." Uncle Jonathan mused when Daniel remained silent, his words a statement rather than a question as he settled back in his chair once more.

"I have said too much."

"Do not concern yourself boy, the Lady's secrets will be safe with me... although it does beg the question *why* she would seek such a condition?" When Daniel remained silent Uncle Jonathan continued to ponder aloud, "And what of the Duke... does he know the truth of things? I understand he detests his brother's children, 'tis understandable he would be eager for more heirs to protect his inheritance, but he is now an old man if he is unable-"

"You appear remarkably well informed Uncle?"

"Information is a valuable commodity, worth its weight in gold sometimes..."

In the Absence of Light

"I have often wondered what exactly the nature of your business is." Daniel looked about the well-furnished study, "it seems to pay well enough whatever it is?"

Uncle Jonathan smiled, "Hard work always has its rewards, my boy."

"What *do* you do?" Daniel asked again, more forcefully.

"I am but humble merchant; I trade in various... *commodities*. Nothing more."

"Wine? Silk? Cloth? Timber?"

"I do not specialise."

Daniel's eyes narrowed, "Mr Greaves never quite struck me as much of a gambler, he is not a man of any particular vice, in fact, is that really how I got that position in the Duke's household?"

Uncle Jonathan sighed before replying softly, "No."

"Then tell me how I came to be in that house?"

"Does it matter?"

"Yes. Greatly."

"The Duchess approached me," his Uncle answered after a long pause, "not directly of course, but via various trusted agents and intermediaries. She was looking for servants of a particular and exceptional quality. I found them and sent them to her. That is all."

"But I had no experience of service. No references, why would she want me?"

"She had certain... *requirements*. I believed you fitted them rather well, and the opportunity would enhance your station in life. It was a situation that was advantageous to all parties."

"Did you procure me for her?" Daniel asked incredulously, "Like some bawdy house mistress?"

"I would not describe the arrangement so disagreeably."

"And what were these requirements, Uncle?"

"She wished young men of fair aspect, good mind and strong body who had not been corrupted by... the temptations of life."

"She was looking for lovers?"

Uncle Jonathan shrugged, "That is what I had assumed, the nobility have their games. I did not question her motives... though I now see she had some greater purpose than mere pleasure."

"But why you? Why come to you to find her... pretty boys to play with?"

"I have a certain reputation for... finding things that may not be readily available. I am discreet, I keep secrets. I am trusted. You wouldn't actually expect a Duchess to trawl around the streets of London themselves looking for... such things? I find the nobility don't care to dirty their hands, which can be most profitable for those who are less concerned about getting muck under their fingernails."

"So you are just a pimp then? A whoremaster? A brother of the Gussit?" Daniel spat, jumping to his feet. He was incredulous at his Uncle's words and wounded that he had been used in such a manner.

"Sit down boy!" Uncle Jonathan commanded sternly.

Daniel hesitated for a moment, his anger pushing him towards the door, but he had nowhere else to go, and no one else to turn to, so instead he slumped dejectedly back into his chair.

"Was it quite so terrible? She is very beautiful; most men would not complain too seriously about being used in such a way."

"She said much the same herself..." Daniel spat bitterly, "...clearly you know me as poorly as she does."

"My dear boy, I meant you no harm by arranging this. I considered it an opportunity, a chance for you to improve your station."

"By becoming a Duchess' whore?"

"That is unfair. I was paid to find her servants; you were paid to be her servant. It was all simply a matter of commerce. There was no whoring of anybody Daniel, she liked you and found a use for you. 'tis the nature of the world that the little man requires a patron amongst the great and the good if he is to progress. I found you a patron Daniel, you should be grateful."

"Thank you so much, Uncle," Daniel replied coldly, "I

see everything more clearly now."

Uncle Jonathan rolled his eyes in exasperation, "You have still not explained why you are hiding, do you believe the Duchess wants you dead now she is with child? Did you do something to make her doubt your discretion?"

"Of course not!"

"You should not sound so doubtful, I have heard of worse."

Daniel shook his head emphatically, "I went back into the burning house to rescue Henrietta's belongings, though, in truth, I went back to die."

"And yet you are here?"

"I decided burning to death was not to my tastes, so I stole her jewellery instead."

"Why on earth did you do that boy?"

"Perhaps I was unhappy with my severance terms."

"And now?"

"Now I am a rich, but dead, man. If anybody recognises me..." Daniel shrugged, "...Jack Ketch will make sure my death becomes more... *permanent*."

"So you want my help?"

"I did not know where else to turn... Father would gladly see me hang after all."

"You don't know your father very well if you think such a thing. He is quite distraught."

"You surprise me."

"You should go and see him."

"No."

"You are his son."

"So is Jacob, he can look after the old tyrant. Being his whipping boy seems to suit Jacob after all."

Uncle Jonathan shook his head sadly, "Daniel I'm very sorry... your brother is dead."

Daniel frowned as if he had misheard the words, "How can that be?"

"He developed an ague; it was unexpected, virulent and he passed in little more than forty-eight hours..."

Daniel had not been close to his little brother in years, he had resented the fact Jacob could not see their father was responsible for Caleb's death, not to mention all their other misfortunes. Instead, he'd trotted around after their father, with large, adoring eyes, even when the heartless old monster beat him senseless for one perceived failing or another. He had become more of an acolyte than a son. Hanging upon the words of his sermons like they were the words of God himself rather than the puerile and bilious ranting of a man so eaten by bitterness that he could not find even a sliver of love in his black heart for his own flesh and blood.

"Was it really an ague?" Daniel asked eventually, his voice cold and emotionless.

"I believe so."

"God alone knew what that man did to him while they were alone."

"You are too harsh... your father loved all of his children very much."

Daniel's laugh was small and distant, "His love must be a strange thing indeed for my back still carries the scars of its caress."

"You should go to him; it would be a kindness for him to know you still live after all."

"I will do that man no kindness. Everything he touched died and the only kindness in telling him that I live would be that it still gives him the opportunity to kill me as he did my brothers and mother."

"He killed no one, Daniel. You are too hard."

"When you were a boy did he ever stand over you and beat you with his belt till the blood run down your back? Did you ever have to listen to him grunting out one of his wretched sermons as he beat you? Did you ever bite down so hard on your tongue to stifle yours screams that your mouth filled with blood just to make sure you heard every word he preached? Did you ever have to stand before him naked and bleeding and recite his sermon back knowing that if you got but a single word wrong he would beat you again for he would know the Devil still lurked in your heart if you had not memorised it? Did you Uncle?"

"No."

"Then don't talk to me about kindness in the same breath you mention that bastard!"

Daniel refused to meet his Uncle's eyes for fear he might see something of his father in them. The news of Jacob's death reminded him how much he hated the man and for a moment he seriously thought about killing him. If he were to end up hanging from Jack Ketch's rope anyway, it might as well be for something he'd really enjoy. He shook the thought away even though it was sweet and tempting. He had only just come to terms with being a thief; he did not want to become a murderer too, however, much his father might deserve it.

"I am sorry for all that has befallen you Daniel, but you cannot stay here. 'tis too dangerous now."

"I would not wish to trouble you more than one night Uncle; I would not wish to keep you from your commerce."

"No, I mean you cannot stay in England, 'tis not so big a place that the fact you still live can remain hidden forever."

"Then where can I go?"

"I do some business in Amsterdam, I have contacts. You will be safer there."

"Amsterdam?" Daniel repeated hollowly, "how might I get there?"

"You are a very rich man now I dare say."

"I suppose."

"Do you have the Duchess' jewellery with you?"

"Most of it is hidden, although I have some pieces with me. I thought to sell them for money."

"Please tell me that you haven't sold anything yet?"

"No, the Duchess' severance has proved enough so far... but it won't take me to Amsterdam."

"I dare say not, come, boy, show me what you have?" Uncle Jonathan's words were eagerly spoken, and he edged forward a little on his chair in expectation.

After a moment's hesitation, Daniel pulled out a piece of cloth from his boot that was wrapped around several of Henrietta's jewel studded rings.

They'd adorned her fingers once...

As he reached over and dropped them into his Uncle's waiting hand, Daniel felt a sense of shame that he had betrayed Henrietta, defiling his love by passing her things from his care. Once they were gone, he could no longer fool himself that he was going to return them to her one day. He could no longer fool himself that he wasn't a common thief.

"Very nice..." Uncle Jonathan muttered, examining each ring in turn by lifting it closer to a candle that burned on the side table next to him, "...but quite unsellable."

"I thought they would be valuable?"

"Oh, they are. Very impressive work, the gold and jewels are of the highest quality, but they are quite distinctive. If you were to sell them it would not take long for their providence to be established, and once the Duchess' rings are identified then two things will become immediately apparent."

Daniel looked enquiringly at his Uncle.

"These rings will tell the world that Daniel Plunkett is alive and that he is a thief."

"Then what am I to do?"

Uncle Jonathan wrapped his thick fingers around the rings and rose to his feet, "Leave matters to me."

From his desk, Uncle Jonathan produced a strong box which he opened and after dropping the rings inside he produced a purse which he tossed in Daniel's direction.

Daniel watched dumbly as the purse landed at his feet with a dull metallic thud.

"They are worth more of course, but that is all the coin I have in the house," Uncle Jonathan explained, quickly locking the strongbox once more, "I will have the stones removed and the gold melted down, they will be worth less, but they will be untraceable to the Duchess or you."

Once the strongbox was out of sight, he eased himself back into his chair opposite Daniel, "I will give you the name of a man in Amsterdam, he is reliable, and I suggest you sell the rest through him. A little at a time. Tell him that you have gambling debts which must be settled, and he will pretend to believe you."

"You seem well versed in selling stolen property, Uncle?"

"Commerce my dear boy, 'tis all just commerce."

Daniel scooped up the purse from the floor; it sat heavily in his hand, "Enough to book passage to Amsterdam?"

"More than enough."

Daniel stared at the purse for a while, shifting its weight from one hand to the other, "What will become of me?"

"Look at this business as an opportunity, buy some good travelling clothes and see the world, Daniel. You can become whatever you wish to be now."

"All I wish for is Henrietta."

"The world is full of pretty women... and now you are a rich man I will wager you will find that to be truer than most men do."

"I will book passage tomorrow."

"No, 'tis too dangerous. You're known around the docks and wharves. You worked there not so long ago remember. You cannot risk being seen. I will arrange for you to sail from Harwich. Until then you can stay here. Your Aunt will be away for a few days, it will be kinder if she thinks you dead. Safer too."

"Thank you, Uncle."

"You are my flesh and blood; you have nothing to

thank me for. I am just glad you are alive."

"I wish I could say the same."

"One day you will. Once you're safe in Amsterdam, you must write. I would like to know that you are well."

"Of course," Daniel nodded, but he knew he never would because his Uncle was wrong, he wasn't alive at all. Daniel Plunkett was dead, and he would give his ashes to the North Sea and let Jack Frost take his soul.

When he arrived in Amsterdam, he would be a new man entirely. Then things would be better.

Chapter Fifteen
The Frost Bride

The Queen's Theatre, The Haymarket, London – 1708

The saloon of *The Queen's Theatre* was so packed Caleb could barely move for the acres of crafted silk and yards of piled and powdered hair, hardly see for the sparkle and shimmer of gold and precious stones and scarcely breathe for the gallons of perfume and cologne that their wearers had evidently bathed in. The Quality of London had arrived in force to see the evening's performance of *Thomyris Queen of Scythia*; although, as always with the Quality, the whole affair had far more to do with *being* seen.

"This won't do at all," Caleb muttered in Alyssa's ear, "simply *everybody* is prettier than me."

Alyssa smiled and continued to fan herself as they stood amongst a milling crowd that was ostensibly waiting for the performance to begin, but, in reality, most of the Quality had ensured they had arrived early to allow their peers ample time to marvel at their wealth, beauty and impeccable good taste while they bitched about everybody else's impoverished attire, ugliness and ostentatious gaudiness.

Nobody was paying much attention to Caleb and Alyssa.

"This seems to be quite the social event," Caleb noted, observing the crowd above the rim of his wine glass, before glancing at Alyssa, "how on earth did you get tickets?"

"Oh, I can usually pull in a favour or two when I need to," Alyssa explained, her face was lightly covered with alum powder and her green eyes sparkled mischievously at him like emeralds pitted in snow.

"One of your gentlemen friends?"

"Don't be so impertinent."

"You must be a great devotee of the opera if you have to call in your favours for a pair of tickets."

"Oh, it's a dreadful bore, and I dear say the majority of the people here feel the same way."

"They do? I'd assumed it must be a particularly popular show, given the turnout."

"Thomyris?" Alyssa snorted, "'tis not even a good opera, and there are few things in life duller than bad opera."

"Then why is everybody here?"

"I didn't realise you were so naive."

"I've been away for some time; in Italy, everybody seems to quite enjoy the opera."

"Foreigners for you," Alyssa sniffed.

Caleb smiled to himself and let his eyes return to wandering across the crowd, which seemed singularly blessed with rich young women eager to flaunt their cleavage and jewellery with equal degrees of brazenness. Caleb didn't know quite where to stare.

He offered a flash of a smile at one passing beauty, but she just looked right through him. He supposed compared to the flamboyant displays of wealth and extravagance that surrounded them, he appeared quite dowdy in comparison, not to mention poor, which was probably why nobody would meet his eye; he was literally beneath most of the patron's sight.

Caleb wore his favoured black frock coat embroidered with silver thread, over a muted cream waistcoat and white silk shirt, an unfussy costume that seemed almost shabby in comparison to the opulence on display. Alyssa, although not as gaudily attired as the other women at the theatre looked, in Caleb's opinion, quite stunning; dressed in a low-cut gown of pearl white silk that shimmered like moonlight reflected on snow, a string of milky pearls adorned her neck while two heavy droplets of silver hung from her ears. Unlike many of the women in the saloon she neither wore a wig nor powdered her hair; instead she had artfully piled it atop her head, save for scores of ringlets that tumbled down onto her pale and powdered skin. Her hair seemed even more vividly red than normal against the paleness of her flesh and the silk of her dress; curls of fire writhing above her snowy skin.

Fire and ice, the thought struck Caleb, she could be Jack Frost's bride; the Queen of the Winter...

He found the imagery vaguely disturbing, and as ever was surprised at how powerfully that childish nightmare still haunted him.

Although the saloon boasted many attractive women, many of whom were more naturally beautiful than Alyssa, he thought her by far the most striking. He doubted he would have been able to drag his eyes from her even if he were not her escort for the night and was, therefore, obliged by good form not to stare too openly at other women.

"See the nervous looking fellow other there?" Alyssa asked, nodding in the direction of an agitated middle-aged man who was moving through the saloon enthusiastically glad-handing the illustrious crowd.

"He seems singularly well pleased to see everybody," Caleb noted.

"So he should be, 'tis Mr Vaughn, the theatre's proprietor; rumour has it that he is terribly in debt."

"That would seem surprising given we can barely move for the great and the good."

"He was of the belief that a man might make quite a fortune from the opera; so, he has retained a large company of artists on most generous benefits. Unfortunately, the company is so great and audiences so poor he now owes a small fortune to the Earl of Manchester. Apparently, he has become so desperate he has even written to Queen Anne begging for money. Sadly, for Mr Vaughn, our monarch has little time for the theatre and even less for the opera so he seems to be heading to ruin; unless he can persuade these good people to return to see his shows."

"You mean they're really not here to see *Thomyris Queen of Scythia?*" Caleb asked as he watched Vaughn wring his hands before a woman whose skirts stretched, at least, three yards wide and whose towering powdered wig was decorated with an intricate nest of interlocked twigs and two stuffed songbirds; from what he had overheard the jury of her peers was still undecided whether her outfit was so cuttingly fashionable it put every other lady in the room to shame, or she had made a complete fool of herself by sticking dead birds in her hair. Their verdict would probably decide whether she could show her face in Society for the next six months.

"Indeed not."

"I assume you know why they are all here then, given you seem so abreast of the latest gossip?"

Alyssa smiled, "Gossip is such a vulgar word Mr Cade,

but as you asked, judging by the commotion by the door I believe the reason everybody is here is just entering the room... *now*."

He followed the direction Alyssa indicated with her fan towards a bustle at the far end of the saloon. A murmur of interest rippled through the room and even the hyperactive Mr Vaughn curtailed his sucking up to see what was happening.

Caleb was more than mildly surprised to see that the focus of the storm of fluttering fans, extravagant curtseys and significant glances was none other than Daniel Bourness, the Third Duke of Pevansea. His son.

Danny was resplendent in a vivid cerulean blue frock coat and a hat so wide and sagging with feathers that Louis Defane would have turned green with envy; if he were not a pile of dust lying in Alyssa's father's cellar anyway. Clinging to his arm was a pretty petite girl bedecked with blonde ringlets, trailing acres of cobalt silk in her wake. Caleb wondered who had consulted who on what colours to wear.

She was smiling radiantly in a manner that appeared equal parts smugness and proprietary, it brought to his mind the image of a fox that had caught the plumpest chicken in the yard and was in no mood to share its meal with any other predators.

The young Duke seemed genuinely amused by the fuss their appearance had made and was nodding and smiling in faint embarrassment as the couple were virtually drowned in an incessant tide of gratuitous toadying and obsequious fawning.

"What, exactly, is going on?" Caleb asked Alyssa out of the corner of his mouth, unable to pull his eyes from the spectacle.

"That young man is the Duke of Pevansea, who is, by a generous country mile, the most eligible bachelor in London."

"He is?"

"Young, single, handsome, titled, rich, intelligent, powerful, a favourite of the Queen, he is also blessed with an attribute that is uncommonly rare amongst the English aristocracy."

"Which is?"

"He isn't a complete shit."

"And that's why everybody is here?"

Alyssa nodded, "His companion for the evening is one of probably no more than half a dozen people in England who thinks *Thomyris Queen of Scythia* is not the operatic equivalent of a steaming pile of rancid horse dung. When word got out that she had achieved the notable *coup d'grace* of persuading the Duke to endure sitting through it with her, every Society mother in London rushed to buy tickets so that they could thrust their daughters at the Duke in the hope the scales might fall from His Grace's eyes, allowing him to see that *their* daughter was his one true love, while realising his current companion is just a money-grabbing, ladder-climbing trollop with no manners, breeding or cleavage."

"Is that why you're here tonight?"

"Me?" Alyssa asked, flapping her fan wildly while placing her free hand over her chest in affront at the suggestion, "I am but a humble Doctor's daughter. I'm not the kind of girl a Duke would be looking to marry; besides I am twenty-three and, therefore, far too old for him anyway. He'll be looking for a young wench to pop out lots of squealing babies for him," she added with a shudder, before looking significantly at Caleb through fluttering eyelashes, "Besides, I am already with the most handsome and intriguing man in the room."

"Fair enough," Caleb was forced to agree.

"Though saying that, obviously I'd leave you here like a shot if he asked to bed me tonight," her mouth twisted in a salacious little grin.

"I'll steal myself for the possibility, who is the girl anyway?"

"Lucy Bedford, the youngest daughter of a Bristol merchant."

Caleb raised an eyebrow, "A merchant's daughter? Maybe you have a chance after all."

"The difference being her father is fabulously rich; he

owns plantations in Virginia and the West Indies and has made an absolute fortune from slaves and tobacco; he has built one of the grandest houses in England by all accounts. The only thing his money can't buy, however, is a title; the Queen thinks he's a grubby little coin counter, so he's been pushing his daughters at all of the young aristocrats in England in the hope of bagging one."

Caleb was about to ask how Alyssa managed to be so well informed when Danny caught sight of them lurking in the corner of the saloon being ignored by everybody else.

"Cade!" he beamed and darted away from a portly middle-aged woman smothered in powder and beauty spots who had brought two equally portly daughters for His Grace's consideration. Lucy shot an icy smile at the woman before hurrying triumphantly in the Duke's wake.

Danny was beaming from ear to ear and pumped Caleb's hand with the enthusiasm of a drowning man who had just found a log floating conveniently by, "What a small world, eh?"

"Indeed, it is Your Grace," Caleb said formally, bowing to the Duke; Alyssa glanced at him curiously throughout her curtsey.

"This is all a bit of a palaver eh? Thought it was going to be a quiet night at the opera, but absolutely *everybody* seems to be here; must be a dashed good show!"

In the Absence of Light

"I'm sure it will be most entertaining."

"You must forgive my manners, may I present my companion, Miss Lucy Bedford. Lucy, this is Mr Caleb Cade who was a dear friend of my parents..."

"Really!" Lucy said with a warm and friendly smile.

"...and this is Miss Alyssa Rothery, the daughter of my most excellent physician, Dr Samuel Rothery."

"Pleased to meet you," Lucy smiled in a manner that suggested if Alyssa came one-inch closer to the Duke she would not be responsible for her actions.

"I didn't know you and Miss Rothery were... friendly?" Danny asked, his eyes sparkling with good humour.

"We share a love of the opera."

"Oh good, perhaps you can explain it to me. Always found it a bit of a bore, but Lucy wore me down in the end; just can't say no to her I'm afraid."

Lucy fairly glowed with happiness.

"Lucy, why don't you and Alyssa chat about the opera for a moment, as you're both such aficionados; I just want a quick word with Mr Cade."

Both girls eyed each other frostily as the young Duke took Caleb's elbow and led him as far away from Lucy as the surrounding throng of mothers and daughters would allow him to move.

"You old dog!" Danny chuckled, glancing at Alyssa "didn't take you long eh?"

"I don't know what you mean."

"Ah, of course not," Danny nodded vigorously enough to set the brim of his hat trembling, "but I have to say she's a fine-looking wench; got something about her alright."

"Lucy is very pretty," Caleb said, feeling slightly uncomfortable discussing Alyssa, "I trust your luncheon date with her went well."

"Ah," Danny replied, pulling a face, "best you don't mention that."

"Did something go amiss?"

"Not at all, I had a marvellous time, it just wasn't with Lucy. I mean, we're not betrothed or anything, but she is quite possessive for some reason."

"And you call me an old dog?"

Danny shrugged, "What is a man to do? 'tis ever so strange, ever since I became Duke women simply throw themselves at me. Everybody says I should be getting married, but it seems rather a waste while I'm in such good form with the ladies. No hurry, whatever Anne says."

"The Queen?"

Danny laughed, "No my big sister, not a week passes without a letter from her extolling the virtues of marriage and parenthood."

Caleb remembered the little girl hiding in Henrietta's skirts as Babbington burned; "How is little Anne?"

"Of course, you haven't seen her since she was

a child; oh, she's a beauty now alright. Got herself married to the Marquis of Marlow five years ago; nice enough chap, but dashed boring, only ever wants to talk about pig breeding for some reason. Still, Anne's sickeningly happy with him. Pops out another nephew or niece for me every year or so."

"How many children does she have?"

Danny shrugged, "Oh, I've lost count, that's one of the advantages of being Duke, apart from the money and women of course, I have staff to deal with that sort thing, birthday presents, Christmas presents, all that bother; best to keep the little blighters happy, though. Who knows, if I fall off my horse like poor Richard before I get hitched and heired-up one of them will end up as Duke. Wouldn't want them saying I was a mean old fellow."

"Enjoy yourself, Danny, life is short, don't end up doing something you don't want. When you meet a woman you want to marry, you'll know it."

"You're a capital fellow Cade, my thoughts exactly, I should be level headed about such matters. No reason to give up the drinking and wenching until I need to, eh?"

"Precisely."

Danny laughed and embraced Caleb, slapping his back in a hearty and rather un-English manner, "Best I keep moving else I might get trapped beneath an avalanche of daughters, come to my club one night so we can have a proper chat."

"I will," Caleb smiled and watched his son disappear once more amongst the throng of skirts and adoring looks. As he moved back to Alyssa's side, his progress was marked by numerous "Good evenings" and welcoming smiles. Nobody still knew who he was, but as he clearly was a good friend of the Duke he was suddenly worthy of acknowledgement and everybody was eager to put right the fact they'd previously ignored him.

"She's a pretty little thing," Caleb said, watching Lucy clinging to the Duke's arm as he raised a glass to his lips.

"Indeed, she is," Alyssa agreed evenly, "though I don't suppose she sucks cock half so well as I do."

Several of the eager mothers looked around sharply. Not because of Alyssa's words, which had been too softly spoken for anyone else to hear, but because the stranger in the modestly adorned coat who, despite appearances, was clearly *somebody*, had inexplicably and rather uncouthly just spurted a plume of red wine out of his nose.

*

It took Caleb barely ten minutes to decide *Thomyris Queen of Scythia* was as turgid and dreary as he'd feared. The show's alternative title was *The Amazon Queen* and even his modest hope that he would be able to enjoy the artistic interpretation of the Amazons, who any scholar of the classics would happily tell you were lithe, beautiful and very scantily clad, was soon dashed.

Rather ridiculously, in his opinion, Mr Vaughn had cast flabby middle-aged women in the role of the Amazonian warriors in the mistaken belief that people preferred ugly actresses who could sing, over pretty ones that couldn't. Caleb wondered if Mr Vaughn would be interested in his ideas on how to get more bums onto the seats of his theatre.

Still, Caleb found some small pleasure from looking down at the sea of heaving cleavage that heaved all the more dramatically whenever the Duke of Pevansea's eyes wandered from the stage (which happened often) and then shuddered with indignation and disapproval whenever Lucy cozied up to the young Duke in order to whisper something in his ear (which happened even more often).

Caleb also noticed that, although the Duke was getting most of the attention, more than a few curious glances were being cast in his direction. Obviously, nobody had a clue who he was and he'd been dutifully ignored in the saloon, but the fact he was a friend of the Duke had marked him as a man now worthy of note and the fact that he was suffering the ghastly *Thomyris Queen of Scythia* from one of the theatre's private boxes, when much of the Quality of London had to make do with a seat in the stalls in order to thrust their daughter's breasts into the Duke of Pevansea's eye line for a few seconds, suggested that he was a man of means as well as mystery.

The fact that he had no more idea than they did how Alyssa had managed to bag the second-best box in the theatre, Danny and Lucy had the Royal Box, did not diminish the vague sense of pleasure he derived from the notion that numerous Ladies of Quality were showing an interest in the son of Puritan rabble-rouser, a one-time footman, a thief, a sharper of hearts and general all round bad egg.

He had never really known why women were attracted to him, even less so the exceptionally beautiful ones like Henrietta and Isabella. On the rare occasions he did look in the mirror he saw nothing particularly remarkable in the reflection; an ordinary looking man, no faults or flaws, but nothing to explain the regularity with which women seemed to fall into his arms. Not that it was something he ever seriously complained about.

He had been curious about it once and had asked several of his conquests why they had been drawn to him. The first had told him that it was because his smile lit up her world and the twinkle in his eye was seductive as the devil himself; the second woman had told him that she found him irresistible because he had a faint, but distinct, aura of evil about him.

He hadn't asked anybody again.

Caleb glanced at Alyssa; in the dim half-light of

the theatre, she looked for once more beautiful than striking. She seemed to be paying no more attention to the opera than he was for her eyes were fixed upon the audience, resting on any one spot for only a moment before moving on, a vague look of amusement resting upon her face alongside a faint crooked grin.

"How did you manage to get a box?" Caleb asked, leaning close to her. Not so much that she might hear his whisper more clearly, but to allow the soft ringlets of her red hair brush lightly against his cheek.

"I told you," she replied without looking at him, "I called in a favour or two."

"So that we could see a bad opera?"

"Yes, 'tis rather dreadful, isn't it?" She laughed softly, "however all the real entertainment is down there in the audience, all those grand ladies and their daughters making a frightful fuss about the Duke and Miss Bedford; they think she is quite the money grabbing hussy apparently.

"They shouldn't worry; I don't think Danny has any plans to marry her."

"Danny?"

"I'm an old friend of the family," Caleb explained.

"Yes, I meant to ask you about that; you're full of surprises it seems."

"Well, life would be boring if you knew everything,

wouldn't it Miss Rothery?"

"Indeed, it would Mr Cade," she turned her eyes on him then and he had to catch his breath for they seemed to glow impishly in the half-light, "but that will never stop me trying."

They regarded each for a while, and Caleb fought down the urge to kiss her; his new-found admirers down below would probably consider it terrible form.

"Very handsome," she said eventually.

"I'm not the kind of man who succumbs easily to flattery."

"I meant Danny."

"Oh, yes I suppose he is... and it's the Duke of Pevansea to the likes of you."

"You know you look a little like him?"

"I do?" Caleb asked innocently.

"Yes, around the eyes most definitely," her crooked grin broke into a fully-fledged smile, "you could be brothers."

"Hmmm, I don't see it myself..."

"Perhaps we should tell people you are a distant cousin; the ladies down there will be most impressed. I'm sure in their eyes that would make you an acceptable second best if their daughters miss out on the Duke."

"How flattering of you to say so, but I'm not in the mood for marriage just yet."

"Why not? You're quite old to be a bachelor."

"And you're quite impertinent for a young lady."

"I prefer to think of myself as endearingly eccentric," Alyssa adjusted her skirts and returned her eyes to watching the audience, "although I think most men find me a wee bit unsettling."

"I don't."

"I've noticed."

"Even when I'm being crude and vulgar?

"So long as you are as crude and vulgar in bed as you are out of it."

"Now who is being impertinent? Not to mention *presumptuous*..."

"It was you who crawled into *my* bed."

"And I have yet to decide whether I shall ever do such a thing again... I am still considering the matter."

"And what must I do to convince you?"

She looked at him again, her eyes wide and unblinking.

"Dance with me."

Caleb raised an eyebrow, "Dance? I know it is a poor opera, but even so I doubt the audience would prefer to see us on stage."

"Later, you will dance with me... and then I will decide what is to be done with you."

With that she turned her full attention back to the

stage, her chin lifted and her nose slightly in the air; evidently the matter was not open for further discussion.

*

Although the *Star Tavern* was little more than a hundred paces from *The Queen's Theatre*, the clientele could not have been more different from the well-heeled gentleman and lavishly dressed ladies they had left at the opera. Caleb, however, was in no mood to complain as he had always felt more comfortable in the company of drunks, wastrels and whores than he had amongst the Quality.

"Isn't it marvellous?" Alyssa beamed from the tavern's doorway, before gripping his hand and leading Caleb towards the bar as if he needed some encouragement.

Back in the *Queen's Theatre* Caleb's sober attire had made him stick out from the crowd of flamboyantly dressed men with their garish coats of every colour, however in the *Star Tavern* his neatly pressed and recently washed clothes made him stand out for exactly the opposite reason. His fingers brushed lightly against the hilt of his sword; the mark of a gentleman amongst the Quality, it was more likely to be seen as the mark of a tempting robbery victim amongst the lower sorts.

The *Star* was by no means a particularly rough establishment, and many of the patrons were probably clerks and artisans; he'd frequented far worse in London and elsewhere, but he struggled to remember being in one with such a well-dressed and attractive woman; a well-dressed and attractive woman dripping in jewellery to boot.

Alyssa was certainly attracting attention as they pushed their way through to the bar, but given Alyssa suffered no worse than a couple of playful grabs for her arse the interest appeared to be motivated by good honest lechery rather than anything more villainous.

Despite the throng, the barkeeper hurried over to them almost as soon as they found a space, being something of a cynic Caleb thought it was more likely he was motivated by the hope of grabbing a closer look at Alyssa's cleavage than by being keenly efficient.

"Good evening Sir, good evening Miss" he grinned, wiping his hands on his grubby apron as he leaned forward to take their order and get a better look at Alyssa, "what will be your pleasure?"

"Two of your biggest jars of your best ale," Alyssa said, leaning purposefully towards the barman before Caleb could open his mouth.

"Right you are Miss..." the barman then set about pouring possibly the two slowest beers in the history of bar keeping as Alyssa remained leaning on the bar, and in doing so provided an exemplary display of her cleavage to the suddenly sweating man. It was a view he clearly intended to enjoy for the longest possible time, along with a dozen of his patrons whose conversations had all inexplicably dried up as they turned to stare as Alyssa.

"Good evening gentlemen," Caleb nodded at the collected gawpers along the bar, "cold tonight, eh?"

He was unsurprised to be totally ignored. Instead, he fumbled for some coins from his purse to pay for the drinks, and by the time the bartender had returned with his change Alyssa had slapped her empty tankard back on the bar. "Another please!"

The bartender looked at Caleb, who glanced at his own drink, which he had not had the time even to pick up yet, before shrugging, "me too."

"Thirsty?" Caleb asked.

To a palpable groan of disappointment, Alyssa turned her back on the bar, rested her elbows on the ledge, and grinned at him. Strangely, despite her fancy attire, she looked as at home here as she had in the saloon of *The Queen's Theatre*.

Once the barman had returned with more drinks, Caleb had hoped to move Alyssa off to a more discreet nook of the tavern, but she was having none of it. "I'm quite happy here, thank you," she said, sipping her latest drink at a more ladylike pace.

"You seem to be attracting a lot of attention," Caleb muttered.

"Oh, really? I hadn't noticed," she smiled innocently;

"you're not getting jealous, are you?"

"Of course, I'm worried you might run off with that fellow over there with his eyes out on stalks and the boil on the end of his nose," Caleb pursed his lips, "and that would be a terrible blow to my vanity."

Alyssa laughed and arched her long white neck back slightly; Caleb had to gulp his beer to fight down the urge to sink his teeth into it.

"I like sex..." Alyssa said suddenly. Caleb was not quite sure whether it was an invitation or an explanation and before he could decide she continued, "...a lot of men don't like that, it frightens them."

"Does it?"

Alyssa nodded emphatically, "Because a woman who openly likes sex has power, the power to manipulate and control men, for men are actually rather simple creatures who think far more with their cocks than their brains and when they are ensnared by a woman they become afraid of their powerlessness. Why do you think men think up so many hateful names for women like me; whore, harlot, slut, slattern, hussy, trollop, doxy, drab? All because I want to take some pleasure from the body God gave me. But you, you're not afraid of my wantonness at all, are you Cade?"

"No."

"And why is that?"

"As you say, I think mostly with my cock," he flashed

his most winning smile at her, "perhaps I have the good fortune to have a cock that knows no fear."

She laughed again, before leaning closer towards him, "Shall we see how you dance then?"

She nodded towards the far side of the tavern where a pair of fiddlers were belting out jigs with feverish energy. Tables and chairs had been cleared to allow people to dance and the space had filled with beaux, whores and sweethearts spinning around each other as those standing to watch clapped their hands and stomped their feet to create a beat for the fiddlers.

Caleb finished both his beers in short order before wrapping his hand around hers and leading her through the crowd. There was little room to dance and Alyssa's flowing dress was not best suited to confined spaces, but the revellers were in good humour, and there were no complaints as they pushed in. There was little formality and less elegance here, so Caleb simply wrapped his hands around Alyssa's waist, and they were soon swirling and spinning as frenetically as everybody else.

The two fiddlers were belting out their jigs with a furious passion; they were both young lads, whose similar dark eyes and locks marked them out as brothers. They were grinning broadly and clearly enjoying themselves as much as the crowd. Londoners loved nothing more than drinking and dancing (with the possible exceptions of public executions, blood sports and being disrespectful to their betters), but were notoriously hard to please. If the fiddlers had been poor, they would not only have gone unpaid but they probably would have been chased out of the tavern and received a beating for their troubles. Luckily for them, they knew their fiddles and the crowd were showing their appreciation by thumping their feet so hard Caleb could feel the floorboards vibrating beneath them.

Alyssa was giggling wildly as they span about the floor, tossing her head so vigorously in time to the music that some of her hair escaped its restraints of clips and pins to fall about her pale powdered face. All the time those bright green eyes sparkled and filled with the laughter that was constantly escaping her throat; which Caleb found he was still highly inclined to bite.

He wasn't sure how long they danced, for time ceased to be something that could be measured as he lost himself in the music and the feel of Alyssa so close to him that he feared he might burst with desire. Later he couldn't remember if they said a word to each other while they had danced, but they didn't need to for the music said everything that needed to be said and when she eventually stepped away from him and pulled his hand he knew exactly what she wanted.

*

He shivered as soon as he stepped outside the tavern, it had become cold enough for his breath to mist the air; although it was spring Jack Frost seemed more reluctant than usual to release the world from his grip this year.

"Are you not cold?" He asked, starting to take off his jacket. Alyssa wore only a light summer shawl over her dress.

She smiled and pulled the shawl away to reveal her bare skin of her chest.

"I love the feel of the winter on my skin, it makes me feel so alive," she shivered, "it's like a thousand tiny pins pricking into your skin."

That didn't sound much like Caleb's idea of fun, but he'd already concluded Alyssa was a "strange girl."

Before he could say anything, she tugged on his hand and led him towards an alley that run alongside the side of the *Star Tavern*, he could still hear the fiddlers inside, and he was surprised the whole building wasn't shaking. The alley was dim and littered with old beer barrels stacked up awaiting a drayman to take them back to the brewery. A full moon hung in the sky and its silvery light was enough to let them pick a way through the clutter. Alyssa stopped near the back of the tavern, where a high wall separated them from the yard at the back of the tavern where patrons could come to piss out the beer that had once filled the barrels around them.

There was a small stretch of wall uncluttered by barrels, and Alyssa stood against it regarding him as the moonlight turned her skin to the colour of frost.

"Did I dance well enough?"

"Well enough indeed," she grinned, pulling up the front of her skirts a little to indicate what she wanted.

"'tis a delightful spot you've picked," Caleb noted looking around him; a dark lump nestling in the shadows of the opposite wall looked suspiciously like a dead dog.

"It has a certain earthy appeal..." she pulled the skirts of her dress up another couple of inches, "...much like myself, in fact."

Caleb stepped forward and gripped her waist, feeling her breath on his face as she tilted her head, but when he tried to come closer, she placed a hand lightly on his chest to stop him. When he frowned, she raised her other hand and opened her palm.

Caleb frown deepened.

"Tuppence for your pleasures Sir!" she insisted.

"Are you serious?"

She pushed him gently away.

Shaking his head he fumbled for his purse before carefully laying out two smooth worn penny pieces in her palm. "Thanking you kindly," she smiled, wrapping her fingers around the coins, "you may continue as you will now."

Slowly she lifted her skirts and petticoats to reveal the silk stockings tied about her thighs with black ribbons. Caleb thought himself a considerate and skilful lover; other than her jewellery it had been the only thing of worth Henrietta had ever given him. However, all such thoughts were seared from Caleb's mind by the sight of Alyssa's smooth white skin and he felt as needy and clumsy as any lusty frustrated virgin as he fumbled with his britches and released his cock. He hissed slightly through his teeth, for the night really had turned exceptionally cold.

He fumbled through his coat pockets and pulled out a pig's bladder sheath which he hurriedly pulled over his cock and used the leather cords wound around it to tie it into place.

"You have no need of that," Alyssa advised watching him with lascivious curiosity, "I'm not poxed."

"Every whore I've ever fucked has told me the same thing," Caleb hissed, his voice sounding harsh and cold in his own ears, but Alyssa just smiled, "then you must treat me the same... just be quick about it."

He returned to her embrace and she hoisted herself up, wrapping her legs around him. Caleb's hands found her buttocks beneath the layers of silk skirts and petticoats that encased it, and took her weight. It was neither the most comfortable nor pleasurable of positions, but his need was so desperate he had no care and managed to find his way inside her after only a couple of fumbled attempts. It was strange, for he found he could take her weight quite easily, she must weigh less that she looked.

Or you are stronger than you used to be...

He pushed the thought away for his lust was too powerful for any other considerations. She gasped as he thrust inside her and he felt her nails digging into him through his coat and shirt. His forehead was hard against hers, and her green eyes bore into him as he thrust ever harder. He moved to kiss her, but she turned her head sharply away.

"My kiss will cost you more than tuppence," she said, her breath harsh and fast.

"How much?"

"You must give me your heart for that."

"What would you say if I told you already had it?"

"I'd call you a liar."

"Clever girl..." Caleb grunted.

He could hear the beat of the music coming from the tavern; in fact, he could feel it, throbbing across the packed earth of the alley to vibrate up his legs. His thrusting pelvis took up the beat of stomping feet and clapping hands as if the revellers inside were providing a musical accompaniment to his own performance.

Alyssa's breathing was becoming as harsh and fast as his own; their frigid breath entwining about them in the cold moon-brushed air.

She buried her face in his neck and in doing so presented the side of her own neck, smooth and white as alabaster. Without thought he bit her. Not hard enough to draw blood, but hard enough for her to cry out, he could taste her perfume harsh and sweet on his tongue, he could feel her hair soft on his face, he could feel the cold silver of her earring against his cheek, but above all he could feel her blood, so close, so powerful and vibrant, just below the skin, her life force, her essence, so terribly close.

He bit her again, and again, each time harder than the last. Alyssa dug her fingers into him more urgently, and her cry became a gasping sob, but she did not struggle or try to break away, so he bit her again harder still, his teeth pulling at her skin so ferociously he thought it might come away in his mouth. He thought of her throat, so delicate and soft and what it would be like to find it with his teeth and tear at it till it came apart and sprayed her hot vibrant blood into his mouth...

He came then, a great racking shudder coursed through his whole body, and he feared he might just drop Alyssa onto the dirt of the alley, but she clung to him all the harder until the last faint shudder had subsided.

They stayed entwined for a little while, once more she rested her head against his forehead a smile lighting her face softly in the moonlight, "That was quite... passionate," she breathed finally.

"I didn't... hurt you did I?" Caleb asked both horrified and excited by what he'd done to her and what, for a moment, he had wanted to do to her.

"Of course you hurt me," she giggled, "but I'm not complaining."

"I don't quite know what came over me," Caleb said, though he knew well enough what it was; the ghost of Louis Defane. That tiniest fragment of the vampire that he had taken within him when he'd drunk his blood.

He moved to let her down, but she squeezed him harder, "No, hold me a little longer; let me feel your warmth."

Caleb nodded and did as she asked.

"You really are quite beautiful," he breathed, after realising he wasn't able to pull his eyes away from her.

Alyssa laughed softly, "And you really are quite a strange man Cade."

"Strange?"

"Most men shower me with compliments, and then once they have gotten what they want they hardly have a good word to say about me; whereas you have not paid me a single compliment until after you have had me."

"Perhaps I did not fully appreciate your beauty until I saw it as it is now, softly painted in the gossamer light of the moon; skin of frost, hair of fire, eyes of emerald..."

Caleb breathed, "...or perhaps it is just the smell of stale piss and decaying dog flesh which hangs about this alley that is addling my mind."

Alyssa hit him playfully on the arm, and he gently let her down laughing, before jumping back to avoid another swipe.

"You are indeed a terrible man!"

"I have never pretended otherwise," Caleb grinned.

"Are you going to leave that just hanging there?" Alyssa nodded at the sheath which hung limply from his flaccid cock by its leather cords as she shook down her skirts.

Caleb untied it and shoved into one of his pockets to wash out later, before fixing his britches.

"Do we look presentable now?" Alyssa asked once he'd finished.

"Well apart from..." Caleb indicated her neck which already sported a collection of dark bruises.

Alyssa looked down at her shoulder and tutted, "Naughty boy..."

She turned her back on him and asked him to help her take down her hair; between them, it only took a few minutes to locate and remove the clips and pins that had held it so carefully in place. Caleb marvelled at its softness and spent as much time running it through his fingers as he did looking for pins. Once it was finally free, Alyssa shook out her locks and let them tumble down to her shoulders. She then wrapped her shawl around herself and all the evidence of Caleb's lust was discreetly hidden.

"How do I look?" She asked, turning to face him again.

"Like an Amazon princess."

"Not a Queen?"

"According to *Thomyris*, the Amazon Queen was old and fat. I'm sure it's historically accurate."

She slipped her hand through his arm, and they wandered back onto the Haymarket, despite the hour there were still a few people about, but no one seemed to notice them, and they made their way back towards *The Queen's Theatre* in companionable silence.

Caleb was surprised to see a throng of people and carriages outside the theatre; the opera must have ground to a dismal end ages ago, but the Quality had clearly not yet dispersed.

As they grew closer Caleb recognised Danny's landau, the leather top of which had now been pulled over to offer some respite from the cold. The carriage was surrounded by a throng of well-heeled ladies and Caleb guessed the fact that the Duke was still here was probably why everybody else had found pressing reasons not to go home yet.

As they walked alongside the carriage, Danny's grinning head popped out.

"Cade! Miss Rothery! Can I offer you a ride?"

Before Caleb could find some excuse to decline Alyssa had beamed her thanks and was clambering aboard no sooner than Danny had opened the door.

"That's very kind," Caleb said, still standing in the middle of The Haymarket.

"No trouble at all; will be the Devil's own job to find a carriage at this hour."

Caleb hoisted himself inside the landau and settled himself next to Alyssa. Lucy was sitting opposite, wrapped in enough furs to suggest someone had depopulated a small forest; she welcomed them with a smile that fell no more than a quarter of an inch from being a snarl.

"You don't mind do you, my dear?" Danny asked Lucy, "can't have old friends of the family wandering around at night."

"Not at all," Lucy replied frostily.

"The Bedford residence driver!" Danny called, tapping his cane against the roof of the carriage.

"Yes, Your Grace!" The driver's muffled response was followed momentarily by the crack of a whip; as the carriage rolled forward, Danny leaned across Lucy to wave at the mothers and daughters still hovering around the steps of the theatre.

"What a turn out, eh? Simply *everybody* was there!" Danny grinned, finally settling back into his seat, before adding with a frown, "Did anyone think to ask Lady Forrester about those dead sparrows in her hair? Quite ghastly."

"'tis a fashion silly," Lucy chided, "and they were nightingales."

"Well, fashion or not, seems daft to me; can understand mounting a stag you've bagged on the wall, but dead birds in your hair... really! Perhaps next time I go out on the town, I'll balance a dead cat on my head and see what people think."

"You are funny," Lucy sighed; acknowledging the young Duke was unlikely ever to grasp the finer sensibilities of fashion.

"I noticed you two didn't come back after the interval; decided to sneak out of that dread- er... delightful opera, eh?"

"We popped out," Caleb offered, by way of explanation.

"We went dancing," Alyssa added.

"Dancing!" Lucy brightened, "Oh, I love to dance, I didn't realise there was a ball tonight?"

"No, it was in a tavern down the road," Alyssa explained, the mischievous twinkle back in her eyes.

"Oh... a tavern? How... *quaint.*"

"I don't know, sounds rather fun to me," Danny beamed, "what did you get up to?"

Alyssa was in full flow before Caleb could reply, "Well, it was tremendously exciting; there were two fiddlers playing these fabulous jigs and after Mr Cade and I downed a few ales, we danced like merry dervishes. The place was full of drunks and whores of course, but that just added to the colour of the place really. And after we had danced until we were fair giddy from all the spinning and twirling Mr Cade took me outside and fu-"

"Found some air!" Caleb interrupted, "it was very smoky in there; no good at all for Miss Rothery's lungs I decided."

Alyssa smiled sweetly.

"My, that does sound fun. Almost wished I'd come along." Danny said brightly, his eyes darting between the two of them.

"The more the merrier," Alyssa grinned.

Caleb kicked her foot.

"Well, it sounds rather coarse to me," Lucy sniffed, "the opera was much more fun, wasn't it Danny?"

"Oh yes. Marvellous." Danny agreed, rather bleakly.

The next few minutes passed in silence as Lucy stared out of the open window at the darkened streets of London and Danny played with his flowing lace cuffs.

"You haven't met Miss Rothery's father, have you Lucy?" Danny piped up eventually

"No."

"Very clever chap; excellent physician... if you ever need a good physician..."

"I'm sure he's very good, but Papa retains the services of Sir Charles Lynton, who is widely considered being the best physician in London."

"Well, I dear say, but Dr Rothery is an uncommonly knowledgeable chap; a member of the Royal Society no less. Isn't that so Miss Rothery?"

"Indeed, Your Grace; my father is blessed with a passionate and consuming curiosity about all manner of things..."

"See, very clever. Not as clever as Sir Isaac of course, but pretty close I'd say."

"Sir Isaac?" Caleb inquired.

"Oh, there I go, dropping names again ha-ha! Sir Isaac Newton, President of the Royal Society and Master of the Mint. Now everybody says he's a genius; quite right too, damned clever fellow," Danny pursed his lips thoughtfully, "can't understand a word he says mind, but dashed clever all the same. Tried reading his thingy on gravitation once; managed three pages before my head started hurting; must be damned clever if you can write stuff that makes a fellow's head hurt. Ever read it, Cade?"

"I believe Dr Rothery did recommend it to me... but I haven't gotten around to it just yet."

"Well, put a couple of years aside if you want to try.

That's what I plan to do when I'm a bit older and not so busy running around... with stuff. Ah, here already, splendid!" The Duke jumped out of the carriage and helped Lucy down onto the street, "I'll just see Lucy home; won't be a tick. Say goodnight Lucy."

"Goodnight," Lucy said coolly, "a pleasure to meet you both."

"Likewise," Caleb said, starting to climb out of the carriage to say goodnight properly, but Lucy had already turned on her heels and was stomping off towards the imposing townhouse the carriage had drawn up alongside.

"Oh, dear," Caleb sighed settling back next to Alyssa, "I think we might have upset her."

"I can't imagine how," Alyssa purred, playing with one of the long fallen strands of her hair.

"Hmmm, you really are a quite scandalous minx aren't you, my dear?"

"Oh, I haven't shocked you with my wickedness have I?"

"Not at all," Caleb grinned, "I don't shock easily."

"Oh good, I do so enjoy a challenge."

Alyssa leaned forward for a moment to look at the house, "How long do you think the handsome young Duke will be inside?"

"No idea. Why?"

She turned her mischievous eyes towards him, "Just

thinking how we might entertain ourselves while we wait..." she reached over and squeezed his knee playfully.

"Excuse me, Miss Rothery," Caleb said aghast, "I think you'll find 'tis my responsibility to take advantage of *you*. 'tis your job to be coy and resistant to my wicked plans."

"There I go, getting it all wrong again; though I must say you're doing a pretty poor job of taking advantage of me. We have been alone for nearly two whole minutes, and yet I remain utterly unflustered, with not so much as a ruffle in my skirts or button half undone."

She moved closer to him, but when he leant across to kiss her, she jerked away.

"I was not joking about that kiss you know."

"And you call me strange; how can you be so free with your favour and yet so miserly with your kisses?"

"'tis not strange, simply contrary; which is how all ladies should behave."

"What harm is there in a kiss?"

"No harm at all, 'tis what lovers do I am led to understand, and when you look upon me as a lover and not a whore you shall be allowed that favour."

"I don't think of you as a whore."

"Yet you take me down a dark alley and pay me tuppence for your pleasures?"

"But-"

She silenced him with a finger laid across his lips, "I am only teasing you; I just consider my heart to be less of a trifle than my body. Is that so terribly strange?"

"You are in all things singularly strange Alyssa."

"That sounds so much nicer than "Miss Rothery" don't you think?"

"Well, if we are keeping things on a business-like footing..."

"Indeed, Mr Cade, indeed, and until such time as you love me I will remain Miss Rothery, if you please," she stared at him demurely out of the corner of her eye, "do you think it would it be so very hard to fall in love with me?"

For most men, it would be the easiest thing in the world, for she was quite intoxicating, but he was not most men. Caleb did not know what part of a man allowed love to flourish, be it his heart, his soul or some other intangible part of his being, but wherever it lay, Henrietta had burned it out of him twenty years ago; burned it as effectively as the flames that had consumed Babbington House.

"Not so very hard," Caleb lied and despised himself all the more for it.

"And yet I do not believe you ever will..."

"We hardly know each other."

"Indeed!" she agreed "better we stick to fucking for now."

Caleb laughed; he swore he had never met a woman

quite like Alyssa Rothery.

Before he could respond, the door of the carriage popped open, and Danny clambered inside. "Lincoln's Inn Fields if you please driver!"

"Phew! Narrow escape." Danny beamed, settling himself into his seat opposite them, "dashed grateful to you two, saved me an awful lot of bother."

"Pleasure to be of assistance," Caleb smiled, "erm... how have we been of assistance exactly?"

"Perfect excuse to get away from Lucy's father, have to see you two safely home and all. If you hadn't had been here I would have suffered hours of ear bending about what a magnificent father-in-law he'd be, what wonderful grandchildren Lucy and I could give him and just how big a dowry he'd provide for Lucy," Danny wrinkled his nose, "never much cared for boastfulness, very un-gentlemanly."

"Just how big a dowry?" Caleb asked before he could stop himself.

"Oh, simply huge; enough to keep a couple of courtesans on the go for an entire marriage I'd wager," Danny looked at Alyssa and pulled a face, "sorry about that Miss, just a little joke."

"Not a problem Your Grace," Alyssa smiled faintly, "I know how boys are..."

"Ah, quite so... and please don't bother with all that Your Grace malarkey. Danny is just fine... though probably not in front of Lucy."

"Of course."

"And how is Miss Bedford, she seemed a mite... *huffy*, if you don't mind me asking?"

"Oh, she's a lovely girl and all, but she has got it in her head I'm going to propose to her every time I see here. When I don't, she gets... well, huffy."

"Perhaps you should put her out of her misery?" Alyssa suggested.

"Oh, I know I should, but if I tell her that I don't want to marry her, she'll get all broken-hearted hearted and weepy. Dear say she won't want to see me again and I do rather like her, despite her dreadful father."

"But you don't love her?"

"Oh, what's love got to do with marriage? A chap has courtesans for that kind of thing. Marriage is about money, influence and producing heirs, love would be a bonus."

"Excuse me if I'm being too inquisitive," Caleb asked carefully, "but do you *need* Mr Bedford's money?"

"Well, I don't need it..." Danny shrugged, "but Father did spend rather a lot of money rebuilding Babbington House, our country seat, what with the taxes to pay for the war with France and the cost of living in London, which is quite frightful. Things aren't as flush as they once were."

"So, you do need someone like Mr Bedford?"

"Or some other means of making money…" Danny looked pointedly at Caleb, before shrugging, "I'm in no fear of the poorhouse, but a fat dowry is always welcome."

"Don't marry someone you don't love," Caleb said, surprised at how forcefully he spoke the words, "there are always other ways."

"I know," the young Duke smiled and pulled out his pocket watch, "speaking of which, if we hurry I might still catch the card game the chaps are running at the club tonight. Who knows, luck might smile on me, after all, eh?"

"You never know," Caleb almost sighed, "you never really know…"

*

"You won't tell anybody about the Duke's money troubles, will you?" Caleb asked Alyssa as they watched his landau turn out of Lincoln's Inn Fields.

"No, will you?"

"Of course not."

"A lot of people would be extremely interested in that little snippet of information."

"It was *very* unguarded of him to mention it, considering he hardly knows us."

"Hardly knows you," Caleb corrected, "I'm almost family."

"Perhaps he's looking for a replacement for his brother; he has no family in London."

"I'm sure he has plenty of friends who can fill that role."

Alyssa shook her head, "His friends are mostly wasters and spongers; if you need to know where the family's money is going, you need to look no further than there. Shame really, he's a rather agreeable boy."

"I don't suppose your father could offer him a big enough dowry eh?"

Alyssa demonstrated her usual ladylike refinement by punching his arm.

"Father's home," she noted, looking up at the window of the Doctor's study which was glowing fiercely from the candles and lanterns within.

"And he will be asking where you've been?"

"Oh, he rarely notices me; his nose is always stuck too far into his books, or too far up one of his patient's rect-"

"I get the picture."

"Still, best he doesn't know we've been together."

"You think he won't approve of me?"

"*Of course* he won't approve, he isn't *that* negligent a father. His known you long enough to work out you're a scoundrel by now."

"Thank you."

"I'll let myself in through the servant's entrance if you don't mind waiting a few minutes in the cold."

"For you..."

She smiled and held out her hand demurely, "You *may* kiss my hand."

"Are you thawing to me then?"

"'tis only my lips that are out of bounds. You may kiss the rest of me freely."

Caleb smiled, and took her hand, which was like ice, and kissed it softly before letting her fingers run reluctantly through his.

"You should dress properly in future, you'll freeze to death."

She walked backwards away from him, "My father may chide me Cade; you, however, may not. You'll just have to accept me the way that I am."

"Will you come to me later?"

"Perhaps," she mused, cocking her head to one side as she continued to walk backwards, "perhaps not."

"I will have to hope for the best then."

She smiled, suddenly and radiantly, "Leave tuppence on your bed table just in case," before hitching up her skirts, turning and running down the side of the house, leaving only laughter in her wake.

"Trouble," a voice said at his side as soon as she'd disappeared from view, "mark my words, she'll be trouble."

Caleb glanced at the memory of his brother who had appeared at his side.

"But what splendid trouble," Caleb sighed, "I could do worse, I'm sure the Doctor would pay a generous dowry. I could settle down, have children. Stop running."

"Eighteen months at most," his brother replied, "eighteen months and you'd be bored. You'd find yourself back on the road with the remnants of your dowry and all her better jewellery in your saddlebag. Just like every other time."

"Perhaps it might be different now?"

"It will only be different if you found someone to love little brother; do you think you could love Alyssa? Or Harriet for that matter? I see it every time as I sit in the back of your mind, like a theatre-goer watching the grand play that is your life; or rather the grand tragedy."

"It hasn't really been that bad; we've seen some things, you and I. Just like I promised."

"I thought we would tour Europe and see all the magnificent works of art; the paintings, the sculpture, the architecture; all the beauty that humanity is capable of. It didn't quite work out like that."

"Yes, it did. We saw the Sistine Chapel, you enjoyed that."

"Michelangelo's work was a marvel," the memory of his brother admitted, "but you only went there to impress that French Count's daughter."

Caleb shrugged, "So, it worked out well for both of us.

You got to see Michelangelo's paintings and I got to see-"

"Yes! I remember very well *what* you got to see. I'm surprised all the Popes of Rome were not spinning in their graves at that point."

Caleb smiled ruefully, but it quickly faded with a sigh, "What should I do?"

"Go inside before we both freeze to death... you know we should have stayed in Italy, it was warm in Italy."

"You can't feel the cold, so what does it matter to you?"

"No, but it is in my interests to keep you alive; though why I bother I have quite forgotten, it does get rather boring watching you getting all in a quandary about the latest woman who happens to have fallen for your questionable charms."

"All I want is to be happy."

"Happy? You've got money, health and women throwing themselves at you with monotonous regularity. If you can't be happy with that, then what do you need?"

"Love," Caleb shrugged.

The memory of his brother snorted, "I have come to the conclusion you are simply one of the perpetually disenchanted; whatever riches life throws your way, you manage to conjure a way of finding misery from them."

"Perhaps..." Caleb walked slowly towards the front door of Rothery's house. He didn't try to find an answer, for he knew his brother had gone again.

He was right of course, he should be able to find happiness. He could make Alyssa love him; that was not a problem, that was never a problem. It was the strange and perverse nature of his own unique curse that he could make women love him with relative ease, but he could never love them in return. Rather than remaining to feel empty, to see nothing reflected back from the mirror of another's love, he broke their hearts, he stole their money, he never stayed still, still, still...

That was what he did, what he was. Nought but a sharper of hearts and Alyssa would probably be his next victim whether he wanted her to be or not.

His suddenly gloomy mood was not particularly lifted when Scaife's sour face greeted him at the door. Before Caleb could disappear to the sanctuary of his own room, the servant indicated with an insistent beckoning hand that he should follow him.

Finding it impossible to argue with a tongue-less man, Caleb followed the servant as he led him up to the Doctor's study; where he found Rothery and the rest of the vampire hunters clustered around the old man's desk, which was covered with even more books, parchments and papers than usual.

"Cade!" Rothery boomed; as Scaife closed the door behind him, he suddenly had the terrible premonition that the Doctor had somehow found out what he'd been doing with his daughter and was about to set Captain Lazziard on him to see honour was served.

However, as the Doctor beckoned him over and set Jute to pouring him a generous brandy, he calmed down a little and remembered his ability to see the future was only marginally worse than his ability to fall in love.

"We've exciting news Cade!" Rentwin enthused, rising from one of the chairs that had been pulled around the Doctor's desk, his head rolling excitedly.

"Where have you been?" Lazziard interrupted, sniffing the air suspiciously.

Caleb wondered how sensitive that large hook nose of his was for under the stink of the tobacco smoke that had infused his clothes when they'd been dancing in *The Star*, the scent of Alyssa's perfume probably mixed headily with the used sheath that sat in his pocket.

"Had a full schedule of sodomizing to keep me busy," Caleb retorted, accepting the brandy from Jute, who looked somewhat aghast at his words. Perhaps Alyssa was starting to rub off on him.

"Thought as much," Lazziard sniffed.

"Come, come, gentlemen," Rothery interceded, "let's have no more of this antagonism, we have work to do."

"We do?" Caleb asked, sipping his brandy.

"Indeed!" the Doctor beamed, looking around at

Lazziard, Rentwin and Archie Jute before announcing confidently, "I do believe we've found ourselves another vampire!"

"Really?"

"And we'd very much like your help in catching it," added the Doctor, backed enthusiastically by Rentwin and Jute and a vague mumble that might have been Lazziard clearing his throat.

Caleb downed the rest of his brandy in one.

Chapter Sixteen

Caleb Cade

The Evangeline, Off the Essex Coast – 1689

England had become no more than a suggestion upon the horizon, all but lost in the grey margins between a sullen bruised sky and the churning gunmetal sea. The young man spent a moment longer staring back towards the coastline before slowly turning his face towards the ship's prow, eyes narrowing against the stinging wind and spray as he stared through the murk towards a future stripped of both certainty and familiarity.

Uncle Jonathan was right, his home was lost to him now; in England, he was a dead man in all but breath. No matter how finely he dressed; somewhere, someone, some day would recognise who he was, or rather who he had been, and he would swing from the Tyburn gallows like a common thief. He wondered if he would have Valentine Cade's bravado if he ever had to stare Jack Ketch in the eye.

His splendid new travelling coat of soft leather was already slick and damp, he couldn't tell if it was the sea or the rain that was responsible; water seemed to be coming at him from every direction in constant sweeps of fine bitter mist that danced wildly to the beat of the incessant wind. Above him, the cries of Dutch sailors and gulls mixed together in a harsh alien serenade while he gripped the rail tightly. The constant motion of the ship made him uneasy, he'd never so much as crossed the Thames under a ferryman's care before, let alone been tossed around at the whim of an ill-humoured sea.

Gradually, however, as it became apparent *The Evangeline* was not in any imminent danger of either capsizing or sinking, his grip slackened enough for a little colour to return to his knuckles. When he felt confident enough that only one hand was required to keep him steady, he let the other wander to grasp the slight weight of the silver locket that hung around his neck.

He resisted the temptation to open it again. He didn't want to lose all he had left of Henrietta to the wind, and carefully tucked it back beneath his silk shirt. Along with the rest of his clothes, it had been the finest he'd been able to purchase in Harwich after the carriage Uncle Jonathan had hired deposited him at the port the day before.

Once the locket was safe, he moved gingerly towards

the very prow of the ship and stared at the great valleys of grey water *The Evangeline* wearily traversed. The ship's Captain, a man whose face was mostly concealed by a vast tobacco-stained beard through which only the odd feature poked through, like the shattered remnants of an old ruin peeking out of the encroaching undergrowth, had mumbled something about there being a heavy swell. The young man had wondered what the actual maritime distinction between a "heavy swell" and a "light storm" was.

The Captain had favoured him with a slow, disinterested look when he'd asked if the crossing to Amsterdam would be bad, before replying in heavily accented English, "My *Evangeline* rolls like a pregnant pig in a mud bath when she sees a heavy sea, but ships are much like women my young friend, generally the prettier they are the more likely they are to misbehave. As you can see my *Evangeline* is a reassuringly ugly bitch, so I reckons we'll all see Amsterdam safe enough…"

"You'll catch your death," his brother announced cheerily, appearing as unexpectedly as ever. He hung over the side of the ship and stared at the churning grey foam bubbling about the ship as it laboured up another swell.

"You can talk," he replied, noting the ink-stained cotton shirt the memory of his brother, as always, wore.

"'tis one of the many advantages of being nought but

a figment of your imagination," the boy grinned, the long hair whipping about his face was perfectly dry, "I never feel the cold or the rain."

The young man smiled faintly before looking out beyond the prow of the ship, "What do you think I'll find out there?"

"Amsterdam hopefully, unless Captain Robben gets it horribly wrong."

The young man gave the memory of his dead brother a cold hard stare, "Am I doing the right thing?"

"I thought doing the right thing was a practice you had abandoned when you stole Henrietta's jewellery or even begun sleeping with her for that matter," the memory said sharply, before softening his tone with a sigh and shrug, "You are a rich young man now, our world has suddenly become so much bigger than before; you can make of it whatever you wish."

"New lands, new experiences..."

"New loves?"

The young man smiled bitterly, "I might spend the rest of my life crossing all of Christendom, but I will never feel love again, not the way I did with Henrietta anyway..."

"That love was as much an illusion as I am; you should find someone who *really* loves you and build a life that is worthy."

The young man shrugged, trying in vain to sweep the

dark locks of his wind-tossed hair from his eyes, "What point is there in looking for something that is real when reality will never be able to hold a candle to the memory of her fictitious love? I will not concern myself with love again, I will spend Henrietta's gold on beautiful women and expensive wine, I will carouse and gamble and debauch. I will be shallow and meaningless. I will be everything our father taught us not to be; including happy."

"You would waste your wealth on such things when you could be most anything you wanted? What will you do when the money runs out as it surely will if you pursue such a tawdry life?"

The young man replied with the certainty of bitter conviction, "Why, then I shall pursue plain women and cheap wine of course."

"'tis a plan, I suppose."

"I am not you brother; I have no gifts, no talents, our feckless fickle God has no grand plans for me. I am just a man, weak and empty and broken hearted; if I do not find something to fill myself with then all there will be left of me is bitterness."

"You believe simple debauched fornication will make you happy?"

"Probably not, after all, love and the Bible both failed..." he shrugged, "I am not much concerned with happiness; I have spent most of my life without it anyway.

Besides 'tis but a wild and fanciful plan I don't suppose women will be much interested in sharing my misery in any case."

"I would not be so sure."

When the young man raised an enquiring eyebrow, the memory of his brother simply nodded across the deck.

When he followed his gaze, he found himself looking at two women clinging to the opposite rail of the ship. One was young and pretty, her cheeks flushed by the cold, strands of blonde hair straying from beneath a bonnet that was tightly tied beneath her chin. She had been looking at him when he'd turned, and she smiled warmly before her companion tugged urgently at her arm, the second woman was older, her face thin and spare of both flesh and warmth; her manner suggested she was her mother, though her clothes, which were plainer and cheaper than the younger woman's, indicated she was more likely a servant.

The two women turned their back on him, resolutely studying the sea instead.

"Perhaps you should go and introduce yourself?"

"I'm not sure that's a good idea; I'm a thief fleeing England to escape the noose, not to mention the fact I'm still quite heartbroken... besides, I wouldn't know what to say."

"It would appear you're going to be a singularly poor

libertine."

The young man scowled, "I don't suppose she would be much interested anyway, probably takes me for some deck hand."

"Deckhands generally do not dress like wealthy young gentlemen, and she is not to know you have only been dressed like a wealthy young gentleman these past few hours. She is quite pretty, though, don't you think?"

"Passable," the young man sniffed, but before he could make further comment he felt a small but insistent tap upon his shoulder.

Turning around he found the two women standing before him, the younger woman smiling up expectantly while, the older one hung on to her arm, scowling ferociously enough to suggest she'd been physically dragged across the deck.

The young woman asked him something before smiling radiantly enough to display her mostly white teeth. He assumed it was a question for she had spoken in Flemish or some such Germanic language that his father had deemed too culturally insignificant to be worth teaching to his sons.

When he had just stared blankly back at her, the young woman's smile faltered a little before she asked, "You are English, perhaps?"

"Mostly, yes..." he heard himself reply, feeling

singularly foolish.

The young woman giggled and whispered something to the older woman whose scowl carved even deeper into her sallow skin as she muttered the word "*Engels*" with as much pleasure as she might have said "*syphilitic.*"

"Would you be so kind as to retrieve my handkerchief?" She asked in careful but perfectly pronounced, English.

"Your handkerchief?"

"Yes, this wretched wind fair ripped it from my poor hand," she explained, pointing to the deck where a lace handkerchief fluttered beneath the pointed toe of her boot. He suspected that if it had been accidentally dropped the wind would have quickly carried out to sea, he wasn't entirely sure what the etiquette was in such situations, but he doubted it involved calling the young lady a liar.

"I would get it myself, but my corsets are quite... *restrictive*," she explained, demurely.

"*Pick it up you fool!*" He heard the memory of his brother hiss, and he quickly did as he bid. He wasn't sure if he should try to wipe off the wet boot print from the delicate lace, but she whipped it from him without apparent care and it disappeared into the fur lined cuffs of her coat in an instant.

"Thank you kindly," she beamed, "may I be so bold as to enquire as to the name of the gallant young gentleman who has shown such kindness in recovering my property?"

"It really was no trouble."

"Oh, that piece of deck looks particularly damp to me; probably full of splinters too, you have done me a great service." She smiled expectantly for a while, before adding, "Your name sir?"

The first thing to flit into his mind were the words *Not Daniel Plunkett*, followed immediately by the sound of his dead brother's voice warning him, "Not Daniel Plunkett!" Despite spending months in hiding before Uncle Jonathan had persuaded him that he had no alternative but to flee England to build his new life, he hadn't given any thought to what name he should take now that Daniel was dead.

After a long moment's hesitation, he combined the only two names he could think of, "Mr Caleb... Cade, of London."

He heard a voice that seemed to be behind him mutter huffily. *"My name and that of the only thief Jack Ketch couldn't hang, I should be mightily offended!"*

"A pleasure to meet you, Mr Cade," she replied, producing a leather gloved hand for his attention, "I am Miss Nicolet Ostrander, of Amsterdam."

Ignoring his brother's words and confident he was on firmer footing with hands than discarded handkerchiefs, he took the offered hand and kissed it lightly. When he straightened up, he found Nicolet smiling broadly while her companion's lips had almost taken on the same colour as her pallid bloodless skin as she was pushing them together with such force.

"The pleasure really is all mine," he said, remembering he was no longer a tongue-tied footman. He was a man of the world now, a man of quality and experience; a *libertine* no less.

"Of course, it is," Nicolet replied earnestly, before leaning forward and asking in a lowered voice, "you appeared to be talking to yourself earlier; I do hope you are not a lunatic. You appear to be the only *gentleman* on this voyage, and it would be such a shame if I would have to avoid you for fear of your mindless ravings?"

"I can assure you that I am no lunatic Miss Ostrander," He smiled reassuringly; "I was simply talking to my dead brother."

Oh, that will set her mind at rest no end...

"Really?" Nicolet said, taking a small step backwards.

He laughed, "'tis not as mad as it sounds. My brother died when I was a boy, we were exceptionally close and it was a terrible loss. I had a childish fancy that, if I tried hard enough, I could make his memory seem real and if I spoke to him and talked about my life I would keep some part of him alive. 'tis a habit I have never grown out of, perhaps it is foolish, but it is not madness. I know he isn't really here."

"I do not think it so foolish Mr Cade; may I be so bold as to ask what you were discussing with him today?"

"My broken heart," he said when nothing else came to mind.

"How intriguing, have you been rejected by your true love?"

"Sadly."

"For another man?"

"Her husband."

"Oh my, you must tell me more, it all sounds so terribly *scandalous!*"

"More sad and tawdry I'm afraid, and what of you Miss Ostrander, what brought you to England?"

"Visiting my cousins, though, in truth, my family sent me in search of a husband, my father has some idea the family's standing would be greatly improved should I be married to an English nobleman."

"And did you mission meet with success?"

"Oh, they were all *most* unsuitable; they were too old, too fat, too ugly, too boorish or too stupid. Some of them even managed to demonstrate all of those lamentable qualities, a feat I had previously thought too difficult for one single man to achieve."

"They are all qualities we English tend to excel in, I'm afraid."

"You are too modest Mr Cade; you do not appear to

suffer from any of them. I do not suppose you are an aristocrat are you...?"

"No."

"Oh-"

"Though my father is," he added quickly, the lie feeling strange and exciting on his lips, it quickened his heart even more than pretty little Nicolet did.

"Oh?"

"We're only a minor family, nothing grand really, just a small house and some land, but the title is... useful."

They spent a moment regarding each other, before Nicolet's companion, who had become ever more agitated as her eyes followed the conversation hissed something in Flemish before trying to pull Nicolet away. Nicolet, however, stood her ground and returned a stream of high pitched Flemish emphasised by the occasional sweeping hand gesture and nod of the head in his direction. When Nicolet had finished, the older woman looked evenly at him for a moment, before something almost, though not entirely quite, like a smile touched her lips and her dark, icy eyes seemed to thaw a little.

"What did you say to her?"

"I told her that you are the heir to a very rich and powerful English nobleman who owns a grand palace, much land, many farms and numerous sheep."

"That isn't exactly true."

I know, but I also told her you were trying to woo me, and she is far more amenable to a rich man's scandalous behaviour than a poor man's."

"That's very... *practical* of her."

"You must excuse my dear old Roos, she has been my maid since childhood, and after my mother died took it upon herself to adopt many motherly duties; particularly the ones that involve nagging, scolding and generally spoiling my fun. Not to mention sleeping with my father, but she doesn't know I know that," Nicolet added with a wrinkle of her nose.

"I won't breathe a word of it."

"No matter, she doesn't speak any English..." Nicolet explained before adding coyly. "...so, have no fear of being *bold* with me Sir, it will go no further."

He raised an eyebrow, was this all it took? Some fashionable clothes coupled with a few airs and graces and pretty women threw themselves at you? No wonder the nobility generally made such a mess of running the country.

"'tis rather too cold and wet for boldness, exposed as we are to the elements, perhaps we should retire below decks, and you may tell me all about Amsterdam, for I have never had the pleasure of visiting your city."

"And in return you must tell me all about your broken heart," Nicolet beamed, "I suggest we retire to my cabin, which is neither warm nor dry, but is unexposed to the elements and Roos can serve us warm tea and cake while she ensures nothing inappropriate occurs?"

"That would be most agreeable."

"Indeed!" Nicolet smiled and he quickly found her swapping Roos' arm for his, the servant did not seem entirely pleased with the arrangement, but under Nicolet's insistent shooing she led them both back along the ship.

He could taste her perfume on the wind and feel her warmth next to him, for the first time since the night of the fire he felt something akin to being alive. Perhaps it would not be so difficult at all to wash away Henrietta's memory; perhaps bedding this pretty young Dutch girl would be enough.

Perhaps...

He briefly glanced behind him in the hope of some kind of reassurance. The memory of his brother, who was still leaning nonchalantly against the ship's rail, offered him a smile of encouragement before fading into the mist.

His smile, however, carried no more conviction than Caleb Cade's thoughts.

The story continues…

Ghosts in the Blood

Monsters live behind all manner of masks.

Dr Rothery and his friends are probably insane, but Caleb has agreed to help them in their search for the vampiric essence so he can stay close to the Doctor's wild and intoxicating daughter. That is what he tries to tell himself anyway.

Could the vampiric essence free him from the grave and allow him to find love? Or is that just the ghost of Louis Defane living in his blood, whispering madness in his mind?

When Rothery and his colleagues capture a vampire alive, Caleb travels with them to Captain Lazziard's remote manor house where there will be no prying eyes to watch them work. As they apply their curiosity to the creature they chain in the cellar, Caleb becomes increasingly unsure who the real monsters are.

When people begin to die Caleb must decide where his loyalties lie; but are his perceptions being manipulated by the ghost in his blood, his own selfish desires for immortality or the fact that the creature Rothery is experimenting on happens to be the most beautiful woman he has ever seen…

Books by Andy Monk

In the Absence of Light

The King of the Winter

A Bad Man's Song

Ghosts in the Blood

The Love of Monsters

In the Company of Shadows

The Burning (Novella)*

A House of the Dead (Novella)*

Red Company

Precious Things (Novella)

The Kindly Man (Rumville Part One)

Execution Dock (Rumville Part Two) *Feb 2021*

The Convenient (Rumville Part Three) *May 2021*

Mr Grim (Rumville Part Four) *July 2021*

Hawker's Drift

The Burden of Souls

Dark Carnival

The Paths of the World

A God of Many Tears

Hollow Places

Other Fiction

The House of Shells

*The Burning and *A House of the Dead* are currently only available by subscribing to Andy Monk's mailing list via www.andymonkbooks.com

For further information about Andy Monk's writing and future releases, please visit the following sites.

www.andymonkwordsandpictures.co.uk
www.facebook.com/andymonkbooks

Printed in Great Britain
by Amazon